Shifted Truths

A Willow's Haven Novel

Clara James

BROKEN SPINE ARCHIVES

Contents

This book is dedicated to my husband, whose name I've taken in part for my pen name.

He is truly my other half, and this book would not be possible without his support.

Trigger Warnings

Graphic violence and gore — vivid descriptions of blood, injuries, and physical trauma.

Murder and death of a parent — an on-page violent killing witnessed by the protagonist.

Trauma, PTSD, and flashbacks — recurring symptoms, panic attacks, and intrusive memories.

Anxiety, depression, and grief — depiction of long-term emotional aftermath and isolation.

Survivor's guilt and emotional self-blame.

Animal attack — extended assault by a wolf, including biting, bone-breaking, dragging.

Physical assault — choking, restraint, and sexualized intimidation during the same scene.

Gun violence — gunshots red, potential injury and death.

Injuries and medical trauma — broken bones, blood loss, visible wounds.

Nightmares / panic attacks

Community prejudice / bigotry

Claustrophobia and confinement — being restrained or dragged.

Prologue

Humans have about 1.5 gallons of blood in their bodies. I've never truly grasped how much that is until now. There's blood everywhere. On my hands, in my hair, streaked across my face, soaking through my clothes like I fucking bathed in it, I want to scoop it up. I want to scoop it up, shove it back into her like that'll somehow fix this. Like it'll undo the horror sprawled out in front of me. But deep down, I know better. She's gone. Those deep, vicious slashes across her throat make damn sure of that, even if my heart's too stubborn to believe it.

I cling to her, sobbing so hard my chest aches. My hand cradles the back of her head; her blonde hair, once soft and glossy, is now sticky and dark, matted with blood. I ignore it. I ignore everything except the woman in my arms.

I rock back and forth, reminiscent of how she used to do the same when I was a child. Soothing motions meant to calm my racing heart and scare away the nightmares. But this is a nightmare I won't wake up from.

My lips move as the choked sound of a lullaby fills the air.

"Hush, little baby, don't say a word…"

If only I had been here. If only I had come home sooner, she wouldn't be dead in my arms.

"Mama's gonna buy you a mockingbird..."

Guilt floods through me as I replay the evening's events in my mind. Jess had come home from college and wanted to celebrate the end of her first year. We got drinks, talked shit, and laughed like nothing bad could ever touch us.

I should've said no. I should have postponed. If I had, then this wouldn't have happened.

"And if that mockingbird don't sing..."

My voice breaks hard on the last line, my hand still combing gently through her ruined hair.

"Mama's gonna buy you a diamond ring..."

My tears hit her face, sliding down her cheeks like she's crying too.

Then I hear it.

A low growl from the hallway.

I inhale sharply as I whip my head around and frantically wipe at my tears with my free hand. My heart seizes in my chest while my ears strain to listen. Part of me is not sure that I heard anything, while my brain wants to rationalize the noise as something mundane. Yet, my arms start to gently lower my mother's body back toward the ground. Something inside me is telling me I need to get out of this house right now.

Her head has barely touched the floor when a louder growl shreds through the silence, followed by the sickening scrape of claws on hardwood.

The hairs on my arms stand on end.

I rise to my feet, eyes locked on the hallway, and then I see it—massive paws, a flash of coarse gray fur, the glint of teeth beneath a long, snarling jaw.

A fucking wolf.

Fight or flight hits hard, and there's no debate. I turn and bolt, legs pumping, heeled feet slapping the blood-slick floor as I sprint toward the still-open front door like hell itself is on my heels.

I make it maybe fifteen steps before it's on me.

The wolf slams into my back like a freight train, and I go flying. My arms shoot out on instinct, but the blood on my hands makes them useless. They slide right off the tile, and I slam face-first into the floor. Pain explodes through my forehead, and I yelp, dazed, my head spinning. I brace myself, body tense and ready for the next hit—but it doesn't come.

I slowly lift my head, careful not to jar it too much and make the already-growing headache worse. The front door gapes open ahead of me like some kind of beacon, and I crawl toward it.

My hands keep slipping, so I drop to my elbows and start army-crawling, dragging myself inch by inch across the floor. As I get closer to the doorway, I spot a crumpled bouquet of flowers wrapped in tissue paper. I didn't notice them when I came in, but I wasn't exactly looking for them. The only thing I saw was my mother's body bleeding out on the living room floor.

There are petals scattered everywhere. Mostly red tulips, their delicate heads bent to the side like they're wilting in grief. Another kind of flower is mixed in—something with a long stem and bright red blooms that look like tiny trumpets. Foxgloves? Snapdragons? I don't know. I don't recognize them. They don't belong here. They leave a stark, jarring contrast against the tan tile.

I push the bouquet out of my way and keep crawling.

When I finally reach the doorframe, I grab it tight. The wood gives me enough grip to pull myself upright. I don't wait. I bolt across the porch and down the steps, heading for my car.

I don't have my keys—they're somewhere in my purse, and my purse is back inside on the floor, probably near my mother's corpse. Doesn't matter. If I can just get to the car, I can lock myself inside and keep the wolf out until Dad gets home.

I reach the car and yank the door open —

— but I don't make it in.

A powerful arm wraps around my torso, pinning my arms to my sides. Another hand grips my throat, and claws dig into the skin.

"Ah, ah, ah. Little girl," a man's voice whispers against my ear, cold and amused. "Where do you think you're going?"

He pulls me flush against him, and I can feel every hard line of muscle along his chest and abs. He leans in and inhales deeply, smelling my hair like a fucking psychopath. My whole body trembles.

"Please," I choke out.

His grip tightens. My lungs scream.

"If you're a good girl—"

I don't let him finish. I lift my leg and drive my heel into the top of his foot, twisting hard. He grunts and loosens his grip just a little. I slam my head backward, nailing him in the face. He curses and staggers back a step, his arms falling away.

I hiss. Headbutts hurt like a motherfucker—not at all like the movies make it seem.

I blink fast to clear the dizziness and bolt for the woods. If I can just get to the trees, I can shift. My raccoon form is smaller, faster, and agile as hell. I can climb, jump, vanish into the canopy. I just have to make it.

The gravel under my feet is brutal, jagged, uneven. I almost twist my ankle more than once as I run. But I push through, desperate to escape this monster who murdered my mom.

"You fucking bitch!" he roars behind me.

I run harder. Breathe deeper. The treeline is two feet away—I can make it.

He slams into my back again.

This time, I get my arm up between my head and the ground, but it still rattles my whole damn skeleton.

The gravel eats into my skin like knives.

Then the real pain hits.

His teeth clamp down on my calf, and I scream. He drags me back; the rocks scraping at my skin, ripping it open. I twist, kicking wildly, trying to catch him in the eye.

He dodges one strike and lets go—but only for a second. I kick again, and this time he grabs my ankle in his mouth and shakes his head violently. My screams hit the sky as white-hot pain rips up my leg. I reach down, trying to pry his mouth open. His teeth feel like they're crushing my bones.

I ball up my fists and start pounding his snout. One blow hits just right, behind his nose—maybe the same spot I headbutted earlier. He yelps and stumbles back, finally releasing me.

He snorts and shakes his head, pawing at his face like he's trying to rub the pain away. Then his eyes lock onto mine.

He dips his head low and growls, deep and vicious. His teeth drip with saliva, and every ounce of malice in his body radiates straight into mine.

I suck in a shaky breath, heart crashing against my ribs.

Oh fuck. I'm going to die.

He lunges.

His jaws clamp down on my ankle again—and this time I hear the bone snap. My scream is raw and feral. I force myself not to yank away. If I do, I'll tear something worse.

Then he's dragging me.

My clothes ride up as he hauls me across the driveway. The gravel scrapes along my ribs and hips, shredding my skin. I twist, reaching for something—anything—to grab onto. There's nothing but rock. Just pain. Endless fucking pain.

Tears stream down my face as I grit my teeth, trying to think, trying to survive.

Then, like a miracle, I hear it—tires on gravel.

Headlights sweep over us. A car screeches to a halt.

A voice shouts.

Gunshots ring out.

The pressure on my leg vanishes.

Warm arms wrap around me, and I scream, thrashing like a wild animal.

"Sarah! It's me!"

Dad. His voice breaks through the fog and I collapse into him, sobbing so hard I can't fucking breathe. He pulls me into his chest, holding me like he's afraid I'll vanish. His large hand runs up and down my back, over and over, whispering, "Shhh, shhh, baby, I've got you."

Eventually the sobs slow. He pulls back, hands cupping my face, eyes scanning every inch of me.

I must look like hell—cuts all over my body from the gravel, bruises, blood. My legs are torn up, one ankle's definitely broken, and I'm still covered in my mom's blood.

His eyes meet mine, pained and frantic.

"Sarah... where's your mother?" he asks.

I flinch. I can't even look at him.

"She's inside."

He lets go of my face and stands.

"No! Daddy—don't. Don't go in there," I beg, grabbing his sleeve in a death grip. "You don't want to see. Please—"

"I have to check on her." He pulls out his phone and hands it to me. "Call the police."

Then he's gone.

"Dad!" I scream, but he's already running toward the house.

I squeeze my eyes shut. He doesn't know what he's about to see, but I do. I know what's coming, and I can't stop it.

His boots hit the steps. Then I hear his voice calling out, desperate. "Kitty!"

And then... silence. Just for a moment.

The sound he makes—it's inhuman. Shattered. And it will haunt me forever.

With shaking hands, I dial.

It rings once. Twice.

"911. What's your emergency?"

Chapter 1

Two years later

I gaze out my bedroom window, staring out at the mountains that surround Willow's Haven. The morning sun spills over the Tennessee Mountains, drenching them in a warm, golden haze. Wildflowers sway lazily in the breeze, and the soft gurgle of a brook nearby mixes with the distant hum of birds. Peaceful, it's absolutely perfect.

But that's the thing about perfection—it's always a lie. I know because it wasn't long ago when my life seemed perfect, before everything went to shit. I tug at the sleeve of my worn-out nightgown, the familiar itch of unease creeping up my spine. Georgia feels a lifetime ago, but it's still there, hanging on like a stain I can't scrub out. Every memory from that place reeks of blood, fear, and the unsolved murder that took my mother.

Leaving? Yeah, that wasn't the tough part. It was the staying that damn near killed me. Every corner of that house held a piece of her—her laugh, her smell, her warmth—and now, all of it's tangled up with the violence that ripped her away. My dad, he tried to fix things, to bury the past in new carpet and repainted walls, thinking it would somehow make it easier to breathe. But it didn't work. The ghosts are always there.

I avoided the living room as if it were cursed. I couldn't step foot in there without feeling like I was drowning in the things we'd lost. But my dad? He just kept himself busy, remodeling, joining support groups, pretending like therapy could sew him back together. Me? No thanks. I knew nobody was going to fix this mess in my head.

The world outside became a minefield—every person, every smile felt like a trap, another face hiding a predator shifter or, worse, the bastard who killed her. Fear ran me ragged, clawing at me until I couldn't tell what was real anymore. That's what Willow's Haven was supposed to be—a reset button, a place where I didn't have to check over my shoulder every second.

And yeah, maybe it worked. The people here, they're safe. At least, that's what I keep telling myself. No predators lurking in the dark. No more late-night panic attacks when I hear a creak in the house. Hell, I've even made a friend here, got a job that keeps my mind busy. It's something, right?

Even so, some days I wake up with that damn knot in my chest, like the air's too thick to breathe. This morning's no different. Light filters in through the curtains, soft and golden, the kind of morning that looks like it should be on a postcard. But my mind's already racing before I can even get out of bed. From my window, the mist still clings to the mountain peaks, trying to lend a sense of calm. The birds' gentle chirping weaves through the quiet, coaxing me into the day.

I stretch, my muscles tight beneath the warmth of the quilt, the remnants of sleep still clinging to me.

"Alright, Sarah," I mutter, dragging myself up. My body feels stiff, like it's protesting the idea of another day. I shuffle across the creaky wooden floor, wrapping myself in the thick robe that's more like a comforting blanket on a cool morning like this one.

I drag myself to the bathroom; the morning routine a welcome distraction. Brushing through my dark brown hair, washing my face, I try to ground myself in the small, simple actions. I splash cold water on my face, then stare at the girl in the mirror. My hair clings to my wet skin; my eyes look more tired than they should. I am grateful for the quiet, though. No sirens, no shadows that stretch too long. Just peace.

The shower's warm spray washes away the lingering tension, and soon, I'm dressed in jeans and my favorite cream-colored sweater. I make my way downstairs, where my dad is already clattering around the kitchen. The smell of pancakes pulls me in before I've even seen him.

"Morning, sweetheart!" My dad's voice greets me before I round the corner. He's already at the stove, flipping pancakes with the ease of someone who's trying too hard to make things feel normal. He's dressed in denim overalls and a plaid shirt, his usual look, but the lines etched into his face are deeper now, the weight of everything we've been through sitting heavy on his shoulders. His boots tap softly against the floor, keeping rhythm with the tune he hums under his breath.

"Morning, Dad," I mumble back, grabbing my coffee and sinking into a chair. Safe as it feels here, that tension is still gnawing at me. The world outside these walls feels fine, but inside? Inside, I'm waiting for the other shoe to drop.

"Sleep okay?" Dad asks, setting a plate stacked high with pancakes in front of me, steam curling up in soft ribbons.

"Better than usual," I admit, sinking into the familiar comfort of our morning routine, the heaviness in my chest loosening just a little.

"See, told ya this place would grow on ya," he says, a smirk on his face like he's got it all figured out. "Now, eat up. Big day ahead."

"Thanks," I murmur, stabbing into the stack of pancakes. It's stupid how something so simple—a damn routine—makes me feel like maybe I've got a grip on things again. There is something to be said about the power of routine, and how it has helped me regain a sense of normalcy in my life. I have always been a person who is not erratic or scattered, but knowing my daily schedule helps me stay calm.

We finish breakfast and I head for my shoes, but the second I think about leaving the house, that familiar panic slithers up my spine. My chest tightens, fingers fumbling with the laces as my brain screams, don't go. Dad notices, of course. He always does.

It's been months since we landed in this town, and it's taken every ounce of willpower just to get used to being around people again. When Mom died, every face on the street looked like a potential killer, every stranger hiding behind a smile. Trying to talk to anyone felt impossible, like my throat was made of lead.

That first year? I was falling, and there was no bottom to hit. Just deeper and deeper into the hole until I didn't know if I'd ever crawl out. The second year was the climb—slow, agonizing, my fingers slipping half the time. I'd reach for the next hold only to lose my grip and slide right back down. But I kept going. Kept dragging myself up, over and over.

These last few months since the move, though... they've been different. The climb's been a little easier. There are no memories of Mom in this house, no ghost of her laugh echoing in the hallway, no room I have to walk past every day that makes my nightmares bleed into real life. Here, there's some space to breathe, to forget—if just for a minute—that everything fell apart.

"Deep breath, honey," he says, his hand warm on my shoulder, steady. "Today's no different from the rest."

I force a nod, my mouth too dry to form words. My dark hair falls over my face as I look down, trying to convince myself everything's fine. The house feels safe — the kind of safe you can wrap around yourself like a blanket. But outside? It's a whole different beast.

"Okay," I whisper, mostly to myself, trying to remember why I'm doing this. Dad's been through just as much—maybe more. Leaving everything behind was his idea, after all. But the look in his eyes says it's not just about him. We're doing this together, one step at a time.

He smiles and gives my shoulder a reassuring squeeze. "I know you will be fine, honey."

Dad grabs his wallet, shoves it into his back pocket, and swings the door open. We step outside, the cool mountain air hitting me first, clean and crisp as I pull it deep into my lungs. We head into town, our feet tapping along the cobblestone streets, surrounded by the picturesque beauty that would've seemed fake if I hadn't been seeing it every day. With each step we take, this town feels a little less like a place we landed in and a little more like home.

Houses line the street, each with its own quirky charm—painted shutters, flower boxes spilling over with color. Neighbors are out, too, waving from their porches with easygoing smiles that almost make me forget the shit we've been through. It's worlds away from where we came from, where every face looked like it could be hiding a threat. Here, though, there's something else—a warmth that I haven't felt in years.

"See?" Dad says, nodding toward the people greeting us like we've known them forever. "Nothing to worry about."

I want to believe him. I do. But that gnawing fear still hangs on, like a shadow just out of sight. I can't help it. I've been here before—thinking it's all good, letting my guard down—and then it happens. The moment it all goes to hell. The smell of blood, the feel of Mom's body cooling under my hands—it comes back in flashes, stealing the air from my lungs. The nightmares haven't fully let go, even here. But here in Willow's Haven, those memories are fading, just a little with each step I take.

As we continue our walk toward the bakery, I continue to marvel at the charming, old-world atmosphere that seems to permeate every corner of this place. Small shops and cafes line the cobblestone streets, their facades blooming with colorful flowers and vines. The air carries the intoxicating scent of fresh-baked goods and brewed coffee, mingling harmoniously with the earthy aroma of the nearby mountains.

"Morning, Sarah! Morning, Thomas!" calls out Mrs. Thompson, the elderly woman who owns the flower shop on the corner. She waves enthusiastically from her perch on a wooden bench, surrounded by vibrant blooms. "Lovely day, isn't it?"

"Hi, Mrs. Thompson!" We reply in unison, causing me to giggle a bit. I grace the woman with a shy smile. "Yes, it's beautiful out."

"Perfect weather for baking," chimes Mr. Johnson as he sweeps the entrance of his barbershop. "I'll be sure to stop by later for some of those delicious pastries!"

"I'm sure Mr. Walters will be happy to hear it," I say. My cheeks flush with pride. "I'll save you some of our best."

My father gives me a proud look and smiles. Once we reach the end of the street, he pulls me into a hug and wishes me a good day before heading off to the library where he works.

As the bakery comes into view, my steps pick up, eyes scanning the storefront like I'm starving. The glass windows glint in the morning sun, showing off colorful designs of fresh pastries, each one looking more tempting than the last. My chest warms as I step inside, the sweet punch of cinnamon and sugar wrapping around me like a cozy blanket.

"Morning, Sarah!" Mr. Walters calls from behind the counter, his voice as cheerful as ever. His salt-and-pepper beard twitches with a grin, and he gives me a nod. "Ready for another busy one?"

"Absolutely, Mr. Walters!" I tie the apron around my waist, settling into my spot behind the counter. He's sturdy, like someone who's been through hell and still finds a reason to smile. With his round belly, trimmed beard, and warm hazel eyes crinkling at the corners, he looks like Santa Claus on his day off. And he's got the jolly part down too.

The bell above the door jingles, and customers trickle in, drawn by the smell of fresh-baked goodness and the easy rhythm of the place. My nerves fade as I fall into the work, focusing on each order, making sure everyone walks out with a smile. It's like the rush keeps the anxiety at bay, like I don't have room in my head for anything else when I'm lost in the hustle.

"Morning, Sarah," Mrs. Davis greets me, already eyeing the display. She's here every week, always after something sweet. "I need something indulgent today. What do you recommend?"

"Morning, Mrs. Davis!" I grin, scanning the case. "How about a chocolate raspberry croissant? Just out of the oven and probably sinful."

"Perfect," she beams, accepting the pastry like I just handed her a piece of heaven. "You never steer me wrong."

"Thank you, Mrs. Davis," I say, feeling a little spark of pride. Her words settle something inside me, a warmth that spreads. "Enjoy!"

As the day rolls on, I lose myself in the rhythm—taking orders, sliding pastries across the counter, hearing the bell jingle as people come and go. The tension that sat heavy in my chest when I woke up? It's gone, replaced by the steady flow of work. The bakery, with its smells, its noise, its routine, has become my safe space, a place where the shadows of my past can't reach me. They're still out there waiting, but here? Here, in this little corner of Willow's Haven, I'm okay. I'm content.

As the afternoon sun spills through the windows, washing everything in a golden glow. I stand behind the counter carefully arranging pastries in neat rows. My hands move on autopilot, but my mind drifts, glancing over at my coworkers as they hustle around. I've gotten used to the rhythm here—the hum of the ovens, the constant chatter—but navigating the social dynamics? That's still a different story.

"Hey, Sarah," Sam calls as he steps out of the kitchen, carrying a tray of freshly baked goods. Heat flushes his cheeks as a grin lights up his boyish face. As the youngest of Mr. Walters' sons, Sam still has that eager, wide-eyed look, like he's ready to take on the world. "Can you stock these?"

I glance at him and nod, taking the tray. His fingers brush mine for a second, and I feel my face heating. Sam, with his tousled sandy hair falling into bright blue eyes and freckles dusting his cheeks, is every bit the sweet high school senior. Tall, lanky, and full of that youthful energy I used to have.

"Sure," I mutter, hoping my blush isn't too obvious. Maybe one day I'll be comfortable around others again, but not today.

He flashes that easygoing grin again. "You're a lifesaver." Then he's gone back into the kitchen.

I barely have time to collect myself before Jordan strides over, Mr. Walters' oldest son. He's closer to my age, with that sturdy build from years of kneading dough and hauling flour sacks. Chestnut-brown hair, always a bit dusted with flour, and hazel eyes that seem to see right through you, even though he carries himself with a grumpy exterior most of the time.

"Need help with those?" he asks, but the smirk on his face says more than his words do. His eyes scan me, and I stiffen under the weight of his gaze. My fingers tremble as I pick up a tray of muffins.

"Uh, no, I'm good," I stammer, trying to keep my voice steady. "I've got it."

Jordan shrugs, clearly picking up on my discomfort but not pushing it. "Alright. Let me know if you change your mind." He lingers for a second longer before heading back to his work, leaving me with a racing heart and that familiar feeling of unease.

I glance down at the muffins, setting them in the display case, trying to steady my breathing. It's not that Jordan—or Sam, for that matter—has ever given me a reason to feel on edge. It's just... me. My nerves, my inability to trust hardly anyone these days.

The bell above the door chimes, pulling me from my thoughts. Laughter rings out, and I look up to see Lila Monroe bouncing through the entrance, her blonde hair catching the sunlight. Lila's been my rock since I moved here, all bright smiles and endless energy. She makes it easy to forget, at least for a little while, that I'm still struggling to piece myself back together.

I catch Jordan scowling as she walks in, his expression darkening before he abruptly retreats to the kitchen. Lila doesn't even seem to notice, but I do; and for a second, I wonder what that was about. Still, I push the thought aside, choosing to focus on Lila's grin as she heads straight for me, her infectious energy already lifting the burden off my shoulders.

"Sarah!" Lila practically bounces across the bakery floor, arms wide as she pulls me into a tight hug, her energy spilling over like always. "I've missed you!"

I laugh as I return the hug. "Lila, it's only been a day."

"Feels like forever," she pouts, her big blue eyes sparkling, the playful gleam in them impossible to miss. That's Lila, though—pure rabbit shifter energy, buzzing like she's got a hundred things to do and no time to waste. We're an odd pair, her all bounce and brightness, me more guarded, but somehow it works.

"Here for Noah's treats?" I ask, knowing how her boss loves the bakery's pastries.

Lila's eyes light up, and she leans in like she's about to share a secret. "Actually, I'm here to whisk you away on an adventure!"

"An adventure?" My stomach flips a little, and I glance around, suddenly aware of everyone watching. The last thing I need is attention. "I still have a few hours left."

She waves her hand like it's no big deal. "Already handled! Talked to Mr. Walters earlier, and he said you're good to leave early. Sarah, you've been working non-stop. You need a break."

I hesitate, torn between wanting to be responsible and the familiar pull of fun with Lila. I glance over at Mr. Walters, who's standing behind the counter, waving me out with a grin.

"You sure?" I ask, still not fully convinced.

"Positive!" Lila grabs my hand before I can argue, already tugging me toward the door. "Let's go! The whole afternoon's waiting for us!"

I barely get my apron off and toss it to Mr. Walters before Lila hauls me outside. The sun hits my face, warm and bright, and I can't help but smile at her relentless enthusiasm. She's a force, that one. And yeah, I'm cautious, always holding back, always thinking too much. But with Lila next to me, dragging me into whatever madness she's cooked up, I feel like maybe—just maybe—I can loosen my grip on the fear that's kept me in the dark for so long.

Maybe one day, I'll let myself fully step into the world I've been so afraid of. But for now, I've got Lila, and that's enough to face whatever comes next.

The warm afternoon sun filters through the trees, casting a golden hue over Lila's small backyard. The wildflowers sway gently in the breeze, their fragrance mixing with the earthy scent of grass. Lila and I sink into the softness of the earth, the grass cool beneath us. A peaceful rustling fills the air, the wind tugging lazily at the leaves above.

"Isn't this just perfect?" Lila stretches out beside me, her hands tucked behind her head, bright brown eyes shimmering with contentment as she takes in the scene. She's practically glowing, her whole body radiating happiness like the sun itself.

I smile, unable to help myself. Even with the small tug of guilt gnawing at me for skipping out early on work, the serenity of the moment makes it hard to care. "Yeah, it really is," I murmur, tucking a strand of hair behind my ear as I glance around the quiet yard.

Lila's voice cuts through the stillness, softer now. "Have you thought any more about what we talked about last week?" Her gaze lands on me, gentle but probing, the weight of the question hanging in the air between us.

I freeze, my fingers instinctively tugging at the hem of my shirt as memories surge forward, ones I've tried so hard to push down. "I... I've been trying," I manage, my voice small, barely scraping past the knot in my throat. "But it's hard."

Lila's hand finds my arm, her touch light but steady. "I get it, sweetie. It's tough, I know. But talking about it might help. You don't have to carry it alone."

I feel a flicker of warmth at her words, her kindness something I'm still not used to. I glance up, meeting her caring eyes, and take a breath I didn't realize I was holding. "Ever since my mom died... I've just been so lost," I admit, the words tumbling out before I can stop them. "She was my anchor, and without her... I don't know how to move forward."

Lila's face softens, her voice like a balm over raw wounds. "It's okay to feel lost, Sarah. You've been through hell, and healing takes time. But you can't keep avoiding shifting until your body forces it. That's dangerous, and you know it. You could really hurt yourself."

Her words hit deeper than I want them to. I've been running from the shift, the way it connects me to everything I'm trying to forget. But Lila's right. I can't keep dodging it forever; eventually the magic will overwhelm me again and I'll either have to shift or risk possibly dying. I nod, fighting back the sting of tears.

Lila squeezes my arm gently. "I'm here, okay? Every step of the way. You're not alone in this."

I let the tears spill over then, blinking them away as quickly as they come. "Thanks, Lila," I whisper, my voice shaky. "I don't know what I'd do without you."

She pulls me into a hug, wrapping me in a kind of warmth that only comes from someone who truly cares. "That's what friends are for," she whispers, her voice light but solid.

We stay like that for a while, just the two of us, letting the quiet seep in. And as the weight of my grief lifts, even if only a little, the afternoon melts into laughter, soft words, and the freedom that comes with finally letting go. When we finally shift into our forms, the weight of our worries seems to disappear entirely, replaced by the joy of running through the grass, free for a moment from everything that holds us down.

In the days after my conversation with Lila, an uncomfortable awareness settles in—I'm more fragile than I want to admit. Every morning, staring into the mirror, I search my reflection for some spark of strength, but all I see are the dark circles under my eyes, like shadows that refuse to leave.

"Deep breaths, Sarah," I mutter, forcing a smile that doesn't quite reach my eyes before I step out into the crisp mountain air.

Today, something feels off as I walk through the quiet streets of Willow's Haven. It's not the neighbors—I trust them enough—but there's this gnawing feeling, a pit in my stomach that I can't shake. I keep my distance, head down, heart guarded like I'm bracing for something. My past has taught me to retreat, to stay hidden behind walls I've built up.

"Morning, Sarah!" Mr. Jenkins calls out, his voice as bright as the flowers he's watering in his front yard. His hose sprays in arcs as he waves, all smiles.

"Good morning, Mr. Jenkins." My smile feels tight as I clutch my bag to my chest. "It really is lovely."

I can hear the hesitation in my voice. My shoulders tense, my pace quickens, and before I know it, I'm practically speed-walking past him, nerves gnawing at me. The small hairs on the back of my neck stand up, and I can't shake the feeling of being watched. My gaze darts around, but I see nothing out of the ordinary. Still, the feeling lingers, and I wrap my arms tightly around myself as I hurry down the street.

At the bakery, I lose myself in the motions—carefully placing pastries in neat rows, my fingers moving with precision. I can handle this part, the work. But beyond that? Conversations shrink to polite smiles, stiff greetings, and the occasional awkward exchange. I keep my head down, hoping my lack of connection doesn't show as much as it feels.

The end of the day brings some relief. My moments with Lila become more important, like they're the only thing keeping me grounded. Her evening visits are a chance to breathe, to stop thinking about the knots inside my head. She keeps telling me I'm stronger than I think, that I need to stop walling myself off. But it's hard. Still, she doesn't give up on nudging me out of my shell.

We're sitting under the oak tree in my backyard, the sky streaked with pinks and oranges as the sun dips below the horizon. Lila's sprawled out on the grass beside me, mischief twinkling in her eyes.

"Now, are you coming to the fair with me tomorrow or not?" She asks, giving me that look. "I could really use the company, and you'd actually enjoy it once you got there."

I chew on my bottom lip, my brain already running in circles. Crowds. Noise. The anxiety winds up inside me. Lila catches the hesitation and, like clockwork, hits me with those puppy-dog eyes, exaggerated to the point of absurdity. She bats her eyelashes dramatically, and I cave.

"Okay, I'll go," I sigh, rolling my eyes but smiling despite myself.

Lila practically squeals, clapping her hands. "Yay! I'll meet you there after work, okay?"

"Okay," I reply, still a little reluctant but trying to convince myself otherwise.

The fair's in Miller's Creek, a town over, but bigger than Willow's Haven. The thought of the crowds already has my stomach in knots. But I take a deep breath. Lila will be there. That makes it a little easier. I remind myself that stepping out of the quiet bubble I've created might not be the worst thing. A break from the routine might even be good for me. Maybe with Lila by my side, I can handle a little more than I give myself credit for.

Chapter 2

JAKE

The scent of freshly worked wood clings to the air, earthy and familiar, as I work in my father's carpentry shop. Each pull of the chisel sends delicate curls of wood spiraling to the floor, slowly revealing the curve of the chair leg taking form under my hands. Sweat beads on my forehead, and I swipe away the strands of dark hair sticking to my face, never breaking my concentration. The rhythm of the work takes hold—cut, shape, smooth—until hours later I finish the chair leg, a solid accomplishment in patience and precision.

I take a moment, admiring the clean lines and the feel of the polished wood beneath my fingers. Then, without hesitation, I turn to the next project, my mind already turning to the details of what's next.

"Hey, Dad, got any spare clamps?" I call out, scanning the cluttered shelves along the walls, my gaze searching for the tool I need.

"Bottom shelf, near the back," he answers, his focus never leaving the intricate carving he's working on.

"Thanks!" I grab the clamps and get back to work, aligning two pieces of wood for a custom bookshelf a local customer has ordered. Carefully, I fit the joints together, making sure every seam is perfect before tightening the clamps to lock them in place.

"Looking good, son." Dad walks over, brushing sawdust off his hands onto his jeans. He's built solid from years of this kind of work, his body sturdy but his demeanor always gentle. Gray streaks his brown hair, his green eyes sharp, reflecting both wisdom and a sadness that never fully leaves. I've got his build, but my eyes are different—light blue, like Mom's.

"Thanks," I say, checking my progress. "I want this one to be flawless."

He chuckles, pride in his voice. "Your attention to detail always amazes me, kid. Just remember, don't get too lost in it." He raises an eyebrow, giving me a hard look. "You tend to growl when you concentrate too hard."

I smirk, nodding. He's right. We walk a fine line, hiding what we are from the town. Wolf shifters don't exactly blend in; we can never let things slip. The need for secrecy hangs over every decision, every interaction. We can't afford to screw up.

"No worries, Dad," I say, tightening the clamp with a little extra force. "I've got it under control." I give the bookcase one last look, checking the clamps again, then I turn back to the bench. I set up another piece of wood for carving and begin, hands steady, focusing on the work in front of me. I'm ready to keep crafting in silence, careful and calculated. Dad clamps a hand on my shoulder and squeezes gently, reassuringly, before turning back to his work.

The shop door creaks open, the bell above chiming through the space as a customer walks in. I put down my tools and make my way toward the showroom up front. I watch as her eyes immediately sweep over the handcrafted pieces on display. I quickly plaster on a friendly smile, making sure my face reads approachable, even though my nerves are still buzzing from earlier.

"Morning, Jake! Marcus!" Mrs. Wilks, the town librarian, greets me with that same cheerful tone she always has. There's something comforting about her, the way she walks in like she belongs here, like this place is as familiar to her as her own library.

"Good morning, Mrs. Wilks," I reply, my voice steady. Dad pokes his head out from the back, smiles and waves, then returns his attention back to his work. That's my cue to handle the front of shop duties. "What can I do for you today?"

She chuckles softly, her eyes twinkling behind her glasses. "I've got this old rocking chair that belonged to my grandmother. One of the legs is getting wobbly. I was hoping you could work your magic on it."

I follow her out to her truck, eyeing the worn, vintage chair resting in the bed. The craftsmanship is impressive, solid and old-school, but yeah, one leg is definitely on its last leg—literally.

"Shouldn't be too hard to fix," I say, giving it a quick once-over. "I'll have it sturdy again in no time."

Grabbing the chair, I haul it out of the truck, Mrs. Wilks trailing behind me as we head back into the shop. The weight of the chair isn't much, but there's something about handling an heirloom like this that adds pressure.

"Thanks, Jake," she says, her smile widening. "You're always so dependable." Then, she leans in slightly, lowering her voice. "You know, there's something about you that's different from the others around here."

Her words send a spike of panic straight through me, my mind immediately racing. Different? What does she mean? Had she overheard something earlier, something from that conversation with Dad? Is she putting the pieces together about us? My pulse quickens as the fear of exposure tightens its grip. The last thing we need is someone catching on to what we really are.

I shake off the rising dread, forcing my smile to stay in place. "Thanks, Mrs. Wilks," I say, trying to sound as casual as ever. "I should have it fixed up for you by next week."

"Perfect," she says, but as she turns to leave, she pauses at the door and casts me a narrow-eyed glance, like she's sizing me up. My stomach twists, and I shift on my feet, doing my best not to let the unease show.

Before I can linger too long on it, she smiles, breaking the tension in the room. "Give me a call when you get it finished," she calls out and disappears out the door. I turn to Dad and raise my brow; he shrugs. What the hell was that all about?

"Hey, Jake!" Charlie's voice rings out, bouncing off the metal walls of the carpentry shop as he comes through the barely closed door. The clang of tools stops for a moment as Dad turns toward the door. Then came the familiar sound of laughter—light and carefree. The twins, Beau and Buckley, barrel in behind him, their feet pounding the concrete floor in a syncopated rhythm that matches their twin grins.

Charlie stands in the middle of the showroom, his hand absently raking through his sandy brown hair, pushing it back only for the strands to tumble effortlessly into his warm brown eyes. He squints against the light, eyes crinkling—the kind that smile even when his mouth doesn't. His frame, lean but solid, speaks to hours spent under the hoods of cars, wrench in hand. His rolled-up sleeves expose forearms streaked with grease. His well-worn jeans cling to his legs, stained and frayed at the edges, but he makes it look like a style choice rather than a necessity. He has a rugged charm, the kind that draws attention without trying—especially from women.

Behind him, the Wilson twins are a whirlwind of energy, their identical brown curls bounce in unison as they skid to a stop. Beau shoves Buckley, Buckley shoves back, their green eyes dancing with a shared joke they hadn't even told yet. They were farm boys through and through, their athletic builds carved from days spent hauling sheep and chasing strays across their parents' fields. Dirt clings to their boots, leaving a trail as they move, their bodies brimming with restless energy. Even standing still, they seem like they were always in motion, always ready to stir up some kind of trouble. With identical faces and matching grins, even those who've known them for years often paused to try to tell them apart.

"Yo," I greet them with a grin, carefully setting down the chair. "What brings y'all here?"

"We wanted to make sure you weren't going to flake on us tonight," Beau says, giving my shoulder an affectionate pat.

"Yeah man. I hear Lila is bringing a transplant, and I wanna get a good look at her. Jordan said she's a real smoke show." Buckley chimes in, a mischievous glint in his eye.

Charlie rolls his eyes while I scoff. "Jordan thinks anything with tits is a smoke show."

Beau burst out laughing while Buckley scowls at me.

"What about Noah Caldwell? He's seen her, said she's got a shapely figure. OH! Or better yet, ask your buddy Grant. He saw her too."

I sigh and pinch the bridge of my nose. "Y'all are nothin' but a bunch of horn dogs."

"Hey!" Charlie mocks outrage. "It's not their fault they've fucked their way through half the town and can't get pussy anymore."

"The fuck you say?!" Beau scowls. "I have no problem gettin' pussy, thank you very much."

"Yeah!" Buckley shouts. "And at least we aren't spending our young, viral years pinning after some pussy that we'll never fuck."

Charlie growls at the pair, and they growl back. "She's not just some pussy." He says as his growls turn menacing. Suddenly, a metallic clang cuts through the shop, making the boys jump. I look down and see a wrench lying on the concrete next to their shoes just before my dad comes barreling out from the back of the shop.

"That's enough!" he shouts, his voice echoing through the space. "You three idiots need to remember that this is a business!"

The three men look at the floor in shame. "Sorry, Papa Marcus." They say in unison.

My father shakes his head at them. "Now, apologize to Charlie."

The twins share a look and then flinch when my father yells out, "Now!"

"Sorry, Charlie."

"Yeah, sorry, man."

Charlie rolls his eyes heavenward and expels a long breath. "It's alright."

"Good, now get the hell out of my shop before you end up doing something else stupid."

"Yes, sir." They all say dejectedly as they leave the shop with their proverbial tails tucked between their legs.

I reach down and pick the wrench up off the floor, holding it out to my father. He takes it from me and shakes his head. "I'm headed to the house; those boys have done got my pressure up. Don't forget Grant is coming by later with a delivery. When you're done, come up to the house and get the list from your momma. She needs a few things from Mac's before you head out this evenin'."

"Yes, sir."

Several hours later, golden light bathes the carpentry shop as the sun begins its slow descent, casting long shadows across the floor. I wipe sweat from my brow just as the familiar crunch of tires on gravel hits my ears. Setting my tools aside, I head outside, knowing exactly who's pulling in.

Grant Sullivan's black pickup rolls up, hauling this week's load of lumber on the trailer hitched behind it. I raise my hand in greeting as he expertly backs the trailer up toward the side doors of the shop.

Grant hops out, unfolding his massive frame from the truck. The guy's built like a wall—easily 6'2" and wide enough to fill a doorway. His muscles bulge beneath his usual flannel, but the look in his brown eyes gives him away—he's a softie at heart. His hair, tied back in a man-bun, and his neatly trimmed beard add to his rugged vibe, but anyone who knows him sees past the intimidation factor.

"Howdy!" I call out, walking over to help with the unloading. "How's the lumber this week?"

"Top quality, as always, Jake," Grant replies, his voice a deep rumble, like distant thunder. Big as he is, there's still a warmth about him you can't ignore.

"Perfect! Let's get this stuff inside." We get to work unloading the wood, the conversation flowing easily between us, like it always does.

"Caught a big one while fishing yesterday," Grant says with a chuckle, the memory still fresh on his mind. "Must've been twenty pounds, at least!"

I raise an eyebrow, impressed. "No shit? How'd you catch it?" I ask, raising a curious brow.

The day I found out Grant was a bear shifter, he was waist-deep in the river, hauling fish like it was no big deal. His grizzly form towered over the water, a massive fish dangling from his jaws before he casually dropped it into a basket on the bank. I hadn't expected to stumble upon another shifter that day. I was just out for a run, sticking to the deep woods like we all did when we wanted to shift in peace, far from the prying eyes of townsfolk. At first, I kept my distance, but when I saw him drop a fish in a basket like some Yogi Bear shit, I knew. No real bear does that.

I watched from the shadows as he waded back into the river, scooped up another fish like it was nothing, and tossed it into the basket. The moment it hit the bottom, he shifted back into his human form, the massive grizzly turning into the man I now called a friend.

I figured I couldn't just lurk in the trees like a creep, so I shifted and stepped out, making sure to call his name loud enough to catch his attention. I'll never forget the look on his face—pure terror — when he realized I'd seen everything. His head snapped up, eyes wide with shock. The color drained from his face and, for a second, he looked like he'd seen a ghost.

I raised my hands, trying to calm him down, explaining I was a predator shifter too. I wasn't there to expose him or anything. Once we got past the initial awkwardness, something clicked between us that day. We've got an unspoken understanding now. Though Grant keeps to himself, we've built a quiet camaraderie that wasn't there before.

Grant's chuckle pulls me back to the present, his grin showing a flash of teeth. I just shake my head, smirking.

"Well, I'd better get going," Grant says, slapping a hand on the side of the truck. "Take care, Jake."

"Thanks again, Grant. We'll probably see you next week," I call, waving as he climbs back into his truck. As I watch him drive away, a sense of calm settles over me. In a world where people like us have to stay hidden, it's good to know there are bonds that go deeper than what the townsfolk see. We've got each other's backs, and that's enough.

Once Grant's taillights disappear, I lock up the shop and head up the trail toward my parents' house. As soon as I step inside, the smell of my ma's cooking hits me, and my stomach growls in response.

"Ma!" I call out, already heading toward the kitchen.

"In here!" her voice rings out.

I walk into the kitchen and immediately wrap my arms around her sturdy frame from behind, pressing a quick kiss to her cheek.

"Hey, baby," she says, her voice warm and filled with that familiar smile. I let her go, and she turns to face me, her piercing blue eyes practically glowing with happiness. I take a second to soak her in—her long black hair, now threaded with more gray, falling in soft waves. The lines around her eyes and mouth, carved by years of laughter, make her look even more radiant. She's tall for a woman, nearly up to my shoulders, and solid like a rock.

She cups my face with both hands, pulling me down to plant a few kisses on my forehead, just like she's done since I was a kid.

I grin as I straighten up. "Dad said you had a list for Mac's?"

She scoffs, giving me a light slap on the arm and rolling her eyes. "I swear, that man would rather do anything than make the trip to town himself."

I chuckle, nodding in agreement. She heads to the fridge, pulls off the list, and hands it over before turning back to the stove.

"I'll be back soon. Try not to give Dad too much hell while I'm gone."

She throws a sly grin over her shoulder that sends an immediate chill down my spine. "Oh, I won't," she says, the mischievous tone in her voice making it clear she's up to something.

I don't want to stick around to find out what. I shove the list in my pocket and start for the door, but before I can take my first step, Dad comes strolling around the corner wearing nothing but brown leather chaps with fringe along the sides.

"Howdy, ma'am," Dad says, trying to sound smooth, one hand on his hip. "I heard you were willin' to help a cowboy pract—" His words die in his throat when he spots me standing there. His eyes widen, and he scrambles to cover himself, looking both mortified and ridiculous as he tries to shield his erection with his hands.

"Nope," I mutter, throwing up a hand to shield my eyes. I don't need to see this, not ever. I stumble toward the door, trying to avoid looking at anything while my mom's laughter rings out behind me.

Navigating the bustling market, the hum of whispered conversations trails behind me, a constant, irritating buzz. I keep my ears perked, hoping to catch fragments of the gossip swirling through the air.

"Did you hear about the rancher in Winchester?" a woman mutters, stealing glances my way. "They say he was attacked by... one of those predators."

"Those predator shifters are nothing but trouble," another voice responds, low but sharp. My stomach tightens. I know that voice. It's the town's resident shit-stirrer, Susan Cummings. I resist the urge to grumble out loud.

Susan stands tall, her silver-white hair in its usual stiff updo, a reflection of her prim and proper attitude. Her high-necked blouse, knee-length skirt, and pointed heels scream I'm better than you, just like she does with every glance, every word. She's always judging, always looking down her nose at the rest of us.

"Can't trust any of them," she scoffs, her voice loud enough for anyone nearby to hear. "Good thing we don't let any of those creatures into our town. Could you imagine?"

My jaw clenches. I've heard this shit my whole life, but it still lands like a punch to the gut every time. They lump us all together, reducing us to dangerous animals, all because of the magic we're born with. I try to shake it off, to ignore the bitterness clawing at my chest, but their words keep pulling me in.

"No, I couldn't," a third woman chimes in. "My granddaughter is a squirrel shifter. This place has always been a safe haven for her since we rid ourselves of their kind thirty years ago."

"Exactly," Susan snaps, her tone dripping with righteousness. "That's what makes Willow's Haven different. We've made it clear—only non-predatory shifters are welcome. It's what keeps this town safe for everyone, especially the children. No need to worry about those dangerous predators causing trouble."

Every word feels like a mountain pressing down on me. I grew up here, in this so-called safe haven, but there's no escaping the way people like Susan look at us—like we're all just one mistake away from proving their twisted assumptions right. I grind my teeth and keep walking, trying not to let their venom sink too deep. But it's hard.

As she continues talking, a tight knot forms in my chest. The lively market around me fades, sounds muffled as if I'm underwater. The irony hits hard—this supposed haven feels like anything but for people like me.

My fists clench at my sides, nails digging into my palms. Part of me wants to bolt, to say fuck it to this town and everyone in it. The sense of being an outsider in my own home wraps around me like a suffocating cloak.

But damn it, this is my home just as much as theirs. I square my shoulders, refusing to be pushed out of a place I have every right to be in. Consequences be damned. If only they knew who we really are, maybe things would be different. We've lived here for generations without harming anyone. That goes for Charlie, the twins, their families, and all the other predator shifters hiding in plain sight.

The first woman nods, eyes darting around as if predators might leap from the shadows. "It's comforting to know that our town is so careful about who comes and goes," she says. "Keeps the community strong and secure."

My heart pounds against my ribcage, each beat echoing louder than the last. The weight of their words presses down, the fear of discovery tightening its grip. It's clear their prejudice isn't going anywhere. Maybe one day we'll have to leave just to keep ourselves safe. Today is not that day. The bitter irony twists like a knife in my gut.

I snatch up the last items on Mom's list and make my way up front. I hurry through checkout, grabbing my bags with slightly more force than necessary. Head down, I weave through the crowd in the parking lot, eager to escape the suffocating atmosphere. My truck offers little comfort as I make my way back up the mountain. The path feels steeper today, every mile heavier.

At the shop, I stash the groceries in the fridge and fire off a quick text to Dad: "Left the stuff in the shop fridge." No way am I heading back to their house after what I saw earlier. The memory of Dad in those chaps makes me cringe. Gross.

Locking up, I head home. A hot shower and a change of clothes might help wash away the tension coiled inside me. Maybe a night out with the boys is exactly what I need to drown out the worries that won't stop gnawing at me.

Chapter 3

"Charlie, I swear, if you don't stop fussin' over me, I'll kick you out of my pack," I mutter, narrowing my gaze at him. My piercing blue eyes meet his steady, unflinching brown ones, but there's no conviction behind my words. He always means well, the voice of reason that keeps our group balanced.

Charlie just grins, running a hand through his messy sandy brown hair, his usual calmness rolling off him in quiet waves. "Relax, Jake," he says with a chuckle. "I'm just trying to make sure you look presentable tonight. You never know when you might meet that special someone." His smirk widens. "So long as you stay out of trouble, that is. I know how hard that is for you;" His tone drips with playful sarcasm.

"Especially when Beau and Buckley are around," I add, glancing over at the twins. They're huddled together, snickering like they always do when they're about to pull something. Their green eyes gleam with mischief, and even from here, I can feel the restless energy radiating off them.

Charlie gives a knowing nod. "Yeah, those two are a handful."

I sigh, clapping him on the back. "Alright, alright. That's enough. Let's just enjoy the festival."

We walk through the festival, the air thick with the sounds of music and laughter, lanterns casting warm glows on the faces of the townsfolk. Families huddle close, couples wander hand in hand, and for a moment, I feel an unfamiliar tug deep inside me. The joyful atmosphere swirls around me, but I can't shake the melancholy feeling in my chest—a longing that sits quietly, growing stronger with each passing step.

Amid the vibrant celebration, I can't shake the quiet tension that lingers beneath the surface. We walk among people who don't know us—who don't know what we are—and that distance feels sharper than ever. The shifter communities remain divided by invisible lines, unspoken tensions; and here we are, hiding in plain sight among those who might wish us harm if they knew.

I glance at the smiling faces, the carefree laughter, and it feels both close and impossibly far. My family is just trying to blend in, to stay unnoticed, but I want more. I long for a connection that isn't built on secrecy and fear, for something beyond the walls we've built to protect ourselves. Watching the townsfolk revel in their joy, something deep inside stirs—an ache for understanding, for unity, for a life where we don't have to hide who we are.

"Come on, let's try some of that food," Charlie says, nodding toward a booth where the air is thick with the scent of sizzling meat and fried dough.

My stomach growls; the smell alone makes' my mouth water. "Yeah, let's do it."

I glance over at Beau and Buckley, already distracted, their eyes locked on a game booth where brightly colored prizes hang overhead. Their hands twitch like they're already scheming. "Stay close," I warn, my voice stern. "No trouble tonight, boys."

"Of course not, Jake," they echo in unison, but the mischievous smirks curling at the corners of their mouths say otherwise.

We wade into the festival, the vibrant energy of the crowd wrapping around us. Laughter rises and falls like waves, blending with the clink of glasses and the hum of conversation. I weave through clusters of people, the glow of string lights overhead casting a warm glow on faces. My gaze catches on a young mother kneeling beside a bawling child, an overturned ice cream cone melting into the pavement at her feet. Her soft whispers try to soothe the sobbing, her hand brushing through the child's hair as tears roll down his flushed cheeks.

I pull my eyes away, realizing too late that Charlie, Beau, and Buckley have disappeared into the sea of people. My heart picks up as I scan the crowd, my focus shifting to the food booth ahead. The small gathering there buzzes with excitement, but none of them are my friends.

Just as I'm about to push forward, something—or someone—crashes into me. I stumble back a step, catching my balance. Looking down, I lock eyes with her—a woman standing just inches from me, her cheeks flushed a deep rose, bright brown eyes wide with surprise. Her lips part, but she looks too embarrassed to speak, her delicate face framed by loose strands of her hair.

I'm frozen, time slowing as her soft gaze holds mine, and something about the way they catch the light pulls me in. There's a vulnerability in her gaze, a kind of quiet sincerity that's disarming, making the crowded festival feel like it's miles away. The clamor of voices, the music, the hum of life around us fades into a distant blur. It's just the two of us, suspended in a moment that feels stretched thin, like time itself is holding its breath.

"Sorry," she says, her voice barely audible even to my wolf hearing.

I give her my best grin, trying to convey calm and friendliness. "No problem," I reply, eyes still locked on hers. She's breathtaking with her dark brown hair that falls over her shoulders and her expressive, bright brown eyes. She looks up at my 6'1" frame from about my chin height, putting her an around 5'4". She's got a pear-shaped body with an ass that looks about ready to burst out of her painted-on jeans. I grunt inwardly while trying not to think about all the things that I would do to an ass like hers.

I blink a few times trying to rid myself of the mental image when her fingers, delicate and pale, curl around a small ball for one of the carnival games next to us. My eyes catch the movement, and without a second thought, I extend my hand toward her. "Here, let me help you," I say, my voice soft but inviting, hoping she'll take the chance to stay just a little longer.

Chapter 4

SARAH

As I pull into the parking lot, a hum of energy vibrates through the air. I step out of the car, heart fluttering, my chest tightening with nerves as I move toward the festival gates. Colorful flags whip in the breeze, their bright hues spinning in a kaleidoscope of motion. Laughter rings out, carefree and contagious, as kids dash between booths, their excitement sparking in the air like electricity.

I pause just inside the entrance, scanning the crowd for Lila when my phone buzzes. A message flashes across the screen:

> Lila: Hey Sarah. I think I have food poisoning. It's bad. Sorry, I can't make it.

My stomach clenches. I quickly type back, thumbs dancing across the keyboard:

> Sarah: It's okay. Hope you feel better ttyl.

A thumbs-up emoji pops up in response, but the sinking feeling lingers. For a moment, I hover there, torn between leaving and staying. The thought of going home feels tempting, as a wave of anxiety tugs at me.

But then another voice, quieter but firmer, pushes back. Why waste gas for nothing—no, I had to stay, if only for a little while.

You can do this.

You can do this.

You can do this.

I think to myself as I move through the crowd.

The festival buzzes around me, a whirlwind of people, sights, and sounds. I feel small, exposed, surrounded by strangers. My fingers twitch slightly, a reminder of my discomfort; the memory of that dark day when I found my mom floods my senses. But I shake it off, planting one foot forward, then another. Fear doesn't get to own me today.

I inch closer to a game booth, my eyes catching the glint of hanging stuffed animals, their colors vibrant in the carnival light. My steps falter—uncertainty flickers, but the chatter around me pulls me onward. I toss a few bills at the carnie and reach for a ball, the game before me suddenly feeling like a mountain I have to climb.

Just as I'm about to throw, I stumble back, my shoulder bumping into someone solid. I whirl around, cheeks flushing hot with embarrassment, and lock eyes with a man. His dark brown hair ruffles slightly in the breeze, but it's his eyes—piercing blue—that pin me in place. My breath hitches. He stands there, calm, easy, like the world doesn't exist beyond this moment, beyond us.

For a brief second, everything fades—the noise, the crowd, the festival itself. It's just him, standing there as if he were meant to be. The nervous flutter in my chest quiets as I take in his presence, the unfamiliar sense of calm settling over me.

"Sorry," I whisper, my voice barely audible amid the din of festival-goers.

He grins, a smile that sends a shiver racing down my spine. "No problem," he says, eyes still locked with mine, like they're seeing more than I'm used to anyone seeing.

His presence feels like a melody woven through the festival's chaotic symphony. Every glance shared between us seems to whisper secrets, unspoken and profound. His blue eyes, deep and clear, hold a quiet understanding that seeps through my defenses, making me feel both vulnerable and oddly safe. When he smiles, it's as if a hidden promise of laughter and adventure flickers in the warmth of his gaze.

"Here, let me help you," he says, extending his hand with a confident ease.

"Thanks," I reply, watching as his expert throw topples the target. The booth attendant grumbles as he hands us a stuffed raccoon while muttering under his breath about lucky shots.

"Wow, you're really good at this!" I exclaim, genuine admiration coloring my tone.

"Years of practice," he states with a playful wink, causing my heart to skip a beat.

He presents the raccoon to me with a triumphant grin. "Here you go!"

"Thank you!" I say, eyes widening with delight as I clutch the plush toy. The joy I feel radiates from me, a warm beam breaking through clouds of uncertainty. "You have no idea how much this means to me."

"Really?" he asks, touched by my enthusiasm. "Well, I'm glad I could get it for you."

A flicker of hesitation passes over me. There's something in his smile, his eyes, that makes me want to trust him. I don't know what it is about him, but something is putting my body at ease and making me feel safer in his presence than I have in a long time. I take a breath while nerves swirl in my belly, but not from fear or apprehension; instead, it's attraction that is giving me jitters.

"You see, winning this particular animal is a bit ironic," I begin, dropping my voice to a conspiratorial whisper.

"Go on," he encourages, leaning in with genuine interest.

"Well," I continue, "I'm actually... a raccoon shifter." I laugh nervously, studying his reaction. He remains calm, inviting me to say more. "So, winning this stuffed raccoon is quite ironic."

"Wow," he says, eyes widening in surprise but showing no judgment. "I didn't expect that—a squirrel shifter or maybe an owl..."

"Really? You didn't pick up on it?"

"I sensed you were a shifter," he says softly, "just not which type. It's kind of hard to pin down really since the magic all feels the same, regardless."

"Yes... it does." I reply, my heart stuttering for a moment as my thoughts turn to Mom and how much better things would have been lately if I could tell which shifters were predators and which ones weren't.

"Hey, you okay?" he asks while tilting my face back up to meet his with a gently brush of his finger under my chin.

"Oh. Yes.," I say, shaking out my thoughts and offering him a warm smile. Cradling the stuffed raccoon close, I take in every detail of his face, suddenly feeling as if I'm standing in the presence of a man so stupidly attractive it has to be illegal—like the universe decided to show off and dumped all its best features into one infuriatingly perfect package. I clear my throat. "I'm Sarah Miller."

"Miller, huh? That's kinda funny given where we are," he chuckles, and I nod in agreement.

"Well, it's nice to meet you, Sarah. I'm Jake. Jake Walker." He extends his hand, and when our fingers touch, a spark seems to jump between us. "Fancy meeting you here."

"Is it strange? I mean, it is a town festival after all," I tease, my shyness melting away as we exchange playful banter.

"True," Jake agrees, eyes locked with mine. "But sometimes, the most extraordinary things happen in the most ordinary places."

"Like winning a raccoon stuffie for a raccoon shifter at a game booth?" I ask with a laugh, sensing there's something heavier beneath the surface—like the universe nudged us into the same space at the exact right time, just to see what might happen.

"Exactly," Jake says, his voice soft. "You never know when fate might step in and change everything."

As the festival buzzes around us, it's like the noise dulls and we're in our own quiet bubble. Just the two of us, standing there like we've known each other longer than a minute, and neither of us is in a rush to break whatever this is.

"Wait..." I gasp, a sudden realization dawning on me when I notice his magic for the first time. "You're a shifter too."

Jake's smile lights up his face as he leans in, his breath warm against my ear. "Yes," he whispers. "I'm—"

Without warning, his warmth rips away, sudden and jarring. One second he's there, solid and steady—and the next, he's on the ground, as if yanked out of existence. Two men are on top of him, pinning him down, laughing like they didn't just shatter the moment and crash straight through me. "Get off of me, you idiots," he grunts, trying to push them away.

I stifle a laugh as the curly-haired men scramble to their feet, pulling Jake up. Just as they get him upright, another man strides over and grips the back of their collars. "I knew I shouldn't have let you two out of your cages," he chides.

"Ah, come on, Charlie," one twin says.

"We can't let Jake be the only one who gets to talk to the pretty lady," the other one adds with a wink, and it finally clicks—they're identical twins. Heat creeps up my neck as the realization sinks in.

"And how exactly did you think your antics would win the lovely lady's attention?" Charlie asks, holding them firmly. He looks like a weary father dealing with misbehaving children.

"I think we did just fine. Didn't we, lovely?" the first twin says, flashing a bright smile at me that gives his face a more boyish charm.

"Don't even think about it," Jake grumbles beside me.

The twins exchange a look before turning back to me. "What's your name, Darlin'?" the second twin asks.

"Sarah," I mumble shyly, barely above a whisper.

"Saraaah," they say in unison, almost like a sigh.

Charlie rolls his eyes and starts shoving the twins back into the crowd. "Come on, you two. Enough of that."

The first twin tries to wriggle free. "Seriously, man?" he complains.

The second twin twists around, giving me one last look. "If you get tired of Mr. Dull and Boring and want some real fun, just let us know, Darlin'. My brother and I know how to show a beautiful woman a good time." He winks at me as Charlie drags them away.

Jake runs a hand over his face. "Christ, Buckley," he mutters under his breath.

I watch, stunned, as Charlie pulls the twins further out of sight. Jake turns back to me, looking apologetic. "I'm sorry about them," he says with a sigh. "Beau and Buckley can be a little..."

"Eccentric?" I suggest.

Jake chuckles, rubbing the back of his neck. "That's one way to put it."

"I hope they didn't ruin your night." His eyes dart around, as if he's afraid I might want to leave after their display.

I blush, feeling a lump of shyness in my throat. "It's quite alright. I haven't been that entertained in a while." His face brightens at my words.

"Alright, Little Trash Panda, where to next?" Jake asks playfully, draping an arm around my shoulders as we wander through the festival.

"Little Trash Panda?" I ask, my cheeks flushing with the nickname. My heart flutters, and I can't help but like it. "I guess I like it," I admit with a shy smile, leaning into his side. His warmth and presence make me feel secure.

"Good," he grins. "It suits you."

Together, we soak in the festival's sights, sounds, and aromas. The energy is infectious, and I feel myself getting swept up in the excitement.

"Ooh! Let's try some of those caramel apples!" I exclaim, pointing to a booth adorned with glossy treats.

"Great idea, Little Trash Panda," Jake agrees, leading me to the booth. We each grab a caramel apple that has thankfully been pre-sliced, the sticky sweetness making our fingers messily delightful.

"UH! This is amazing!" I declare while trying not to devour the whole thing in one go.

Jake chuckles. "Looks like you've got a little something right here," he teases, tapping his own nose. I quickly wipe away the caramel, laughing.

"Thanks," I say, rolling my eyes playfully while also blushing.

We finish our treats, and I pull out a small packet of wet wipes from my purse, offering Jake one. He takes the offered wipe and cleans each finger, making my mouth water as I get a good look at his thick fingers and the bulging veins that run along the back of his hands. He catches me staring and smirks. I quickly dart my eyes away, looking anywhere but at him. I aggressively scrub at my own hands until those same fingers wrap around mine, halting my movements.

He stays silent, taking the wipe with his other hand before threading our fingers together. I chance a glance at his face to find him grinning down at me.

"Come on. Let me show you around, Little Trash Panda."

I nod in agreement and motion for him to lead the way.

As we stroll hand in hand through the festival, I steal glances at Jake. Despite his broad, intimidating frame, he moves with a quiet, effortless grace—like a shadow slipping through moonlight. It amazes me how someone so strong can carry himself with such calm, easy gentleness.

As the sun sinks below the horizon, spilling pink and orange across the sky, we wander deeper into the festival. When we stumble across a comedy show, Jake wraps an arm around my shoulders, pulling me close as laughter fills the air, blending with the mild warmth of the evening and the buzz of carnival magic.

"Hey," he murmurs, eyes flicking toward the glowing Ferris wheel in the distance, "how about a ride?"

"Sounds like fun," I say, though my voice barely masks the rush pounding in my chest. Every step toward the Ferris wheel winds the tension tighter—like my heart's holding its breath, waiting. I can't stop the thoughts spiraling in my head. What happens at the top? Will he reach for my hand again, anchoring me in that quiet way he does—or will he close the space between us, tilt the world on its axis, and kiss me like he means it?

In line, our fingers intertwine, and a thrill of excitement runs through me. Despite knowing each other only a short time, it feels like we've been waiting to connect. The festival's buzz fades as we step into the small carriage. Jake's gaze lingers on me, his eyes reflecting the dimming light around us.

"Come on, Little Trash Panda, let's see the view from the top," Jake murmurs, his breath warm against my ear. As the wheel begins its ascent, I feel a magnetic pull drawing us closer, a connection strengthening with each passing moment.

"Wow," I exhale, taking in the sweeping panorama of the festival below. "It's so beautiful up here."

"Almost as beautiful as you," Jake whispers, and warmth rushes to my cheeks. His words settle over me like sunlight, soft and steady, filling my chest with something bright and fluttering.

"Thank you," I murmur, meeting his gaze. The Ferris wheel lights shimmer in his eyes, casting reflections that pulse with the rhythm of the ride, while the distant festival sounds blur into a quiet hum around us.

"So," he says, his voice low but curious, "tell me about your family."

There's something in the way he looks at me—so present, so genuinely interested—that makes the words come easier than I expected.

"Well, my dad and I moved to a town close to here from Georgia a few months ago. My mom passed away two years ago, and we needed a fresh start." Jake wraps his arm around my shoulder, giving a comforting squeeze. "I'm sorry to hear about your mom," he says, his voice tinged with empathy.

"It's okay. We're taking it day by day. The move has actually been good for us," I continue, feeling more at ease. "He ran a bookstore back home. It was easy for him to get a job at the library with Ms. Wilks. I think she might have a bit of a crush on him," I add with a nervous chuckle. The thought of my dad with someone new leaves a sour taste on my tongue. "As for me, I've always loved nature. It's kind of fitting, considering..." I gesture to the stuffed raccoon, a playful smile on my lips.

"Ah, yes," Jake laughs, acknowledging my shifter nature. "Nature seems to be a common passion among shifters."

His eyes widen, a look of recognition dawning on his face. "Wait... Your dad works for Janet Wilks?"

I nod slowly, a hint of uncertainty in my expression.

"So, you're living in Willow's Haven," he says, his grin growing wider. "You're the new transplant. Well, I'll be damned."

My eyes must look comically large as I stare at him. "You live in Willow's Haven too?"

"Yep, sure do. Small world, huh?"

I laugh, the surprise mirrored in his amusement. "It really is."

We let the revelation hang between us for a moment. Then my curiosity takes over, prompting me to lean in, eager to learn more.

"What about you?" I ask, a quiet spark in my voice. "Tell me about your family."

Jake hesitates, then begins. "My father's a carpenter. I work with him at his shop up the mountain. He likes to stay close to my mother. They lost my younger brother when I was very young. My mother's strong, but it still worries him." He sighs. "Charlie and the twins have become like adopted children to her. They keep her busy and, in a way, help heal her heart." He chuckles.

"I'm sorry about your brother. I can't imagine how hard that must have been. Has your family always lived here?"

He smiles, a touch of nostalgia in his eyes. "Yes, and no. My dad grew up here, but he moved us back after my brother passed. This town seems to have a knack for taking in wounded souls and helping them heal."

"That sounds comforting," I say, my voice soft. I think of my own wounds and how healing seems just out of reach. Having them soothed would be a weight off my chest, but I'm still not sure if I'm ready for that.

"What about your dreams?" I ask genuinely interested.

"Working with my dad is my dream," Jake says, his eyes bright with passion. "I want to build our family business into a nationwide brand. I think deep down he wants that too."

I see the fire in his eyes, and my heart swells with admiration. "That's a beautiful dream, Jake. I believe you can achieve it."

"Thank you, Little Trash Panda," he says warmly, brushing his hand against mine. "What about you? What's your dream?"

"I'd love to work with animals one day," I share, my confidence growing. "Maybe at a rehab center or sanctuary—somewhere I can actually help them heal."

"That sounds like a passion worth fighting for," Jake observes, squeezing my hand gently.

As we continue sharing stories, my shyness fades under Jake's warm gaze and genuine interest. Our laughter flows freely as we tease and talk about our dreams, the connection between us deepening. The Ferris wheel carries us high above the festival, but the view is secondary to the comfort and understanding we find in each other's company.

Chapter 5

The Ferris wheel creaks as it hits the apex, the city lights below smearing into ribbons of motion and noise. Cool air grazes my skin, but it's Sarah I feel—her presence steady and electric, grounding me in a moment that hums with quiet tension. The carnival shrinks to a background murmur, like a dream slipping out of reach. Up here, it's just us—suspended in the hush between steel and stars, hearts beating in the pause before gravity remembers we exist.

"Sarah," I breathe, my voice barely carrying over the faint hum of the machinery. "I don't want this night to end."

She turns toward me, her soft eyes reflecting the faint glow of the distant lights. "Neither do I," she whispers, the words soft, fragile. "But all good things..."

She doesn't finish. She doesn't have to.

I look at her, the gravity of the moment settling deep as I tell myself that I need to say something, anything, to get this girl to understand just how badly I want to keep seeing her. "It doesn't have to be the end for us."

Her gaze locks onto mine, her lips parting slightly, a question hanging between us. The ride pauses at the top, and my gaze goes to her lips. They look soft and sweet. The slightly plumper lower lip just begging for me to bite it gently before allowing my tongue to dance along with hers. She pulls that enticing lip between her teeth, and I lose all sense of being. If I don't taste her lips in the next five seconds, I'm not sure I'll survive the sixth. I reach out, my fingers brushing a strand of her brown hair back behind her ear, lingering just long enough to cup her cheek.

"Sarah..." I exhale her name. "I'd really like to kiss you."

Her lip slips free, leaving a slick shine behind that catches the light—and my full attention. I couldn't tear my eyes away—even if the world caught fire around us. She draws in a breath and leans in, close enough that her exhale brushes my mouth, soft and warm, like a promise hanging between us. "I'd like that," she whispers, her voice brushing my lips like foreplay—soft, wicked, and full of promise. One word away from a moan. One breath away from begging.

I don't hesitate. I close the gap, our lips meeting softly at first, testing the waters. But the moment she responds, a soft moan escaping her, my restraint breaks. My hand slides to the back of her head, fingers threading into her hair as my tongue traces her bottom lip, asking for more. She opens for me, like a flower reaching for the sun, and I dive deeper, her soft gasps wrapping around me. She tastes like heaven and sin, a sweetness that sinks into me, and I know—right here, I'd give her anything.

Time bends, the world forgotten, until the gentle lurch of the Ferris wheel reminds us it hasn't stopped for us. Reluctantly, I pull away, stealing a few lingering kisses before resting my forehead against hers, trying to catch my breath.

"Christ," I mutter, catching her gaze. Her dazed look nearly undoes me. Her lips are swollen from our kiss, and it takes everything in me not to dive back in. This woman, I swear, is going to be the death of me. I can feel it deep in my bones.

As the Ferris wheel begins its slow descent, the lights and noise of the festival seep back in, reality crawling its way between us. The moment's ending—but it doesn't feel like one. When we step off and drift through the thinning crowd, her hand in mine, there's a pull deep in my chest that whispers this is only the beginning.

We reach the parking lot, the night air cool against my skin, but it does nothing to quiet the heat still burning low and steady inside me.

"I want to see you again," I murmur, dragging her against me. My fingers press into the curve of her waist, not soft—just enough to let her feel it, how tightly I'm strung, how badly I want her. She's in my space, in my blood, and I'm not ready to let her go.

"I'd like that," she whispers, mimicking her words from earlier. I stifle a groan and remind my dick that he can't have her, not yet.

I kiss her one last time, slow and possessive, dragging it out like I'm branding the taste of her. Then, I pull back just enough to hand her my phone. She takes it with that same damn lip caught between her teeth, a shy smile tugging at her mouth as she taps in her number—like she doesn't know she's killing me one sweet second at a time.

I release her, slow and unwilling, like letting go of something I already know I'll crave the second she's gone.

"Goodnight, Little Trash Panda," I say, the nickname slipping out with a grin. "I'll call you."

"You better," she teases, slipping into her car with one last smirk that damn near levels me. I watch as her taillights fade into the dark, my body still humming with the imprint of her—her mouth, her laugh, the way she fit against me like something I'd been missing.

The festival noise dulls behind me, rides powering down one by one until only the chirp of crickets and the hush of wind remain. Still, my smile holds steady.

"She's going to be my wife," I murmur to the night, watching my breath curl in the cool air. The moon throws silver across the pavement, painting the empty lot in quiet promise. I turn toward my car, every thought soaked in her—her scent, her voice, the taste of her lips still burning on mine.

The drive home is fucking torture. Every red light punishes me; every mile reminds me how good she felt pressed against me—soft, warm, made to fit there.

By the time I walk through my door, my fingers are already twitching for my phone. It takes everything I've got not to call her. Hell, if I thought she wouldn't think I was desperate, I'd hit dial without hesitation.

Tomorrow can't come fast enough. Not when every part of me already wants more.

Chapter 6

I sit on the edge of my bed, phone in hand, staring at Sarah's name glowing on the screen. My heart's hammering, a mess of excitement and nerves twisting in my gut. Ever since the festival last week, she's been stuck in my head—her laugh, her mouth, the way her body melted into mine.

We've been texting nonstop—memes, banter, late-night jokes—but I haven't had the balls to actually call her. Not yet. That kiss won't leave me alone, and hell, I swear I can still smell her perfume on my jacket.

I want more. I want her voice in my ear, her heat against me. But fuck, I'm sitting here nervous as a long-tailed cat in a room full of rocking chairs.

I take a deep breath and hit the call button. The line rings, and instantly my brain goes into overdrive. What the hell am I even going to say?

My fingers tap a restless rhythm on my thigh, trying to settle the chaos swarming in my chest. It's ridiculous—just a phone call, but it's got me more twisted up than I care to admit.

Each ring cranks up the tension. My mind spins through every scenario. What if she doesn't answer? What if she does? What if I say something dumb and ruin it all? I'm seconds from hanging up, convincing myself voicemail would be safer. Cleaner.

Then — "Hello?"

Her voice cuts through the silence like a warm light in a dark room. Just one word, and the nerves drop out of me in a rush.

Shit. Now I actually have to speak.

"Hey, Sarah. It's Jake," I manage, aiming for casual but hearing the stiffness in my own voice. Idiot. Of course, she knows it's me.

My nerves hijack my mouth. "I, uh, was wondering if you'd want to go on a date."

Great job, dumbass. Real smooth. My heart stutters as silence stretches on the other end—long enough to make me wonder if I already screwed this up.

I rush to cover it. "It'd be real laid-back, nothin' too fancy. Just a chance for us to hang out, chat a bit, maybe grab a bite to eat. What do ya think?"

The pause that follows feels like it's stretching out forever. I'm already bracing for rejection, but then her voice comes through, soft and warm. "That sounds real nice, Jake. I don't have another day off 'til Sunday, though. Unless you're free today—I'm actually off right now."

"Great!" I utter, barely keeping the grin out of my voice. Truth is, I already knew she was off today—small towns make it real easy to learn things you're not technically supposed to know.

"Yeah, I'm free. Let's make it happen. I mean—only if you're good with that. We could go today. How about I pick you up around noon?"

"Oh, um, yeah, that sounds good, if, you know, that's okay with you..." she says, her voice a little hesitant but sweet.

She gives me her address, and I can't stop the stupid grin from stretching across my face. As soon as we hang up, I fist-pump the air like a damn teenager. Hell yeah. I can't believe I actually pulled that off.

"Alright, I'll see you then. Be sure to come hungry."

"Okay. See you then."

We say our goodbyes, and the second the call ends, adrenaline kicks in like a shot of espresso. There's this buzz under my skin—something electric, something hopeful. And hell, I'm already thinking about where this might go.

My palms are suddenly sweaty, so I wipe them on my jeans and head for the shower. Noon's not far off, and I've got work to do if I'm gonna pick her up looking like anything more than a mess.

Today, I don't want to be a half-ass snack. I need to show up looking like the whole damn meal.

A few minutes before noon, I pull up to Sarah's small bungalow on the edge of town. My eyes catch on the red roses lining her front garden—starting to wilt, just like the weather shifting into fall. There's a flicker of nervous energy in my gut as I park and step out of the truck, shaking out my hands to kill the jitters.

Deep breath. I walk up, ring the bell.

The door swings open—and there she is. Bright eyes lock onto mine, and for a second, I forget how to breathe. She's stunning—hair pulled back in a ponytail, a simple sundress hugging that petite frame in all the right ways. She's wearing some nude colored leggings underneath, which I find odd but don't comment on. The weather is warm enough today for that curve hugging dress, and I thank every God I can think of for this blessing.

"Hi, Jake," she says, voice soft, a little shy. She twirls a piece of hair around her finger, that sweet smile playing on her lips.

"Hey, Sarah. You look..." I pause, exhale, trying not to sound like I've been mentally undressing her since Tuesday. "Amazing."

And I mean it. Too much. My dick perks up like it heard its name called. I immediately counterattack with mental images—my dad strolling into the kitchen in nothing but those hideous leather chaps the other day. That does the trick. Crisis averted.

She blushes, her cheeks blooming that soft pink that makes it real hard not to stare. "Thank you. You look nice too."

I offer her my arm, trying to play it cool even though my pulse is anything but. "Shall we?"

"Um, sure," she says, slipping her hand into the crook of my arm like it's the most natural thing in the world. We walk to the truck, talking about little things—weather, the town, the flowers in her yard—anything to keep the nerves at bay.

I help her into the passenger seat, shut the door gently, and then slide behind the wheel. The engine rumbles to life, and I pull onto the street, excitement thrumming just under my skin. She's right here beside me, and this date? Yeah, it's finally happening.

Chapter 7

As we pull up to the scenic overlook, my breath catches. The mountains stretch across the horizon, casting long shadows over the town below. The sky is wide and open, streaked with early afternoon gold. A hush settles over *everything*, the kind that seeps into your chest and makes you feel the quiet.

I turn to Jake with a smile, the enormity of the moment grounding me.

"Wow, this is beautiful," I say, eyes scanning the view. "I didn't realize this was so close to town. You can see everything from up here."

Jake's blue eyes spark with quiet pride. "I'm glad you like it," he says, voice low and sure. "I wanted to take you somewhere special. Somewhere we could actually talk. Just us. No distractions."

"Really?" I murmur, surprised by the thoughtfulness. Normally, I'd be bracing for tension, for that flicker of fear that always shows up when I'm alone with someone new. But with Jake... it's different.

There's no tightness in my chest. No urge to keep my distance. Just a slow, unfamiliar ease sinking into my bones.

For the first time in a long while, I feel like *me*—the version of me I thought I'd lost somewhere along the way.

We climb out of the truck and stand side by side, quietly soaking in the view. The wind stirs the trees, rustling leaves like whispers around us. For a long moment, neither of us speaks—we just *exist* in it, breathing in the stillness.

"Shall we sit?" Jake nods toward a bench nestled beneath a wide oak tree, its shade spilling across the ground like a welcome invitation.

"Sure," I say, following him over.

We sit, and the silence between us doesn't feel awkward—it feels earned. Easy. Like I've been here beside him a hundred times before. The nervous energy from earlier has melted away, replaced by something softer. Calmer.

It's not surface-level comfort, either. It's something deeper—a quiet understanding that doesn't need words. We're not filling space just to avoid the quiet. We're *sharing* it. And that kind of peace? It's rare.

"How'd you find this place?" I ask, still marveling at the view. "With a view like this, you'd think it'd be crawling with tourists."

Jake grins, a mischievous glint flashing in his eyes. "Tourists won't find this spot," he says. "It's on private property—back forty of my folks' land."

"Really?" I glance around, seeing it all with fresh eyes.

He nods, then gestures to the massive oak behind us. "That tree? My great-great-grandparents planted it when they settled here. And this bench?" He taps the worn wood beneath us. "My grandparents put it in. They used to sit here every fall, just watching the leaves change. My parents still come out every year and do the same."

"I bet that's a sight to see," I murmur, imagining it—flaming reds, burned oranges, bright golds blanketing the hills. Back home, the trees just turned brown, dropped their leaves, and left everything looking like a graveyard of twisted branches.

Jake's voice drops, warm and sincere. "I could bring you back in a few weeks, when it's in full color. If you'd like."

I smile, heart lifting with the offer. "I'd love that." It's been on my bucket list for years—something I thought I'd never get around to.

He leans back against the bench, arm draped casually across the backrest, close enough that I feel the warmth of him at my shoulder. "Tell me something I don't know about you," he says, eyes on me now, inviting.

I pause, then smile softly. "When I was a teenager, I used to sneak out at night to go stargazing. It was the only time I felt... calm. The stars made everything feel smaller. Manageable. Like I wasn't drowning all the time."

His eyes light up, sincere and curious. "Really? I've always loved stargazing too. Maybe we could do that together sometime."

The idea of lying beneath the stars with Jake sends a quiet warmth through my chest. "I'd like that," I say softly, surprised by how easy it is to picture—how right it feels.

I can't believe how quickly I've opened up to him. Normally, I'm locked down tight—especially since losing my mom—but something about Jake disarms me. His presence, his voice... it settles something inside me. Like my body instinctively knows I'm safe here. With him.

"Are you hungry?" he asks after a few more minutes of easygoing conversation, his voice pulling me gently from my thoughts.

"Famished," I admit, blushing as my stomach agrees with a low growl.

"Let's set up over there, closer to the edge," he says, reaching for my hand and pulling me to my feet.

He heads to the back of the truck and grabs a picnic basket and blanket. I take a moment to breathe in the view—the mountains rising like giants in the distance, the town sprawled below us like something out of a postcard. Jake's picked the perfect spot.

"That sounds great," I say, following him over.

He spreads the blanket out with practiced ease, smoothing the fabric before placing the basket down in the center. There's a soft breeze brushing against my skin, the first hint of autumn clinging to the air.

"Shall we?" he says, gesturing for me to sit.

I lower myself onto the blanket, the moment feeling strangely intimate—like something sacred in its simplicity.

Jake opens the basket, and the scent of fresh food drifts up, making my stomach growl louder this time. "Wow, everything looks amazing," I say, eyeing the chicken salad sandwiches, the colorful mix of fruit, and two stainless-steel thermoses nestled in the corner.

"Thanks," he says, a quiet pride tugging at his smile. "I made it all myself. Wanted to make sure it was something you'd like."

"Really? You didn't have to do all that," I say, genuinely touched by how thoughtful he's been. But I can't help being impressed—it's obvious he went out of his way—every detail chosen to make this moment special. And it makes me feel... cared for. In a way I haven't felt in a long time.

"I wanted to," he says simply, handing me a sandwich. "Now, let's dig in."

The first bite is heaven—perfectly seasoned, the balance of flavors spot on. The fruit is crisp and sweet, a bright contrast to the savory richness of the sandwich. I take my time, savoring each bite, stealing glances at Jake as he eats with the same quiet appreciation.

"Jake, this is honestly one of the best chicken salad sandwiches I've ever had," I tell him, going in for another.

He beams, eyes lighting up. "Thanks, Sarah. That means a lot."

Everything about this moment feels easy—the food, the view, the soft rhythm of conversation between us. It's not just shared interests; it's something deeper. A quiet connection that feels rare, like we just... click.

As we talk, I find myself opening up without even realizing it. His laid-back energy draws the words out of me. But even in the laughter and the comfort, there's a part of me that stays guarded. A sliver of distance I can't quite shake.

There's something about Jake—something just under the surface—that I haven't figured out yet. I want to trust him, and maybe I will. But not yet. Not all the way.

For now, I push that feeling aside. I focus on the moment—the breeze lifting my hair, the mountains stretching out in front of us, and the man beside me who somehow makes the world feel a little lighter.

As I lean back on the blanket, a subtle ripple brushes over me—like static in the air, only it's not physical. It's energetic, tugging at something deep in my gut. Jake's aura presses against mine, just faintly, but enough to make the hair on the back of my neck stir.

It's not aggressive, not obviously threatening... but there's something wrong about it. Too heavy. Too wild. A tension coiled just beneath the surface that makes my instincts sit up and pay attention.

I've never been great at reading auras—never saw the point. But this one's impossible to ignore. It feels familiar in the worst way, like I've felt it before but can't remember when—just that it meant danger. His presence doesn't match the calm smile on his face. It's like standing next to a fire that hasn't caught yet—quiet, but full of potential to burn.

I glance at him. Still relaxed. Still smiling. But something primal stirs in the back of my mind. Something that whispers: Not safe.

"You okay?" he asks, his voice gentle but laced with curiosity.

I nod quickly. "Yeah. Just... zoning out."

He lets it go with a small smile, but the strange pressure doesn't lift.

Jake's a shifter—I've known that from the start. But now, some buried part of me is screaming to figure out *what kind*. And at the same time, I'm scared to know.

I take a sip from the thermos, the cold water grounding me as I shove the nerves and doubts down deep.

I'm just being paranoid.

"Your life here seems so idyllic," I say, curiosity tugging at me. "Tell me more about it. Do you live close to your parents' place?"

"Yeah, actually," Jake replies, a warm smile tugging at his lips. "My cabin's just a short walk through the woods from their house. It's quiet, secluded. I love being close enough to visit whenever, but still having my own space. And the shop's nearby, so I only really take the truck when I need to head into town."

"Sounds lovely," I murmur, picturing a cabin tucked among the trees—quiet, safe, untouched.

Then Jake shifts the spotlight back to me, his gaze steady. "Do you like living on the edge of town?"

"Absolutely," I say, my face lighting up with the answer. "It's the perfect balance. Back in Georgia, we lived close to Atlanta—sirens, traffic, constant noise. Sure, you'd hear birds, but not like you can here. We had a patch of trees around our house, just enough not to see the neighbors. But it wasn't anything like here. And stargazing? Forget it. You needed a telescope just to get past the light pollution."

I pause, glancing at the horizon. "Here, it's slower. Calmer. I wake up to birdsong every morning, and at night... you can actually see the stars. It's a mix of what I'm used to and what I always wanted."

"Wait," he says, a curious look on his face. "How did you go stargazing if the light pollution was so bad?"

I snort a laugh. "Funny story, that. So, I, um, had this friend. His name was Rico. He wanted to be an astrologist when he grew up. He used to check out books from the library—anything and everything to do with space. He was fascinated by it."

Jake smiles, giving me this look like it's the most fascinating story he's ever heard.

"So... Rico used to steal his mom's car late at night. He'd swing by my place, and we'd drive an hour—sometimes more—just to find a spot where the sky was actually dark. No lights, no noise. Just the two of us and a sky full of stars."

Jake lets out a low whistle. "Damn. That's commitment. How old were you two when you started sneaking out like that?"

"Twelve," I say, smirking a little at the memory. "Maybe twelve and a half. Rico had just figured out how to put the car in neutral and roll it down the driveway so it wouldn't wake his mom."

Jake laughs, eyes wide. "Twelve? You little rebel."

I roll my eyes, but I'm grinning. "It wasn't that bad. We weren't out doing anything stupid—we just wanted to see the stars."

"Yeah, yeah," he says, nudging me lightly with his shoulder. "Just two innocent kids committing grand theft auto for a better view of Orion's Belt."

I burst out laughing. "Okay, technically it wasn't grand theft. He always put the car back before sunrise."

Jake chuckles. "Still, I'm impressed. And here I thought you were the quiet type. Turns out, you were out living your best little delinquent life."

I shake my head, but my smile won't quit. "Not delinquent. Just... curious. And a little restless, I guess."

Jake's voice softens. "I get that."

"I still stargaze," I say, voice low and raw. "But it's different now. Every time I look up, I think about how the sky just kept going, like nothing happened. Like it didn't give a single shit that Rico died screaming in his own living room."

I swallow hard, the bitterness thick in my throat.

"But I keep doing it. Not because it comforts me. Not because it helps. I do it because he loved it. Because it was our thing. We used to lie there for hours, making up constellations and naming them after dumb movie characters. It was his escape... and he let me be a part of it."

My voice cracks.

"Now it's just me. Same stars, same silence. But it's for him. It's the only part of him I still have."

Jake reaches over, lays a hand on mine—solid, warm, steady. He doesn't offer an apology. Doesn't try to patch the hole.

He just stays there with me, quiet in the wreckage.

And somehow, that's enough.

For a long moment, neither of us says anything. The wind rustles the trees, carrying the weight of everything I just said out into the open air like a secret that finally stopped rotting inside me.

Eventually, the silence softens. Not heavy anymore—just still. Safe.

We keep talking, slower now, but easier too. And I can't help but notice how focused Jake is—his eyes never leaving mine, like every word I say matters. It's a rare feeling, being listened to so completely. It makes me feel seen in a way I haven't in a long time.

As we trade stories about our lives, the conversation pulls me in deeper, making it easier to let the heftiness slip off my shoulders. I don't even realize I'm opening up until the words are already coming out.

"You know," I say, glancing at the old barn off in the distance, "I've always been fascinated by abandoned buildings. There's something about their history—the stories left behind—that just pulls me in."

Jake raises an eyebrow, curiosity lighting his face. "Really? I don't think I've ever met anyone into that kind of thing."

"Most people think it's weird," I admit with a small shrug. "But I find it... comforting, I guess. Like the past leaves echoes, and those places still remember."

He nods slowly, thoughtful. "That actually makes sense."

I tilt my head. "What about you? Any unusual interests?"

Jake hesitates when I ask, just for a second. Then he says, "I bury caches."

I raise an eyebrow. "Caches?"

He shrugs, a little sheepish. "Yeah. Survival stuff. Knives. Fire starters. Rations. First aid. All stashed out in the woods."

I blink. "Okay... but why?"

He doesn't look at me right away—his eyes drift toward the treeline, his voice quieter when he finally answers. "Because things can go sideways fast. And not everyone around here is as friendly as they pretend to be."

The words hang heavy in the air, unspoken things tucked between each one. I wait, but he doesn't elaborate.

"So... you're just always ready to disappear?" I ask, trying to keep my tone light, though my stomach tightens.

Jake's jaw flexes slightly. "If it comes to that, yeah. Better to be prepared than caught off guard."

There's something in the way he says it—like he's not talking about some vague worst-case scenario. Like he's lived through it before.

I nod slowly. "That's... intense."

He glances over at me. "Yeah. But necessary."

I don't push further. Not yet. But something about his answer itches at the back of my mind—like my instincts are trying to tell me something I haven't quite figured out.

Chapter 8

After my confession, we fall into silence again. It's not uncomfortable, but I can feel it—her mind spinning behind those quiet eyes. Questions. Doubts. Instincts she probably doesn't even know she's picking up on.

And, fuck, I want to tell her the truth. Just say it—I'm a predator shifter—and be done with the waiting. But living in this town has beaten that impulse out of me. Around here, admitting you're a predator is like lighting the fuse on your own funeral pyre. People don't give a damn who you are once they know what you are.

It's always the same bullshit—the safety of our children—as if predator shifters are monsters lurking in closets. As if we're defined by fangs and instinct instead of choices and restraint.

We're not dangerous.

We just have bigger teeth.

The tension in the air thickens. I shouldn't have mentioned the caches. It slipped out—too honest, too revealing. But part of me wanted her to know. Wanted to offer her a glimpse of the real me, the part I bury for everyone else.

I shift my weight beside her and speak before she can retreat into her thoughts.

"Sarah," I breathe, my voice cutting through the crisp morning air like a thread. "Care to join me for a stroll in the woods?"

Her brown eyes lift to mine, curiosity flickering behind them like a flame. She gives me a small, shy smile. "I'd love to," she murmurs.

We step into the trees, and the world changes around us. The brilliance of the overlook fades behind us, replaced by the dappled hush of forest light. Sun filters through the canopy in golden shards, casting shifting patterns across the ground. The wind weaves through the branches, whispering low and steady, like the woods themselves are breathing.

Each step draws us deeper into the quiet. Leaves rustle like silk. The scent of damp earth and slow decay wraps around us, grounding everything, pulling us away from the significance of unspoken truths and into something simpler.

Here, it's just her. Just me. And the calm.

But even in this stillness, I feel the wolf stirring beneath my skin—silent, alert, watching her with a kind of longing I don't have the right to feel.

Not yet.

She glances over her shoulder, a soft smile playing on her lips, and the last of my restraint creaks under the magnitude of it.

"I love it here," I murmur, taking a deep breath to steady myself.

Sarah nods, a few strands of dark hair slipping loose from her ponytail and framing her face. She tilts her head back slightly, inhaling. "It's like you can smell everything for miles," she says, her voice laced with quiet wonder.

We keep walking, but my focus is slipping fast. My eyes betray me—dragging over the lines of her body, the way her sundress hugs her frame and moves with her like it wants you to follow the curves of the hem as she walks. I swear I've never appreciated an article of clothing more.

The hem sways with each step, teasing flashes of the curve of her ass, and I have to swallow hard. My hands ache—physically ache—to slide up her thighs, to cup the perfect curve of her ass and pull her in close. Biteable doesn't even begin to cover it.

I drag my gaze back to the trail before I do something stupid. Like licking my lips. Or reaching for her.

Or forget I'm supposed to be playing it safe.

I try to keep my eyes on the path, but it only takes a few more steps before they drift right back to her. This time, it's her breasts that steal my attention. Her dress dips just enough to tease the rise and fall of her chest with every breath. They bounce softly with each step, and fuck—my brain short-circuits.

All I can think about is how they'd feel in my hands. How full, how warm, how heavy. I wonder what color her nipples are—soft pink like cherry blossoms... or deeper, like raspberries. The image slams into me, and I choke down a curse.

Focus. Focus.

"Jake," Sarah says, voice gentle, eyes fixed on the ground. "Thank you for inviting me here. This has been the best date I've ever had."

Her words hit me harder than they should. When she looks up, her smile is bright, honest, full of warmth.

I grin, heart thudding harder than I'd like to admit. "I'm glad you're enjoying it," I say, and fuck if that doesn't feel too small for what I mean.

We keep walking deeper into the woods. At some point, without even thinking, our hands find each other. Fingers slide together like they've been waiting for this.

The world quiets around us—just the soft rustle of leaves, the crunch of old foliage beneath our feet, and the warmth of her hand in mine like an anchor I didn't know I needed.

"Listen," I whisper, gently pulling her to a stop. "Do you hear that?"

Sarah tilts her head, focusing. "Is that... a bird?" she asks, eyes scanning the canopy.

"Yeah. Sounds like it's in distress," I say, concern threading into my voice. I tighten my grip on her hand and guide her toward the sound.

We push through a thicket, and there it is—a small bird, hanging upside down, tangled in a thin length of rope. Its feathers ruffle, wings fluttering weakly as it struggles.

"Oh, poor thing," Sarah murmurs, her voice soft with worry. "We've got to help it."

"Yeah," I agree, watching her closely. There's no hesitation in her—just that fierce, clear-eyed determination I'm starting to recognize. "Let's see what we can do."

"Let me try," she says, stepping closer with deliberate care. Her focus stays locked on the bird, every movement slow and intentional.

"Careful," I warn, torn between admiration and concern. "It might peck you."

"I will be," she replies, not taking her eyes off the bird. Her voice lowers, gentle and soothing. "Hey, little one," she whispers, a quiet comfort meant more for the bird than me.

Her fingers gently brush against its feathers, and almost instantly, the bird's frantic flapping slows. It's like her touch alone is enough to calm it. She lifts the tiny creature into her palm, her eyes meeting mine in a quiet moment of understanding. We're in this together—focused, determined.

The bird, sensing her gentleness, trembles less as she strokes it with slow, careful fingers.

"We're here to help you," Sarah whispers, her voice barely louder than the breeze rustling through the leaves.

I watch completely captivated. There's something about the way she moves—so steady, so soft—it's like she's meant for this. Born for it.

"Go slow, Sarah," I whisper, not wanting to startle the bird. "It could still peck."

She nods without looking at me, her focus absolute. "Alright, little one. I'm going to get you free. Nice and slow."

"You're doing great," I murmur, a smile tugging at my lips. Her patience, her calm—it's damn near mesmerizing. And as I watch her work, I'm not the least bit surprised she wants to open an animal sanctuary. It suits her. She's a natural.

"Alright," I say, shifting my focus to the tangled rope. "Let's see what we can do to help."

Sarah nods, a fire of quiet determination lighting up her eyes. We move closer, carefully examining the knots. Our fingers brush as we work, small sparks passing between us with every touch—but we stay focused. For now.

"Okay," Sarah whispers, her breath warm against my ear. "I think if I pull here, I can slide this piece out. That should give me enough slack."

"Are you sure?" I ask, concern creeping in. "I don't want to make it worse."

She shoots me a look—half confident, half sassy. "Jake, I've untied knots before."

"Right. Sorry," I mutter, stepping back as she delicately works at the rope. Her fingers move with care and precision, tugging at the tangled strands. Slowly, the bird settles in her grip, its beady eyes locked on us, sensing we mean no harm.

"Almost there," Sarah murmurs, her body tensing with focus. "Just a little more..."

With one last twist, the knot slips free. The bird lets out a soft, relieved chirp, and we both exhale at the same time, the tension breaking in a wave of quiet relief.

"See?" Sarah smiles, her eyes crinkling at the corners. "We did it."

"Only because of you," I say, unable to keep the admiration out of my voice. "You were incredible."

She blushes, tucking a loose strand of hair behind her ear. "Thank you. But you were a great help too. Couldn't have done it without you."

I almost laugh—knowing damn well she did most of the work—but I let it slide.

The bird wiggles in her hands, chirping louder now, as if urging us to let it go.

"It's telling us it's time," Sarah says, her smile reaching all the way to her eyes.

"You ready?"

"I am."

She takes a deep breath, then lifts her hand. The bird lingers for a beat—just long enough to make it feel like a goodbye—then spreads its wings and soars into the sky.

Sarah watches, her gaze wide with wonder. "It's flying again," she whispers, like anything louder might shatter the moment.

I feel a rush of pride—not just for helping the bird, but for the quiet connection we've built in the process.

"We did that," I say, smiling at her.

Our eyes meet, and something electric sparks between us. My heart kicks hard in my chest.

"Thank you, Jake," Sarah says softly, her voice warm and sincere. "For helping me."

We both know she did the heavy lifting, but she's still thanking me—and somehow, that means more than if I had done anything heroic.

"Of course," I murmur, shaking my head with a smile.

Her eyes hold mine, and the air between us shifts—thicker now, charged. There's a pull I can't ignore, something magnetic in the way she looks at me. It's more than friendship, more than kindness. It's want—slow and building.

"Is everything okay?" she asks, tilting her head. A loose strand of dark hair brushes her cheek, and I want to reach out and tuck it behind her ear just to feel her skin.

"Yeah. Everything's... great," I manage, though my throat's dry as hell. I swallow hard. "I just... I've never met anyone like you before."

Her cheeks flush, a soft pink blooming up her neck. She glances down. "You don't have to say that."

"I mean it," I say, my voice steady now, my gaze locked on hers. "You're different. In the best possible way."

"Thank you," she whispers, her fingers twisting together in her lap. "You're pretty amazing too."

"Am I?" I ask, grinning.

She laughs, but it's quiet, nervous. "Definitely. You have this... strength about you. It's comforting."

"Strength?" I echo, raising a brow.

"Maybe it's your confidence," she says, biting her lip. Her eyes flick up to mine, linger for a second, then dip toward my mouth. "Either way... I feel safe when I'm with you."

"Sarah..." I whisper, the space between us charged, humming with anticipation. I want to tell her everything—rip the truth out of me and lay all at her feet. That I'm not just a guy with a quiet cabin and a love for the woods. That there's a part of me made of teeth and instinct and secrets. But fear knots tight in my chest. I think back to that night at the festival—the night I nearly told her everything. It hit me like a compulsion, this need to tell her everything. To stop hiding. To just be.

Thankfully, the twins knocked some sense into me—literally. It was a brutal reminder of what this town does to predators like me the second we stop pretending.

The silence stretches, thick and tense, but I can't look away. Her eyes hold too much—curiosity, hesitation, something that feels dangerously close to trust.

"Sarah," I whisper again, like her name might anchor me.

We move without speaking, like we've done this before in another life. Lips meet in the middle—soft at first, tentative. But the heat between us doesn't stay gentle for long. The kiss blooms like wildfire, slow and consuming. It tastes like something I've missed without ever knowing it.

My blood sings, my hands ache to pull her closer, and the wolf stirs beneath my skin, hungry for more.

When we break apart, the world feels slower. The trees still sway, the air still moves, but I'm stuck in the space between her lips and mine. I slide my arm around her waist, needing the contact like air.

"Come on. Let's start headin' back to the truck," I say, grinning down at her. She beams back at me, that smile so bright and pure I want to etch it into my memory forever.

"Okay," she murmurs, her arm wrapping around my waist as we walk.

I don't want this day to end. With her, everything feels lighter, simpler. She's like a cool breeze cutting through the heat or a warm fire in the middle of winter. I barely know her, but already she's wrapped around my heart. She could lift me up or shatter me with a single word—and that thought should scare the hell out of me.

But all it does is make me want more.

Chapter 9

JAKE

A few days later, I'm wrapping up at the shop, putting away tools when my phone pings. A smile pulls at my lips before I even check it—I know who it is.

Sarah.

Sarah: Hey handsome. Are we still on for tonight?

Jake: What, and miss a date with my favorite Trash Panda? Not a damn chance.

Sarah: lol. Do you have other trash pandas I should know about?

Jake: Nah, babe, you're more than enough panda for me.

Sarah: Flattered.

Jake: Finishing up now. Gimme a bit to clean up, and I'll be over. Got something special planned for tonight.

Sarah: Oooh. Sounds intriguing. Don't take too long. I'll be waiting. ☒

Jake: I won't.

I shove my phone into my pocket, finishing the last few cleanups at the shop. Tonight's the night. I'm finally taking her to that old abandoned barn we saw from the overlook.

Got permission from old man McMillian earlier this week. Not easy, but worth it. I already know she's gonna love it.

But first—shower. No way I'm showing up smelling like stain, paint, and acetone.

I clean up fast, throw on my best jeans and a fresh shirt. Keys, wallet, boots. Out the door.

When I pull up to Sarah's place, she's already at the curb, waiting—like she's been counting down the minutes. She slides into the truck, buckling up with that bright little smile that gets me every damn time.

"My dad's watching his shows," she says, before I can even ask. "Didn't want the doorbell interrupting Jeopardy."

I chuckle and nod, shifting the truck back into drive. The ride's short, filled with easy talk and dumb jokes, the kind that only seem to happen when she's around.

By the time we hit the outskirts of town, the sun's melting into the horizon, washing everything in orange and gold. I turn onto a gravel road, tires crunching as we pull into McMillian's lot. We park near the edge of the property and head into the trees.

Sarah's eyes go wide. "Where are we going?"

I grin and keep walking, the sound of her boots crunching behind me.

"Trust me," I say. "You're gonna love it."

We push through the underbrush, thick weeds brushing against our legs until the old barn comes into view. It stands there, weathered and forgotten, but still holding that rustic charm beneath the fading light. The air smells of hay, and the soft rustle of leaves fills the quiet.

I open the door for her, and we step inside.

Her breath catches as she takes it all in. The interior is lit by strands of fairy lights, casting a warm glow over everything. In the center there's a blanket spread out with a picnic basket, candles, and a bouquet of wild-flowers.

Sarah's eyes sparkle as she looks at me, pure delight lighting up her face. "Is this the old barn we saw from the cliff?"

I nod. "I know a guy who knows a guy. No worries about getting shot or arrested."

She laughs, walking slowly around the barn, taking it all in. "This is amazing, Jake. I can't believe you did all this for me."

I throw my hands out dramatically. "Yeah, I know. Another romantic-ass picnic. Really pushing the boundaries of originality here."

She smirks. "Well, it's working."

I nod, mock-serious. "Clearly. Who knew all it took to impress a girl was fairy lights and not getting arrested for trespassing?"

She snorts. "You're ridiculous."

I shoot her a grin. "Yeah, but don't pretend you're not into it. Now sit down and prepare to be fed mediocre sandwiches under questionable structural safety. Real date-of-the-year stuff happening here."

We settle onto the blanket, sharing stories and laughter as the evening unfolds. The barn creaks with every gust of wind, the structure squeaking but standing firm, even though I can't help but wonder if it might fall on us. Then again, I spent hours in here yesterday hanging from the rafters to run those fairy lights, so I know it'll hold. The stars begin to dot the sky, and the whole place takes on a magical feel, like something out of a dream.

Time slips by as we talk, the conversation easy and warm. I keep wanting to kiss her again, but I hold back. I'm trying to take it slow—let her set the pace.

Eventually, we wander outside, the cool night air brushing against our skin as we walk hand in hand through the meadow with the moonlight lighting our path.

When we reach the old spruce tree, I stop and turn to her. "I've been thinking a lot about us—about you," I say, the words tumbling out, unfiltered. "I feel like there's something real here, and I want to see where it leads."

Sarah looks up at me, a soft smile tugging at her lips. "I feel the same way, Jake. Since the day we met, it's felt like I've known you forever. It's insane... but kind of perfect, too."

I smile, soaking her in—the way the moonlight plays off her hair, the glow in her eyes. "Can I kiss you?"

Her smile deepens, and she loops her arms around my neck, pulling me in. Her lips find mine, soft and warm. I cup her face, letting my thumb trace her cheekbone as I run my tongue along the seam of her lips, asking—gently—for more. She opens to me, and our tongues meet; the taste of her hitting me like a punch to the chest.

Every instinct tells me to grab her by that perfectly rounded ass and lift her up, press her body flush against mine so we're at the same height—so she can feel every inch of what she's doing to me while I kiss her stupid. But I hold back, trying to be a good boy, trying to let her lead. I can feel the heat building between us, the tension coiled tight just under the surface—but dragging her against me and letting her feel exactly how hard I am wouldn't exactly count as playing it cool. So I deal with the dull ache building in my back from leaning down too long, and just focus on this—on the way her lips move against mine, slow and soft and goddamn perfect.

As we linger beneath the ancient spruce, the moonlight casts a soft glow around us, wrapping us in a quiet intimacy. I groan softly, reluctantly pulling away from her lips—but not before stealing a few more slow kisses. She exhales sharply, like she's just as disappointed as I am that it's over.

With a tender smile, she looks up at me. "It's so beautiful here tonight. Thank you for bringing me."

I return the smile, warmth spreading in my chest. We decide to explore more of McMillian's land, and I let her walk a few steps ahead—just enough time to discreetly adjust my dick before catching up and sliding my hand into hers.

Eventually, we make our way back to the barn, its rustic, weathered charm standing stark against the star-filled sky. We settle on the ground near the barn, leaning against its old wooden walls, gazing up at the vast expanse above us. The stars stretch endlessly, each one a tiny point of light in the darkness, painting the night sky with the beauty of the universe. It's breathtaking—but when I glance over at Sarah, the sky dims by comparison. She lights up the night around us—like her very presence outshines them all.

I watch her quietly for a moment. Emotions ripple across her face—happiness, contentment, awe... then a flicker of sadness. I know she must be thinking about her friend who loved stars—Rico. I want to share that moment with her. To let her know it's okay to grieve him, even in my presence. I'm not intimidated by the ghost of a sixteen-year-old boy who never got to see the amazing woman she grew up to be.

"Tell me more about your juvenile delinquency days," I say, my voice low and easy. "What's another favorite memory of Rico?"

She gives me a grateful look, her lips curving just before she lets out a long, steady breath.

And then she talks.

For the next thirty minutes, she tells me stories—some funny, some bittersweet, some that seem to carry the profundity of a thousand sleepless nights. I don't interrupt. I don't need to. I just listen, letting her voice fill the space between us as the stars spin quietly overhead.

There's a softness in the way she remembers him, even when the pain creeps in at the edges. Like every memory is a fragile artifact she's only now daring to touch again.

By the time she finishes, her voice is quieter, slower, like the words took something out of her. She leans her head gently against my shoulder, and I don't move. I stay right there, steady, silent—honored to hold the space.

And in that moment, I don't think about what I'm hiding. I don't think about what might happen later.

All I think about is her. And how lucky I am to be the one she's telling these stories to.

After a while, I turn to her, feeling the pull of the moment. "You know," I say, a grin tugging at my lips, "the stars up there are breathtaking, but none of them shine as brightly as you do."

Sarah's cheeks flush, but she bursts into laughter, snorting in a way that makes her flesh flush even more. "Jake!" she howls, "That's so sweet but so corny."

I feign offense, putting on a mockingly serious face. "Come on, it wasn't *that* bad."

She's laughing even harder now, tears streaming down her cheeks, and I can't help but join in. Her laughter echoes through the night, blending with the soft chirping of crickets, creating a melody that feels like the soundtrack to a perfect moment.

The drive back to Sarah's house wraps us in a comfortable silence—the kind that lingers when something real just happened. The night still hums between us, charged and heavy in all the best ways. When I pull up to her place and kill the engine, I glance over. She's already looking at me.

I lean in and press a soft, lingering kiss to her lips. Something slow. Sweet. Just to say thank you without words.

"Tonight was special," I murmur, my voice low, honest.

She nods, her eyes catching the moonlight. "It really was, Jake."

I should leave it at that. But all I can think is, fuck being a good boy.

I kiss her again—harder this time. No restraint. Just need. My fingers slide into her hair, tugging her closer as I devour her mouth. She sighs into me, and I grunt against her lips, my cock already rock hard and straining against my jeans. Her scent is everywhere, her taste addictive, and I don't want to stop. Not now. Not ever.

I tear my mouth from hers just long enough to kiss down her jaw, then bite down gently on her earlobe. Her gasp is sharp, and it lights me up.

My lips brush her ear, my voice rough and strained. "Can I touch you?"

She keens, nodding fast, but I don't move yet—not until I hear her say it.

"Please touch me, Jake."

I don't waste a second.

One hand stays locked behind her neck, keeping her close as my lips crash against hers. The other slides down her shoulder, fingers brushing the strap of her dress until it slips free. Her skin is warm, soft, and when the strap falls, it leaves just enough of a gap for me to catch a teasing glimpse of her bra strap beneath.

Between kisses, I trace the edge of her bra cup before sliding my hand inside, cupping her breast. It's firm and full, fitting perfectly in my palm like it was meant to be there.

A sound escapes her—half gasp, half groan—as I roll her nipple between my fingers, feeling it harden against my touch. I push the fabric down, lifting her breast free, unable to look away from the way her rosy nipple peaks in the low light. My mouth waters, and I can't resist the urge to taste her.

I kiss my way down her chest, savoring every inch until I finally close my lips around her nipple, suckling slowly and deep.

She throws her head back with a sharp, breathy "Ah!"—and fuck, the sound makes my cock jump. I need to hear it again. I need more of her. Every soft sound, every shiver—it's all I can think about now.

I shift fast, sliding into the middle of the seat and pulling her onto my lap. Her skirt rides up around her waist as my hands roam from her knees to her thighs, gripping her hips. She pulls back for a second, eyes locked on mine—wild, dark, full of want—and then she crashes back into my mouth, her kiss hungry and fucking desperate.

My hands slide higher, tugging down her other bra cup, freeing both breasts. I pinch her nipples—rosy, stiff—with just enough pressure to pull a gasp straight from her throat. She grinds against me, rubbing her pussy along the seam of my jeans, and fuck, she's going to make me lose it.

One hand keeps working her nipples, rolling, kneading, teasing those sweet little gasps out of her while the other slips back down her thigh. Pulling the fabric of her dress up more, I plunge my hand underneath it. I reach the soaked fabric of her panties and pant, fingers sliding the fabric aside so I can run them over her slick pussy. She jerks when I graze her clit, sucking in a sharp breath.

I tease her, light strokes just to hear those whimpers spill from her lips. She trembles, her whole body aching for more, and when she grumbles in frustration, I give her what she wants—shoving one finger deep inside her soaked cunt.

The way she clenches around me? Fucking sinful. Just thinking about how she'll feel wrapped around my cock has me clenching my jaw to keep control.

I curl my finger, dragging a gasp out of her, then slide in two more—stretching her, filling her. She's so goddamn tight.

I break the kiss, breath ragged, lips at her ear. "Grind up on my fingers, baby."

She doesn't even pause. Her hips roll, grinding hard, chasing that release. Every rock of her body sends shockwaves through me, her moans breaking into sharp, breathless sounds as I curl my fingers again, hitting that spot that makes her shudder.

My mouth replaces my hand on her breast, my thumb taking over, rubbing tight, relentless circles on her clit.

"Oh fuck, oh fuck, oh fuck," she cries, her voice breaking, hands tangled in my hair as she buries her face into my shoulder. Her pussy clenches around my fingers like a vice, and I press harder against her clit—just enough to send her crashing over the edge.

"Jake!" she cries, her body locks up, a raw, guttural moan ripping from her throat as she bites down on my shoulder and cums hard, unraveling right in my lap.

I keep fucking her with my fingers, dragging every last spasm out of her until she finally collapses against me—spent, panting, limp. A grin pulls at my lips. My fingers remain buried inside her, slick with her cum, and fuck me, but I have no intention of pulling them out until I've wrung another orgasm from her trembling body.

But the universe seems to have other plans.

The porch light starts flickering on and off.

I freeze, blinking. "The fuck?"

Sarah whimpers and leans back to glance over her shoulder. "Shit."

"What is it?" I ask, heart still pounding like I'm mid-sprint.

"It's my dad," she mutters, rubbing her temples. "That's his way of saying stop fucking around and get my ass inside."

My concern shifts real fast—from the moment to my immediate survival.

"Oh," I manage, suddenly feeling very naked despite being fully clothed.

She leans close, whispering in my ear with a smirk. "Relax. I'm a grown woman. He's flashing for the neighbors' sake."

I huff a laugh into her neck. "Man's got some damn good timing."

She joins in, her laughter dissolving into snickers.

Slowly, I pull my fingers from inside her, and we both sigh—hers full of disappointment, mine thick with frustration. I help her fix her clothes, even as she pouts sliding off my lap.

"I didn't get to touch you," she mutters, lips forming that perfect little pout.

I grin, shaking my head. "I'll survive."

"But—"

The porch light flashes again, and she groans—pure fucking annoyance this time.

"Goodnight, Jake," she says, sliding out of the truck, cheeks still flushed, legs still shaky.

"Goodnight, Sarah," I murmur, watching her until the front door shuts behind her.

I crank the engine, cock still painfully hard, throbbing against my jeans as I pull onto the road. I can already hear that bottle of warming lube in my nightstand whispering sweet nothings, because there's no way in hell I'm sleeping without jerking off to the memory of her moaning my name.

And because I'm a goddamn glutton for punishment, I lift the fingers that were just buried inside her to my nose and inhale.

Fuck.

This is gonna be the longest fucking drive of my life.

Chapter 10

The day unfolds like any other. I roll out of bed, shoot Jake a text, and go through the motions—get ready, eat breakfast with Dad, stroll into town. Same routine. My coworkers wave, the boss gives his usual nod, and I dive into work.

But today, something simmers just beneath the surface—a lingering heat from last night. That date. Jake has me buzzing, still feeling the way his fingers played my body like a damn fiddle. It was electric. I walked into work just like I had a secret stitched beneath my skin.

Nothing, I thought, could kill this high.

Until it did.

Mid-morning, shit hits the fan. I'm behind the counter, flashing smiles at the regulars, when a family wanders in—strangers. The dad's in front, two kids glued to his sides like letting go means floating off into the void. I slide into autopilot, slipping on my best customer service face.

"Good morning!" I chirp.

"Mornin'," he grunts, not really looking at me.

The kids—two preteens—press their faces to the display case like it holds the secrets of the universe. The mom's by the door, bouncing a fussy baby that's building up to a full-blown meltdown.

"Dad!" the older boy tugs on the guy's pant leg, relentless. "Dad! Dad!"

"Yeah," the dad mutters, half there.

"Can we get some cinnamon rolls? Pleeeease."

"No!" the younger girl screeches. "Cinnamon rolls are gross. I want a strawberry danish!"

"We don't have to get the same thing, stupid," the boy shoots back, glaring at her.

"Charlie!" The mother's voice slices through the air like a whip, her glare matching the father's *'you-better-fall-in-line'* look. "Apologize to your sister."

Charlie mumbles a half-hearted apology while his sister sticks her tongue out in victory.

The father rubs his temples like it's the only thing keeping his skull from cracking open. He rattles off their order, and I quickly bag it up, grateful to move things along.

The bell jingles as more customers file in. The father swipes his card and gives me a tired smile. "Oh, um, we're a little lost. The cell reception's been cutting out, and the GPS is acting up. Could you point us to the interstate?"

I hand over his receipt, my heart sinking a little. "Oh, uh, I'm actually pretty new here myself. I've only been in town a few months."

He nods, still looking just as lost.

"Mr. Walters!" I call out. My boss steps out from the back, wiping flour off his hands. I quickly explain the situation, and he steps in without hesitation, leading the man to a side table to help with directions.

Then—**crash**.

A chair hits the floor hard, cutting through the noise like a gunshot. The baby lets loose a wail, loud and piercing, just as the kids kick off another round of bickering.

A deep, guttural growl slices through the chaos.

The father's patience snaps like a twig. His face darkens, veins bulging in his neck as he snarls;

"Charlie, Bailey. Sit. Down. Now."

The kids freeze, eyes wide, and scurry off to a corner, too scared to test him. The air turns heavy, sharp with tension. I turn back to my station, trying to shake it off—but the buzz from earlier? Completely gone.

Then it hits me—the man isn't just a shifter.

He's a predator shifter.

My heart thuds hard against my ribs. A cold sweat blooms across my palms. I can't move, can't breathe, like something primal in me just hit the panic button as fear digs its claws into my chest.

That's when a voice cuts through the shop—sharp, venomous.

"Your kind aren't welcome here."

I turn. It's the small, older woman standing near the door, dressed to the nines like she just stepped out of a 1950s magazine ad. Her tone is ice cold, her words aimed like a blade at the man.

"Excuse me?" the father growls, low and dangerous. His kids huddle tighter to their mother, who's now clutching the baby like a shield, her stunned eyes bouncing between her husband and the old woman.

"You heard me," the woman spits. "You and your kind aren't welcome in this town. We don't need predator filth anywhere near our families."

A rumble starts in the man's chest. His body coils tight and ready to snap.

I stumble back instinctively—right into someone. A solid wall of heat and muscle stops me.

I twist my head around, heart in my throat.

Jordan.

His jaw's clenched, dark fury simmering in his eyes. His hands close gently but firmly around my arms as he pulls me behind him, shielding me without a word.

"I can't believe this!" the man snaps, voice rising with raw fury. "It's the twenty-first century, for Christ's sake! Did we fall into a damn wormhole when we entered this backwater town? What the hell is your problem, lady?"

His wife's eyes flick nervously around the room, catching the hard, judgmental stares of the other customers. She lays a calming hand on his shoulder, her voice low but steady.

"Richard. I think we should leave."

Richard's jaw flexes. He glances at her, then at the kids—both huddled close and scared—and for a beat, his anger falters. His shoulders drop just slightly, but then his gaze snaps back to the old woman.

That's when Mr. Walters steps forward, voice even and carrying gravitas. "Susan."

The name alone is a warning.

"They haven't done anything wrong. They're paying customers, and they deserve to be treated with respect. You can't just run folks out of town because they happen to be predator shifters."

Susan lifts her chin, somehow managing to look down her nose at a man twice her height.

"I can and I will, Henry Walters. You know damn well we don't tolerate those things coming through here—even in passing."

Richard moves indicative of taking a step toward her, fury radiating off him—but his wife tightens her grip on his shoulder, giving him a small, firm shake of her head.

He stills, body coiled tight, muscles trembling with restraint.

Mr. Walters lets out a long breath, rubbing his hand down his apron like he's trying to wipe the situation off with the flour. The air is thick—tension buzzing, hearts pounding.

"They're just passing through, Susan," he says, tone measured, wearied. "No harm done."

There's a flicker of something in his voice—regret, maybe—but it fades quickly into something more neutral.

"I'll walk them out and give them directions. I'm sure they won't be passing back through."

Susan scoffs.

"See to it they understand it's best if they don't," she hisses, her words sharp as shattered glass.

Jordan steps forward, his jaw tight. "I'll help you take the trash out."

"Un-fucking-believable," Richard mutters under his breath, eyes dark with anger.

Mr. Walters shoots his son a look that could cut steel. "Absolutely not. There are customers that need tending to. I won't be long."

"But—"

"No buts! Do as I say and get back to work." His voice is iron, sharper than I've ever heard, and Jordan scowls, clenching his fists, before reluctantly nodding in agreement.

The bell jingles as Mr. Walters, Richard, and his family leave the shop. The door barely clicks shut when the tension in my body snaps like a dam breaking. A sharp gasp escapes me, and I can't stop the silent tears that roll down my cheeks. My whole body trembles, the weariness of it all crashing in at once.

Then, warm arms wrap around me, pulling me close. Jordan's voice floats above me, steady and calm despite the storm in his eyes. "Give me a second, folks. I'll be right back."

He gently guides me into the kitchen, and Sam appears, glass of water in hand, his face soft with concern. Jordan hands me off to him, his fingers lingering for a second longer than necessary before he steps away to tend to the customers. Sam helps me into a chair, his presence grounding as he presses the cool glass into my shaking hands.

"Here, drink this," he murmurs.

I take a few tentative sips, the water calming the fire in my throat. Deep breaths follow, the chaos in my chest slowly easing, though the burden of what just happened still sits heavy on my shoulders.

The cold water slides down my throat, each sip easing the tightness in my chest. Sam stands nearby, his eyes on me, making sure I'm steady. His silence is a comfort—he knows better than to ask if I'm okay.

We both know I'm not. Not after that.

"Take your time," he murmurs, his hand briefly resting on my shoulder before pulling away.

The clatter of the shop carries through the doorway, the bell ringing as customers move in and out. Normal life, continuing on just feet away, like the world hadn't just tipped sideways for me. I glance at Sam, his eyes tracking toward the front. He's itching to check on Jordan, but he stays put, solid like a pillar holding me up.

I manage a shaky breath, my voice barely above a whisper. "Thanks, Sam."

He just nods, not making a big deal of it. He never does.

The door swings open, and Jordan walks back in, his eyes immediately finding me. His gaze softens for a moment before flicking to Sam.

"How is she?" Jordan's voice is rougher than usual, his concern barely hidden.

"She's okay," Sam replies, shooting me a glance. "Just needs a few minutes."

Jordan kneels down in front of me, his eyes scanning my face, taking in the tear streaks and the pale look I probably can't hide. "You did good out there," he says, voice low, laced with something that feels like pride. "Handled it better than most would."

I let out a shaky laugh. "I don't know about that..."

"You did." He's firm, his hand briefly brushing mine before he stands again, his eyes hardening as he turns toward Sam. "What the hell was that, though?" There's no bite in his tone, no real shock—just animosity.

"Susan's never held back," Jordan adds grimly, "but I didn't expect her to call them out like that."

Sam shrugs, his jaw tight, fingers dragging across his stubble. "Nobody around here thinks she overstepped," he says, though there's a slight pause in his words, his gaze flicking away before meeting Jordan's again. "You know that. Predator shifters... they bring trouble. Always have."

His voice stays even, but the way his thumb nervously taps against his side gives something away. He shifts his weight, like he's trying to settle into the words—but they don't quite sit right.

"People don't want them here," Sam continues, his tone hardening again. "And honestly, I can't blame them."

But the tension in his shoulders doesn't disappear. For just a moment, his eyes harden—like he's biting back something he'd rather not admit.

Jordan nods, his expression hardening. "She was right to say something. It's not safe with them around. We all know what happened when we let a predator shifter get too close."

The words hit like a punch to the gut. My breath catches. A sharp pang stabs through my chest, old fear clawing its way back to the surface. My mother's face flashes through my mind—her body, the aftermath. Murdered. Because of a predator shifter.

I don't even try to push the fear away. I can't.

Jordan looks at me, his voice softening, though his stance stays firm. "You know it too, Sarah. Susan did what needed to be done."

I nod, barely able to breathe through the lump in my throat. No one in this town thought Susan went too far, and deep down... a part of me couldn't, either.

They were right—predator shifters weren't safe. They were dangerous. And I knew that more than anyone.

Despite that, watching them get forced out like that—it felt wrong. Didn't it?

Even if the fear in me screamed otherwise.

I finally find my voice, the shakiness clinging to it. "What happens now? With Richard and his family?"

Jordan sighs and runs a hand through his hair. "Dad's probably walking them to their car. He'll make sure they know the roads. But... they won't be coming back. People like Susan make sure of that."

He looks at me again, eyes steady. "You're safe here, Sarah. That's what matters."

I take a deep breath, the burden of it all pressing down like a boulder. This town... it finally started to feel like home. A place I could settle.

But now I see the cracks.

Still, I can't ignore the truth—predator shifters terrify me now. I never used to fear them... not until that night. Not until one of them tore my world apart and left me with scars to prove it.

That fear gnaws at me.

And worse—it makes people like Susan make sense.

It makes sense, doesn't it? Keeping predator shifters out keeps us safe. Keeps me safe. But then, something in me twists with discomfort. They're still people. Watching Richard and his family get driven out—it felt wrong. Even if that voice in the back of my mind insists it was for the best.

I can't deny the unease crawling up my spine. How long can I stand by and live in a place that shuts people out for what they are? For the fear they bring?

The cracks are showing. And as much as I agree with the town's caution, I can't ignore the nagging truth—maybe this kind of safety comes with a price I'm not sure I'm willing to pay.

The bell above the shop door jingles again. Jordan glances toward the front, his shoulders tensing—then easing when he sees it's not another customer.

Mr. Walters steps into the kitchen, his usual stride slower, more deliberate. The moment his eyes meet mine, his expression softens. There's pity there—gentle, but unmistakable.

"Go on home, Sarah," he says, voice low with quiet compassion. "We've got it from here."

I manage a small nod, my throat tight. The massiveness of the day presses down on me like a stone as I gather my things. Without another word, I step out into the warm sun, the guilt sticking to me like humidity in July.

The door clicks shut behind me, and with it, the last hour locks itself in my chest. That woman had a baby in her arms. The man just wanted directions. I watched them get driven out like stray dogs, and I didn't say a damn thing.

Because I am scared.

Because a long time ago, a predator shifter tore my world apart. And even now, with all these years and scars between us, the fear still wins.

I tell myself it was safer this way. That this town is just doing what it has to. That I'm doing what I have to.

But if that's true… why does it feel like I helped break something I can't put back together?

Chapter 11

I step out of the hardware store, squinting against the sun, and spot Henry Walters standing outside his bakery. He's escorting a family that looks more than a little upset. They move stiffly, shoulders tight, like they're carrying something heavy they can't set down.

Tossing my purchases into the cab of my truck, curiosity tugs at me, so I head down the street.

As I get closer, I catch Henry giving the family a polite but strained wave as they pull away from the curb. His smile, when he finally turns to greet me, doesn't quite reach his eyes.

"What's goin' on, Henry?" I ask, my gaze following the SUV as it disappears down Main Street.

Henry rubs the bridge of his nose and lets out a sigh thick with frustration. "The father growled at his kids when they wouldn't stop acting up."

"Growled?" I echo, my brow tightening. That doesn't sound like a reason to run someone out of town.

Henry catches my look and shoots me a pointed glance. "Susan was in the shop."

I let out a low curse. "Shit."

"Yeah, my sentiments exactly," he mutters. "I tried to defuse things, but you know Susan. Once she gets started, she doesn't stop."

I nod, my expression souring. Susan Cummings is infamous for driving predator shifters out of town the second they slip up. It doesn't matter how small it is—she turns it into a scene.

Henry's shoulders slump as he goes on. "I gave 'em an under-the-table refund and sent them up to the old gas station off 43. Lord only knows what'd happen if they ended up lost near Ol' Hickory's place."

I wait, gut telling me this wasn't just idle shop gossip. There's more here—something I need to be part of.

"You think you could head up and show 'em the way out?" Henry asks, voice low. "I told 'em I'd meet 'em there, but... I've got a few things to handle at the shop."

I nod, catching what he's not saying. Henry's a deer shifter—kind, well-meaning—but not the kind that makes folks like that family feel any safer after what just happened. They'll trust me more.

I clap a firm hand on his shoulder, then turn and head back to my truck.

Gripping the steering wheel, I feel the seriousness of it settle in. I know exactly what this is about. And I hate it. But there's no getting around it—I'll do what needs to be done. I pull out my phone, shoot a quick text to Dad to let him know what's going on, then toss it onto the passenger seat.

With a sigh, I start the truck and ease out onto Main Street, heading toward 43. The engine rumbles beneath me, steady and familiar, but it doesn't do much to settle the twist in my gut.

Gravel crunches under my tires as I roll up to the old gas station. The same SUV I saw earlier parked there, looking awkward and out of place in the empty lot. I park, take a deep breath, and step out with my hands raised in a show of peace. The last thing I want is to spook them more than they already are.

The driver's side door opens. The man steps out with a pistol in his hand—pointed at the ground, thankfully. That's something, at least.

"Howdy!" I call, keeping my voice calm. "Henry told me y'all had a run-in with our resident Cowardly, Unoriginal, Neurotic Tool—if you catch my drift."

A faint smirk tugs at the man's mouth before he tamps it down.

"Who are you?" he asks, voice firm but not hostile.

"Jake Walker," I reply.

"That supposed to mean something?" He raises an eyebrow, clearly still wary.

"Not really," I say with a shrug and a small smile. "Henry just wanted to make sure you found the interstate. Asked me to help."

He studies me for a beat, sharp eyes not missing a thing. "That so? And why should I trust you?"

I glance around the lot, making sure we're alone. "Just... don't shoot," I say. Then I shift.

The change washes over me like a wave—seamless, silent, instinctive. My skin shimmers, shape melting and reforming as fur unfurls in a muted silver cascade. I drop low, limbs folding inward as the illusion of humanity fades, replaced by the quiet grace of my other form.

In the span of a breath, I stand as a timber wolf—lean, wild, and utterly unremarkable to the untrained eye. No towering beast, no monstrous distortion—just a wolf, the kind that walks the tree line unseen, nature's perfect ghost. My coat is a mottled mix of ash and charcoal, blending easily into shadow and stone. My paws press into the gravel, steady and sure, my tail low in a show of calm. My ears flick toward the wind, but my amber eyes stay locked on him.

No threats. No words. Just truth.

The man's eyes widen—but not in fear. His posture loosens, tension bleeding from his shoulders.

He lets out a short laugh and heads back to the SUV, still shaking his head. "Lead the way, wolf."

I shift back, climb into my truck, and guide them out—past the edge of town, onto the winding road that spits out near the interstate.

Once they're back on track, I give them a quick nod and turn around, heading back the way I came. No reason to dwell. Just another day, another reminder of how things work around here.

Chapter 12

JAKE

Sarah sits across from me at a small, dimly lit diner. It's been over a week since our last date, but the sound of her moans still echoes in my head, the way she came on my fingers playing on repeat. My cock's been half-hard ever since.

She's been sending me wicked texts all week—especially the one this morning that damn near broke me. I don't think I've jerked off this much since I was a teenager. Just as my mind begins to drift—her thighs, her mouth, the way she bites her lip—my phone buzzes.

Mom.

"Jake, sweetheart, you missed the family gathering," my mother says, her voice warm but laced with that gentle frustration only she can pull off. "Your daddy might see you every day, but I sure do miss you."

Across the table, Sarah arches a brow, clearly amused. I try to play it casual. "I've just been busy, Mom."

"Yes, your father mentioned your lady friend," she says, curiosity creeping in. "But busy or not, family's important. I expect to see you at the next one, alright?"

I smile, despite myself. "Alright, Mom. I'll be there."

When I hang up, Sarah's grinning. "Looks like your mom's getting jealous of all the attention you're giving me."

I snort. "She's affectionate, but not the possessive type. Thank God she's not one of those 'no one can love my son like I can' moms."

Her smile lights me up, sending these warm, fuzzy feelings coursing through me. It's too damn easy to picture coming home to her—it's the kind of life that feels too good to be true. But that's where things have gotten complicated lately. When I'm with her, the rest of the world fades away—nothing else seems to matter.

Then my mind drifts back to the other day. To what those strangers experienced when they came to town. Treated for being different. Different like me. And how Sarah reacted to it.

I wasn't there to see it, but Henry said she was pretty shaken up—not because of what Susan had done, but because they were predator shifters. That hit like a punch to the gut. If she knew about me... would she even give me a chance?

Worse—would she turn out like everyone else in this town?

I wanted her to be different. Hell, I needed her to be worth it. But the doubts keep creeping in, no matter how hard I try to shove them down.

I try not to dwell on it, letting my thoughts drift back to the phone call with my mother—to everything I've been avoiding. I haven't just been neglecting my parents, but Charlie, the twins, and their folks too. I want to be with Sarah, but my family... they've got to be a priority.

Those gatherings are the only place where I can let my guard down. Talk about the struggle of being a wolf shifter if it comes up. It's like finally breaking the surface after holding my breath too long—that first gasp of air that fills your lungs and reminds you that you're alive. I know the twins have probably been raising hell with Charlie in my absence. I can practically picture the chaos, and Charlie's righteous indignation. The thought makes me grin.

But beneath the smile, the enormity's still there.

Then I glance up and everything shifts.

Sarah sits across from me, lips pursed in concentration as she studies her menu. Her brows knit just slightly, and, fuck if that little crease doesn't make my heart stutter. There's something about her—something that's been haunting me since the last time we touched.

The tension's still there, crackling like a live wire between us. Every look, every text she's sent over the past week, has just added fuel to the fire. She knows exactly how to keep me wanting, and I don't think I've gone a full night without dreaming about her.

My cock stirs just watching her tuck a strand of hair behind her ear.

Family, guilt, pressure—they can all wait.

Right now, I've got a beautiful woman sitting across from me, and all I can think about is getting her alone. I want her grinding down on my lap, moaning in my ear while I work my hand under those jeans—slow at first, just enough to tease her, to feel how soaked she already is for me. I want to hook my fingers in her panties, tug them aside, and slide deep inside her until she bites her lip trying not to cry out my name. I want to feel her thighs tremble around my hand, her breath stuttering as she chases that high, desperate and aching.

And when she finally falls apart for me, I want to kiss her through it, slow and dirty, so she knows exactly who she belongs to when her body's still shaking in my arms.

Her eyes flick up from the menu and catch mine—like she knows exactly where my head's at. There's a flash of mischief in her gaze, a small smirk tugging at her lips, and, fuck me if that look alone doesn't make my cock twitch. She shifts in her seat, slowly crossing one leg over the other, and I swear to God I hear the denim of her jeans strain. My fingers curl around the edge of the table. If she weren't wearing those jeans, I'd already have my hand between her thighs, teasing her until she was dripping down them.

And just like that, the guilt's gone. All that matters is her.

She drops her menu on the table and flashes me a bright smile. "I think I'm just gonna get a burger and fries. What about you?"

My eyes drag over her body, menu completely forgotten. "I'm not sure. All I can think about right now is dessert."

Her cheeks flush a deep red, and I smirk as I take a slow sip of water, watching her glance around the restaurant like she's trying to keep it together.

"Well..." she says, her lips curling into a devilish grin. "I could really go for a popsicle."

I damn near inhale my water the wrong way, coughing hard as she giggles across the table.

"You are so wrong for that," I croak, wiping my mouth, still hacking.

Her smirk only widens, one brow cocked like she's proud of herself. "Yeeeah. I deserved that," I wheeze between the last of the coughs.

If I weren't already desperate to get my hands on her, now I'm downright feral.

Chapter 13

Somehow, we make it through dinner without jumping each other's bones. I have to keep squeezing my thighs together, chasing just enough friction to stop myself from lunging across the damn table. The plans I've got for this man once we get to the truck? Debaucherous.

I toss my napkin onto the empty plate just as the server approaches with the check. Before either of us can reach for it, she smiles and points toward a booth across the diner.

"The guys over there covered it," she says with a wink. "Have a great night!"

Jake and I glance over, and his grunt makes me grin. The Wilson twins are grinning like idiots, waving like they just won the lottery.

"Thanks!" Jake hollers, giving them a half-hearted wave before offering me his arm.

I loop mine through his, fingers wrapping around his bicep. Even through his shirt, I can feel the warmth of his skin, the tension thrumming beneath it. As we walk toward the door, I flash a bright smile at the twins. They wave back, way too pleased with themselves.

"That was sweet of them," I whisper once we're outside, the cool night air brushing against my cheeks.

"Yeah, it was," Jake murmurs, giving my hand a gentle squeeze.

The breeze carries the scent of fresh-cut grass and lingering grease from the diner. I lean into him as we walk to his truck, that fluttery warmth in my chest turning molten. He opens the passenger door, and I slide in, fumbling a little with the seatbelt as he shuts the door and heads around.

The engine rumbles to life—low, steady, and just dirty enough to send a vibration straight through me. I take a deep breath, trying to calm the nerves fluttering in my stomach. That line about the popsicle wasn't just a tease. I've been thinking about making up for that very interrupted moment in his truck all week long.

As Jake pulls onto the road, I unbuckle my seatbelt and slide across the seat. Before he can react, I drape one arm over his shoulders, my other hand landing firmly on his thigh. I lean in, kissing the side of his neck, trailing soft, wet kisses up his jawline before sucking his earlobe into my mouth. My hand squeezes his thigh and inches toward the growing bulge between his legs.

"Drive slow," I whisper, my fingers brushing over the outline of his cock.

His hands tighten on the wheel, knuckles white, a deep groan rumbling from his chest. Spurred on, I free my other hand and make quick work of the button on his jeans. I'm practically aching to wrap my hand around him. The thought alone sends heat pulsing between my legs.

I nip the pulse point in his neck as I slide my hand into his jeans and finally wrap my fingers around his cock. His breath shudders out, jaw clenched so tight I can hear the grind of his teeth. I stroke him, slow and deliberate, kissing and sucking at his neck, loving the way his whole body tenses beneath me.

"Sarah, *fuck*," he rasps through gritted teeth, voice ragged.

Hearing him fall apart like that only makes me bolder. I pull his cock free, and my breath catches.

Holy shit, he's thick.

I knew he wasn't small, but seeing how my fingers don't even meet around him? That does something feral to me. Just the thought of him inside me makes me press my thighs together, hard.

Licking my lips, I take the head of his cock into my mouth, savoring the taste of his pre-cum as my tongue swirls around him. He hisses through his teeth, and I start bobbing my head, my lips stretching to accommodate every inch. My hair falls forward, brushing his thighs as I take him deeper, the soft drag of my tongue matched by the growing tension in his body. His sharp exhale sends a shiver through me, and when his fingers tangle in my hair, gripping tight, I know exactly how close he is to losing control.

I hum around him; the vibration making him groan louder as I work him deeper into my mouth. My tongue flicks along the sensitive underside of his cock, and his raw, low moan tells me I've found the right spot.

"Ah—God. Don't stop, baby," he pants, his voice thick with need.

I pull back just enough to suck the head again, my cheeks hollowing as he pulses against my tongue. Slowly, I take him in inch by inch, until I swallow him whole, his cock buried deep in my throat.

"Fuuuuuck," he croons, his hand gripping my hair tighter, hips twitching beneath the strain of holding still.

I pull back, stroking him with one hand while my mouth works him in rhythm. Each motion deliberate—slick, hungry. I alternate between bobbing down and pumping him with my hand, dragging out every delicious sound he makes. His breathing quickens. He's close. I feel it.

A light tap on my shoulder—his silent signal. I ignore it.

A second tap. Firmer. I don't stop.

"Sarah—fuck, baby," he growls through clenched teeth. "You're gonna make me cum."

I moan around him, letting him know that's exactly what I want. The vibration pushes him over the edge.

"Ah—fuck—I'm cumming," he gasps, his voice breaking. I feel him twitch in my mouth before his release hits the back of my throat. I swallow it down, savoring the heat and salt of him, sucking softly until the last pulse fades.

I slowly pull off with one final swirl of my tongue, then slide back into my seat and buckle up, lips tingling, satisfaction warm in my belly.

Jake's eyes glisten, his chest still rising and falling with sharp breaths.

I shoot him a grin, mischief dripping from my voice. "That was the best popsicle I've ever had."

Jake glances at me—then bursts into laughter, his whole body shaking as he tries to catch his breath. "*Fuck*, woman," he manages between laughs, his face lit up, the tension in his eyes completely gone.

I can't help but snicker, smug satisfaction curling through me. Nothing beats seeing that smile on his face—*especially* when I'm the reason for it.

Still grinning, he tucks himself back into his jeans with one hand, chuckles tapering off as silence settles between us. It's a good silence. Comfortable. Warm.

When he pulls up in front of my house, I unbuckle, lean over, and press a soft kiss to his cheek. I linger just long enough to make him want more.

"Goodnight, Jake," I purr, letting the heat linger in my voice.

He exhales a low laugh, his grin lazy and crooked. "Goodnight, Sarah."

Chapter 14

As promised, I show up to the next family gathering. The familiar sounds of laughter and the mouthwatering aroma of barbecue hit me the second I step into my parents' backyard. The late afternoon sun casts everything in a soft golden glow, making the place feel timeless.

My aunt and uncle are in from California, their kids tearing through the yard, adding another layer of noise and chaos to the already lively scene. I barely make it past the cooler when Brent and Annie spot me, pulling me into a conversation about Sarah.

Beau and Buckley are suspiciously quiet for once—hovering nearby but staying out of the conversation. Likely because they know better than to run their mouths with their mom in earshot. Still, I catch them eyeing me with that familiar glint, and I know they're up to something. They always are.

The backyard hums with an easygoing energy you only get from family—blood or chosen. Conversations layer over each other, kids dart around underfoot, and every few minutes someone laughs loud enough to rise over the noise. The warmth isn't just in the food or the setting—it's in how everyone clicks together like no time has passed at all.

I load up a plate and do my best to steer clear of the twins' line of fire. But I can feel them plotting. The second they start whispering and side-eyeing each other, it's game on. I focus on the food, pretending not to notice. Maybe if I stay busy enough, I'll dodge whatever nonsense they're cooking up.

As the sun sinks lower, casting long shadows and coating the yard in gold, I spot Charlie—less lucky than me. The twins ambush him from behind a tree, unloading twin cans of neon silly string. He just stands there, covered in bright green and pink strands, and shoots me a look that screams You owe me. But the twitch in his mouth betrays him—Charlie's more amused than pissed. He's always had a soft spot for those two, more tolerant of their antics than anyone else.

But of course, the twins aren't satisfied with just one victory. They're already moving on, quietly swapping people's belongings when no one's looking. Glasses, hats, phones—it doesn't take long before everyone's wearing the wrong stuff, and the confusion erupts into laughter. The whole yard is buzzing with a special brand of chaos only a family this close can generate.

Their mom, finally fed up with the mischief, turns the tables. She spins some wild tales about a woodland sprite that only calms down when it's offered shiny pebbles. And the twins—gullible as ever—eat it right up. Next thing we know, they're darting around the yard on a full-blown rock hunt, totally committed to the quest. The rest of us watch, thoroughly entertained, as they run around with more enthusiasm than half the kids here.

Across the yard, Charlie catches my eye, and we both shake our heads, trying to hold back our laughter. He wanders over and leans against the tree beside me.

"How the hell did she pull that off?" he mutters. "You'd think they were six, not grown-ass men, the way they're chasing invisible sprites."

I chuckle, nudging him. "You know Annie's grandfather immigrated from Ireland. They've still got some of that old-country belief in 'em."

Charlie barks a laugh. "Well, I'll be damned. Whatever works, I guess. They're more trouble than harm, anyway."

"True," I say, smiling as the twins trip over each other near the grill. "But you gotta love 'em. Wouldn't be the same without their chaos."

As the sky fades into twilight and stars peek through, someone lights the bonfire. Warm, flickering light dances across everyone's faces, casting the entire scene in something that feels like memory already. We circle up, passing marshmallows and swapping stories. The fire pops and cracks, blending with laughter, while the night settles cool and easy around us.

Mom finally finds me, her eyes twinkling as she surveys the scene.

"I thought you'd bring that girl around to meet the family," she says, her voice full of playful teasing.

"She's not ready for this level of chaos," I reply, smiling back at her.

She sits on the log beside me, her smile warm and gentle.

"What makes you say that, baby?"

I sigh and glance around the bonfire. The crackle of wood creates a haunting melody to the sudden silence that's settled over the group. They can all sense the shift in my posture, the tension rolling off me.

Aunt Rosemary stands and makes her way to Uncle Dillon, bending to kiss his cheek.

"I'm going to put the kids to bed," she says loudly enough for everyone to hear. "Do you need anything from the house?"

Dillon glances at me. I give him a small shake of my head. He turns back to his wife with a smile.

"I'm alright, baby. Thank you."

Rosemary nods and gathers up the kids, who grumble their way back toward the house.

We wait in silence until they're out of earshot.

"What's going on, son?" Dad asks, his voice low with concern.

I let out a harsh breath. Open my mouth. Close it again. Shake my head.

Everyone leans in slightly, waiting.

It takes me a minute to gather my thoughts. I was the one who used codewords for "we need to talk"—guess I better follow through now.

"I'm conflicted," I start. "Sarah is amazing. She's bright, smart, beautiful. She's all I think about—and she's everything I could ever hope for in a woman."

Mom smiles and tears up instantly.

"Oh, honey, that's wonderful," she says.

I turn to her, sadness tugging at my features. Her smile falters.

"She's got some trauma, Mom. I don't know the whole story, but whatever it is—it's made her deathly afraid of predator shifters."

Her breath catches.

"What?" she whispers, confused. "I thought her family were transplants. Surely they're not..." She can't even finish the thought.

"I don't know," I say, looking around the circle. "All I know is what Mr. Walters told me."

"This about that bakery incident last week?" Dad asks.

I nod.

"Sarah was working the counter. Henry said that by the time he came out to check the noise, she was standing there frozen—white as a sheet. Looked like she'd seen a ghost. After he escorted the family out, Jordan and Sam had already pulled her into the back. Said it was clear she was having a panic attack, so he sent her home early."

"Poor thing," Mom murmurs. She's always been soft-hearted—even toward people who don't deserve it.

Charlie leans forward, elbows on his knees.

"So you think it was because they were predator shifters?"

I nod again.

"Feels like too big a coincidence otherwise."

Beau shakes his head slowly, like he's trying to wrap his mind around it.

"Makes sense she'd hate our kind," he mutters.

"What?" I stare at him.

"Think about it, Jake. What's our town known for? Prejudice against people like us. What kind of people do you think would choose to move here?"

Buckley crosses his arms and leans forward, his voice quiet but firm.

"Beau's not wrong," he says. "Folks like that don't end up here by accident. Either they're hiding somethin', or they fit right into the way this town thinks."

He glances over at me, brows furrowed. "If she flinched just 'cause a couple predator shifters walked in, that ain't just fear—that's history. Deep-rooted kind."

The words hit like gravel in my gut.

"I know that," I snap, sharper than I mean to. "You think I haven't thought about all of that?"

Everyone falls quiet again. The fire crackles, spitting embers into the dark like punctuation marks.

I scrub a hand down my face. "I get it, okay? I get that this town is poison for people like us. But she's not like that."

Beau lifts a brow. "You sure?"

I hesitate. Just for a second. And that second costs me.

"I'm not saying she's some bigot," Buckley adds quickly, trying to soften the blow. "I'm just sayin'—if she's got trauma, if she's been fed fear her whole damn life... lovin' you might not be enough to unlearn all that."

That lands harder than anything else.

I exhale, my voice low. "I don't want to walk away from her."

"We're not tellin' you to," Buckley says, a little gentler now. "But don't lie to yourself about what this is either. If she finds out what you are... how do you think that ends?"

I look down at my hands, the calluses, the scars. I've done everything right to pass, to blend in, to be safe. And still, there's a part of me that wonders if all it'll take is one truth too many for her to run like everyone else.

Uncle Dillon clears his throat, a sharp sound that slices through the tension like a knife. "You know, Jake, you could always come out to California. Hell, I'll help you get set up. There's a whole damn country out there that doesn't act like these hillbilly hicks."

The words land like a slap. A few heads snap his way.

Mom stiffens beside me, her spine going ramrod straight as she turns toward him. "You don't get to call them that," she says, voice clipped and cold. "You know why we stayed. And you used to respect that."

Dillon scoffs, tossing his hands in the air. "*Used* to. Until I had to watch my sister, keep living in a place that would string her up from a fucking tree—*literally*—the second they find out what she is. This is *madness*, MaryAnn. Don't sit there and act like this town is safe. It never was, and it sure as hell isn't now."

He gestures toward me. "Jake can't even date a woman without worrying about her finding out the truth. He's being judged for *what* he is, not *who*. How fucked up is that, huh? And Marcus? He should be ashamed of himself for making you stay here."

Her jaw tightens. "Don't you *dare*."

But Dillon's already leaning in, voice hard. "Your *husband's* family built this place generations ago—not yours. You came here with him after his parents died, after that wreck took your baby boy and turned your world upside down. Don't pretend like that didn't break you. You thought moving here was about legacy. But this town? It changed. It's not the place Marcus grew up in, and dragging you and Jake into it was a mistake."

Marcus shifts beside the fire, his expression unreadable. The silence draws everyone in. Then he stands.

His voice isn't loud, but it lands like a hammer. "You think I don't know that?"

Dillon opens his mouth, but Marcus cuts him off with a look.

"You think I don't know what this place has become? You think I don't wake up every goddamn day knowing I brought my family into a town that'll see us as animals if they ever find out the truth?" His voice catches slightly, but he pushes through. "I grew up here. It wasn't always like this. People used to wave at each other. Kids played together no matter what their parents were. But something changed. And by the time I realized it, we were already buried too deep."

He glances down, jaw tight. "My parents died on that highway with my son in the backseat. There was no time to think about where to go. I brought MaryAnn and Jake here because this was the only place that still *felt* like home. I thought I could keep them safe."

His eyes lift and lock on Dillon. "I stayed because this house is the only thing I had left. Because walking away would've felt like giving up on everything my parents built. And yeah, maybe that was pride. Maybe that was grief. But don't stand there and act like it was cowardice."

The fire pops loudly. Nobody speaks for a beat.

Then MaryAnn reaches over, lacing her fingers with Marcus's. Her voice is soft but unshakable. "It was *my* choice to stay here, Dillon. Not his. *Mine.*"

Dillon stares at them, anger flickering into something closer to regret.

Dillon's jaw works, like he's chewing on words that taste like ash. The fire throws dancing shadows across his face, but the anger in his eyes fades, replaced by something raw—worry.

"I didn't mean to come at you like that," he mutters, voice low. "I just—" He blows out a breath and scrubs a hand over his face. "I'm scared, MaryAnn. For you. For Jake. For all of us. You know I shoot my mouth off when I'm scared."

His gaze drifts to me, softer now. "This place... it ain't safe for people like us, and we both know it. Maybe it never really was. I see you, kid, trying to hold it all together. Hiding what you are. Watching what you say. Walking on eggshells just to date someone without it blowing up in your face." He shakes his head. "You shouldn't have to live like that."

I glance at my parents—Dad's still stone-faced, Mom's eyes shining with tears she won't let fall.

Dillon looks between them, then back to me. "I'm sorry. I wasn't trying to throw blame around. I just—" His voice cracks, just a little. "I don't want to lose anyone else."

The silence that follows isn't hostile anymore. It's heavy, but shared.

Mom finally nods, her fingers still clasped with Dad's. "We know. And we love you for it."

Dad doesn't say much, but he reaches for a stick and pokes at the fire. His way of cooling things down.

Dillon sinks onto the log across from us, elbows resting on his knees, staring into the flames. "I just miss the days when we didn't have to worry about being hunted in our own backyard," Dillon says, his eyes fixed on the fire. "Back when I could shift and run with my nephews without wondering if it'd get them killed. I'm not trying to pick a fight—I just want y'all safe. That's all."

Aunt Rosemary's voice calls softly from behind as she returns from the house, brushing her hands together as if dusting off the last of bedtime duties. She stops short when she sees the tight circle we've formed around the fire and the tension still hanging heavy in the air.

"What happened?" she asks, her eyes narrowing as she takes in the rigid postures and the shadows etched across everyone's faces.

Dillon sighs, rubbing the back of his neck like a guilty kid caught with his hand in the cookie jar. "I might've... said a few things while you were inside," he admits, voice low. "Got a little fired up."

Rosemary crosses her arms and fixes him with a death glare that could make a grown man forget his own name. "Define *a few things*, Dillon."

Dillon winces. "I may have called the townsfolk hillbilly hicks and told MaryAnn and Marcus they were digging their own graves by staying here."

"Dillon," she hisses through clenched teeth, shooting a quick, apologetic glance toward Mom and Dad. "Really?"

He holds up his hands. "I know, I know. I already apologized. I just—I lost my temper. I'm worried."

Rosemary glares at him a beat longer, then exhales slowly. She turns toward me, her expression softening. "Jake, sweetheart," she says gently, "we can all argue and bark at each other 'til sunrise, but the truth is, everyone here just wants what's best for you."

I nod, swallowing the knot in my throat. Rosemary knows her husband better than anyone. She didn't have to be here to know what he said and how it affects all of us. We've had these conversations before.

She steps closer and places a hand on my shoulder. "So tell us what you want. Not what Dillon wants. Not what your mama or daddy want. What's sitting heavy on your heart right now?"

I sigh heavily and lean forward, elbows on my knees, burying my face in my hands.

"I don't know," I admit. "I was hoping for some kind of clarity, but now I'm just more jumbled up."

Rosemary rubs slow circles on my back—soothing, maternal.

"Why don't you try telling us how you feel about her?" she suggests gently. "Maybe that'll help."

I nod, my head still hanging low.

"I can't think around her," I say, my voice quieter than I expect. "She's in my head all the time—dreams, thoughts... hell, even when I'm trying to focus, she's there."

I drag a hand down my face and glance around the fire, everyone watching, waiting, but nobody speaks.

"It's not some passing thing. It's deeper. I don't even know how to explain it." My chest tightens. "The idea of leaving her?" I shake my head. "It feels like being gutted. Like I'm losing something I didn't even know I had."

A half-laugh escapes me, low and breathless. "Hell, the first night we met, I almost told her I was a wolf shifter. Wasn't even thinking about the risk. I just wanted her to know everything about me—so I could learn everything about her."

I look down at my hands, at the calluses, the dirt beneath my nails, like maybe the answer's buried in the lines of my skin.

"It's like... from the second I met her, something in me clicked into place. Like she fits where nobody ever has. She's not just in my heart; she's under my skin. In my bones. And I don't know what the hell to do with that."

Charlie chokes on his drink. "You *almost* did what *now*?"

Buckley barks out a laugh. "He said he nearly outed himself without even thinkin' about it."

"Yeah," I say with a wry grin. "If it weren't for those two knuckleheads crashing into me, it would've been out of my mouth before you could say 'bless you.'"

Mom gasps. From the corner of my eye, I see Dad silently pull her to his side.

"Holy fuckin' shit," Beau mutters.

"*Language*!" Annie snaps at him, glaring.

"Sorry, Momma," he says, not sounding even a little sorry.

Beau shifts in his seat, eyes narrowing like he's finally seeing something clearly. "Y'all know what this means, don't ya?"

I frown. "What're you talkin' about?"

Buckley's grin vanishes, replaced by something more serious than I've ever seen on him. "Holy hell," he breathes, just as Uncle Dillon mutters, "Jesus Christ," under his breath.

Dad's eyes go wide. Mom's hand flies to her mouth.

Aunt Rosemary's hand freezes mid-circle on my back.

Even Brent and Annie exchange a look like someone just dropped a live grenade between their boots.

The silence stretches long enough to make my skin crawl. No one moves. No one breathes. It's like the fire's gone still too, its crackle muted beneath the magnitude of whatever realization just hit everyone but me.

Aunt Rosemary's voice breaks the hush, soft and trembling, like she's telling a ghost story meant only for me.

"Jake, honey... does your skin feel kinda buzzy when you're away from her for awhile? Like you've been holdin' a sander too long?"

I blink at her. "Yeah, but I work with sanders, so—"

Before I can finish, Dad speaks, his voice low but steady. "That kind of feeling doesn't linger all day, son," he says, cutting through my excuse like a blade through bark. "Not unless it's magic."

I sit back slowly, spine straightening. My pulse drums in my ears.

"What're you sayin'?"

Mom turns toward me, her eyes glassy. "Do you remember the old stories, baby? The ones about Gaia? About how shifters came to be?"

I nod, confused but listening.

She swallows hard. "There's more to them than bedtime tales."

Uncle Dillon speaks up, voice low and solemn. "Before the written word, there was war. Cruelty. Innocents caught in the middle, slaughtered like animals. And when they cried out—Gaia listened. She gave magic to those who needed to run... and power to those who had to stay and fight."

His voice takes on a rhythm, a cadence I've only heard when they talk about the really old stuff—the history that isn't written down, only remembered.

"To the weak, the sick, the young—she gave the shapes of prey. Rabbits. Squirrels. Deer. Quick-footed and quiet. Meant to vanish."

Rosemary continues, picking it up like a chorus they've all sung before.

"To the protectors, she gave the form of predator—wolves, lions, foxes and bears. Claws like sharpened mercy. Teeth like truth. Not to rule—but to guard."

Buckley leans forward, eyes locked on mine. "And from that magic, passed down in blood and bone... came the Bond."

I stare at him, still not tracking. "What bond?"

Beau answers, voice quiet for once. "The one where two people's magic recognizes each other. Like roots tanglin' underground. You ain't got no say in it. It just... happens."

"They're called soulmates," Mom says softly. "Not fate. Not destiny. Just two threads of Gaia's magic... singin' the same song."

I stare at the fire, my stomach churning. "That's not real. That's just legend."

"No, Son," Dad says, his voice firm. "It's real. Your mother and I? We're soulmates. So are Dillon and Rosemary."

"And Brent's parents were, too," Annie adds. "It ain't rare. Folks just stopped talkin' about it like it's real."

"Because the world got cruel," Rosemary says. "And cruel things hate magic they can't control."

I swallow hard, the pressure in my chest growing by the second.

"You think that's what's happening to me?" I ask, scanning the faces around me. "You think this thing I feel for Sarah—it's a soulmate bond?"

Nobody says anything for a moment.

Then Mom nods, tears sliding down her cheek. "I do."

Dillon's voice softens. "That's why it hurts so much to think of walkin' away. The magic's in you now, runnin' wild, starvin' for her."

"It's a choice," Dad says gently. "Always has been. But the magic... it don't lie."

My heart slams against my ribs like it's tryin' to break free. I shoot to my feet, pacing a tight circle in the dirt, gravel crunching under my boots.

"I didn't *choose this*," I snap, louder than I mean to. "I didn't ask for some damn magic to crawl under my skin and tie itself to her. I didn't sign up to feel like I'll *die* if I walk away!"

My voice cracks, and I hear the echo ripple across the yard. Even the fire seems quieter.

"I don't want to *need* her," I grit out. "I want to *want* her. I do—but how the hell am I supposed to know what's real when this bond is pulling the strings?"

The silence settles in like fog—thick and clinging.

Then Dad rises. Not fast, not forceful. Just solid.

"You're scared," he says plainly, like he's naming something I didn't know I was allowed to admit.

I don't answer.

He steps closer, gaze heavy. "You think I wasn't?"

That makes me freeze.

He nods toward Mom. "When I met your mama, I felt it. Same as you. Like gravity shifted and my whole world spun sideways. I didn't eat for two days. Couldn't sleep. Thought it was just lust or adrenaline or maybe I'd hit my head too hard during a Lacrosse game."

A faint smile ghosts his lips. "But then it didn't go away. And the more I got to know her, the worse it got—in the best damn way. The bond didn't make me love her. It just peeled back every layer of bullshit that would've let me pretend I didn't."

He looks up at me, eyes glassy with memory. "When one shifter's magic calls out and the other calls back... that's what we call a soulmate bond. It ain't fate. Ain't some prophecy written in the stars. It's older than that. Wilder than that."

I stare at him, chest rising too fast. "Then why does it feel like I'm not in control?"

"Because you're not," he says simply. "Not all the way. The bond doesn't take your choices, Jake—it just *amplifies* what's already there. What you feel for her? That's *real*. It's *yours*. But the magic... it deepens it. Makes it louder. And yeah, that can be scary."

He leans forward, hands rubbing together like he's warming up the memory.

"Back in the old days, they said the bond felt like standin' too close to a thunderstorm. That hum in your bones, that pull in your gut? That's the magic singin' for hers. Not to chain you—but to find her. Because it thinks you *fit*."

He lets the words hang for a moment, heavy and quiet.

"It's a choice, Jake," he says again. "It always was. You can nurture that bond, grow it into somethin' strong. Or you can let it wither. But either way—the feelings? They came from *you*. The bond just made sure you couldn't lie to yourself about it."

The fire crackles, but nobody speaks. The night presses in, thick with smoke and memory, and I feel the gravity of all their eyes on me.

I sit back down slowly, the adrenaline draining out of me in a rush. My hands hang loose between my knees. Everything feels too big—too loud inside my chest.

"I don't know what to do," I admit, voice low. It's the most honest thing I've said all night.

No one tries to fix it. No one offers advice I didn't ask for.

Then Charlie shifts his weight beside me, elbows resting on his knees. His voice is calm, solid. "You don't gotta have the answer tonight."

I glance over. He's watching the fire like it holds the whole damn truth in its flicker.

"Love's messy," he adds. "Magic just makes it louder. But you don't have to wrestle it all at once."

Buckley elbows Beau. "He's gonna start singin' sad country lyrics if we don't change the subject."

Beau smirks. "Long as it ain't about trucks and dead dogs, I'll allow it."

A few laughs rumble through the circle. It's not enough to erase the momentousness, but it eases something sharp around the edges.

Uncle Dillon grunts as he pushes off the log. "I'm gettin' whiskey. Jake, you want one?"

I shake my head, half-smiling. "Maybe later."

Aunt Rosemary stands and rubs my back once before following him. "You don't have to carry it all tonight, baby. Let it settle some."

My mom reaches over, her hand curling gently around my shoulder, grounding me. Her grip's soft, but it holds more strength than anything I've got in me right now.

The conversation dies down, replaced by the low murmur of family voices and the crackle of burning wood. The circle breaks apart slowly—one by one, each of them drifting off into their own thoughts and private reckonings.

Mom's touch lingers, that one small promise that I'm not alone in all this. Even when the truth feels too heavy to bear.

As the night deepens, I step away from the glow of the fire, the chill of the air clinging to my skin. I walk across the yard, the world around me dim and quiet except for the echo in my head.

The bond. The pull. Her.

I don't know what any of this means yet. I just know I'm conflicted—and everything's bound to change if Sarah ever learns the full story. About me. About our magic. About what this thing between us really is.

For now, I force a smile when I glance back toward the house. Pretend like everything's fine. Like my world hasn't just been flipped on its damn head.

But deep down?

Every piece of me trembles with what this new path might cost.

Chapter 15

It's been three days since the family gathering, and my head's been a damn mess ever since. I still don't know what to do about Sarah and me. All I know is—I need her.

I need her like I need fucking air.

And hell if I know whether that's my emotions or the damn bond talking. Everything inside me feels too loud. Too tight. I want to hold her. To wrap myself around her and breathe her in like she's the only thing keeping me alive. I want to taste her lips, hear my name fall from her mouth like a prayer while I worship every inch of her skin.

I drop the tool in my hand with a sharp clatter and rake both hands through my hair, trying to ground myself. The buzzing under my skin's getting worse. I haven't seen her in days, and I'm about ready to crawl out of my damn body just to find her. Just one look. One touch. That's all I need.

I rub my arms like that'll do a damn thing to ease the ache. It doesn't. Never does. But I do it anyway.

Sighing, I go back to gathering tools, cleaning the shop for the night. Dad had to leave early—something about a parts run that couldn't wait.

Normally we close up together, but tonight it's just me. The shadows stretch longer, the quiet settling in as thick as the scent of sawdust and oil, wrapping around me like the magnitude of everything I still haven't figured out.

Then it hits me.

That buzz beneath my skin flares, sharp and electric.

A second later, the bell over the door jingles.

I glance up, ready to bark at whoever's come in this late—but the words die in my throat.

She's standing there.

Box of pastries in her hands, mischievous little grin on her face, and just like that, everything calms. The buzz eases. The ache quiets. My whole goddamn world narrows down to her.

"Hey there," she says, stepping inside like she owns the air around her. Sugar and warmth trail behind her, soft and familiar.

My mouth tips into a smile before I can stop it. "What brings you here? Not that I'm complainin'."

She smirks and lifts the box. "Thought you might need some sweetness after dealing with all those unruly customers."

I laugh, tension bleeding out of me like air from a cracked tire. "You have no idea."

We end up in the back corner of the shop, settled among wood shavings and drying stain. She talks about her day—crazy customers, Sam's latest pastry disaster—and her laughter fills the whole damn space.

And I just sit there, staring at her, feeling like maybe for a second, everything's okay.

Like maybe my whole world won't go to shit at any moment.

I take a bite of one donut and hum in delight. She blushes at my reaction, and I feel that familiar heat stir in my gut.

Damn, this woman's really gonna be the death of me.

A pang of guilt hits me square in the chest. She's so damn beautiful. Delicate, even. All I want to do is wrap her up in my arms and keep the world the hell away from her.

The trouble is... I don't know if that's me talking—or the bond.

Everyone keeps telling me the feelings are mine, that the bond only amplifies what's already there. But the fact that it exists at all feels like a fucking elephant on my chest. It's like I don't get to *choose* how deep I fall.

I wonder if she feels it too. That desperate pull. That buzz under the skin that sparks the second we're apart and eases the second she's near. It's intense. Consuming.

I clench my fists, trying to keep from devouring her whole.

I should tell her about the bond; I should tell her about everything. She deserves to know. Deserves the choice. Even if it kills me when she walks away... it's a risk I have to take. Keeping it from her ain't fair.

My mind's spiraling when she leans in and kisses me.

Instinct takes over. I wrap my arms around her and pull her in, deepening the kiss. My pulse kicks up, pounding in my ears. She tastes like sugar and cinnamon and something that wrecks me. I slide my tongue against hers, swallowing the soft moan that escapes her.

I grip her tighter, drowning in the heat of her body. For one second—just one—I think, *fuck it*. Fuck everything. All that matters is her mouth on mine and the way she melts in my arms.

I break the kiss long enough to brush my fingers against her cheek, then tangle them in her hair and pull gently. Her gasp sends a jolt straight to my cock.

I trail kisses along her jaw, down to that soft, sensitive spot just behind her ear.

"Jake," she breathes. My name, a whisper, a plea, a fucking prayer.

And I almost lose it. Almost bend her over the worktable and take her right then and there.

But I let go.

I *have* to.

She stares up at me, eyes hazy with want, lips swollen from the kiss. I groan, my dick straining against my jeans. I step back, try to steady my breathing, and *will* my body to calm the hell down.

She smiles like she knows exactly what she's doing. "I thought you might wanna go for a walk. It's a pretty night out, and you've been cooped up in here all day."

I return the smile and nod. "Yeah. That actually sounds real nice."

She nods in acknowledgment and smiles again; this one is bright and sultry.

She turns, and I spin back toward the workbench to finish up. Out of the corner of my eye, I catch her admiring the shop like it's a cathedral.

With her back turned, I reach down and adjust myself—my cock still hard as fuck and aching behind the zipper.

Motherfucker, I think. *I'm so fucking screwed.*

I finish putting away my tools as the last rays of sunlight fade, casting long shadows across the shop. After a final check on the locks, I take Sarah's hand and lead her toward the worn path that cuts through the trees behind the building.

The air is crisp, heavy with pine and the promise of night. The sounds of the forest shift as the animals settle, the rustle of leaves and distant chirps fading into something quieter, softer.

By the time the light of my cabin comes into view, half-hidden by trees and shadow, that restless buzz under my skin has eased a little.

"This is home," I say with a smile, nodding toward the front porch. "Not far from the shop, as you can see."

She looks up at me, eyes bright with curiosity. "You weren't kidding about walking to work every day."

I furrow my brow. "You walk to work every day—why can't I?"

She snorts. "I live in town, not the middle of the woods. People actually wave when I pass."

"Touche," I admit, grinning as I squeeze her hand.

An idea flickers. "You wanna come in for a bit? I could make you some tea. Or coffee, if you're not afraid I'll burn water."

Her smile widens, and she nods.

Without another word, I tug her toward the porch—already wondering how the hell I'm gonna keep it together once she's inside.

I bring her inside my modest home, the scent of cedar hitting me the moment I open the door. She steps into the living room behind me, her eyes scanning the space. It's not big, but it's mine.

A comfy loveseat sits in front of the fireplace, a TV mounted on the wall above it. Pictures of family and friends line the mantel—smiling faces frozen in time, watching over the room. To the right, a short hallway leads to the laundry room, bathroom, and two small bedrooms. To the left is the kitchen, outfitted with wood cabinets that almost disappear into the walls, a spacious fridge, and a large stove.

"Make yourself at home," I tell her as I head toward the kitchen. I get a pot of coffee brewing, the familiar ritual steadying my nerves, then walk back into the living room.

Sarah's sitting on one end of the loveseat, her eyes still drifting over everything. She looks so perfect there. Like she belongs.

My dick twitches at the thought, and I grit my teeth, trying to shove it down. Not now.

She shivers a little, and I notice the chill in the air. It's not quite cold enough for a fire, but fall's coming fast. I grab the blanket from the back of the couch and drape it over her shoulders.

She flashes me a soft smile, pulling the blanket tighter. It smells like home—clean laundry and faint woodsmoke. I watch her inhale deeply, like she's breathing it all in.

"Sorry it's a bit chilly," I say as I ease down beside her, the quiet hum of the coffee pot filling the silence.

"It's alright," she murmurs. "I get cold pretty easy. The blanket helps. Thank you."

Without thinking, I lean in and brush a kiss across her forehead.

When I pull back, our eyes meet—and the air between us thickens.

I can feel it—that heat building in my chest. That need. And I know she feels it too. It's in the way her eyes darken, the way her breath catches.

It's a hunger. Mirrored in her eyes.

"I could kiss you right now," she murmurs, her voice barely a whisper.I swallow, my throat tightening. "I wouldn't stop you," I reply just as quietly, my voice thick with anticipation.

With sudden, determined motion, Sarah tosses the blanket aside and straddles me, her lips crashing into mine with a hunger that rips through me like wildfire. I meet her with equal force—our mouths clashing, tongues tangling in a rhythm that's messy, desperate, perfect.

She rocks against me, soft sighs escaping her lips as friction builds. I groan into her mouth, hips lifting to meet hers, grinding in sync. The sound of rustling fabric fills the room, blending with her breathy moans and my harsh exhales.

She pulls back, panting, her eyes locked on mine—dark, wild, full of raw need. Her fingers rake through my hair, tugging just enough to make me grunt. I grip her tighter, sliding my hands up her back, feeling the heat of her through the thin fabric of her shirt.

I kiss her again—harder this time, almost rough—chasing more. More of her. More of this. My hands slip under her shirt, finding bare skin, smooth and warm beneath my palms.

She breaks away again, her lips brushing my ear. "Show me your bedroom," she whispers, voice low and breathless.

She doesn't have to ask twice.

I grip her hips and stand, and she wraps herself around me without hesitation. Our mouths crash together in a fevered kiss, teeth grazing, tongues claiming. I press her tighter against me, my hands sliding down to cup her ass, grinding her into my aching cock. She moans, tightening her grip, her legs locked around me like she's never letting go.

I stagger toward the hallway without breaking the kiss—it feels like breathing her is the only thing keeping me alive. My back bumps the bedroom door, and it swings open, hitting the wall. I step inside and kick it shut behind us.

Then I press her to it, pinning her there. My lips trail from her mouth to her jaw, down her neck to the hollow of her throat. She gasps, arching into me, her fingers buried in my hair.

Moonlight spills through the window, painting her in silver and shadow. Her skin glows, her eyes burning with hunger and something deeper.

She's flushed, breathless, utterly fucking beautiful — and she's fucking *mine.*

"Are you sure?" I whisper, my voice low and strained, every muscle in my body pulled tight with restraint. As much as I ache for her, I'd stop if she wanted me to.

She runs her fingers along my jaw, her eyes dark and steady. "I'm sure," she breathes.

Groaning, I capture her mouth again, slower this time—savoring the way her lips mold to mine, the soft hitch in her breath. Her legs loosen from around my waist as my hands find the hem of her shirt. She slides down my body, pulling the fabric over her head as she goes. It hits the floor just as I spin her gently, guiding her backward toward the bed.

Her jeans slip down with ease, her shoes kicked aside in one fluid motion, clothes scattering in our wake. When the backs of her knees hit the edge of the mattress, I give her a light push, watching the bounce of her breasts in her bra as she lands. Fuck, she's perfect.

I strip off my shirt and shove my jeans down in one quick motion, dropping to my knees between her legs. She props herself up on her elbows, watching me with parted lips, like she already knows what's coming.

Good. She fucking should.

I grip her thighs, smooth and warm beneath my palms, and pull her to the edge of the bed. Her hands find my shoulders, then my hair, as I kiss her—deep and claiming. Her bra comes loose beneath my fingers, and she tosses it across the room like it's nothing.

I cup her breasts, running my thumbs over her nipples until she gasps, breaking the kiss. I lower my mouth, sucking one nipple between my lips. It hardens under my tongue, and I graze it lightly with my teeth before moving to the other, giving it the same attention. She fists her hands in my hair, arching into me, begging without a word.

I pant against her skin, my cock already leaking pre-cum, aching for her. Kissing my way down her stomach, I reach the waistband of her panties. My fingers hook beneath the fabric, and she lifts her hips without a word, letting me slide them down her legs. I toss them over my shoulder, savoring the sight of her laid out naked before me. Her thighs are slick, trembling in my hands. I spread them wide, slinging her legs over my shoulders, and grin up at her like a man starved.

"You're so fuckin' pretty like this," I murmur, breath hot against her soaked pussy. "Bet you taste even better."

My cock throbs just looking at her—slick, spread, ready for me. I lean in, groaning as my tongue drags through her folds in one slow, deliberate stroke. She jolts with a sharp inhale, her hands flying to the blanket beside her. She tastes better than I ever imagined—warm and wet on my tongue, like something I was born to crave. I savor every drop like it's owed to me, like her body was crafted to be devoured by my mouth alone. She's mine, and I want her to feel that with every flick of my tongue.

When I suck her clit into my mouth, her arms give out, a raw, broken moan spilling out as her hips buck against my face. I grip her tighter, locking her down. She's panting, legs twitching, her whole body chasing every movement of my tongue.

I slide one arm across her waist, pinning her in place as my other hand trails down, fingers slick with her arousal before I slide one inside her. She's so warm, so fucking tight. I curl my finger just right, and her whole body jerks, a cry ripping from her throat as she falls apart.

"Fuck, that's it," I growl against her, adding another finger, curling then while pumping slow and deep as her orgasm slams into her. She gushes around me, soaking my hand, her cries bouncing off the walls.

I press a final kiss to her pussy before dragging my mouth up her trembling body—tasting sweat, lust, and everything that's mine. I pause at her breasts, giving each nipple a rough flick of my tongue before catching her mouth in a hungry kiss. She moans into me, biting my lip just enough to make me groan.

My cock's aching, straining inside my boxers, but I'm not done wrecking her yet.

I pull back, watching the hunger in her eyes as I move around the bed. Her gaze follows me, lingering while I open the drawer and grab a condom. She smiles, scooting higher on the mattress, eyes dark with need. As I strip off my boxers, her teeth catch her bottom lip. One hand comes up to cup her breast, fingers teasing her nipple as her gaze drops to my cock.

I stroke myself slowly, but the impatience builds quickly. I crawl onto the bed and press my body to hers, kissing her deep. She whimpers, rolling her hips up, her slick pussy gliding against me—and I hiss, breaking the kiss to tear open the condom with my teeth.

I roll it on fast, and the second it's in place, she wraps her legs around me, dragging me closer.

Chuckling, I cup her cheek, leaning in close. "Easy, baby. I've got you."

She squirms beneath me, breathless. "Jake... please."

I know I'm... well, girthy compared to most men, and the last thing I want is to hurt her. I brush my lips over hers, steadying my hips.

"Tell me if I hurt you," I murmur, lining myself up. Her body's already begging for me—hot, soaked, ready—and I sink into her with a gasp. Her heat wraps around me like a vice, tight and perfect, and I gasp at how good it feels.

"Fuck," I breathe. "You were made for me."

She moans, her back arching as I bottom out, buried to the hilt. I hold there for a second, letting her adjust, fighting the sharp edge of hunger threatening to snap my control. My mind flickers to what it would feel like without the condom, skin on skin—and I have to grit my teeth to keep from losing it.

"Jake..." she gasps, breath hot against my neck.

That's all it takes.

I start to move—slow, deep strokes, dragging every inch of me against her walls. Her gasps turn to soft cries, hands gripping my shoulders, her legs locked around me as I build a rhythm. Every thrust has her clenching tighter, every grind dragging another sound from her lips.

Her body trembles beneath me, close already, her voice rising with every breath.

"Oh God... don't stop. Don't stop. Please don't stop."

I thrust harder, her pussy gripping my cock as she cums, her body shaking beneath me. I ride her through it, pushing her higher until she's panting, limp and trembling. And then I start again, building her up, driving her over the edge two more times. By the time she crashes through her last orgasm, I pull out, her soft whimpering only spurring me on.

Sitting back on my knees, I flip her onto her stomach and guide her onto all fours. My hands trail down her spine as I line up behind her. Her ass looks too fucking perfect to resist—I grab it tight and sink back into her in one hard, hungry thrust. She gasps, back arching, and I don't wait. I fuck her deep, my pace relentless. Her moans turn guttural, her arms giving out as she presses her face into the pillow. Her hips tilt higher, giving me deeper access, and I take it, slamming into her again and again. My balls tighten, the pressure building fast.

I reach around, fingers circling her clit, and she unravels—screaming my name as her pussy clenches hard, milking my cock as I cum with a groan, emptying into the condom in thick, pulsing waves. I don't stop until her body goes slack beneath me, her final tremor fading into soft shudders.

Still panting, I pull her close and we collapse sideways on the bed, our limbs tangled, sweat-slicked skin pressed together. I nuzzle into her neck, kissing her shoulder, my cock still buried inside her. She wiggles slightly, teasing me, and I grunt, wrapping an arm tighter around her. Her fingers trail lazy lines across my arm, and for a moment we stay like that—skin to skin, soaked in the warmth and weight of each other.

When I finally soften, I press one more kiss to her shoulder and ease out of her, careful and slow. "I'll be right back," I murmur into her ear, dragging myself from the bed and heading toward the bathroom.

The light flicks on, and I blink against the sudden brightness. Closing the door behind me, I remove the condom, knotting it before tossing it into the trash. I grab a washcloth from the shower, run it under warm water, and wipe away the remnants of our time together before tossing it in the hamper.

When I open the door, Sarah's already there, standing naked in the soft glow spilling from the bathroom. Her skin glows, her body lit in golden hues. My palms itch to touch her again, but I step aside, watching the way her ass jiggles as she walks past me. The door clicks shut.

I hunt for my underwear, which I somehow kicked across the room. Just as I sit on the edge of the bed, pulling them on, Sarah steps back out. My eyes track her every movement—her breasts bounce slightly with each step, and my mouth waters at the thought of tasting her rosy pink nipples again. Fuck, this woman is like a drug—she's worked her way into my system, deeper than skin, running through my veins like she's part of me. I doubt I'd ever be free of her, even if I bled the life force from my body at her feet.

She straddles me again, arms curling around my neck, and I kiss her without hesitation. Her tongue traces my lower lip, and I give her what she wants, what I always will. Her kiss is slow and deep, and when she finally pulls back, I rest my forehead against hers, holding her close like I never want to let go.

"Stay," I whisper, brushing kisses across her mouth.

She sighs, lips brushing my jaw. "I can't," she breathes against my ear.

I nibble gently at the spot where her neck meets her shoulder. "Stay," I murmur again, more insistent now.

I want her here. In my bed. Wrapped around me as we sleep. I want her scent on my sheets, her warmth in my arms. I want her always. But she kisses me again—soft, apologetic—and shakes her head.

"I want to," she whispers, "but I can't."

I exhale against her mouth, one last kiss sealing the ache in my chest. "Okay," I murmur, voice low.

I slide her off my lap and stand. "Let's get you dressed. I'll walk you to your car."

She groans softly but rises, gathering her clothes. I do the same, the quiet between us filled with rustling fabric and moonlight.

We walk the familiar path back to the shop, the cool night air sharp against my skin, still overheated from everything we shared. She slips into her car, backs up and swings around. I raise a hand in goodbye. She mirrors the motion before driving off, her taillights shrinking to specks in the dark.

I don't turn back until I see her brake lights disappear at the end of the drive. Only then do I head toward the cabin.

Later, I lie in bed, her scent still clinging to the sheets. It's the best night's sleep I've had in a long time. But even in my dreams, I'm bracing for morning—because that's when it'll hit me all over again. She's not here.

Chapter 16

"You were home late," my father, Thomas, says as he walks into the kitchen, his voice gruff but steady.

I glance up, offering a small smile before taking a slow sip of my coffee, savoring the warmth spreading across my tongue. "I went to see Jake."

Without a word, he heads for the counter and pours a cup of coffee. He adds the perfect amount of cream and sugar, stirs, then turns to face me. "Is he good to you?" His brow arches, a mixture of concern and curiosity in his tone.

I nod, the words stuck in my throat. He sits down across from me, his hands wrapped around the cup, turning it slowly as he sighs. The silence between us is thick with unspoken worry. I know what's on his mind. Since losing my mother two years ago, it's been like our lives hit a wall, frozen in that moment. Everything changed that night—my dreams, my ambitions, all of it seemed to wither away with her. My father left grasping at pieces of the life we once had, clung to me, while I just float along, aimlessly.

But then there's Jake. He's like a lighthouse on the shore, cutting through the fog and chaos. When I'm with him, I don't feel lost anymore. I'm not afraid.

"Sarah." My father's voice pulls me out of my thoughts, the usual gruff-ness edged with emotion. "I know you're not my little girl anymore. I've known that for a long time. I asked you to come here with me because I can see your pain. It mirrors mine. I wanted to give us both a place where we could feel safe." His voice cracks slightly. "Your mother's loss... it's thrown our lives into chaos. And the last thing I want is for you to let it consume you."

Tears spill down my cheeks, hot and unstoppable, as he reaches across the table, his rough hand gently grasping mine. He presses a soft kiss to my knuckles, the touch filled with a tenderness that breaks me a little more.

"If this Jake fellow makes you happy," he continues, "then I'm happy for you. I just want you safe, that's all. Just give your old man a call if you're going to be out late, okay?"

"I didn't mean to worry you, Daddy," I murmur, my voice thick with emotion.

He nods, his expression softening. "I know, baby girl. You haven't need-ed to check in with me for a long time—not since high school, when your mom made me realize you needed to figure things out for yourself." He sighs, squeezing my fingers a little tighter. "But I'm terrified of losing you too. It's something I'll have to work through."

I give him a watery smile, squeezing his hand in return. "I know, Dad. And there's no reason I can't check in with you. I worry about you too, you know."

He releases my hand, and I wipe away the stray tears still lingering on my cheeks. For a moment, it feels like we've reached an understanding, the weight between us slightly lighter. But then he stiffens, turning to face me fully.

"You did use protection, didn't you?"

I choke on the coffee I've just sipped, coughing hard as I grimace. "Ew. Dad. No, we are not talking about that."

His expression wavers between discomfort and the need to know, his eyes boring into mine. Once I finally get the coughing fit under control, I sigh heavily. "If you must know... yes. We did." My eyes dart around the room, suddenly fascinated by everything but his face.

"Good. Uh," my dad stumbles, clearly uncomfortable. "As much as I'd still love them, I'm not ready to be a grandfather yet."

"Dad!" I practically shout, my face burning, probably a deep shade of red from how hot it feels.

He pushes his chair back, the scrape loud in the quiet kitchen, standing like the room's suddenly too small for him. "Yes... well... I should be getting to work." He mumbles, heading toward the exit.

I huff to myself. Crap, I really need to remember to mention the weird tingling I've been getting lately. Maybe one of my medications is acting up or something. I don't know if itchy skin is a side effect of any of them, but something's gotta give. The fact that it comes and goes at random is just plain weird. Even just *thinking* about asking Dad now is giving me the heebie-jeebies.

A shudder runs through me as his silhouette disappears down the hall, relief settling in. But before I can fully relax, his voice suddenly echoes through the house—panicked.

"Sarah!"

I freeze for a split second before shoving my chair back and sprinting toward the front door, my heart pounding. The hardwood floors seem to slip beneath my feet as I skid to a halt behind him. He's standing in the doorway, frozen, staring at something on the porch. The light from outside streams in, illuminating the horror before us.

I gasp as I step up beside him, the sight in front of us sinking into my brain. A dead cat lies on the porch, blood pooling around its body, but it's the message scrawled next to it in blood that makes my blood run cold. WHORE is written in thick, bold letters across the wood planks. The blood is still wet, glistening in the sunlight.

My eyes meet my father's—wide, panicked, searching. Without thinking, I rush forward, kicking the carcass off the porch. It's not until my foot hits the still-warm body that I realize I'm barefoot. Normally, the thought alone would make me gag, but all I can think of is getting rid of the mess.

I hurry to grab the hose, turning the water on full blast and spraying the porch until the blood disappears, swirling into the grass. I drop the hose and turn back. He's still frozen, staring at the empty spot where the cat had been.

I move quickly, grabbing his shoulders and forcing him to look at me. He seems to snap out of it, pulling me inside and slamming the door shut. He hugs me tight, his hands trembling as they run through my hair.

I feel the fear radiating off him—thick, suffocating—the same fear settling deep in my bones. The warmth of his arms is such a contrast to the cold, horrifying reality of what we've just seen.

"Dad, what the hell is going on?" I whisper, my voice barely a breath.

He pulls back, keeping his hands on my shoulders, his eyes searching mine for answers neither of us has. "I don't know, sweetheart. I really don't. But someone's trying to scare us, and I won't let anything happen to you," he says, voice firm but tinged with worry.

My mind races, a hundred questions swirling in my head, but I force myself to focus. "Maybe we should call the police. This... this isn't okay."

His grip tightens for a moment as he considers my words. "We can't. We don't have any evidence. All we've got is a dead cat on our lawn—one that could've crawled there and died for all they know."

I nod, biting my lip, mentally kicking myself for reacting so quickly and washing away any trace of proof. Vulnerability wraps around me like a second skin—the chilling realization that someone out there is targeting us, invading our home with a message meant to terrify.

My dad guides me to the living room, and we sink onto the couch, the silence heavy with fear. I can tell he's trying to stay composed, but the tension is thick—both of us struggling to process what just happened.

After a long moment, he finally breaks the silence.

"We need to be careful, Sarah. Keep an eye out. If anything else happens, we'll call the police."

I nod, trying to push away the suffocating pressure building in my chest. But it's hard to shake the feeling of being watched, of our safety shattered by some unseen threat. The idea of someone out there harboring that much hate—it makes my skin crawl.

"We need to clean up. Go about our day," he says quietly, though his voice carries the weight of everything we just saw.

Reluctantly, we head outside to finish the job. He grabs a shovel, and together, we bury the poor cat in a corner of the yard. It feels like a twisted ritual—an innocent life caught in the middle of something darker than either of us understands. As the last bit of dirt falls, it feels like the weight of the world presses down even harder.

The sense of stability I'd just begun to find with Jake feels distant now—replaced by the grim reality that's crept into our lives. The illusion of safety we've been rebuilding since my mother's death has been shattered, and in its place is something far more fragile.

After we clean up, my father walks me to work before heading to the library. I try to focus, to quiet my nerves, but every sound in the bakery sets me on edge. Every customer feels like a potential threat. Mr. Walters notices the tension, probably assumes I'm coming down with something. By lunchtime, he sends me home.

I can't decide if I'm grateful or terrified at the thought of being alone.

Jake texted me a few times throughout the day, and I did my best to sound normal. But it kills me that the memory of last night—something that felt so right—is already tainted by whoever did this.

Thankfully, my father gets sent home early too—his boss must have picked up on the same unease mine did.

By nightfall he's on high alert, pacing the house like a guard dog. I can't sleep either. We take turns peering through windows, scanning the darkness outside. Every creak, every gust of wind makes us flinch. Both of us are on edge, bracing for whatever might come next.

When morning rolls around, sunlight filters through the kitchen windows, but it does little to lift the heavy atmosphere in the room. I sit at the table, clutching my third cup of coffee—the warmth barely cutting through the weight in my chest.

Across from me, my father jerks awake every few minutes, fighting the exhaustion written all over his face. I grunt softly, my head pounding like I'm dealing with the worst hangover of my life—only without the fun night to justify it. Yesterday's stress sits deep in my bones, making everything feel slow and dull.

He startles awake again, and I reach out, wrapping my fingers around his hand, giving it a gentle squeeze. He looks at me with a tired smile, the kind that barely touches his eyes.

"Daddy, why don't you call in and take a nap?" I ask, knowing he's running on fumes.

He rubs his temples, the lines of fatigue etched deep into his face. He considers it for a moment, then sighs.

"I appreciate the concern, Doodle Bug, but I can't just leave you alone."

I nod, appreciating his strength, even if it makes me worry more.

"Maybe we should think about getting some security cameras," I say, grasping for anything that might make us feel safe again.

He nods slowly. "We'll look into it. But we also need to figure out who would do something like this. It's not just a prank—it's personal. Targeted."

The incident weighs between us. The fear of the unknown gnaws at the edges of whatever peace we had left. We share a look—tired, unsettled—both of us sensing that something darker is at play.

His expression softens, tinged with sadness and a hint of pity. I know what he's thinking. The last thing he wants is for me to slip back into the fear and nightmares that took hold after Mom died.

"Did anyone know you were going to see Jake that night?" he asks gently.

My mind flashes to the word scrawled on our porch—WHORE—in blood. The morning after that incredible night with Jake. That memory doesn't feel like mine anymore. It's been tainted, corrupted. I rack my brain trying to remember who I told.

"I told Lila," I murmur. "But she wouldn't do something like this. And I haven't talked to her since, so she wouldn't even know about..."

I trail off. I can't bring myself to say it out loud.

Dad nods. He knows Lila. Sweet, protective. Not the type to hurt anyone.

He runs a hand through his graying hair, jaw tight in thought. "Alright. Then we need to be cautious about who we share this with. No need to stir up panic if we're wrong."

I nod. He's right. We can't start pointing fingers without proof, and the last thing we want is to start a wildfire in a small town.

"Let's keep it between us for now. Watch. See if anything else happens. Maybe it really was just... some sick one-time thing."

He squeezes my hand again, and a quiet understanding passes between us. In that moment, without another word, we agree: this stays between us. A silent pact to protect each other in the best way that we can.

The tension doesn't leave—not really—but the decision gives me a small sense of control. Just enough to breathe.

After checking the porch and finding no fresh horrors, we both decide to call in to work. Some rest is long overdue.

Chapter 17

The ping of my phone pulls me from a restless sleep, the image of that poor cat playing on an endless loop in my mind. I try to shake it, but the memory clings to me, bleeding into my dreams, twisting into nightmares where my mother lies across the floor—only sometimes she is the cat, murdered because of me. Other times, it's just the cat, its blood staining the living room floor, pooling like a warning.

I rub my face, trying to clear my head, and reach for the phone. Jake's name flashes across the screen, and despite everything, a small smile tugs at my lips. His text brings a sliver of calm to my frayed nerves.

Jake: Hello, beautiful. I haven't heard from you today and wanted to check on you. Mr. Walters said you weren't feeling well.

Sarah: Hi (smiley face emoji) I'm feeling okay. Just tired.

> **Jake:** Anything I can do for you?

> **Sarah:** I don't think so. I think I just caught a small bug. Dad has it too, but we're on the mend. Should be back to normal by tomorrow.

My fingers tighten around the phone, the lie tasting bitter in my mouth. I hate not telling Jake what's really going on, but I don't want to worry him over something that might turn out to be nothing. The phone pings again, pulling me from my thoughts.

> **Jake:** Okay. Let me know if you change your mind.

> **Jake:** I miss you.

I blush at his last text, warmth spreading through my chest. I can practically feel his arms around me, hear him telling me everything's going to be okay. Without overthinking, I type my reply.

> **Sarah:** Miss you too.

I set the phone down and toss the covers off, heading for the living room. My father's already there, freshly showered, sitting on the couch. The TV's on—some game show—but he doesn't seem to be watching it. The tension in the room is thick, and all I want is to rewind to a few days ago, back before everything unraveled.

I settle beside him in silence. He wraps an arm around me, presses a kiss to the top of my head, and I melt into the hug. It's comforting—reminding me I'm not alone, that no matter how old I get, I'll always be his little girl.

The day drifts by in a haze. The routine helps—a few chores, dinner, small talk and laughter—but the unease never fully fades. It dulls a little, settling into the background like white noise. But it's still there, humming quietly.

The next morning, sunlight filters through my window as I pull myself out of bed. My father's already in the kitchen, flipping pancakes. Over coffee, we chat casually, but yesterday's peace feels thin—like it might shatter under the wrong breath. The cat... the message... it all still lingers.

I glance at the clock, knowing I need to get ready for the bakery. A knot forms in my stomach. Every part of me wants to stay home, but I won't let fear win. Not again.

After a quick shower, I throw on jeans and a cozy sweater that'll double as my work uniform. It feels like armor—thin, but better than nothing. When I return to the kitchen, Dad's already dressed, his face lined with worry. We both hesitate near the front door.

I grab my coat off the hook and slip it on. He steps closer, hand on the knob, and I hold my breath. When he finally opens the door, the porch is clear.

I exhale. Relief hits in a slow wave. No blood. No corpse. No messages.

We step outside. I scan the yard just in case. My father watches me closely, concern etched deep into every line of his face. I force a smile, give him a small nod, and he locks the door behind us.

We walk in silence. He watches the town. I watch the cracks in the sidewalk. But neither of us says what we're both thinking—because saying it would make it real.

We part ways outside the shop, exchanging a quick hug before I watch him walk toward the library. Stepping into the bakery, I'm greeted by the familiar scent of freshly baked bread—warm and yeasty, wrapping around me like a comforting blanket.

Mr. Walters smiles as I cross the floor. "Morning, Sarah!" he calls.

"Morning," I say, grateful for the routine.

I slip into the back and get ready for the day. A few minutes later, the bell above the door jingles, and I glance up to see Lila striding in with her usual bright smile.

"Hey, girl!" she chirps, completely unaware of the storm simmering beneath my calm exterior. She places her office's order and, true to form, immediately launches into chatter, pestering me until I cave and promise to meet her later.

I shake my head, watching her with a mix of amusement and exasperation as Jordan, standing nearby, rolls his eyes behind her back.

The rest of the day passes in a blur. I move on autopilot—serving customers, making small talk, and keeping myself busy so I don't have to think.

"Goodnight, Mr. Walters!" I call, shrugging into my coat and waving as I head for the door.

"Goodnight, Sarah!" he calls back, his voice warm and steady.

Outside, the cold hits instantly—early winter air biting at my skin as the sun slips below the horizon. I never cared for this time of year. The early sunsets, the biting cold... everything feels heavier, darker.

The sky fades from burned orange to dusky violet as I head toward Main Street. I texted my dad to let him know I'm safe, my boots crunching against the sidewalk with every step. A shiver crawls down my spine—sharp, invasive, and not from the cold. I freeze mid-step, scanning the quiet street. Everything looks normal. Too normal. But that feeling—eyes on me, breath held just out of reach—won't let go. My heart picks up. I shove my hands into my pockets and quicken my pace, every footstep echoing louder than it should.

When I finally step into the diner, the heat slams into me like a wall, and I let out a sigh of relief. I tug off my coat, my cheeks tingling from the sudden temperature change.

Across the room, Lila waves so hard her whole body moves. Her energy is ridiculous—but contagious. I smile and wave back, making my way toward her. Before I even reach the booth, she's out of her seat, throwing her arms around me like it's been years. Her presence is calming, instantly washing away the unease I felt just moments ago.

I melt into her hug, tension bleeding from my shoulders as I catch the familiar scent of her vanilla perfume.

"Sarah, you have no idea how much I needed this tonight," she says, pulling back with a grin that's impossible not to return.

"Same," I admit, meaning it. Just being near her calms me more than I expected.

We slide into the booth and, for a moment, I let myself sink into the familiar rhythm of diner life—the clink of silverware, the murmur of conversations, the low hum of comfort.

After we order coffee, Lila launches into a recap of her chaotic day at the attorney's office, her voice fast and bright, like music I didn't know I missed.

Once the server finally returns to take our food order, Lila waits until he's out of earshot, then leans forward suddenly, her eyes lighting up with mischief as she grabs my hands across the table.

"Okay," she practically squeals. "I've been dying to know how it went with Jake the other night. Did he like the pastries?"

My cheeks heat instantly, and I lean in, making sure no one else is close enough to overhear. "It was a-mazing," I say, wiggling my eyebrows at her, unable to hide my grin.

Her jaw drops, and she quickly claps her hands over her mouth, eyes wide with excitement. "Girl!" she whisper-yells, barely containing herself. "You two..." She finishes her sentence with another squeal, and I nod, confirming what she already suspected. Even though everything with Jake had been tainted by the incident afterward, I'm choosing to focus on the night itself—the part that made me smile.

"Oh. My. God," Lila practically drums her fingers on the table in excitement. "Tell me everything. Was it good? Did you, you know...?" She winks dramatically, then leans in with a lowered voice. "OH! OH! What about his package?" She gestures with her hands, slowly pulling them apart until they reach an absurdly exaggerated size.

I can't help but laugh, the tension of the past day finally lifting. I shake my head, grateful for the momentary escape.

"Yes, it was. Yes, I did. And no, we're not talking about that."

"Oh, come on!" Lila practically yells, drawing a few glances from nearby tables. I quickly shush her, but she just grins, wide-eyed and unapologetic.

"I'm sorry!" she whisper-yells, still buzzing. "I'm just so happy for you! I haven't been laid in *three years*, okay? I'm living through you right now."

"Wait, seriously? Three years? Like *years* plural?"

"Ugh. Yes," she groans. "I don't know if you've noticed, but most of the guys around here are married or—ew, no. Just no."

I pause, considering. "What about Jordan?"

Lila's face twists like she just sucked on a lemon. "Jordan? *Jordan Walters*? Um, no."

"Why not? I'm pretty sure he's into you."

Her face scrunches again. "He *hates* me. And trust me, the feeling is mutual."

"Hates you? Really?" I raise an eyebrow. "Why would you think that?"

She sighs dramatically, eyes narrowing like she's recalling some ancient high school trauma. "It's a long story, but let's just say it involves a failed group project, a misunderstanding over a stolen lunch, and an unfortunate incident with a bottle of ketchup. We never quite recovered."

I lean in, fully intrigued. "Failed project, stolen lunch, *and* ketchup? You can't drop that and not tell me more."

Lila smirks, clearly enjoying the suspense she's created. "Alright, picture this—senior year. We got paired up for a history project. Jordan was known for being a slacker, and I, naturally, was the overachiever. So we clashed. On everything—topic, timeline, deadlines."

I sip my coffee, fully invested now. "Go on."

She rolls her eyes. "Presentation day rolls around. I'd done all the work. Jordan shows up empty-handed, claiming he 'forgot.' I was *pissed*. Later at lunch, I accidentally knocked over a bottle of ketchup—right onto his tray. He didn't believe it was an accident. It was a messy scene, both literally and figuratively."

I chuckle, picturing the entire scene. "And that's the 'lunch misunderstanding' part, huh?"

Lila nods. "Exactly. He is convinced to this day that I deliberately ruined his lunch. And ever since then, it's been this back-and-forth cold war of passive-aggressive jabs and us avoiding each other like the plague."

I try to stifle my laughter but fail. "But you didn't steal it—you just ruined it."

"Well…" She grimaces. "He didn't see it that way. So he stole my lunch in retaliation."

That's it—I lose it, laughing outright.

"Oh, but it gets worse," she mutters, scowling.

"How could it *possibly* get worse?"

She leans forward, lowering her voice like she's about to drop a bomb. "The lunch he stole? It was made by my Nonna. For my birthday. Her famous meatloaf, mashed potatoes, and the most decadent chocolate cake you've ever seen. It was sacred. A gift. And he *devoured* it."

My laughter falters, sympathy creeping in. "Oh, that's rough. I can't believe he really thought you ruined his lunch on purpose."

Lila nods, eyes flashing with a mix of frustration and lingering hurt. "It was a comedy of errors that spiraled out of control. We failed the project—he didn't do his part, and I didn't have everything I needed to finish it alone. My GPA dropped. I *still* get mad thinking about it."

"Lila," I gape, "you're *actually* still holding a grudge."

She glares into her coffee. "I don't usually hold grudges. But that was the first bad grade I ever got. It was *traumatic*."

I reach for her hand and squeeze it. "God, I'm sorry."

She squeezes back, her voice laced with bitterness. "He never even apologized. Freaking *butthole*."

That breaks me. I choke, then snort, then spiral into uncontrollable laughter. Heads turn, but I can't stop. I wave my hands around, trying to compose myself, but it only makes it worse.

Lila joins in, shaking her head as she gasps for air. Soon we're both doubled over, tears streaming down our faces.

"You should've seen your face when you tried not to laugh!" she sputters between fits of giggles.

I wipe my eyes, struggling to catch my breath, but the laughter keeps bubbling up. By the time we finally calm down, the server arrives with our food, giving us a bemused look. Lila just shakes her head, and we pull ourselves together, diving into our meals.

As we eat, we swap high school stories, letting the laughter carry us. By the time I leave the diner and head home, my heart feels lighter. For the first time in days, I can focus on the good again.

Lila will never know just how much I needed that distraction—or how deeply I value her friendship.

Chapter 18

SARAH

I jolt awake, my heart pounding in the quiet darkness. My eyes scan the room, adjusting quickly to the dim light, but nothing looks out of place. Still, unease crawls along my skin, prickling at the edges of my senses. I toss the covers aside and slip out of bed, my bare feet padding softly across the floor. Everything is still. The room, the house—silent.

Something pulls me toward the window. Maybe it's the need to see for myself that the world outside is quiet. I peer into the night. The moon is hidden behind thick clouds, casting everything in inky blackness, but my raccoon-shifter sight cuts through the dark. Shapes form—trees, the edge of the yard, the porch steps. Nothing's moving. No figures. No threats. The yard is empty.

I exhale slowly, but the unease lingers, coiled tight in my chest. My gaze sweeps over the yard again. Still nothing. Still nothing.

Then, suddenly, the hairs on the back of my neck rise. A cold shiver trails down my spine.

I'm being watched.

I can feel it.

My eyes dart back to the window, searching for something—any-thing—but the shadows outside remain still. My pulse spikes. I scan the room again, each corner heavy with silence.

With a sharp tug, I yank the blinds closed. The thud of the slats hitting the frame is oddly grounding. I breathe a little easier, telling myself I'm just paranoid. Jumpy from the cat incident. It was a sick prank, nothing more. In a few days and this tension will fade.

I crawl back into bed, clinging to that lie like a lifeline. Eventually, sleep returns.

Until—*Tink*.

I jolt upright, covers flung aside. My feet hit the floor. Ears straining.

Tink.

There it is again—a soft tapping, like something striking glass.

My gaze shifts to the window. The blinds still hang in place, unmoved. But the sound came from there.

Tink.

My heart hammers. I rise slowly, inching toward the sound, every muscle tight.

Tink.

My fingers hover near the cord. I force a deep breath, steadying my nerves.

Tink.

I yank the cord. The blinds fly up.

Nothing.

Just the empty yard.

My shoulders drop—but then a bird suddenly flutters past the window. I yelp—a sharp, startled sound—as I clutch my chest. My heart races, breaths shallow.

Leaning my forehead against the cold glass, I groan. "It was just a bird. Just a fucking bird."

Relief drips through me, slow and cold. I drop the blinds again and crawl back into bed, too tired to care anymore. As soon as my head hits the pillow, sleep pulls me under once again.

Morning arrives far too quickly, and I grumble as I drag myself downstairs, following the smell of freshly brewed coffee. Yawning and stretching, I mutter under my breath, annoyed by that damn bird. It woke me up three more times last night with its incessant tapping. Whatever species it is, it's about to face extinction if this keeps up.

I round the corner into the kitchen to find my father finishing his coffee. I trudge over to the pot, still grumbling, while he hands me a mug with a smirk plastered across his face. The amusement in his eyes only fuels my irritation, and for a split second, I consider pouring my coffee on him.

"Late night, Doodle Bug?" he asks, chuckling softly.

I glare at him, giving him my best *go-fuck-yourself* look. "A damn bird kept waking me up last night. Tapping on my window."

"A bird?" he echoes, raising an eyebrow as I slam the pot back into place.

"Yes, a bird," I snap, sinking into a chair at the table with my mug. "Just *tap, tap, tap*. All night long. Ugh."

"That sucks, baby girl," he says, patting my shoulder as he sits beside me, still smirking.

"Oh, I'm so glad my suffering amuses you," I mutter, shooting him a look.

He shakes his head; the smirk softening into something gentler. "I'm not laughing at your pain, Doodle Bug." His expression turns a little nostalgic. "You just reminded me of your mother. She was a bear when her sleep got interrupted too."

The mention of Mom hits me in the chest. I remember plenty of mornings where she'd stomp around the house half-asleep and grumbling. Dad would always make her extra-strong coffee and wrap her in one of his big bear hugs until she softened.

I take a sip of my coffee, the bitterness grounding me a little. "Well, it's not exactly fun waking up to a bird knocking on your window over and over," I mutter, still holding on to a shred of grumpiness.

Dad chuckles again. "Fair enough, Doodle Bug. Maybe we can figure out a way to keep that bird away from your window tonight."

I nod, appreciating the offer. "Yeah, let's do that. I need a decent night's sleep." I pause, then sigh. "For now, I should go get ready for work."

He stands when I do, pulling me into one of those signature bear hugs—the kind that melts tension straight out of my bones. I sink into it, letting the warmth ease the last of my irritation.

He kisses the top of my head before letting go. "You've got this, kiddo."

"Thanks, Dad," I mumble, a soft smile tugging at my lips as I head out of the kitchen. My mood is noticeably lighter than when I came in.

The day at the bakery blurs by, a steady stream of customers keeping me busy, leaving little room for my thoughts to wander. The routine offers a strange comfort, something to anchor me while the tension hums quietly at the edges of my mind.

But still—on and off throughout the morning—I keep getting that prickling sense of being watched. Yet, when I glance out the window or scan the bakery, I find everything is perfectly normal. Customers chatting. Coffee brewing. Sunshine spilling through the glass. And yet... something feels off.

I'm starting to wonder if I'm just paranoid when Lila bursts in during her lunch break, all bright smiles and laughter, blissfully unaware of the weirdness festering at home.

"Hey, girl!" she chirps, flashing a grin.

Jordan barely acknowledges her, scowling as he disappears into the back. I roll my eyes as the door swings shut behind him. Denial runs deep with that one.

As the evening draws closer, a mix of exhaustion and unease settles in my bones. The thought of going home dredges up that damn bird again—it's tapping etched into my mind like a warning I don't know how to interpret. That eerie feeling hasn't left me, not completely.

I wave goodbye to Mr. Walters and the boys, tugging on my coat before stepping out into the chilly air. The walk home feels longer today, the icy wind doing little to soothe my nerves.

My phone pings in my pocket, and I grab it quickly, a smile tugging at my lips when I see Jake's name.

> Jake: Good evening, beautiful. When am I going to see you again?

Just like that, the knot in my chest loosens a little. My fingers fly across the screen.

> Sarah: I don't know. Depends on if you know a good hitman.

> Jake: (Raised eyebrow emoji) I might know a guy.

I snicker, imagining his playful expression. Part of me knows he's joking, but there's also that small chance he's not. Best not to push the joke too far.

> Sarah: There's a bird that kept me up last night, tapping on my window.

Jake: You want it to sleep with the fishes, huh? (Fish emoji)

Sarah: (Crying laughing emoji) No, not really. I just want it to leave me alone.

Jake: (Thinking emoji) First time this has happened?

Sarah: Yeah, probably looking for food or something.

Jake: (Laughing emoji) Nature's alarm clock, huh?

Sarah: More like nature's annoying neighbor. I just want a good night's sleep.

Jake: I get it. Let me think on it. I'll see if there's a humane way to convince it to find a new spot if it keeps up.

Sarah: Thanks, Jake. I don't want to hurt it, just need some peace.

Jake: Gotcha. I'll come up with something. How's your day been otherwise?

Sarah: You know, just the usual bakery chaos. What about you?

Jake: Same old, same old. Carpentry work, nothing too exciting.

Jake: How about this weekend?

Sarah: How about this weekend what?

Jake: Don't play coy with me, Little Trash Panda.

I laugh, shaking my head as I type back—grateful for the distraction, even if that feeling of being watched still lingers just beneath the surface.

Sarah: I would say I'm free, but there's this guy I've been seeing... keeps calling me "Little Trash Panda." Not sure I want to encourage him, you know?

Jake: Sounds like a real charmer. Can't blame you for being hesitant.

Sarah: Yeah, he's kind of annoying. Always trying to be sweet and thoughtful… ugh, the worst.

Jake: Oh, the worst? That guy sounds like a nightmare. You should probably just give him a chance, you know… for charity's sake.

Sarah: Mmm, I don't know. The way he insists on making me laugh and checking in on me…super clingy vibes.

Jake: Careful, I might start sending you flowers just to seal the deal.

Sarah: Flowers? Who are you, a gentleman? Where's the hitman energy I asked for?

Jake: Hey, I can multi-task. I'll handle the bird and win you over this weekend.

Sarah: Fine, I guess I'll pencil you in. But only because of the bird.

Jake: I want to take you somewhere.

Sarah: Oh?

I pause mid-step, waiting for my phone to buzz again. But the silence stretches. No new message.

Slipping the phone back into my pocket, I glance around. The glow of the streetlamps spills across the pavement, casting long shadows in the darkening street. For a moment, I feel oddly at peace—alone but calm, the quiet settling over me like a blanket.

Then, like a frigid breath on the back of my neck, it creeps in.

That feeling.

The prickling along my skin. The tension that coils tight in my chest. I'm being watched.

I freeze, eyes scanning the empty street for movement, for anything out of place. But everything looks normal. Still.

The wind howls down the road, sharp against my skin, and I shiver, yanking my coat tighter. My footsteps crunch against the scattered leaves, brittle and dry beneath my boots. Each step breaks the silence with a sharp crackle, like nature's warning shot. The street is too quiet. Still. Like something's waiting.

I quicken my pace. Not quite running, just enough to escape the weight pressing against my spine without drawing attention from anyone who might glance out their windows.

When the house finally comes into view, I take the porch steps two at a time. My breath comes in sharp, fast pulls as I shove open the front door and slip inside.

Warmth rushes over me. Familiar. Safe.

In the living room, my dad sits in his favorite chair, a book open in his hands. He glances up and smiles, calm and unaware of the way the night still clings to me—how the unease hasn't fully let go.

"Hey, Doodle Bug. Feeling better after a day's work?" His voice is gentle, cutting through the quiet.

I manage a smile, trying to push away the lingering anxiety. "Yeah, a bit. Jake wants to take me somewhere this weekend."

Dad sets his book aside, expression thoughtful as he processes the news. "Just for the weekend?"

I nod, feeling the heat rise in my cheeks as my mind flashes back to the last time I saw Jake. The memory lingers—warm, vivid—making my face burn even hotter.

Dad shifts in his chair, unease thick in the air. His discomfort is obvious, his eyes avoiding mine. "Do you think it's a good idea? Do you feel safe being alone with him?"

The tension creeps in, tangled with memories and awkwardness. My mouth moves before I can stop it. "I'll be fine," I blurt out, a little too quickly.

He shifts again, clearly trying to avoid the mental images neither of us wants. "Alright," he says after clearing his throat. "Just be safe, and, uh... yeah."

Heat creeps up my neck, settling deep in my chest. His cheeks are flushed too, and we sit there in mutual embarrassment, silently agreeing not to push this conversation any further. It's an unspoken rule—*just don't go there*. But he's still my dad. Worrying is part of the job.

We're both adults, but that doesn't make tiptoeing around this any easier. He clears his throat again, like he's trying to physically shake the thoughts loose. I don't even want to imagine what just crossed his mind. Thank God we can't read each other's thoughts.

He reaches for his book, a silent escape. But halfway there, he pauses.

"Oh, I almost forgot—Janet invited us to Thanksgiving with her family. Thought we might enjoy the company."

Janet, his boss at the library, has always been sweet. But a small knot tightens in my gut. The idea of Dad dating again... it feels too soon. It's only been two years since Mom passed. The thought of him moving on twists something raw in me.

Sensing my hesitation, Dad quickly adds, "Janet's married. Her husband, Doug, works over at the tackle and bait shop. If she were single, I wouldn't have even considered it. I'm not looking to date anyone, not anytime soon... if ever."

Relief washes over me—followed by a pinch of sadness. I was wrong about Janet. But I also don't want him to be alone forever. I don't say that, though. I just nod and offer a soft smile. "It sounds nice. If you're up for it, I'll be glad to go with you."

He smiles back, gratitude softening his features. "Thanks, sweetheart."

I turn to leave, calling over my shoulder, "I'm going to heat up some leftovers. Want anything?"

"Nah, Doodle Bug. I'll grab something in a bit—just got to the good part."

I snicker as I head to the kitchen. You'd never guess by looking at him, but my dad has a soft spot for historical romance novels. Sure, he likes science fiction too, but those love stories? That's his guilty pleasure. He probably checked that one out under the guise of it being for me. I don't mind. If anyone ever asked, I'd play along. No questions asked. Not that anyone ever does.

Dinner passes quietly. With Dad occupied in the living room, I take out my phone and scroll through social media. Still no reply from Jake.

Rude.

Once everything's cleaned up, I make my way upstairs, the exhaustion of the day finally settling into my bones. The moment my back hits the mattress, my eyes start to close—but before I can drift off, my phone pings from the nightstand. I reach over, grab it, and open the messaging app, a smile already forming on my lips.

Jake: Meet me at my cabin Friday night?

Sarah: Hoping for round two, huh?

Jake: Well, round one was pretty... inspiring.

Sarah: Inspiring? Wow, you're really pulling out the fancy words.

Jake: What can I say? You bring out the poet in me.

Sarah: I'm sure that's not all I bring out.

Jake: You're not wrong.

Sarah: Oh, I know I'm not wrong. I've seen how "inspired" you get.

Jake: Hard not to be when I've got a body like that crawling all over me.

Sarah: Crawling? Babe, I was doing all the work; you were just along for the ride.

Jake: All the work? You sure about that? Seemed like you were the one moaning my name.

Sarah: That's because I was trying to motivate you to keep up.

Jake: Keep up? You were lucky I didn't break you in half.

Sarah: Break me? Baby, you were the one looking ready to tap out.

Jake: Tap out? Trust me, round two's gonna have you begging for more before I'm even halfway done.

Sarah: Begging? Oh, honey, you've got it twisted. I'll be the one making you beg to keep going.

Jake: Big talk for someone who was trembling around my cock.

Sarah: Trembling from trying not to laugh at how hard you were trying to impress me.

Jake: Keep that energy, Trash Panda. You'll be the one calling for mercy the next time I'm buried in your cunt.

Sarah: Mercy? Baby, I don't even know the meaning of the word. You'd better rest up—I don't want to be responsible for breaking you.

Jake: You couldn't break me if you tried, Trash Panda.

Sarah: I guess we'll see. (Winking face emoji)

Jake: I guess we will. Just turn down the gravel drive right before you'd turn to get to the shop. That'll take you straight to my cabin,

Jake: Sleep tight, Little Trash Panda.

Sarah: Goodnight, Jake.

I toss the phone back onto the nightstand, pulling the covers up and sinking into their warmth with a deep sigh. The soft fabric wraps around me, offering comfort I desperately need—though it does nothing to help with the ache now blooming between my thighs.

Maybe, just maybe, that damn bird was a one-time nuisance. And maybe tonight, I'll actually get a chance to catch up on some much-needed sleep.

Chapter 19

The bird definitely wasn't a one-time thing. For the last three nights, it's woken me up multiple times, pecking away at my sanity and any hope of decent sleep. Last night, I even hurled a pillow at the window, yelling for it to *"shut the fuck up."* That worked for all of five minutes before it was back at it—like it was mocking me. At this rate, the damn bird was going to drive me over the edge. If I wasn't excited about a weekend away with Jake before, I sure as hell am now.

After arriving home last night, I'd packed my bag with a renewed sense of urgency, desperate for a couple of days of peace. Grabbing it off the floor, I rush out of my bedroom, the thud of my feet pounding down the stairs filling the quiet house. My father's already waiting for me by the side door. Without a word, we both step outside and pile into my car.

The engine rumbles to life as I hit the button for the garage door. Backing out, I take a deep breath, trying to shake off the fatigue that's been clinging to me for days. The irony of driving such a short distance to work isn't lost on me, but with plans to head straight to Jake's afterward, there's no point in walking today.

I park behind the bakery, but before I can open the door, Dad reaches over and grabs my hand.

"Drive extra safe going up the mountain later," he says, his voice carrying a hint of concern. "And make sure you let me know when you've arrived. That you're safe."

I give him a soft smile, squeezing his hand in return. "I will, Daddy. Promise."

He nods, looking a little more at ease. Then we step out, and he pulls me into a big bear hug, pressing a kiss to my forehead before heading off toward the library. I watch him for a moment, the weight of his concern lingering, then head into the shop.

The familiar warmth of the bakery hits me the second I step through the door—the smell of fresh pastries and cakes wrapping around me like a blanket. Jordan and Sam greet me with a wave as I hang up my coat, and the comforting atmosphere settles in my chest, sending a gentle wave of euphoria through me. This place always feels like home.

I glance around, noticing the absence of Mr. Walters. "Sam? Where's your dad this morning?" I call out.

Without looking up from his task, Sam replies, "Dad's out sick today. Jordan and I had to threaten to cancel Thanksgiving if he didn't stay in bed and rest."

I snort. "You two don't mess around."

Jordan huffs from the back. "He's as stubborn as a mule. I wouldn't be surprised if he tries to sneak in later."

Shaking my head, I dive into my work, with the thought of Mr. Walters sneaking in somehow more amusing than surprising.

But as the day drags on, the tension shifts.

Sam and Jordan grow more fidgety. Their dad doesn't show, not even once. And from the way they talk, he'd need to be practically on his deathbed to miss a day of work—even with the threat of no Thanksgiving. By closing time, Jordan is practically shoving me out the door, locking it behind me before I can even wave goodbye. That unease that's been gnawing at me all day? It sinks deeper, curling low in my stomach like it knows something I don't.

I slide into my car, and the cold hits me like a slap. I crank the heat and wait for the engine to warm up, watching my breath fog the windshield. Everything feels... wrong. Mr. Walters still hasn't called or texted. The boys were trying way too hard to act normal. And that bird—whatever the hell it is—hasn't let up.

The town slips away behind me as I turn toward the mountain. Trees close in on both sides—tall and skeletal, their bare branches clawing at the sky, while thick evergreens loom in between like silent sentinels, watching. The sun's nearly down, the road cast in that dim gray light that makes everything look hazy and off.

I check my phone. No new messages. Jake hasn't texted again, and the signal bars flicker like they're barely hanging on.

Perfect.

The road curves sharply, the trees thicker now, swallowing the last hints of daylight. The air turns colder, biting through the warm cocoon of the car. I glance in the rearview mirror, half-expecting to see headlights behind me—but there's nothing. Just darkness and my reflection, pale and uneasy.

Something feels like it's watching me.

Not a car. Not an animal. Something else.

I grip the steering wheel tighter, my knuckles going white. It's just your imagination, I tell myself. Just nerves. You're tired. Sleep-deprived. You'll get to Jake's, he'll wrap you up in those big arms, and everything will be fine.

But the hairs on the back of my neck stay standing.

And even as I turn onto the gravel road that leads to Jake's cabin, part of me knows—somewhere deep down—that whatever's been watching hasn't stopped.

It's just getting closer.

The gravel crunches beneath my tires as I wind up Jake's driveway, trying to shake off the unease that's been riding shotgun all day. Everything's fine. If something serious was wrong with Mr. Walters, surely one of the boys would've called by now. They aren't cruel, and they know I'd be worried.

The headlights bounce off the trees, and as I round the final bend, Jake's cabin comes into view, warm light spilling from the windows into the cold darkness. The front door swings open, and Jake steps out, a grin spreading across his face as he spots me pulling in. His breath hangs in the air, a foggy cloud, as he walks over to my car and opens the door for me.

I slide out of the car, immediately wrapping my arms around him, pulling him close. His scent—that familiar mix of wood, earth, and something that's just him—surrounds me, making me feel like I'm home. He presses a soft kiss to my lips.

"Hey," I murmur, leaning up to kiss him again, this time a little longer.

"Hey yourself," he replies, his grin widening. "Where's your bag?"

"Backseat," I answer, nodding toward the car.

Jake pecks my lips again before walking over to grab my bag from the back. He opens the door of his truck and sets it down next to his own. "We've got a bit of a drive ahead of us," he says. "You wanna use the bathroom before we hit the road?"

I consider it for a second, then nod. "Yeah, probably a good idea."

"The door's open," he says, nodding toward the cabin. "Just twist the bottom lock and pull it closed when you're done. I'll go warm up the truck."

"Got it," I reply, heading toward the cabin while he walks to his truck.

Just before I reach the porch, I pause—eyes flicking to the treeline. A soft rustle. Nothing's there. At least, nothing I can see. I force myself to look away and step inside. Warmth greets me the second I step inside, a welcome contrast to the cold bite of the night. I make my way to the bathroom, quickly taking care of business. On my way back, something catches my eye—a row of photos hanging along the hallway. I slow down, taking a closer look. There are pictures of Jake with his parents, some of him with his friends, all smiles and laughter.

One photo in particular grabs my attention. It's of Jake's parents, much younger. His mom is holding a little boy, probably no older than two, while a young Jake stands in front of his father, grinning. They all look so happy, carefree. My chest tightens at the sight. Jake once told me he lost his little brother when they were kids—something he rarely talks about. Seeing the boy in this photo makes it real in a way words never could. I wonder how long after this photo was taken that tragedy struck. Without thinking, I reach out, my fingers brushing against the frame. I'm lost in thought when a gentle hand lands on my shoulder, startling me. I jump, spinning around to face him, my heart still racing.

"Sorry," he says, voice soft, apologetic. "Didn't mean to scare you."

I take a deep breath, trying to calm myself. "No, it's okay. I was just... thinking."

He glances at the photo I was staring at, and his face softens, but there's a flicker of sadness behind his eyes. The air between us shifts—warmth replaced by the weight of memory, unspoken but heavy enough to settle between us. I drop my head, embarrassed at getting caught being nosy.

Jake clears his throat, breaking the silence. His voice is quiet but heavy with emotion. "That's my little brother," he says. "Been a while since I looked at that picture."

I look up to meet his eyes, now filled with a mixture of longing and pain. Wanting to ease the moment, I offer a small piece of myself. "I understand. Pictures have a way of bringing back memories—both good and bad. What was his name?"

He nods, appreciating the gentle curiosity. "Yeah. They do. His name was Michael," he says, his fingers tracing the image of his brother. There's a brief silence, heavy with the weight of unspoken memories.

"Do you want to talk about him?" I ask softly. "How long after this picture did you lose him?"

The question lingers in the air, and for a moment, he looks like he might open up. But then he lets out a quiet sigh, a mixture of sadness and something resigned. "Not tonight," he says, his voice barely above a whisper. "We've got to get going."

I nod, understanding. Some memories are too heavy to share, even with someone close. Without another word, I follow him out into the cold, the chill biting at my skin, echoing the weight Jake carries and the silence that now rides with us into the dark.

A few hours later, we pull up to a cozy hotel nestled in the heart of Gatlinburg. Snow drifts lazily across the windshield, a fine powder catching the glow of the city lights in the distance. The drive had been a pleasant distraction, filled with debates over music, favorite songs, and artists. The heaviness from the cabin still clung to us when we pulled out of the driveway, but the longer we drove, the easier it became to breathe. Jake had seemed deep in thought for a while, and I didn't push him, letting the quiet be its own conversation. Eventually he handed me his phone, open to Spotify, and asked me to pick some music. That's when I discovered his not-so-secret love for Ariana Grande, courtesy of his playlist titled "Ari da best."

Now, standing in the parking lot, I watch the snow settle around us as Jake grabs our bags from the backseat. His arm wraps around my waist, pulling me close as we head toward the hotel entrance. Inside, the lobby is the standard gray-on-gray palette—modern, neutral, forgettable. Faux crystal chandeliers hang above us, casting a sterile light across the room. While Jake checks us in at the front desk, I step back, pulling out my phone to text my dad. I let him know we've arrived safely and include the hotel's phone number in case he needs to reach me. He sends a quick thank-you text back, and I slide my phone into my pocket just as Jake walks over and hands me a key card.

As we step into the elevator, I feel a small sense of anticipation, wondering what the night holds. But when we get to the room, I pause in the doorway, taking in the two double beds instead of the one I expected. Jake catches my expression and shrugs, a sheepish smile tugging at his lips. "Didn't want to assume."

I chuckle, appreciating his thoughtfulness even if I find it a little amusing. "No worries, Jake. I get it."

He nods clearly relieved, and we start unpacking. The room fills with a comfortable silence as we settle in, the air buzzing with that unspoken excitement of being somewhere new together. After a few moments, I catch Jake's eye.

"So," I say, breaking the quiet, "What's on the agenda for tomorrow?"

Jake's lips curl into a playful grin. "I'm surprised you didn't ask earlier."

"Oh, trust me, I've been dying to know, but I'm trying this thing called patience." I roll my eyes. "It's not going great."

He laughs, that deep, rich sound that always makes my stomach flip. "Well, you're in luck. First, we're hitting up this local diner I found. Word is, they've got the best pancakes in town."

My eyes light up at the mention of pancakes. "That sounds amazing! I'm always up for a good breakfast."

Jake nods, a grin spreading across his face. "After that, we're going to Ober Mountain for some skiing and snow tubing. What do you think?"

I raise an eyebrow, curiosity piqued but also a little wary. "Skiing?"

He nods again, his excitement palpable. "Yeah! It'll be fun."

"I've never been skiing."

Jake steps closer, taking my hands in his; the warmth of his fingers eases my nerves. "That's okay. They have beginner trails and instructors. Plus, if you hate it, we'll find something else to do. No pressure."

The thought of trying something new, especially in front of other people, sends a little spike of anxiety through me. I've never been a fan of being the center of attention, but the fact that Jake will be there, right beside me, makes the idea a little easier to swallow.

I offer him a small smile. "Alright, skiing it is. But don't expect me to be an Olympic pro."

He laughs, the sound light and easy, making me feel a bit more at ease. "No worries. We'll take it slow, whatever pace you're comfortable with."

"Okay." I exhale, feeling a little more relaxed.

Jake cups my cheeks in his hands, his thumbs brushing along my jaw, and it makes my heart flutter.

"You need to get some sleep, Little Trash Panda," he murmurs, voice low and fond.

"Only if I get a goodnight kiss," I reply, grinning up at him.

His lips curve into a wicked smile before he leans down, pressing a soft kiss to mine. It starts soft, sweet—but as he pulls away, I grab the back of his neck and pull him in again, deepening it. A soft moan escapes me, heat coiling low in my stomach. I feel bold in his arms—because with him, I can be. I feel wanted. Safe. Like I'm not too much.

He wraps his arm around my waist and yanks me closer. My breasts press into his chest, my nipples hardening beneath the thin fabric. My pussy throbs, already aching for him, while my mouth waters at the thought of tasting him. His hands slip under my shirt and drag upward, rough palms gliding from my waist to my shoulders. The calluses on his fingers send sparks skittering across my skin.

I find his waistband and pop the button open with one hand, unzipping his jeans with the other. He unclasps my bra beneath my shirt, and the sensation makes me shiver—the weird, annoying looseness of it beneath the fabric driving me nuts. I strip off my shirt and bra in one motion, letting them fall to the floor.

I drop to my knees in front of him without hesitation, sliding my hands down his abdomen, fingers curling around his thick cock. He exhales sharply when I stroke him, hips twitching forward. I pull him free from his pants and wrap my lips around him, moaning as I taste the salt of his pre-cum.

"Fuuuuck," Jake hisses, his head falling back when the head of his cock hits the back of my throat.

He tangles his fingers in my hair and grips tight. I moan again, taking him deeper, my jaw stretching to fit his girth. I can't relax it all the way, but I open as wide as I can, letting him fuck my mouth. Slow, deep thrusts. Each one brushes my throat, testing my control.

I hold my breath as he pushes in deep, fighting the urge to gag. His cock hits the back of my throat with each thrust, and I take it, greedy for the sound of his ragged breathing and the way his fingers tighten in my hair.

His voice drops to a gravelly growl. "You look so fucking perfect like this."

I hum in response, letting him take what he needs—letting him fuck my mouth the way he wants. And loving every second of it.

With Jake in control, fucking my mouth with slow, deliberate thrusts, my hands drift upward. I roll my nipples between my fingers, pinching until they ache. Each jolt of pain zings straight to my core, my pussy throbbing with need. I'm soaking through my panties, desperate for the feel of his cock buried deep inside me.

Still on my knees, I reach up and hook my fingers in the waistband of his jeans and boxers, tugging them down his legs. He lets go of my hair, pausing his thrusts as I stroke his cock a few more times—slick licks, one last kiss to the tip—before rising to my feet.

Jake cups my face, pulling me into a deep, hungry kiss. His tongue swipes across mine, teasing, tasting, and it only makes the ache worse. I tug his shirt up his torso, and when he breaks the kiss to let me pull it over his head, I throw it aside.

He steps out of his pants, reaching for his wallet and pulling out a condom. It drops to the floor along with everything else.

"You might want to go ahead and put that on," I purr, already shimmying out of the rest of my clothes.

His brow lifts, amused—but he does as he's told, rolling the condom down his thick cock with practiced ease. The second it's on, I press a hand to his chest and shove him onto the bed. Before he can even blink, I'm crawling up his body and straddling his lap.

His hands land on my hips as I reach down and wrap my fingers around his cock, guiding him toward my entrance. He groans, low and rough, when I sink down—slow at first, teasing us both. Inch by inch, I take him, relishing the stretch until he's fully seated inside me.

I sit there for a second, letting the feeling of him buried deep settle into my bones. One of his hands plays with my breast while the other grips my hip. I grind against him, slow and steady, dragging him along that perfect spot inside me.

My moans build with every grind, higher and needier as the tension coils tighter. Then Jake's finger slips between us, finding my clit. With every motion, he presses against it, and I shatter. He lets out a guttural groan as my pussy pulses around his cock. He lifts my hips and thrusts up into me, long and deep, prolonging my orgasm until my cum is dripping down his length. Just when I think I can finally relax, he rubs my clit again—fast, ruthless circles that send me spiraling.

"Oh fuck, Jake," I whimper, barely holding on as another orgasm rips through me.

My pussy clamps down on him hard, and Jake's grip on my hips tightens as he slams into me, again and again, chasing his release. With a guttural moan, he stills, buried deep, his cock twitching as he fills the condom.

We collapse in a tangle of limbs and sweat, panting, grinning like fools. My body feels like melted wax as I slide off his lap and curl against his side.

He knots the condom and sets it aside on the nightstand, then wraps an arm around me.

His warmth, his scent, his heartbeat against my back—it's perfect. I never want to move again.

Chapter 20

The next morning, we set out early, the cold biting at our cheeks as we made our way to the diner. True to its reputation, the pancakes are the best I've ever had—fluffy, buttery perfection that leaves me feeling warm and content. After breakfast, we head to the ski resort. The tram ride up the mountain is equal parts thrilling and terrifying, but the crisp air and promise of adventure set my heart racing.

At the top, the resort buzzes with activity—people bustling around, laughter echoing over the snow-covered slopes. We rent our gear and get a quick lesson from an instructor before heading to the beginner's hill. I glance nervously at Jake, who flashes me his confident, reassuring smile.

"We've got this," he says, adjusting his skis like it's second nature.

I take a deep breath, trying to remember everything we were just told. My first few attempts are awkward—wobbling, sliding, barely keeping upright—but Jake stays close, steadying me with patient encouragement.

We finally start down the slope, and slowly, I find my rhythm. The chilly wind rushes past my face, trees blurring in my peripheral vision. Fear melts into exhilaration, and by the time we reach the bottom, Jake lets out a triumphant cheer. We exchange a high-five, grinning like kids.

I want to kiss him, adrenaline still humming through my veins—but with all these layers of gear between us, I settle for another run down the slope instead.

Each trip gets easier, and more fun. By the time we break for lunch, my nerves are gone, replaced by a glowing sense of accomplishment.

At the base, we finally strip off our heavy gear. Freed from all the padding, I waste no time. I wrap my arms around Jake and kiss him—soft, lingering, the kind that makes you forget about the cold. He grips my waist, pulling me close until a loud growl escapes my stomach, cutting through the moment.

Jake laughs. "Alright, let's feed you before you get hangry."

We grab lunch at the café, then spend the rest of the afternoon on the mountain coaster and snow tubing. While skiing was fun, tubing quickly became my favorite. There's something reckless and free about it—just sitting in a tube, letting gravity take over while wind and laughter carry you down.

The hill is a glittering winter wonderland. We drag our tubes to the top, hearts pounding with anticipation. One push and we're flying. Wind tears through my hair, and Jake's laughter echoes beside mine.

At the bottom, we sprint back up like giddy kids for another round. And another. And another.

By the time the sun dips behind the mountains, our cheeks are rosy, our bodies aching, but our spirits are sky-high.

That evening, back at the hotel, the warmth from the day's adventures lingers in our bones. The lobby has a setup of coffee and hot chocolate, and we waste no time pouring ourselves a cup to warm up from the inside.

I take a sip, groaning in delight. "Mmm, that's so good,"

Jake raises an eyebrow, that familiar smirk tugging at the corner of his mouth.

I give him a look. "What?"

He just shakes his head, the smirk deepening as he keeps his eyes on me.

"Seriously, Jake," I say, narrowing my eyes. "What is it?"

"You make a sound like that when you cum," he says in a low voice, leaning closer.

Heat rushes to my face. I smack his arm, frantically glancing around. "Jake!" I hiss, mortified and aroused all at once.

He chuckles, leaning in to murmur against my ear. "What? I love that sound." His voice drops lower, rougher. "Now all I can think about is your sweet pussy wrapped around my dick."

Desire pools low in my belly. I grab his wrist, tugging him toward the elevator without another word. Not caring who sees us anymore. Jake laughs, following eagerly as I practically drag him across the lobby.

As soon as the elevator doors slide shut, he pulls me into him. His lips crash into mine, tongue teasing along the seam of my mouth. I open for him instantly, the taste of hot chocolate still lingering on our tongues as we kiss.

All I can think about is his mouth on other parts of me. I moan, pressing against him.

The elevator dings. We break apart just in time as the doors open.

An older couple steps in. I lean back against the wall, trying to catch my breath and pretend I'm not seconds from jumping Jake's bones.

"Good afternoon," the older man says cheerfully.

"Evenin'," Jake and I echo in unison, trying to sound casual.

I shift awkwardly, shrinking against the wall, my face still hot from the kiss and what I know is about to happen once we get to our room.

The lady scoffs, turning toward her husband.

"You see, Harold! I told you the elevator was going *up*, not down.

"I realize that, dear. It'll go back down shortly. No need to fuss," the man replies, pulling her close.

She scowls, but he kisses her forehead, and she relaxes into him.

I smile—until Harold casually squeezes her ass.

"Stop that, Harold! We're not alone, and you *promised* me a nice dinner," she scolds, swatting at him.

The old man just grins—wolfish and shameless—and winks at us like we're all in on some joke.

Jake nearly chokes trying not to laugh. Harold's hand shamelessly gives her ass another squeeze. She rolls her eyes, but doesn't pull away.

Harold leans down to whisper something in her ear.

Her voice rings through the elevator: "*HAROLD!*"

By the time the doors open on our floor, Jake and I are barely holding it together. We mutter polite goodbyes and practically run down the hallway, bursting into laughter once we're out of earshot.

"I wonder what he said to her," I gasp, wiping tears from my eyes.

Jake shakes his head. "Trust me—you don't want to know. It was dirty."

I gasp, pretending to be scandalized. "Well, in that case, he'd better buy her that nice dinner first."

Jake fumbles with the keycard, still laughing. When the light turns green, the laughter fades. The simmering heat returns to his eyes. He opens the door. My pulse quickens, thighs rubbing together in anticipation.

The moment the door clicks shut, I leap into his arms, crashing my mouth against his, tasting the heat of him, savoring every greedy, open-mouthed second. His hands grip my ass, pulling me tighter as he grinds his hard cock against my pussy through our clothes. I moan into the kiss, grinding back, the friction dizzying and dirty and not nearly enough.

Jake hisses between his teeth as I unwrap my legs and slide down his body, my feet hitting the floor. I back away, breathless, stripping out of my clothes in a frenzy, desperate to feel skin on skin.

His eyes rake over me with pure hunger as he yanks his shirt over his head and shoves his pants down. Our clothes tangle together in a messy heap on the floor.

Jake grabs my waist and crushes our bodies together. His lips find my neck, trailing hot, possessive kisses along my skin. His teeth graze my collarbone, just enough to make me shiver and gasp, and my pussy throbs in response.

We stumble backward toward the bed, every inch of my body aching for him. The back of my knees bump the edge, and Jake eases me down, his hands firm and commanding. I crawl backward across the mattress, my eyes locked on him as he follows—every inch of him hard, ready, and dangerous. His cock juts out proudly, thick and leaking, and the sight of it makes my mouth water.

I want to taste him. I want to wrap my lips around his cock and hear him lose control.

Jake crawls up between my legs, and his mouth starts a slow, torturous path up my inner thighs, lips and tongue dragging fire across my skin.

"Jake," I breathe, just as his tongue flicks across my pussy.

I cry out, hips jolting at the sudden, delicious contact. But I want more—I need more. I push at his chest, flipping the script. He lets me, grinning like he's already won.

I straddle his hips and kiss my way down his chest, savoring the way his muscles tense under my tongue. I drag my mouth over the sharp lines of his abs, then down to the thick, pulsing length of him.

"Oh no, you don't," he grunts, voice rough and wrecked as my tongue glides up his shaft.

Before I can take him deeper, Jake grabs my shoulders and yanks me up his body, his cock leaving a trail of pre-cum along my belly. He kisses me hard—hungry, claiming—then shifts, flipping me so I'm facing his cock while he settles beneath me.

His hands grip my ass, guiding me down until my pussy hovers over his mouth.

Then his tongue is on me.

I gasp as he licks a broad, slow stroke up my slit, ending with a firm circle around my clit that makes me see stars. My hands tremble as I grip his cock, stroking him once, twice, before pulling the head into my mouth.

He hums into me.

Having Jake's cock in my mouth while his tongue works me over is a damn dream. The rhythm of his tongue—firm, relentless—dances along my pussy, sending electric shocks through every nerve. I moan around his cock, lips sliding over him in time with each flick of his tongue against my clit.

His hand slips from my hip, and I almost protest—until I feel his fingers sliding into me, slow and deliberate. They curl just right, hitting that perfect spot. I gasp, moaning around his cock, the vibrations pulling another groan from him as he thrusts deeper into my mouth.

I try to keep my rhythm, but it's hopeless—every movement of his tongue wrecks my focus. I grow sloppy, messy, chasing the pleasure, and he doesn't seem to mind one bit. If anything, it spurs him on.

He adds a second finger to my soaked pussy; the stretch makes me cry out. My mouth pops off his cock as I suck in a ragged breath, hips grinding against his face with no shame. I grab his cock again, stroking it blindly while I ride the edge of release.

Jake fucks me with his fingers, firm and fast, while his mouth clamps down on my clit. Every flick of his tongue, every thrust of his hand, pushes me closer—until I finally shatter.

"Ah! Fuck! Yes! Jake!" I scream, my whole body convulsing, my pussy clenching around his fingers as the orgasm tears through me.

He growls into me, lips never leaving my clit, drawing it out until I collapse forward, boneless and panting. Slowly, he slips his fingers from my pussy, and I feel his hand glide down my thigh—then lower, trailing over my calf.

The second his fingers brush over the scars, my whole body jolts like I've been burned.

I try to play it off, shifting my leg away, but Jake notices. His hand pauses, then returns—gentler now—as his fingers trace the raised lines like he's trying to understand them. His touch is feather-light, almost reverent, but it makes my stomach twist into knots.

This is the first time he's seen them.

My breath catches in my throat. I squeeze my eyes shut, trying to force the memories back into the dark corner where they belong.

I hate this. I hate how exposed I suddenly feel.

I yank my leg from his grip and roll away, heart pounding as I meet his gaze. He looks stunned—brows drawn tight, his mouth slightly open like he's about to ask something. The concern on his face cuts deeper than anything else.

"I don't want to talk about it," I snap, the words too loud, too sharp.

Jake nods immediately, the question dying on his lips. No pressure. No push.

He climbs up over me, lowering his mouth to mine in a deep kiss grounding me back into the moment. I melt into him, my tension bleeding out, his weight and warmth a shield from the thoughts clawing at the edges of my mind.

He grinds against me, his cock sliding along my slick folds, every stroke brushing my clit and making me squirm. His hand moves between us, two fingers plunging back into my pussy, curling in sync with the grind of his hips.

My orgasm builds fast and sharp.

I gasp his name as I cum again, my legs trembling, my body wrecked and eager all at once.

Before I can catch my breath, I feel him shift. A drawer opens. The soft crinkle of a condom wrapper cuts through the quiet. I'm too blissed out to move, just barely aware of the bed dipping again.

Then I feel him—Jake, thick and hard, latex-wrapped and ready—pressing against my entrance.

And I want him. All of him. Now.

"Wait," I pant, pressing a hand to his chest. "I want to watch."

He smirks down at me, leaning back just enough for me to see his thick length poised at my entrance. My eyes stay locked on the sight as he guides himself inside, inch by inch, filling me. The heat between us builds as he presses in deeper, each inch igniting my already sensitive nerves.

"Oh God," I pant, reveling in the sensation as he finally bottoms out, fully seated inside me.

"Fuck, Sarah," he groans, his voice all gravel and heat, sinking into my skin like a brand.

Our eyes meet, and the intensity there mirrors everything I'm feeling. Slowly, he moves, pulling out just to push back in, his rhythm teasing me, almost torturous in its restraint. I arch my hips, matching his movements, and the friction sends pleasure radiating outward, but it's a slow build—more of a simmer than a blaze.

"Jake... please, fuck me," I beg, my voice breaking with need.

He growls, lowering his head to take my nipple into his mouth, sucking hard. I cry out, my whole body responding, clutching tight around him as he quickens his thrusts, filling me in a deeper, harder rhythm. Each stroke brings me closer to the edge, and I can feel him adjusting his angle just enough to brush against that perfect spot inside.

"Oh, God!" I gasp. "Right there... don't stop!"

He growls low, increasing his pace as my muscles tighten, pleasure curling low in my belly and spreading outward. The tension builds, and then I'm there, crying out as my orgasm slams into me, ripping a scream from my throat as he keeps thrusting through it, making me tremble, unravel, come undone.

His hands grip my hips tightly and, with a few more deep thrusts, he lets out a guttural sound as he reaches his own release, collapsing against me with a final shudder. He kisses me gently, his breaths evening out as he comes down, his body warm and solid against mine.

Later, we lay entangled in each other, content in the quiet after everything. My cheek rests on his chest, listening to the steady beat of his heart, his fingers tracing lazy circles along my arm. Sleep pulls at my eyelids, and I let out a soft sigh, snuggling closer, his warmth and familiar scent grounding me in a way I never thought possible.

With my thoughts drifting, I marvel at how perfect he's been since the moment we met. Thoughtful, strong, and caring. My heart swells, my mind envisioning a future with him—moments, days, a lifetime. How did I ever get this far without him? He's the anchor I didn't know I needed, a light that seems to guide me even when I didn't think I needed one.

I love you. The thought pulses through my mind, echoing with every beat of my heart: I love you. It's so clear, so certain. The words fill me, gaining strength each time I repeat them silently to myself. *I love you; I love you; I love you.*

I nestle closer against his warmth, savoring the comfort of his steady heartbeat beneath my cheek, letting that quiet admission wash over me. The rise and fall of his chest, the gentle way his fingers trail up and down my arm—it's all so easy, so right.

His hand pauses briefly on my arm, his breath catching for just a second, and I think nothing of it as he resumes, holding me even tighter. My eyelids grow heavy, the warmth of his body easing me into a calm I've never quite felt before.

As I drift into sleep, blissfully unaware that I whispered it aloud, I rest fully in his embrace, knowing that here, I'm safe.

Chapter 21

I love you.

Those words echoed through my mind all night, reverberating in the quiet between us. I don't know if she meant to say it or if it slipped out, but hearing it made my heart feel like it could lift off. I lay there, watching her sleep, her soft curves molded against me, her breaths warm and steady on my chest. I wanted to wake her just to hear her say it again, to know she was really mine. Instead, I stayed still, holding her close and letting the thought settle in, imagining those words spoken to me in the light of day.

When the morning sun streams through the flimsy hotel curtains, I blink my eyes open, still wrapped around her. I can't shake the thought—I've fallen for this woman hard and fast, in a way that makes me both ecstatic and terrified. There's no denying I want her; I want to keep her by my side and protect her from everything. I know the bond is helping to pull us together, but the way she said those words, reverently like a prayer, I don't believe that was the bond talking. Everyone had been trying to tell me that it doesn't force you to love someone, but until those words left her lips, I didn't want to believe they were true.

Guilt washes over me when I think about the bond. I still don't know if she's aware of it, and by continuing our relationship, I am allowing it to grow strong between us without her consent. Then there's the other thing I haven't told her, the part of me that's kept hidden from everyone. I'm a predator shifter. A wolf shifter, to be exact—the same kind of creature our town's people still talk about with fear and distrust. It's backwards, and it's fucked up, but that's the world I live in, and I can't ignore the fact that Sarah's family moved here most likely to get away from predator shifters. Those scars on her calf? They tell a story of pain—pain inflicted by someone like me. Not me, but close enough that it might not matter when she finds out. I don't know exactly what happened, but it wasn't all sunshine and rainbows.

I think back to the night we met. I almost let my nature slip to her right then and there. Something came over me—like I couldn't hold back, even if I wanted to. If it hadn't been for the twins, I probably would have told her right there in the middle of the crowded fairgrounds. At least we would have been in Miller's Creek that night and not Willow's Haven. Even so, its dangerous information. And as much as I want to give her everything—I'm not ready to risk losing her. Not yet. I need to find out what happened to her and find a way to tell her about our bond. I just hope that she'll accept it, accept me, for who I am when the time comes.

I push those thoughts aside as Sarah starts to stir beside me, her hand resting warm against my chest. Her eyes flutter open, and when they meet mine, she gives me a sleepy smile.

"Good morning," she murmurs, her voice thick with sleep.

"Good morning," I say back, matching her smile. I wonder if she remembers what she said last night. If she does, she doesn't bring it up—just stretches with that lazy grin, her bare skin brushing mine like it's the most natural thing in the world. I glance at the clock on the nightstand. Almost check-out time. I tell her she can take the first shower while I make us some of the sub-par hotel coffee.

She leans over, looping her arms around my neck and kissing me, soft and slow. "You're a saint," she mumbles before slipping out of bed and tossing the covers aside.

Fuck. Watching her walk across the room, completely naked, has my morning wood throbbing with interest. That perfect sway of her hips? It's a damn problem. I grit my teeth and press down on my cock like that's going to do a damn thing.

"Down, boy," I mutter, knowing full well it's useless. With a sigh, I toss off the covers and drag myself over to the cheap little coffee maker, already missing her warmth in my bed.

Chapter 22

The drive home is as smooth and easy as the one that took us away, with Jake handing me his phone to pick our playlist. Every few minutes, he glances over at me with that smile—the one that says more than words ever could. Occasionally, he lifts my hand to his lips, brushing a kiss across my fingers in a way that turns my heart to absolute mush. Affection just radiates off him, and I savor every second of it, soaking in how natural it feels. Even though the trip is only three hours, it flies by. With Jake, everything feels timeless.

The mid-afternoon sun glints off fresh piles of snow as Jake steers us up his driveway, the cabin nestled like a postcard against the frosty landscape. A pang of sadness tugs at me as we pull in—I don't want this trip to end. But I need to check on my dad, and on Mr. Walters. Not hearing anything from his sons while I was gone is probably a good sign—he's likely on the mend.

Jake puts the car in park and kisses my fingers one last time before climbing out. The moment he steps into the cold, his breath fogs in soft clouds. I brace myself and grab the door handle. By the time I step outside, he's already grabbed our bags, his quick efficiency leaving little for me to do. He sets his down by the porch and crosses to my car to stash mine in the back seat.

I reach for the driver's door, but Jake places his hand over mine, stopping me gently. I glance up, and his gaze locks me in place—those ocean-deep eyes doing dangerous things to my insides.

"You're not really plannin' to run off without a proper goodbye, are you, Little Trash Panda?" His smirk has that wicked edge I've grown to crave.

I shake my head, laughing. "No, you silly goose. I was just gonna start the engine, let the car warm up a bit while I give you that 'proper goodbye.'"

His gloved fingers slide over the back of my hand, wrapping around it warmly. "I was thinking we could head up to the shop and let it warm up there. I've got a surprise for you."

"Oh?" I arch an eyebrow. "Will I like this surprise?"

His smirk deepens as he nods, not giving anything away. "You'll see."

"Alright, then. Get in the car." I open my door, pulse already picking up.

The drive up to the shop is so short I barely have time to roll down the window for visibility. I park, shut the window, and leave the car running as I hop out and follow him inside.

The rich scent of fresh-cut wood hits me the second I step into Jake's workshop. I breathe it in deep—it's warm, earthy, familiar. It clings to Jake too, mingling with his rugged soap. Honestly, I could breathe it forever.

Jake guides me to the back of the shop, past several projects he and his dad have clearly been pouring their hearts into. There's a couple of beautifully assembled tables waiting for stain or paint, their wood gleaming under the shop lights. A partially built frame—maybe for a swing—sits nearby, flanked by stacks of wood marked with pencil lines and measure-ments.

He leads me to a table nestled against the back wall, cluttered with minor projects—cutting boards, coasters, and what looks like a tiny, detailed birdhouse. He picks it up and sets it gently in front of me, and my heart skips. The longer I stare at it, the more my eyes blur. Jake has crafted the most enchanting birdhouse I've ever seen, and it's obvious he's poured his whole heart into it. It's not just a box with a hole; it looks like a miniature fairy cottage, with intricate vines and tiny flowers carved along its surface. Each petal, every leaf, is so delicate it looks painted with the lightest brush. Rich, earthy colors enhance every detail. Beside it, a small feeder painted to match completes the set. The craftsmanship is unreal.

Jake's watching me closely, a mix of anticipation and worry flickering across his face. I feel a tear slip down my cheek as I turn to him, grinning.

"It's beautiful, Jake," I say, my voice a little shaky.

Relief and pride brighten his face. "I thought it might help with that pesky bird," he says with a grin. "Give it somewhere it can feed and make a cozy little nest."

I laugh, touched by his thoughtfulness. "That's a great idea."

He nods, still watching my reaction closely. "I was thinking I could come by tomorrow while you're at work and hang it up for you. Right next to your window. You'll be able to just open the window to refill the feeder."

"Oh, so you know which window is mine, huh?" I tease, raising an eyebrow.

Jake grins, wrapping his arms around my waist and pulling me close. "Not yet, but you could mark it for me. That way I'll know which one to climb up to when I want to sneak in."

I laugh, a playful smile tugging at my lips. "Please. I can just picture you trying to climb in through my window. I doubt you could even get these guns through it." I give his biceps an appreciative squeeze, loving the amusement in his eyes.

Jake shakes his head with a soft laugh. "Come on, Little Trash Panda. Let's get you back to your car. It should be good and warm by now."

Nodding, I follow him outside into the cold air, already warmed by everything he's just done.

It surprised me how much it had snowed farther south during our trip, but coming back to find a few inches blanketing the ground here was even more unexpected. The snow crunches under my boots as we make our way to my car, the icy wind slicing through the trees and sneaking beneath the hem of my sweater dress. I shiver, instantly regretting not layering up with leggings or stockings. The dress brushes my ankles, and my boots reach just below my knees, but the tops of my thighs are going numb from the cold. Every step brings a small burst of warmth as I rub my legs together, trying to keep the chill at bay.

As we reach the car, I let out a sigh of relief. The engine's warmth spills out as I open the door, easing the sting on my thighs. The windows are nicely defrosted—thanks to my foresight in starting the heat before we stepped inside the shop—and the light dusting of snow has already melted away.

Jake steps in behind me, wrapping his arms around my waist and pulling me back against him.

"Have I told you how sexy you look today?" His voice is low and rough, and the way his eyes travel over me sends a jolt of heat straight through my core.

I smile, swatting his shoulder. "Oh, please. There is nothing sexy about this hot mess express standing in front of you."

"Oh, I beg to differ," he growls—and then his mouth crashes into mine, the kiss fierce and consuming.

I slide my tongue along his, coaxing him deeper, sparks flaring between us as he groans into my mouth. My hands tangle around his neck, trying to pull him closer despite our thick jackets. The kiss turns dizzying fast, and a pulse of need throbs through me, leaving me aching. If we don't stop soon, I'm going to end up begging him to take me against the hood of the car.

Reluctantly, I break the kiss, brushing a few soft pecks against his lips before pulling away entirely. His breath leaves him in ragged puffs, his dark eyes locked on mine.

"Still don't believe me?" he asks, voice low and rumbling.

It takes me a moment to register what he means, but when I do, I let out a defiant little scoff. His eyes flash—a brief flicker of something feral—before he slams my door shut and pushes me back against the car. He shrugs off his coat and lets it fall to the ground. Before I can even question him, he's on his knees, hands sliding up under my skirt.

I gasp as he grabs my panties, tearing them at each seam with one swift tug. "These are mine," he growls, stuffing the torn fabric into his pocket.

His hands press against my thighs, slowly tracing upward as he lifts my skirt with him. When he reaches my knees, he spreads my legs as far as they'll go without tipping me over, and I can barely think past the haze of desire. Jake's head disappears beneath my skirt—and the first warm glide of his tongue against my pussy sends a violent shiver through me that has nothing to do with the cold.

My breath catches as his tongue flicks over my clit, a moan ripping from my throat. His hands slide higher along my inner thighs, lifting one leg up over his shoulder. The new angle gives him full access—and he doesn't waste a second.

I can't hold back the guttural sounds spilling from me as he devours me with brutal precision. With my leg draped over his shoulder, he's got me exactly where he wants me, and he's making damn sure I know it.

"Oh, fuck, Jake," I cry out as he slides a finger into me, curling it perfectly against that glorious spot inside. My breaths come ragged, and the leg I'm balancing on begins to shake.

Then, he slides in a second finger and latches his mouth onto my clit.

I'm gone.

His fingers slip out of me, gentle but firm, as he lowers my leg from his shoulder. My knees are jelly. I sag against the car, still swimming in the blissed-out aftermath, struggling to breathe.

Jake rises, his hands gripping my hips to keep me steady, with that smug, sinful look in his eyes.

"Do you still doubt it, Little Trash Panda?" he murmurs, voice thick with self-satisfied heat.

I should probably say no. I should be satisfied after the mind-numbing orgasm he just gave me. I should probably climb into my car and get out of the cold.

But I can't.

My body's still thrumming, wanting more—and some wild, reckless part of me wants to see what he'll do if I say otherwise.

My pussy clenches as I lift my chin defiantly and utter the one word I know I shouldn't, but can't resist:

"Yes."

A smirk cuts across his lips, and he's on me in an instant, mouth crashing into mine—rough, possessive, devouring. I taste myself on his tongue, and a moan escapes me, raw and needy.

The sound of his zipper being undone barely registers before he shoves my skirt up around my hips and lifts me, pinning me to the car. I wrap my legs around his waist, the heat of his cock pressing against me—so close it's unbearable.

The warmth of the car bleeds through my jacket as he thrusts into me in one smooth, brutal stroke, filling me to the hilt.

I gasp, my head falling back as his mouth moves to my neck. He holds still, buried deep, his cock pulsing inside me as his hands clamp down on my hips.

The fire racing through my body makes me whimper—a broken, pleading sound he seems to understand without question.

Jake moves, his thrusts slow but impossibly deep, dragging against that sweet, devastating spot inside me.

"Jake..." I breathe, trembling, the need building fast—too fast.

"I've got you, baby," he pants against my lips, keeping that deliberate rhythm. My pussy clenches around him with every stroke, each one stoking the burn—but it's not enough. Not fast enough. Not hard enough.

"Jake, please," I whimper, breathless. "Please, please, please—I need to cum."

"Fuck," he growls, voice ragged as he slams me harder into the car, restraint shattering. His thrusts turn fierce and fast, slamming into me with savage need, filling the ache that's been clawing through me.

Each breath comes out as a desperate moan as the tension coils tighter and tighter inside me.

"Jake... oh God..." My voice breaks, breathless and high, the pressure so close to snapping.

Hearing me fall apart only pushes him further. He pounds into me, each thrust hitting that perfect spot with ruthless precision until I break — "Fuck. Jake... I love you!"

The words rip out of me as I cum, hard and wild, my pussy gripping around him so tight it forces a guttural groan from his lips.

Thank God Jake's holding me—my legs are jelly, my whole body melting from the sheer force of release. A buzzing sensation rushes through me, and something tightens in my chest like a tripwire.

I suck in a sharp breath as the buzzing fades to a soft tingle at the back of my mind. The sensation is strange—familiar and unfamiliar all at once—and I can't quite make sense of it.

I push it aside, focusing on my breath, trying to calm the frantic beat of my heart. Slowly, it settles, but I can still feel the weight of him inside me, anchoring me as I float back down.

Then I see it.

A shift on his face.

Satisfaction fading.

Panic takes its place.

"Shit. Fuck," he mutters, glancing between us—his eyes darting down where our bodies are still joined. A warm, slick sensation spills around him. As his cock softens, he pulls back, eyes wide with alarm.

"Sarah," he blurts, panic overtaking his voice. "Oh, shit, baby. I'm so sorry."

He's frantic, guilt-ridden, like he's scrambling to find a way to explain it all before I break in front of him.

"I... I wasn't wearing a condom. I meant to pull out, but you were gripping me so tight, and I just... I couldn't—"

His face is stricken, reminiscent of having committed some unspeakable sin.

And I can't help it. I laugh.

It bubbles up involuntarily, even as he stares at me in horror. I catch my breath, shaking my head as I reach up and brush a hand across his cheek. "It's alright, Jake. Really. I have an implant."

Relief crashes over his face, and for a second, it makes my heart skip.

But then—quietly, sharply—something stings.

It's not that I'm ready for kids. I'm not.

But part of me wonders: did he panic because the idea of that future—with me—terrifies him?

Am I really that unthinkable as the mother of his children?

The questions rush in too fast, swirling like a storm behind my ribcage. I barely notice as Jake gently lowers my legs, smoothing my skirt back down, steadying me as he always does. The stiff wind bites at my skin, but I hardly feel it.

Not until his fingers lift my chin, pulling my gaze back to his.

"Hey," he murmurs softly and steadily. "What's going on in that head of yours?"

The question breaks something open in me. He sees me—really sees me.

It's like he already knows where my thoughts have spiraled, because then, with a kind of quiet sincerity that wrecks me, he says:

"It's not that I wouldn't want to see your belly grow with my child someday, Sarah. I panicked because we haven't talked about kids... and the last thing I ever want is to make that choice for you."

His words sink deep—past the fear, past the noise.

He's not pulling away. He's holding a space for me. For us.

Then he leans in, brushing his lips over mine—soft and lingering, like a vow.

When he pulls back, his voice is raw and unguarded.

"I love you too."

And just like that, my heart soars.

Chapter 23

Sarah's scent clings to me, a mix of sweetness and something uniquely her, lingering in my nose as I maneuver the heavy extension ladder toward the back of her house. Each step crunches softly in the layer of snow dusting the ground; the sound is oddly satisfying against the stillness of the morning. My mind is a mess, tangled with images of her—her soft moans, the way her body fit against mine—and the thought brings a smile to my face despite the chill in the air. I can feel her in the back of my mind, like a calming balm on my soul. The buzzing under my skin is gone now, and I can't help but wonder if it has something to do with the bond. I'll ask my parents about it later. Right now, I've got more important things to handle—like getting this birdhouse hung and solving Sarah's pesky bird problem.

As I round the corner to the backyard, my eyes immediately scan the second-story windows. I'm looking for a sign, something to tell me which one belongs to her. When my gaze lands on it, I can't help but chuckle. Written in bold, bright red letters—lipstick, if I had to guess—is my name, backwards from her side but perfectly readable from mine. Of course, she'd make it easy for me. I shake my head, my grin widening as I walk closer.

Stopping just below her window, I spot something unusual at my feet: a pile of small, round pebbles, partially buried in the snow, catches my attention. I set the ladder down and crouch to inspect them. They're gray, smooth, and almost perfectly round, like tiny marbles. Most of them are uniform, though a few have tiny holes dotting their surfaces. I roll one between my fingers; the texture is strange but oddly satisfying.

Glancing around, I try to figure out where they might have come from. There's no landscaping nearby that matches, and the snow hides any clues of how they got here. Maybe they're some sort of decorative stone I've never seen before, though I can't imagine why they're piled here, directly below her window.

Without fully understanding why, I slip the pebble into my pocket. Feels dumb, but something about leaving it behind doesn't sit right. Something about it that feels off—too deliberate, maybe—but I push the thought aside and turn back to the task at hand.

The icy tips of my fingers sting as I wrestle with the cold metal of the ladder, its unforgiving chill digging into my skin. The fingerless gloves I'm wearing are useless against the biting cold, but they make gripping and maneuvering easier than bulky full-coverage gloves. As soon as I've got the ladder adjusted into place, I shove my hands into my pockets, relishing the heat from the hand warmers I had the good sense to stash there before stepping out of my truck.

The wind slices through the air, carrying the sharp scent of snow and pine, and I shiver against its force. I head back to the front of the house, moving quickly to grab the tools and the birdhouse I made for Sarah out of the cab. The rush of cold seems to cut straight through my jacket, urging me to hurry. Once everything's in place, I take a step back and look up at the birdhouse now hanging snugly beside her window.

It's small, but it carries so much of me—each carved vine, each painted flower, a testament of hours of thought and care. The way it hangs there now feels right, like it belongs, just as much as I hope to belong in Sarah's life. An unbidden smile tugs at my lips as I admire my work.

The wind brushes past again as I make my way back to the truck, tugging at the edges of my jacket and filling my lungs with crisp air. My fingers graze the smooth, round rock still in my pocket, a strange but fitting keepsake of the day. Driving away, with the sight of the birdhouse etched into my memory, I feel a quiet satisfaction settle over me—a warmth that not even the frigid air can steal.

Chapter 24

The back door slams against the frame with a force that makes me jump as Jordan shuffles into the bakery. I'm not about to say it out loud, but he looks like hell—like a zombie in designer jeans who stumbled into the wrong universe. He's moving in slow motion, shoulders slumped, and the sunglasses he wears do nothing to hide the deep exhaustion radiating off him. When he finally takes them off, the dark circles under his eyes could be mistaken for bruises. His attempt at nonchalance is about as convincing as a cat pretending it's *not* plotting world domination.

His hair's combed, and his clothes aren't rumpled, but his face is hollow, his skin dull, and he looks like he might collapse if a stiff breeze hits him. When his bloodshot eyes meet mine, he grimaces. A weak, half-assed "Mornin'" floats across the air like he could barely muster the energy to say it.

"Mornin'," I reply, giving him a little wave, though I can't stop myself from staring. What the hell happened to him?

Before I can ask, the back door bangs open again—this time with enough force to make me wince. Sam bursts in with a chaotic energy that could power a small country. His loud, boisterous "Good mornin'! Good mornin'!" practically echoes through the shop, and I half-expect him to break out into a dance routine on the display case. His presence is like a wrecking ball of enthusiasm, and Jordan reacts like a man who accidentally adopted the world's most hyperactive puppy. He flinches, face twisting into a murderous glare, and if looks could kill, Sam would've dropped dead on the spot.

Sam, completely unfazed, slaps his brother on the shoulder with enough force to rock Jordan forward. "Aw, what's wrong, big bro? Feeling a little hungover?" His tone drips with mock concern, and his grin is wide enough to make the Cheshire Cat jealous.

"Fuck. You. Sam," Jordan grinds out through clenched teeth, his voice rough and raspier than usual.

Sam's grin only grows larger. "Awwww, don't be like that, bro. It's not my fault you can't hold your liquor."

I raise an eyebrow at Sam, my curiosity officially piqued. "Oh? Are you going to fill me in, or do I have to guess?"

Sam's grin turns downright wicked. "Oh, you haven't talked to Lila this morning, have you? I imagine not. She's probably sporting one hell of a hangover too." He pauses, clearly relishing the moment as I stare at him expectantly.

"Are you going to explain, or are you just here to gloat?"

Sam chuckles under his breath before turning fully toward me, his eyes twinkling with mischief. "Well... our dear Jordan here got into a little altercation with Lila last night."

I gasp—the word *altercation* sets off alarms. Sam holds up his hands quickly, laughter bubbling up again. "Relax, relax. No one got hurt. They didn't beat on each other or anything."

I ease slightly, though I can't help narrowing my eyes at Jordan. "Then what happened?"

Sam's chuckles turn into full-blown cackles, his shoulders shaking as Jordan glares daggers at him. Sam wipes his eyes, trying to collect himself enough to speak. "Oh, you're gonna love this. So, our genius over here thought the best way to settle their little... disagreement... was to challenge her to a drinking game."

I blink, trying to process what I'm hearing. Sam barely gives me time to catch up before continuing, voice full of glee. "He actually thought he could out-drink Lila. And you know what his reasoning was? Because she's—and I quote—'nothing but a poor wittle wabbit shifter.'" Sam mimics Jordan's voice, throwing in an exaggerated pout for good measure.

I whip my head around to glare at Jordan, who has the good sense to look sheepish. His lips press together in a tight line, and his shoulders slump even further as he mutters something under his breath that sounds suspiciously like, "Shut the fuck up."

"Dumbass forgot her grandpappy's been running moonshine in these hills for sixty years. Lila's been his taste tester since she was five." Sam can barely finish the sentence without breaking into laughter again, his voice pitching higher with each word.

"She wasn't even slurring when he passed out," Sam adds, gasping for breath. "Funniest shit I've ever seen."

Jordan shoots him a look that could strip paint, his face a mix of exhaustion and humiliation. If I thought his earlier glare was murderous, it's got *nothing* on the one currently plastered on his face. He looks like he'd rather see Sam as a smear on the bakery floor than standing upright in front of him. With the way Sam's still cackling, it's clear Jordan will *never* escape this story unscathed.

And as if the universe wanted to twist the knife, the bell above the door jingles. Lila waltzes in like she owns the damn place.

Her entrance is nothing short of victorious. Wearing a perfectly tailored outfit that screams effortless chic, her blonde hair cascades over her shoulders in soft waves, and her blue eyes sparkle with mischief. She radiates smug satisfaction as she removes her sunglasses, her gaze locking onto Jordan like a predator toying with its prey. A smirk curves her lips, and she practically sings, "Good morning!" loud enough to echo up the mountain and into the next town over.

Jordan groans and mutters, "Christ, woman," and slinks into the kitchen, clearly retreating to lick his wounds. I shake my head at Lila, trying to stifle a grin.

She meets my look with wide, innocent eyes. "What?" She asks in an exaggerated tone of faux sincerity. "He started it."

Sam, still recovering from his bout of laughter and grinning ear to ear, slaps Lila on the back. "So, you finally set him straight, huh?"

Leaning against the counter, Lila shrugs, her smirk widening. "Oh, he set himself up. I just made sure he stayed there."

I can't hold back my curiosity any longer. "What exactly happened?" I ask, leaning in.

Lila's smirk turns devilish as she winks at me. "Well, your dear Jordan decided to argue with me about the quality of Jackson's liquor. Naturally, he figured a drinking game would settle the score. But—" she pauses for dramatic effect—"he underestimated me. Forgot my grandpappy's moonshine is legend around here, and I've been his taste tester since I was five. I may be a 'wittle wabbit shifter,' as he called me, but I can drink anyone under the table."

Sam chimes in, still grinning. "She wasn't kidding. She knocked back shots like they were water. Jordan didn't stand a chance."

I pictured it vividly—Jordan, full of misplaced confidence, facing off against Lila in a battle he couldn't possibly win. The thought of him passed out on the floor while she remained smug and composed had me snorting with laughter.

"You two seriously need to bang it out," I snort between laughs.

Sam gives me a wide-eyed look, while Lila looks like she's about to vomit right there on the floor.

"Gross, Sarah! Why would you say something like that?"

I shrug and shoot her a look that clearly says, really?

"The sexual tension between you two is ridiculous. Jordan may act like a dick to you, but come on—he totally wants to bang you. It's obvious."

Sam's gaze bounces between me and Lila as she makes an exaggerated gagging sound. I just shake my head as she wraps up her little dramatics.

The kitchen door swings open, and Jordan emerges, balancing a tray of scones. His glare toward Sam and Lila could have frozen lava, but when he looks at me, it softened into a sheepish smile. He places the tray on the counter with more force than necessary and turns back toward the kitchen.

Lila reaches out and pats his back in mock sympathy. "Don't worry, Jordan. You'll recover. Someday."

Jordan's only response is a look of pure venom and a grumbled, "Don't you have somewhere to be?" before he disappears into the kitchen. Lila's laugh trails after him, unabashed and triumphant.

Tapping her fingers on the counter, Lila turns to me. "As much as I'd love to torment Jordan all day, unfortunately, he's right. I have places to be." She glances at the menu board. "Noah sent me for pastries and coffee. Can you get those started for me?"

As I pack up her order, she calls to Sam, "Hey, how's your dad? I didn't get a chance to ask yesterday."

Sam's grin eases into something gentler. "He's doing good. You know how he gets about this place, though. Mom practically had to tie him down to make him rest. But he'll be in later."

"Good to hear," Lila says, her tone genuine. Then her attention swings back to me, and her mischievous grin returns. "And you," she points, "I want to hear all the hot gossip about your weekend later. Don't even think about leaving anything out."

She grabs the bag of pastries and her coffee, waving cheerfully as she heads for the door. "Don't have too much fun now!" she calls over her shoulder.

Sam and I exchange amused looks, shaking our heads as the bell jingles behind her. "She's a damn tornado," I mutter, smiling despite myself.

"Yeah," Sam replies with a chuckle. "But a damn entertaining one."

I turn to Sam and cross my arms. "I'm not going to get into why you were at a party when you're only seventeen. I ain't your momma." I glance at the clock on the wall. "However, ain't you supposed to be in school right now? It's eight o'clock."

Sam gives me his best smile, like he's trying to weasel his way out of somethin'. "Aw, come on now, Sarah. I couldn't miss the show. That showdown's been brewin' for years."

I raise a brow and cock my hip, giving him my best don't-care stare.

"Well... show's over. You better hightail it to school before your daddy finds out you're skippin' class."

A genuine smile crosses his face as he gives me a two-finger salute.

"Yes, ma'am. Tell Jordan I said 'later.'"

I nod and watch him walk out the door, then shake my head. It wasn't that long ago I was seventeen, but it feels like I've aged a lifetime in the last five years. I sigh, shove the sad thoughts back, and get to work.

The bell above the bakery door jingles mid-morning and in walks Mr. Walters, true to his word. He looks a little tired, his steps just a touch slower than usual, but he's upright and in good spirits. Relief blooms in my chest as I greet him warmly; his familiar smile reassures me that he's on the mend.

The rest of the day blurs into the rhythm of customers, laughter, and the scent of fresh pastries. By closing time, my feet are screaming in protest, and I dread the walk home. Still, I remind myself it's only a few blocks. I shrug into my coat, the thick fabric settling heavily on my tired shoulders, and brace myself for the chill outside.

The winter air hits me the moment I step outside, sharp and biting, cutting through the thick wool like an unwelcome guest. Shoving my hands deep into my coat pockets, I set off, my steps quick and determined. The snow crunches underfoot with each stride, the fresh flakes dusting the town like powdered sugar on a beignet.

The streets are quiet, serene in their snowy stillness. A soft smile tugs at my lips as I admire the picturesque scene, the rooftops and trees already coated in white. Soon, the town will be aglow with twinkling Christmas lights, a sight I can't wait to see. This is my first holiday season here, and the thought of spending some of that time with Jake sends a warm flutter through my chest.

But first, there's Thanksgiving. Janet's invitation looms in my thoughts. The gesture is kind, and I know Dad appreciates it. But it still stings—the unspoken pity behind her offer gnaws at me. I resolve to make the best of it, though. After all, it is just Dad and me now, and the holidays can be a lonely stretch without the company of others. Maybe after Thanksgiving, Dad and I can find a tree, string it with lights, and create some new memories in this little town.

Life had changed so drastically since losing Mom. The pain of her absence still lingers, but this town—its charm, its people—has eased the ache in ways I hadn't expected. Jake, Mr. Walters, even Sam and Lila—they all make me feel like I belong here, like I'm part of something bigger than myself.

The icy wind bites at my shoulders, sneaking past the layers of my coat to send a shiver rippling down my spine. I pause mid-step; a sudden, inexplicable sensation prickles at the back of my neck. Someone is watching me. My eyes dart around the neighborhood, scanning for anything unusual.

Children laugh and squeal down the street as they toss snowballs at each other, their red cheeks and bundled bodies oblivious to the chill. A man down the street shovels his driveway with steady, rhythmic motions.

Across the way, a woman pulls a bag of groceries from the trunk of her car. Everything seems perfectly ordinary.

But the feeling doesn't go away. It clings to me, heavy and insistent, like an unseen presence just out of sight. My breath hitches as a deeper chill slides down my back, one that has nothing to do with the cold wind whipping through the streets.

I quicken my pace, my boots crunching against the snow as I try to shake the unease. My shoulders tighten, and I can't help glancing over my shoulder one more time. Nothing. No one out of place. Still, the sensation lingers, stubborn and unshakable, urging me to move faster.

The glow of the house comes into view, soft light spilling out through the curtains like a guiding light in the night. I let out a breath of relief as my shoulders relax. The scent of something savory carries on the cold air as I approach, coaxing me to quicken my steps further. By the time I reach the door, my fingers are tingling from the chill. I open it, stepping into the warmth and comfort of home.

Inside, Dad is in the kitchen, an apron tied snugly around his waist. The hum of a familiar tune floats in the air as he stirs a pot on the stove. The scent of simmering herbs and roasted something—chicken, maybe—wraps around me like a hug. Dad glances over his shoulder, his warm smile is a beacon in the cozy glow of our home.

"Hey there, Doodle Bug! How was your day at the bakery?" he asks, flipping off the stove and giving the pot on the burner a final stir.

"Good, Dad," I say, shrugging out of my coat and hanging it neatly by the door. "Mr. Walters showed up around mid-morning. He seems to be feeling better."

"That's great to hear," he replies, wiping his hands on a kitchen towel before pulling me into a quick hug. "Dinner'll be ready in just a few."

"Thanks, Dad," I say, stepping back. "I'm just gonna pop upstairs real quick."

My footsteps echo against the hardwood floor as I hurry upstairs, my anticipation building with each step. Jake had mentioned he'd be by to hang the birdhouse, and I can't wait to see it. The door to my room creaks slightly as I push it open. I make a beeline for the window, eager to take in his handiwork.

The first thing that catches my eye is the bold, bright red lettering I scrawled backward across the window—a cheeky little message meant just for Jake. But what steals my breath is the delicate orange flower sitting on the windowsill. I pick it up gently, the soft petals brushing against my fingers and jaw as I bring it closer to inspect it. A smile spreads across my face, growing wider as I glance out the window and see the birdhouse nestled exactly where Jake said it would be. It was beautiful in the shop, but it's breathtaking now, framed by the soft winter light.

Satisfied, I tuck the flower into my hand and make my way back downstairs. Dad looks up when I enter, his eyes immediately catching on the bloom in my hand.

"What a lovely marigold," he says, a knowing smile tugging at his lips.

I blink, glancing down at the flower. "Is that what this is?"

He nods, reaching into the cabinet for a glass. Filling it halfway with water, he hands it to me. "Here. It'll keep for a few days if you put it in water."

"Thanks, Dad," I say, placing the flower gently into the makeshift vase before setting it on the table.

"I take it Jake came by?" he asks, his tone casual but tinged with curiosity.

"He did," I confirm, a hint of excitement creeping into my voice. "The birdhouse is up now, so hopefully that god-awful bird will get the hint."

Dad chuckles, shaking his head. "One can only hope."

I laugh and sink into the seat he slides my way. As I dig into the plate he sets before me, I quickly shoot Jake a text: Thank you, the birdhouse is perfect.

The rest of the evening passes in a comforting rhythm of small talk and holiday planning. After dinner, I head back upstairs to wind down for the night. Jake left a small bag of birdseed by the back door, so I scoop some out and fill the holder on the birdhouse. The cold nips at my cheeks, but I feel a warmth inside knowing Jake thought of even the smallest detail.

Later, as I curl up under the covers, with the marigold resting in its glass on my nightstand, I send a silent prayer into the night. Please, whatever gods or cosmic forces are listening, let that damn bird get the hint.

Chapter 25

The bakery is bustling from morning to night, a frenzy of activity in the days leading up to Thanksgiving. Customers pour in like waves, collecting pies and treats for their family gatherings. Mr. Walters, true to holiday form, is in the kitchen whipping up his signature creations—special pies and delicacies he only makes once a year. The cranberry and pear pie, in particular, is flying off the shelves, the demand overwhelming. Tomorrow's Thanksgiving, and I can't wait to go home and put my feet up.

As I head for the door at the end of the day, Mr. Walters stops me, a warm smile on his face.

"Don't forget this," he says, sliding a perfectly golden pie toward me.

"For me?" I ask, startled by the gesture. The sweet, tangy aroma of cranberries and pears drifts up, making my mouth water.

"Consider it a little something for you and your dad," he replies with a wave of his hand, brushing off my thanks. "I know you two are going to Janet's house tomorrow, and trust me, she'll love you after this."

"Thank you," I say, clutching the pie to my chest, my heart warmed by his kindness.

Thanksgiving Day arrives, snowflakes swirling outside as the comforting scent of roasted turkey fills the air. Janet's home is warm and inviting—a kind of place where laughter seems to seep into the walls, wrapping everyone in its embrace.

"This is for you," I say, handing her the pie as we step into her kitchen.

Her face lights up like a kid on Christmas morning. "You didn't!" she gasps, clutching the dessert like it's a rare treasure.

"Mr. Walters insisted," I explain with a smile.

"Thank God for that man," Doug chimes in from the doorway. "She was downright inconsolable when she missed the list this year."

We laugh as the pie takes its place of honor at the center of the dessert table. Janet's family welcomes us like old friends, sharing stories and jokes that dissolve any lingering awkwardness. For the first time in a while, I feel the warmth of a community embracing me and Dad, covering us in a sense of belonging that we hadn't realized we were missing.

The weekend after Thanksgiving, Dad and I bundle up in layers and trek out to find the perfect Christmas tree. Snow crunches under our boots as we wander through rows of evergreens, the air thick with the scent of pine and punctuated by bursts of laughter when one of us slips on an icy patch. The chill nips at our cheeks, but the search fills us with a shared joy that makes the cold seem almost welcome.

"Too short," Dad says, pointing to a stout little tree.

"And that one's crooked," I counter, pointing to another.

Eventually, we find it—a majestic tree that seems to whisper, *take me home*. We mark it with the ribbon the sales clerk gave us, then make our way to the checkout. One credit card swipe and a precarious car ride later, the tree now sits proudly in our living room.

A soft golden glow spills from the string of bulbs draped across the tree, casting flickering shadows along the walls. The room hums with quiet warmth, punctuated only by the rustling of tissue paper as Dad pulls out an ornament. He pauses, holding up a glittery star, its edges worn with time.

"Look at this," he says, his voice softer than usual. The delicate glitter catches the light, and for a moment, it seems to glow with its own peaceful brilliance.

I swallow hard, the weight of unspoken memories pressing against my chest. I reach for it, the texture rough against my fingers as I gently take it from him. The star feels heavier than it should, a piece of the past lingering in the present. It was one of Mom's favorites. She'd taken me to a little niche store when I was about a year old, and I picked it out from hundreds of others. It had a place of honor on our tree every year since.

Carefully, I lift it toward the tree, my hand trembling just enough to notice. As I hook it onto a branch, it sways slightly before settling into place. The room holds its breath, the absence of her presence felt as much as the fullness of her love.

December unfolds like the first shake of a snow globe, the town coming alive with twinkling lights and festive decorations. Every lamppost wears a wreath, every storefront glows with holiday cheer. The bakery, bustling with customers eager for cookies and cakes, hums with a chaos that somehow feels comforting. The warm scent of cinnamon and sugar hangs in the air, wrapping around me like a hug.

Amid the rush, quiet moments sneak in—moments where I let myself take it all in. The people we've met, the life we're building here—it's more than I ever hoped for.

Outside my window, Jake's birdhouse hangs proudly, its intricate carvings now dusted with snow. My feathered nemesis seems to have finally taken the hint, and for the first time in weeks, mornings are peaceful. With every uninterrupted night's sleep, my mood lightens.

As I step outside the house each morning, a vibrant marigold waits for me on the porch, its petals a fiery burst of orange against the winter frost. The sight never fails to tug a smile from me, a joy blooming in my chest. I pluck the flower gently from its spot, the cold stem pressing against my fingers, and carry it inside. The vase by the door holds a growing collection now, each flower a small, perfect reminder of Jake's thoughtfulness.

The gesture—romantic as it is—keeps me wondering. Where is he finding marigolds in the dead of winter? The question lingers in the back of my mind, but I don't ask. I don't want to ruin the magic of it.

Jake's hopeless romantic streak makes me adore him even more, but not everyone shares my sentiment. Each time Dad sees a new marigold, his brow furrows a little deeper, the corners of his mouth pulling tight. He stays silent, the unease in his expression speaking volumes.

Finally, I can't keep my curiosity at bay. "What's with the face every time you see these flowers?" I ask one morning, holding up the latest marigold for emphasis.

Dad shrugs, the motion far too casual to be genuine. "Nothing. It's fine."

I roll my eyes, not buying it for a second. "Seriously, Dad. It's just Jake being sweet. What's the problem?"

His lips press into a thin line, his gaze sliding toward the flower as if it were some kind of unwelcome guest. "No problem," he says, the tension in his voice betraying him. "Probably just... the whole courtship thing. It's a dad thing."

I snort, shaking my head as I tuck the marigold into the vase with its companions. "You mean you're freaking out because your little girl is being courted? By someone who treats her well?"

His silence speaks volumes, and I can't help the grin that spreads across my face. Whatever his reservations, they clearly aren't enough to outweigh the obvious fact that Jake is putting in the effort. Dad might be nervous, but that doesn't mean I have to be. Jake is proving, flower by flower, that he is exactly the kind of man I want in my life—and no amount of dad jitters is going to change that.

Later that night, I can't help but smile as I pull up to Jake's house. Grabbing the gift from my passenger seat, I brace myself for the frosty evening air. Snow swirls around me, dancing in the glow of the cabin's porch light as I stand outside his door, my fingers gripping the small, carefully wrapped box in my hands. The crisp air bites at my cheeks, painting them pink, and my breath clouds in front of me with each exhale. A flutter of nervous excitement churns in my chest, and I force myself to take a steadying breath.

Lifting a hand, I knock—the sound echoing softly in the quiet of the night. For a moment, there's nothing but the faint howl of the wind and the crunch of snow underfoot as I shift nervously. Then, muffled footsteps approach from inside.

The door swings open, and there he is—Jake, his smile wide and warm, the kind that reaches his eyes and melts the icy air around me. His flannel shirt is slightly unbuttoned, and the cozy cabin glow spills out behind him, wrapping me in its welcome.

Before I can say anything, he grabs me by the waist and pulls me into a deep, searing kiss. His lips are warm and familiar, melting away the cold that seeped into my skin.

"Hi," I mumble against his lips, a hint of a smile blooming at my own.

"Hi yourself," he murmurs back, voice low and teasing.

"Merry Christmas Eve."

"Merry Christmas Eve, Little Trash Panda."

I brush my nose against his, giggling softly before stepping out of his embrace. Jake takes the coat I shrug off—his hands grazing mine in a way that sends a pleasant shiver down my spine—and hangs it neatly by the door. His hand finds the small of my back, guiding me into the cozy living room, where a roaring fire colors the space with a warm, golden glow. He has a few Christmas decorations up: a small tree that's sparsely decorated, garland across the mantle, and one lone stocking.

I sink into the plush couch with a sigh, the heat of the fire seeping into my bones. Jake hands me a glass of wine before settling beside me, his thigh brushing against mine. He places his own glass on the table and turns toward me, his gaze soft and intent.

"Dinner will be ready soon," he says, his voice velvety and deep—the sound alone making my heart skip a beat. "But in the meantime..." He reaches into his pocket, pulling out a small box wrapped in elegant silver paper with a tiny red bow perched on top. "I wanted to give you this. Go ahead, open it."

I blink at the gift, warmth rising to my cheeks. The wrapping is almost too pretty to tear, but the excitement bubbling inside me wins out. Jake's eager expression is infectious, and with a little squeak of anticipation, I peel away the paper. A soft chuckle escapes him as he watches my enthusiasm.

Underneath, a sleek black box rests in my palm. My fingers tremble as I flip open the lid, and my breath hitches at the sight inside.

"Oh my God, Jake. It's so beautiful," I whisper, voice breaking with emotion. "Thank you."

Nestled inside is a delicate raccoon pendant hanging from a fine chain. Its simple design is elevated by tiny black gems that sparkle like stars, adorning the raccoon's eyes, body, and tail in intricate detail. Two white gems mark its eyes. It's stunning, and my heart swells at the thought and care he's put into choosing it.

Jake's smile widens as he leans closer. "Do you like it?" His voice holds a flicker of nervousness, as if unsure of my reaction.

Tears well in my eyes, and I fling my arms around him, burying my face in his neck. Jake chuckles, his arms tightening around me as his lips brush my hair. "I'll take that as a yes."

I nod against him, unable to form words through the lump in my throat. He holds me close, his warmth and steady presence grounding me until the tears subside. I finally pull back, wiping at my cheeks with a sheepish smile. Jake reaches for the necklace, his fingers brushing mine.

"Let me put it on you," he offers, voice gentle.

I turn, gathering my hair to the side as he clasps the chain around my neck. His fingers linger briefly against my skin, sending another pleasant shiver down my spine.

"The gems are all diamonds," he says softly, adjusting the pendant to rest perfectly against my chest. "Fifty-one black ones and two white."

My fingers trace the pendant as a smile spreads across my face. I turn to him, gratitude shining in my eyes. "Thank you," I whisper.

Jake leans in, pressing a delicate kiss to my cheek. "Seeing your reaction is the best present I could ever get," he says, his tone teasing yet heartfelt.

I raise a playful eyebrow. "Oh, really? In that case, I guess I'll return your gift, since mine apparently won't measure up."

His laughter fills the room as he wraps an arm around me, pulling me into his chest. "Not a chance, Little Trash Panda."

I giggle, swatting at him lightly before handing him the small gift box I've been holding. "Here," I say, watching his face light up as he takes it from my hands.

The box in Jake's hands looks like a crime scene of wrapping paper and tape—a sharp contrast to the pristine silver paper his gift came in. The cartoon snowman pattern and mismatched folds tell an obvious story: I am not a gift-wrapping aficionado. My mom had always loved wrapping presents, taking joy in making each one look like it came straight out of a magazine. A pang of sadness hits me at the memory, but I push it away, focusing instead on Jake as he examines the box with an amused smile.

"Looks like Frosty had a rough night," he teases, carefully turning the package over in his hands.

"Don't judge me!" I protest, a blush heating my cheeks.

"Not judging," he says, finally finding an edge to peel. "Just admiring your... technique."

His fingers make quick work of the paper, revealing a polished wooden box underneath. I watch with bated breath as he flips open the lid, revealing a set of five detail carving tools nestled inside. He freezes for a moment, staring at them, his expression unreadable. My heart clenches, but then his hand reaches out to stroke the tools, and a smile breaks across his face.

"They're beautiful," he murmurs, running his fingers along the smooth handles.

Relief floods me. "I, uh, didn't know if you already had a set or not," I say quickly, nerves bubbling up again.

"I do," he admits softly, "but not like these. Mine are shaped more like pencils."

"Well," I start, shifting closer, "these are called palm-handle tools. They're supposed to be more ergonomic." I reach into the box and pick one up, turning it so the rounded end faces us. "And... I had your initials engraved on the ends."

Jake's gaze snaps to mine, his blue eyes wide with surprise. He gently takes the tool from my hand, turning it over to admire the detail.

"I stand corrected," he says after a moment, voice thick with emotion. "This is the best present I've ever gotten."

Warmth blooms in my chest as I lean in to kiss his cheek. Before I can fully sink into the moment, the oven timer buzzes from the kitchen, breaking the spell. Jake groans, reluctantly setting the box down on the coffee table.

"Dinner calls," he says, rising to his feet.

I laugh softly, picking up my wine glass for a sip. I feel restless sitting here by myself, so I stand and wander over to the fireplace. The mantel is lined with framed photos, and my curiosity gets the best of me.

"Need any help?" I call toward the kitchen, running my fingers along the edge of the mantel. The sound of shuffling and a few clatters comes from the other room.

"No, I'm good!" Jake's voice rings out.

I smile, letting my attention drift back to the photos. One shows a much younger Jake with Charlie and the twins, their grins wide and full of mischief. I shake my head, imagining the trouble they must have caused. My eyes move to another picture—Jake and Charlie, likely in their teenage years, sitting on a pier. Their summer-tanned skin glows in the sunlight, their expressions carefree.

But it's the third person in the photo that makes me pause. A blonde girl stands with Charlie's arm slung around her waist. She's dressed in a bikini top and jean shorts, her bright smile aimed up at Charlie with an unmistakable look of admiration. I lean closer, running my fingers along the edge of the frame, curiosity stirring inside me.

Who is she?

The sound of Jake's boots on the hardwood draws my attention toward the kitchen. I lean against the mantel, a playful smile tugging at my lips.

"You know," I call out as he steps into view, "you're going to have to stop spoiling me. Between the flowers and the pendant, you might end up setting some pretty high expectations for yourself, mister."

Jake pauses mid-step, his brows pulling together in confusion. "Flowers?" he repeats, the word hanging in the air like an off-key note.

My smile falters. The warmth in my chest turns icy cold. "The flowers," I say, trying to keep my voice steady. "The ones you've been leaving on my porch every morning."

Jake tilts his head, confusion deepening. "Sarah... I haven't been leaving you any flowers."

His words hit me like a physical blow. My stomach flips. I start to pace in front of the fireplace, my thoughts spiraling. The calm, cozy atmosphere of the room evaporates, replaced by a creeping dread.

If Jake hasn't been leaving the flowers, then who has?

My mind scrambles through the timeline. The first flower appeared the day he installed the birdhouse. And that flower... it had been sitting inside my bedroom. On the windowsill.

Inside.

A cold realization snakes down my spine, squeezing the air from my lungs. My breath comes fast and shallow as the room blurs at the edges.

"Sarah!" Jake's voice cuts through the haze, his hands gripping my arms. His touch grounds me, but only just. "What's going on? Talk to me!"

I blink, sucking in a ragged breath. My eyes land on the mantle just over Jake's shoulder. A small, smooth object sits there—something I hadn't noticed before. My body stiffens. For a moment, the world holds its breath.

"Sarah," Jake says again, softer this time.

I reach out with trembling fingers and pick it up. The stone is gray, almost perfectly round, its surface smooth but covered in tiny pitted indents.

My heart stumbles. I've seen these before. Not often. But I know what this is.

I turn the stone in my hand and hold it up. My voice shakes. "Where did you get this?"

Jake frowns. "From your house," he says slowly, "The day I put up the birdhouse. There was a pile of them under your window in the back. They're just landscaping rocks, right?"

The stone feels too heavy now. My chest tightens with something close to panic.

"I'm so sorry, Jake. I have to go," I whisper, stepping out of his grasp.

"What? Wait!" His voice jumps from concern to alarm as I grab my coat and head for the door. "Sarah, what's going on? Talk to me!"

Tears blur my vision as I shove my arms into my coat and fumble with my keys. "I'm sorry," I choke out. "I can't explain right now. I just... I have to go."

Jake follows me out into the snow, the crunch of his boots close behind. The freezing wind cuts through my clothes, but it's nothing compared to the terror clawing at my ribs.

"Sarah, stop! Please, just tell me what's wrong," he pleads, his voice rough. "You're scaring me."

I shake my head, unable to form the words. He reaches out, but I pull away, sliding into the driver's seat and slamming the door shut. Through the glass, I see his face—his eyes full of worry, confusion, fear.

"I'll explain later," I manage. My voice barely breaks through the engine's growl.

In the rearview mirror, Jake stands alone in the yard, framed in porchlight and snow. I can almost hear him yell, *what the fuck?* Into the night. But I don't stop.

My fingers grip the wheel, knuckles white, and a single thought drowns out everything else:

I need to get home.

Chapter 26

The door slams shut behind me, echoing through the house as I barrel inside, my boots thudding against the floor. Dad jolts up from his chair by the fire, his book tumbling from his hands to the floor. He clutches his chest, his face twisting in startled annoyance.

"Christ, Doodle Bug! You about gave me a heart attack," he grumbles, bending to scoop up his book. He huffs, flipping through the pages as he realizes he's lost his spot. But when he looks up at me, his expression shifts. The annoyance melts into immediate concern, his brows knitting together as his eyes scan my face.

"What's wrong?" he asks, his voice steady but filled with worry.

I open my mouth, but the words refuse to come. My chest feels tight, the panic gripping me too hard to allow speech. Instead, I lift my arm and hold out my clenched fist, the small rock cold against my palm. His gaze shifts to my hand, and he crosses the room—his movements purposeful but careful. His rough fingers gently unfold mine, exposing the smooth, round stone nestled in my palm.

He sucks in a sharp breath, his body going rigid. His fingers hover over mine before carefully picking up the rock. He scrutinizes it, turning it over in his hand. When he speaks, his voice is hoarse, barely above a whisper.

"Where did you get this?"

I take a shaky breath, willing my thoughts to organize into something coherent. The words tumble out, soft and broken. "Jake. Birdhouse. Backyard."

Dad exhales abruptly, his hand tightening around the rock. Without hesitation, he storms to the coat rack, ripping his jacket from the hook and shoving his arms into the sleeves. His feet slide into his boots in hurried, clumsy motions. The door flies open, letting in an icy gust of wind that makes me shiver. My brain barely registers the frigid air before I'm following him outside, my boots crunching against the snow as we round the house to the backyard.

Dad moves like a man on a mission, his eyes scanning the yard, his breath coming out in white puffs. The snow lies undisturbed, a pristine blanket covering the ground. He stops and turns to me, his voice sharp and clipped. "Did he say where he found it?"

I nod, my finger trembling as I point toward my bedroom window. "Under the window."

His jaw tightens, and he turns back to face the spot. The tension in his posture grows as he approaches the window slowly, as if bracing for what he might find. The snow squeaks softly under his boots. He pauses, sticks his foot out, and scrapes at the snow beneath the window.

A sharp inhale cuts through the air, and his shoulders stiffen. My heart pounds, my legs moving toward him on autopilot. I don't want to see—I don't want to know—but my body ignores the warnings from my brain. By the time I reach his side, he's crouched down, brushing away the snow with his hands.

A small yelp escapes me, muffled by the hand I slap over my mouth. Dozens of the tiny rocks lay nestled in the snow under my window, smooth and gray, identical to the one Jake had found. The sight makes my stomach churn. There are too many to count, but at least three dozen glisten faintly in the faint light.

Dad straightens, several rocks in his hand, his face grim. He looks up at my window, then back down at the pile. Without a word, he pulls his arm back and tosses one at the window.

Tink.

The sound sends a chill down my spine, dread flooding my chest like ice water. He throws another.

Tink.

My throat tightens, bile rising as the noise reverberates in my head, taunting me with its familiarity. A third rock strikes the glass with the same hollow *tink* before falling back into the pile at his feet.

The sound hangs in the air, heavy and suffocating. Dad's hand drops to his side, the rocks slipping from his grip as he turns to look at me, his face pale and tight. My hands feel like lead, my legs rooted to the spot. The blood drains from my face as the weight of the realization settles in my chest.

Someone has been here.

Someone has been watching.

My limbs go numb, breath shallow, vision narrowing in on the offending heap of stones. It's like the ground beneath me is threatening to give way, dragging me down with it. Dad stares at the pile, his jaw clenched, shoulders rigid with tension.

"Sarah," he says, voice low but steady, "go grab a bucket. Or one of the small trash cans from the bathroom."

I freeze, mind racing in a thousand directions but unable to land on a single thought. His fingers wrap gently around my arms, grounding me.

"It's going to be okay, Doodle Bug," he says, his voice softening. "Just go get what I asked for."

I nod, the words barely registering, and force myself to move, even though my legs feel like they're moving through concrete. I throw one last glance at the rocks before stumbling toward the house. The warm air inside doesn't do a damn thing to stop the chill that's settled under my skin. I fumble under the kitchen sink and pull out the empty coffee container from the trash. The smooth plastic is cold in my shaking hands as I head back outside through the porch door.

Dad meets my eyes briefly as I hand him the container. His fingers brush mine in a fleeting moment of reassurance. Without a word, he crouches and starts scooping up the rocks. I watch him for a second, my breath curling in the air, then kneel beside him. We work together in silence, the stones cold and smooth and wrong against my skin, until every single one is inside the container.

Back in the house, the coffee tub sits ominously in the middle of the kitchen table. Our coats are still piled on the floor. Two untouched mugs of cocoa steam beside the container like they don't realize everything's changed.

The marigold flowers sit in their glass vase next to it—bright, cheerful, and completely out of place. They feel like a goddamn mockery now.

The silence is thick. Dad stares at the rocks like he's trying to will them into making sense. We each pick up our mugs and take tentative sips.

Finally, he speaks, voice low and tight. "Sarah, we need to figure out what's going on here. This isn't something we can ignore."

I nod, strained, eyes flicking between the container and the flowers. My hands shake as I set my mug down. "Jake said the flowers aren't from him."

Dad stiffens. His fingers tighten around his own mug. "What?"

"It's not him," I repeat, voice cracking. "He looked confused when I brought it up."

Dad leans forward, hand covering mine, firm and steady. "Tell me everything."

So I do. I tell him about the conversation with Jake, the rock, the look on his face when I asked about the flowers. I tell him about the first one—how it wasn't on the porch at all, but inside my room. On the windowsill.

Dad's jaw tightens. His gaze drifts back to the rocks, then returns to me. "If Jake didn't leave the flowers..." He trails off, and the unspoken implications hang between us like a guillotine.

My voice barely comes out. "There's been one on the porch every day, Dad. The first one was before Thanksgiving. It's Christmas Eve now."

The weight of that lands like a brick.

Dad doesn't speak right away. His brow furrows, eyes darken, and when he finally speaks, his voice is firm. "We need to be vigilant. This isn't a prank. Especially after..." He glances toward the vase. "After the cat."

I swallow hard. My stomach rolls. The image flashes in my mind again, and I fight the urge to gag. "Should we call the police?" I whisper.

He considers it for a long moment, then shakes his head. "We don't have enough. The rocks and flowers don't prove anything. And the cat... we should've called then, but now it's too late to connect the dots. They'll just say it's a secret admirer. Or a prank."

I want to argue, but he's right. I huff out a frustrated breath, jaw clenching as I stare into the swirling steam above my cocoa. My thoughts won't settle, swirling like the snow outside. Something's digging at me. A nagging thought I can't quite catch. Those rocks... there's something about them. Something important.

I turn the thought over and over, frustration building until it hits me like a jolt of lightning.

"Wait," I blurt, breaking the silence. "Aren't the rocks custom-made?"

Dad lifts his head slowly, eyes locking onto mine. "They are," he says, voice edged with weariness. "I had them made for your mother. The year you were born."

The memories flicker across his face like a film reel—his expression softening, shadowed by grief. The room feels heavier; the air tinged with bittersweet echoes of a past we both still carry.

I trace my fingers over the smooth surface of the rock in my palm. Its familiar texture sparks something deep—images of our old home in Georgia flashing behind my eyes. The garden. The flowers. Mom's voice as she hummed while planting. These rocks had never been just decorations. They were her dream made real—a reflection of Dad's love, handcrafted to her exact vision.

"She always hated the shape of regular landscaping rocks," I say softly, more to myself than him. "Said they ruined the look of the garden."

Dad nods, a faint smile tugging at one corner of his mouth. "She did. Wanted everything just right. I found a company that could make 'em the way she liked—round, mostly smooth. She loved those damn rocks."

My fingers close around the one in my hand. It's cool, grounding. The garden feels so close in my mind—Mom's beaming smile, the neat rows of flowers, the way those perfect rocks were tucked between the blooms like pieces of her. She didn't just plant things. She designed joy into every inch of that yard.

"We left them behind," I murmur, the words weighted with regret.

"We had to," Dad says quietly. "They belonged there. She belonged there."

His gaze drops to the container on the table. For a moment, neither of us speaks. The air stretches thin between us, heavy with everything we don't say.

My chest tightens. I remember the day we left Georgia—how it felt like losing her all over again. The rocks were too many, too heavy. We didn't have the room, the strength, or the heart to bring them. And now, some of them are here. Under my window. A thousand miles away from where they were supposed to stay.

"They're not just rocks," I say, voice low, trembling. "They're a message."

Dad's shoulders tense. His jaw clenches as the reality sets in.

"They didn't show up here by accident," I whisper. "Whoever's doing this... they followed us."

He goes still.

"They knew," I continue. "They knew what these rocks meant."

Dad exhales sharply, running a hand through his hair. "Even with that... I don't think it's enough to take to the police."

I grunt in reluctant agreement; the helplessness clawing at my chest. "So, what do we do?"

"We wait," he says, voice steady, though I can hear the unease underneath. "We keep our eyes open. If something else happens, we'll have more to go on."

The warmth of the kitchen fades quickly as I move through the motions of cleaning. The prickle at the back of my neck intensifies with each movement. Each step feels like a performance under a watchful eye I can't see. The snow outside lies still, untouched and pristine—yet the feeling of being watched gnaws at me. My eyes flick to the windows, scanning for shadows, movement, anything.

Nothing.

Just the winter night stretching on, cold and endless.

Later, as I climb into bed, the feeling doesn't leave me. Each creak of the house sends my heart into a stuttering rhythm. The rustle of wind against the windows makes me flinch. I pull the blanket tighter around me, seeking solace where none can be found.

My phone buzzes on the nightstand, and relief washes over me at Jake's name lighting up the screen. There are several unread messages from him, and a pang of guilt forms in my chest.

I smile faintly, my fingers brushing over the raccoon pendant resting against my chest, its cool surface grounding me.

> Jake: Hey Little Trash Panda. Did you make it home okay? Is everything alright?

> Jake: Baby, please reply. I need to know you're okay.

> Jake: I'm really worried, baby. If I don't hear from you soon, I'm driving down the mountain, snow or no snow.

His concern warms me—but it also tightens the knot in my chest. Should I tell him? Should I confide in him about the strange occurrences that have me doubting my sanity?

My fingers hover over the keyboard, indecision paralyzing me. Jake and I haven't been together long. What if he thinks I'm overreacting? Or worse—what if I drag him into something dangerous?

I grip the phone tighter. As much as I trust Jake, the absurdity of the situation feels too heavy to share. How could I explain the creeping fear that someone followed us from Georgia? That someone's leaving gifts at my window like it's some twisted game?

In the end, I keep it to myself. For now.

> Sarah: Hey! Yeah. Sorry about that. I didn't mean to worry you or freak you out.

His reply is immediate, the three dots blinking like they can sense my hesitation.

> Jake: What happened?

I take a shaky breath; the lie forms quickly in my mind to cover the jagged edges of truth. My fingers move deliberately, though each word feels like a betrayal.

Sarah: Ugh. I'm so embarrassed. It's so stupid.

Jake: ?

Sarah: The rock that was on your mantel is from our house in Georgia.

Sarah: They were ones my dad had made for my mom.

Sarah: Like custom made.

Sarah: Anyway… I thought we left them all behind, but apparently Dad brought a few with us.

Sarah: I never expected to see them again, and I guess it just kinda caught me off guard.

The seconds stretch into eternity as I wait for his reply.

Jake: Shit, baby. I'm sorry. If I'd known, I'd have left it where I found it.

Sarah: It's okay. You couldn't have known. I didn't even know.

Jake: Still. The last thing I ever want is to upset you.

The guilt presses harder. I grip the pendant like its weight could anchor me.

Sarah: I know.

> Sarah: I need to get some sleep. Thank you again for the wonderful present. I love you.

> Jake: I love you too. Goodnight, Little Trash Panda.

I set the phone down, my chest heavy with the weight of my words. Keeping the truth from Jake feels like a sharp thorn lodged in my ribs, but for now, it feels like the safest choice—for both of us.

The house settles around me as I try to sleep, but rest won't come. The shadows feel closer. The air, thicker. Every sound—the groan of the wooden frame, the whistle of the wind—amplifies the tension twisting inside me.

I check the blinds again and again, peeking into the darkened backyard. But there's nothing there.

Only snow.

Only silence.

I close the blinds tightly, but the sense of unease doesn't leave. The marigolds on the porch. The rocks beneath my window. The ghost of my mother's murder. They swirl in my mind like fragments of a nightmare I can't wake from.

Questions rise like waves, crashing hard and fast.

Who could be doing this?

Why now?

What do they want?

My thoughts spiral, and sleep doesn't come easily. When it finally does, it's restless—fractured by dreams I can't recall and fears I can't escape. Each time I wake, the red glow of the clock reminds me that the night is crawling by in slow motion.

Finally, the alarm blares through the room, pulling me from the haze of half-consciousness. I groan, pulling the blanket over my head, but the day doesn't wait.

It's Christmas morning. And no matter how much I want to, I can't hide in bed forever.

Chapter 27

The door clicks shut behind me, the cold left outside as I step into the warm, cozy embrace of the house.

"Ma!" I call out, my voice cutting through the quiet hum of the holiday.

"In the kitchen!" Her voice rings out, clear and familiar.

As I move through the living room, the smell of roasting meat and warm spices fills the air, teasing my stomach. My father steps out from the hallway, his broad figure bringing with it an aura of quiet strength. The image of him striding into the kitchen in those godforsaken chaps flashes in my mind, and I suppress a shudder. Pushing the memory aside, I throw my arms around him in a firm bear hug. His palm lands lightly on my back—his way of showing affection without words.

"Merry Christmas, Pop," I mutter into his shoulder.

"Merry Christmas, Son," he replies, gruff but warm.

The hug ends, but the connection lingers in the air—a silent acknowledgment of love and respect.

I head into the kitchen, where Ma is bustling around, orchestrating the chaos of pots and pans with her usual grace. She turns as I enter; her face lighting up with a smile only a mother can wear.

"Jake, darling—Merry Christmas!" she says, crossing the room to wrap me in a hug. Her arms are strong, comforting, and smell faintly of nutmeg and vanilla.

"Merry Christmas, Ma," I reply, feeling a pang of guilt for the trouble I'm probably about to cause her.

She pulls back, but her eyes linger on me—sharp and knowing.

"Are you still seeing that girl? Sarah, was it?"

I groan internally. Leave it to Ma to dive straight into my love life.

Before I can answer, Pop ambles in, making a beeline for the deviled eggs. Ma catches him in her peripheral and swats his hand away with hawk-like precision.

"Marcus Aaron Walker, don't you dare," she scolds, light but firm.

Pop smirks, the picture of a man who lives to push buttons. I bite back a grin. He could just ask nicely and she'd probably let him have one—but where's the fun in that?

My amusement fades when Ma's gaze snaps back to me, sharp enough to slice steel.

"Yes, I'm still seeing her, Ma," I admit, voice steady despite her stare.

"Humph," she mutters, tone laced with judgment and reluctant approval. She glances at Pop, her expression clear as day: Go on, then. This isn't just Christmas. It's intervention day.

Pop clears his throat, his face sobering. "Have you told her yet?"

I shake my head, avoiding both their eyes.

Ma plants her fists on her hips, letting out a loud tsk. "She's your soulmate, Jake. You can't keep putting it off. It's been well over a month since the bonfire."

The answer comes fast, even if saying it feels like tearing my ribs open.

"I know, Ma. I do."

Pop lets out a long-suffering sigh, looking skyward like he's praying for strength.

"Son," he starts, grave now, "We know it's hard, but you can't keep it from her. If she's like the others in this town, this'll be the worst betrayal she's ever felt."

Ma nods. Her voice softens, but there's steel under it. "We've worked hard to keep our family—and our friends—safe. If she finds out the wrong way..." She trails off. The rest doesn't need saying.

"She could put all of us at risk," Pop finishes.

"I know, Pop. I know," I mutter, the words bitter on my tongue.

Their concern slices through me. It's not just about Sarah knowing who—what—I am. It's about the ripple effect it'll cause if it goes wrong. The prejudice in this town isn't just a shadow. It's a monster waiting for any excuse to bare its teeth. But how the hell do I tell Sarah the truth without losing her? And if I don't—how long before the truth finds her another way?

The thought of confessing the truth to Sarah weighs on me like a mountain pressing down on my chest. My mind won't quit, churning with fears I can't shake. What if she doesn't accept it? What if she looks at me with fear, disgust—or worse—betrayal? The idea of her rejecting not just *me* but the very fabric of our lives sends a cold jolt through my veins.

Worse still is the risk of her exposing our secret to the narrow-minded jackals in this town. Willow's Haven has been home to my family for generations—a fragile balance between humans, non-predator shifters, and the predator shifters hiding in plain sight, like us. One misstep, and that peace shatters. The thought of being driven out, of losing everything we've worked so hard to protect, is a nightmare I can't afford to let come true.

Ma's gaze softens as she studies me, her lecture giving way to something gentler.

"Jake, sweetheart," she says, voice quieter now, "You can't build a future on lies. If you don't tell her soon, then you need to let her go. So long as you haven't solidified the bond, it will eventually break."

Her words land deep, thudding heavy in my chest. She's right. I can't keep hiding from Sarah. She deserves to know. *All* of it. Even if it breaks us. I suck in a breath and nod slowly, the truth settling in my bones. I'll tell her. Whatever happens after, I need her to know me—*all* of me. Even if it costs me her love. The thought slices clean through me, but the alternative? Losing her slowly under the weight of secrets? That'd be worse.

I nod. "I'll tell her. Soon, I promise."

Pop claps my shoulder and smiles. "Good man."

I get distracted watching him wrap his arms around Ma, pressing a kiss to her neck. She squeals and swats at him with her spoon, though she's smiling as she leans back into him.

A thought finally pushes through the fog in my head. "Hey—speaking of the bond... I'm not feeling that buzzing sensation anymore. After our trip, I started noticing this, uh... I don't know how to explain it—just this trickle of awareness in the back of my mind. It's like I can feel her all the time. Her emotions or something. It's—"

A loud crash from the stove cuts me off. I spin around. Both my parents are staring at me like I just announced I joined a cult.

"What?" I ask, heart thudding.

Pop's voice drops to a whisper. "You've solidified the bond, son."

"What? No," I say quickly, rewinding every moment with Sarah. "We haven't done anything different. How would that even happen?"

They look at each other. Pop's ears turn red, then his cheeks.

Is he seriously blushing?

"Um... hello?"

He clears his throat. "Well... to fully lock in the bond, you kind of have to... you know."

I stare. "I don't."

Ma smacks his arm with the back of her hand. "You have to have sex. Without protection."

I nearly choke. "And with mutual... you know, satisfaction," she adds.

"I'm sorry. What?"

Pop rubs his neck, avoiding my eyes. "You've got to practice making babies, son."

I blink. "I'm not sure I'm hearing you right."

Ma rolls her eyes and pinches the bridge of her nose. "Honestly, you two. It's just sex. Stop acting like I asked you to wrestle a gator."

I stare at her. Pretty sure my brain just froze.

"Sex, Jake. No barriers. Shared release. That's what locks the bond," Ma says with exasperation.

I scrub my hands down my face, trying to erase the memory of hearing my Ma say that.

"Why didn't you tell me this months ago?"

"We figured you were being careful," Pop says with a groan. "We hammered it into you when you hit puberty, remember?"

"Sonofabitch."

Ma gives me a warning glare but lets it slide.

"What happens now?"

"Nothing bad," Pop says. "You'll stay connected to her. Emotionally, magically. If she's in danger, you'll know. You might be able to sense where she is—but it's not like tracking her with a GPS."

I exhale. "Okay... that doesn't sound terrible."

"It's not, baby," Ma says gently. "Just... harder to undo. Before, you could've walked away and the bond would fade. Now? It's near impossible to break. It'll require magical intervention."

"What do you mean by magical intervention?"

"A witch, baby. And not just any witch, one that is connected to Gaia."

My eyes drop to the floor as a wave of guilt rushes over me. I should've talked to her well before now. I'm such an asshole.

Then Ma hits me with a question that makes me stumble back a step.

"So... does that little indiscretion of yours mean I should start knitting booties?"

"Ma!" I practically shout. "Absolutely not."

She just grins and shrugs like she didn't just drop a bomb for fun.

"It's a perfectly reasonable question, Jake. If you're gonna go around spreadin' the population paste, then you need to be prepared for the consequences."

"Christ, Ma," I groan. "It was one time."

"Once is all it takes, boy. Ask your father." She points her spoon at him.

Dad stiffens, his blush deepening.

"Dad?" I ask, brow raised.

"She... uh. She's right." He shifts like he'd rather be anywhere else but in this kitchen. "You were a welcome but surprising... uh... result of the first time your mother and I..."

"Nope!" I shout, cutting him off. "Nope. I don't need to hear any more. I got it."

Dad exhales like he just avoided a firing squad.

She swings her gaze between us, lets out a big ol' sigh, and plants her hands on her hips. "Sex, Jake. Say it. Sex! It ain't nuclear launch codes; it's biology. If you're old enough to do it, you're old enough to talk about it without actin' like I pissed in your Cheerios."

Dads had enough. He walks out without a word, leaving me alone in the lion's den.

"I *can* talk about it," I snap. "Just not with you. I'd rather believe I was dropped off by a stork who signed a non-disclosure agreement."

She throws her head back and cackles, loud and gleeful. "Oh, honey. That stork *railed* me in the back of your daddy's truck. Bent me over the tailgate, hollerin' louder than a Baptist choir on Easter Sunday."

I recoil like I've been shot and practically sprint for the door, her laughter chasing me all the way out.

The rest of the morning plays out peacefully—a stark contrast to the storm behind my ribs. We share a few quiet hours together, my parents leaving me to my thoughts, before the hum of conversation returns and the clinking of dishes grounds me in the warmth of home. But by noon, that calm is shattered in true Wilson family fashion—by the whirlwind arrival of Brent, Annie, their twin terrors Beau and Buckley, and our old friend Charlie.

The house explodes with noise and chaos.

Beau and Buckley waste no time. Their latest masterpiece? A rubber snake left smack in the middle of the kitchen counter. Ma shrieks loud enough to raise the dead, her dishtowel flying through the air while the boys dissolve into breathless giggles. Annie just sighs and mutters something about tying them to the porch.

"Beau! Buckley!" Ma snaps, her voice sharp enough to flay skin. "You apologize *right now*, or you won't see a single bite of lunch."

They don't need telling twice. The apologies tumble out in unison, faces scrunched into their best fake-sorry expressions. Charlie and I exchange smirks, leaning against the wall like spectators at a three-ring circus. Just as the dust starts to settle, the doorbell rings.

Ma breezes past, already calling out, "Jake, honey, come help me real quick!" as she disappears down the hall.

I don't bother replying—she knows I'm already moving. As I round the corner, I spot Grant stepping into the living room. A grin breaks across my face, and I close the distance.

"Merry Christmas, buddy," I say, pulling him into a quick hug.

He might play the quiet, gruff card, but Grant's got a loyal heart under that armor. Not many people get to see it. I'm lucky to be one of them.

"Merry Christmas, Jake," he says, voice low but warm.

Before we can say more, the twins launch themselves at him like wolves on fresh meat, knocking him flat in a blur of limbs and shrieking laughter. I chuckle and shake my head, already backing out of the room to go help Ma. Some things never change.

In the kitchen, I help Ma bring everything to the table and pour drinks. The clink of glasses and hum of quiet chatter make the perfect backdrop to the raucous laughter spilling from the living room. Love and chaos wrap around me like a warm blanket, a reminder of just how damn lucky I am to have this family.

The dining table buzzes with an energy only a loud, messy, tight-knit family can generate. Beau and Buckley, forever up to no good, jab at each other with forks when they think no one's watching, their giggles half-swallowed by the clatter of silverware. Charlie keeps the pace going with his usual arsenal of sharp one-liners, earning belly laughs from everyone except Ma, who throws him a look that lands somewhere between exasperated and fond. Across from me, Grant raises his glass of eggnog—so spiked it's practically a hazard—and toasts my dad for providing the "best Christmas spirit" of the season.

The mood is festive, alive, full of everything I should be grateful for. And yet, the unease coiling in my gut refuses to loosen. Every time I glance at my parents, their fleeting looks of concern jab at me like pinpricks. They're trying to hide it, but their worry cuts through the noise like a siren. I don't need to hear the words to know what they're thinking: Sarah. And me. And the secrets sitting heavy between us.

Their glances say what they won't: that she's in danger. That I'm playing with fire. That the truth I've kept buried could ruin her, ruin *everything*.

I stab a piece of turkey with my fork, but the smell turns on me—too rich, too much. I set the fork down. My stomach churns as I glance around the table, at the people I'd do anything to protect. The twins, wild and full of light. Charlie, always grinning. Grant, humming contentedly as he leans back in his chair. *This* is what's at stake.

And tomorrow, I'm the one who might set a match to it.

The thought skips through my mind like a stone over water, refusing to sink. Tomorrow, I'll tell Sarah everything. I'll hand her the truth—no filters, no shields.

The fear of her reaction is a living thing inside me, gnawing at my ribs. But it still doesn't compare to the ache I feel when I imagine losing her. If she looks at me with disgust...If she walks away without looking back...

But I *have* to do this. I can't keep hiding behind silence. Especially now that we've solidified the bond.

Across the table, Ma catches my eye. She doesn't say a word, but her gaze is steady, full of quiet understanding. She knows. I give the barest nod. She returns it with a thin, tight smile. Beside her, Pop clears his throat. His eyes meet mine for a second, softening at the edges. He knows too.

I love Sarah in a way that's carved into bone. She isn't just someone I'm dating—she's it. My balance. My reason. The thought of losing her feels like imagining the sun going dark. But this isn't just about love. It's about trust. It's about giving her the truth, no matter how dark or dangerous it might be.

Her grief is still fresh, delicate. Losing her mother cracked something deep inside her, and I've spent every moment since trying not to deepen the break. Seeing that damn rock—watching it undo her in real time—was a brutal reminder of how raw her wounds still are. But she deserves the truth. If I want her to stand beside me—if I want her to *choose* me—then I have to give her the chance. Tomorrow, I'll lay it all out. The truth of who I am. What I am. The world she's unknowingly stepped into. And I'll pray she doesn't run. I'll hope that the love between us is enough. And I'll do everything I can to prove I'm worth staying for.

My eyes blink open the next morning to the bright light streaming through the window. I groan, squinting at the open curtain, silently cursing myself for not closing it. The second groan comes when the view outside comes into focus—like the universe is having a laugh at my expense.

Thick snow blankets everything, pristine and untouched; it's a scene you'd find on a calendar. But to me, it's a curse. The drifts climb halfway up the front door, daring anyone to even think about stepping outside. My stomach twists as reality settles in: we're not leaving this mountain anytime soon.

Last night, fueled by one too many drinks, I crashed here—my parents' house, my childhood room. It felt like a good idea at the time, a cozy dose of nostalgia. But now, staring out at the frozen world, all I feel is dread. The storm hit harder than expected. Relentless. Suffocating.

It's cut off every path back to town. And the cherry on top? No cell service. No way to reach Sarah. No way to explain why I won't be showing up—why I've gone silent. The weight of what I need to tell her presses heavier than the snow piling up outside. The house feels more like a bunker than a refuge now—wood fires and backup generators the only thing keeping the cold at bay.

I sigh, rubbing at my temples, trying to shake the tightness in my chest. My brooding is interrupted by the sound of familiar footsteps. A second later, my dad appears in the doorway, steady as ever, a steaming mug of coffee in each hand.

"Here," he says, offering me one.

I take it, the heat from the ceramic a welcome relief against my chilled fingers. I sip slowly, the bitter taste grounding me just enough to dull the panic creeping up my spine.

Dad glances out the window as he drinks, his eyes scanning the white-washed world. "I'll get on the radio soon," he says, calm but firm. "Let Ranger Kyle know we're safe. After that, I'll check on the others."

I nod, my voice snagging in my throat before I manage to speak. "Could you... ask Kyle to pass a message to Sarah? Let her know I'll call as soon as I can."

The thought of her—waiting without an explanation—gnaws at me. She doesn't know about the storm. Doesn't know why I disappeared. For all I know, she's worried. Or worse—she's already thinking the worst of me. The only thing giving me comfort at the moment is feeling her in the back of my mind. She's calm and safe, and that's all I need to know.

Dad's hand lands on my shoulder, solid and steady. "Of course, son," he says. One firm pat, then he turns and disappears into the kitchen, leaving me alone with my coffee, my thoughts, and the snow.

I grip the mug tighter and stare at the flurries outside, wondering how long this isolation will last—and how much damage it'll do before I get the chance to make things right.

Chapter 28

SARAH

Restlessness claws at me, each day dragging on as if time itself has slowed. It's been almost two weeks since Jake and his family became stranded on the mountain. Ranger Kyle stops by every few days—his easy-going smile and calm reassurances doing little to soothe the gnawing ache in my chest. He's younger than I expected for someone in his role, uniform crisp, demeanor confident, but his comfort evaporates the moment he steps out the door.

I'd be falling apart if it weren't for the steady feeling of calm in the back of my mind every time I think of Jake.

I try to keep busy, drowning my unease in work and chores, but every task feels hollow—a meaningless distraction from the heavy silence filling my days. New Year's came and went without celebration, its passing only serving as a bitter reminder of how far apart we are. I dread the possibility that I might not see him until spring. The thought of months without him leaves a dull ache in my chest.

As if the waiting weren't enough, my so-called "stalker" has thrown me another curveball. For months, the orange marigold on my porch had been a sinister constant. Every morning, it waited—silent, intentional. But on New Year's Day, everything changed.

When I opened the door, instead of the usual marigold, I found a single gardenia nestled among a pile of pink camellias. I froze. The unexpected shift felt just as unnerving as the marigold once had. The next morning, there were only camellias. And the next. Now, each day brings the same soft pink petals. No note. No explanation. Just more questions: *Why? Who? What are they trying to tell me?*

The nightmares are back.

Almost every night, I wake up screaming, my father shaking me awake, his arms around me as I cry myself calm. Neither of us has slept more than a few hours at a time this past week.

This morning, I pace in front of the door, my steps tracing a well-worn path. Hesitation chains me in place. My stomach twists, dread coiling tighter with each pass. On my tenth—or maybe eleventh—lap, my father's hands land on my shoulders, grounding me. His steady presence snaps me out of my spiral.

"Sarah," he says, gently prying my fingers from my mouth. I hadn't even realized I'd been chewing my nails again.

His voice is soft but laced with worry. "You're going to end up with an infection if you keep this up."

Heat rises to my cheeks, shame mingling with frustration. I glance down at my raw nail beds, embarrassed. He's been just as shaken by all this as I have—his usually calm demeanor fractured by the same helplessness that's been eating at me. Over the past week, he's poured himself into unraveling this mystery, calling in old favors, reaching out to friends, doing anything he can to make sense of it all.

Even his best friend, Mark, got involved—driving over to our old house in Georgia to investigate. But his report only made things worse: everything there was untouched, exactly as we'd left it. Which meant that whoever had taken the rocks—and delivered them back—had stolen them directly from our old property, not from some dump or recycling center. Mark even spoke to the new owner, some guy named Victor Langley, but apparently he didn't notice anyone creeping around. Then again, he travels a lot for work.

The knowledge sends a fresh chill down my spine. Whoever's behind this didn't stumble on those rocks by accident. They planned it. They've been watching.

The steady deliveries—the marigolds, now the camellias—play like a looping message I can't decode. They feel intimate. Deliberate. A message written in gestures that only I'm meant to understand. And no matter how hard I try, the meaning stays maddeningly out of reach.

My father's hands land on my shoulders, steady and grounding. His warm grip pulls me from the spiral. His gaze is level, but concerned.

"I know you're upset," he says, voice low and measured, like he's trying to anchor me. "But obsessing over it won't help. Take a few deep breaths. Then we're getting you out of this house. I'd feel a hell of a lot better knowing you're at the bakery, surrounded by people. You'll be safer there than alone here."

The thought of stepping outside, into a world where someone might be watching, sends a ripple of anxiety through me. But I can't deny the strange comfort the bakery offers—its familiar walls, the kindness of Mr. Walters and his sons, and the quiet understanding they've always extended when I've needed space to breathe.

"I'll walk you," Dad adds firmly, already reaching for his coat. No room for argument.

Guilt stabs through me. "Dad, you don't have to do that. I've got a later shift today, and Janet'll give you hell if you're late."

He cups my cheek, the roughness of his palm grounding in its familiarity. "You come first, Doodle Bug. Always."

I swallow the lump in my throat and nod. "Then let's go now. I can hang around the shop till it's time to clock in."

He gives a small nod of agreement, and I finally reach for my jacket. My chest feels tight with the effort it takes to face the world, but I do it anyway.

As we step outside, the cold bites at my skin. But it's not the weather that makes my heart race. My eyes flick toward the edge of the porch—

Another camellia. Soft pink. Resting on the snow like it belongs there. My stomach churns. I force myself to look away.

Beside me, my father moves quietly. He bends, scoops up the flower without a word, and tosses it into the trash bin by the steps. He says nothing about it. He doesn't need to. His actions speak for themselves.

The crisp morning air seems quieter than usual as we walk, my father keeping a steady pace beside me. Each step feels heavy, weighed down by the sense of unease that clings to me like a shadow. As we reach the halfway point, a familiar sensation crawls across my skin—the prickling awareness of eyes on me. I can't stop myself from glancing over my shoulder, scanning the quiet street and rows of snow-laden houses. Nothing seems out of place. Dad stops and looks around too, his gaze sweeping our surroundings before continuing on.

By the time we reach the bakery, the feeling has burrowed deep into my chest, like an itch I can't scratch. I turn to Dad, pressing a quick kiss to his cheek. "Thanks, Dad," I whisper, not trusting my voice to hold steady.

He nods, his expression softening. "Be safe," he says, lingering a moment before heading toward the library.

The familiar chime of the bakery doorbell is a balm to my frayed nerves. The warmth of the shop wraps around me like a blanket, the scent of sugar and coffee soothing the tension in my shoulders. For the first time all morning, I exhale fully, the invisible weight of fear easing just a little. Whoever—or whatever—was following me, I have a feeling they wouldn't cross the threshold of this safe haven. Mr. Walters greets me with a smile and offers me a pastry and a cup of coffee while I wait to clock in. I return his smile and accept his kindness.

Once I'm clocked in, I find myself unexpectedly grateful that Dad convinced me to come. The hum of customers, the clink of coffee cups, and Sam's endless stream of cheerful banter manages to chase the shadows from my thoughts. By the time we're locking up, I feel like a strange mix of exhausted and calm, the storm in my chest having finally settled.

Jordan flips the lock on the front door with a satisfying click while Mr. Walters and I finish cleaning. The shop smells of sugar and cinnamon—a scent that feels like home. As I wipe down the counters, the distant buzz of my phone pulls my attention. I pause mid-wipe and glance toward Mr. Walters, who gives me a knowing nod, his permission clear without a word.

Abandoning the rag, I make a beeline for the back where my coat hangs. Jake's name glowing on the screen sends a wave of relief through me. My heart lifts just seeing it. Without hesitation, I answer, pressing the phone close like it might somehow close the distance between us.

"Jake," I exhale, his name escaping with all the pent-up emotion I've been holding in.

"Hey, Little Trash Panda," he greets, his voice wrapping around me like a warm blanket.

The sound of his nickname for me makes my chest ache in the best way. "I'm so happy to hear from you. I've missed you so much," I say, the weight of the last week spilling into my words.

"I've missed you too, baby," he replies, his tone warm and soothing. "I called as soon as I could. Cell service is still a little iffy up here, so it might be a few days before I can call again."

"I'm just glad you're okay," I breathe, the tension I've carried since Christmas beginning to ease. "I've been so worried."

"Hasn't Ranger Kyle been keeping you updated?" Jake asks, a faint edge of irritation in his voice.

"Oh—no, yes, he has," I fumble. "It's just different hearing it from you."

He chuckles, and I can practically see the smile in his voice. "Ah, I get it. Well, we're all doing fine up here. Although Mrs. Wilson's about ready to toss the twins into a snowbank."

His laugh is infectious, and I can't help but join in. "They're that bad, huh?"

"Like two feral raccoons in a pantry," he says, and his amusement is so vivid I can picture the chaos.

"Don't they have their own place?" I ask, curious now.

"Yeah, they do—just up the mountain from their folks. But like me, they got stuck at their parents' house. Too much eggnog, not enough foresight."

I smile, the image of Jake, and the twins snowed in playing clearly in my mind. "So you haven't been home?"

"Not yet," he admits, a note of frustration slipping in. "The snow's been bad. But it won't be too much longer, good Lord willin'."

My heart warms at the reassurance, though the ache of missing him lingers. "What about getting into town?"

Jake hesitates, and I hear the sigh that follows. "Not sure yet, baby. But don't worry. Soon as I can get down the mountain, I'm comin' to see you."

His words feel like a warm hand on my heart. "I can't wait. Keep me updated, okay?"

"You bet your pretty little ass I will," he says, voice low and teasing.

Before I can reply, a voice calls faintly in the background—his mother. Jake sighs, clearly reluctant.

"Sounds like I've gotta go. Mom needs something. And you don't keep that woman waiting."

"Okay. I love you," I say, the bittersweet tug of ending the call already gnawing at me.

"I love you too, Little Trash Panda," he replies, his words laced with tenderness.

The connection lingers, the silence stretching just long enough for me to think he's hung up. Then, Jake's voice drops into a husky whisper that sends a jolt straight through me. "Can I call you later tonight so I can hear your sweet voice in my ear while I pleasure myself? My imagination can only get me so far, and I'm starting to forget all the little sounds you make when I'm buried deep inside you."

A sharp gasp escapes me, and my cheeks flame as I slap a hand over my mouth. My eyes dart around the room, relief flooding me when I see Mr. Walters and his sons still engrossed in their tasks at the front of the bakery. "Jake," I hiss, trying to sound admonishing but failing as my voice trembles with a smile.

He laughs, a deep, wicked sound that only intensifies the heat pooling low in my belly. "I'll call you tonight, baby," he murmurs, his promise thick with intention.

Before I can respond, his mom's voice calls out again, louder this time, and the line disconnects.

Lowering the phone from my ear, I shake my head, trying to tamp down the smile tugging at my lips. My cheeks still burn, and my pulse thrums with a mix of embarrassment and excitement. Taking a deep breath, I will the warmth to subside, though the thought of Jake's words lingers, leaving me unable to fully suppress the grin splitting my face.

I glance toward the front of the store, relieved that no one seems to have noticed my flustered state. Jake always knows how to leave me completely undone, even from miles away.

Each passing day without hearing Jake's voice feels like another weight added to the ever-growing pile of frustration pressing on my chest. Nights stretch into mornings with no calls, no messages—no end in sight. The mountain storms are relentless; each flake of snow further solidifies the wall between us. My fingers itch to dial his number, but I know it would only go unanswered.

I groan, the sound echoing in the stillness of my room, and drop my head into my hands. The ache of missing him is more than physical; it claws at my mind, making my chest feel hollow. As the storm outside rages on, a stubborn thought forms in the back of my mind: next time, there won't be this much distance between us. Whether that meant him staying with me during bad weather or us braving the cabin together, I'd make sure this never happened again.

The notion startles me. I've never felt this way about anyone before—never entertained the thought of living with someone, sharing my space so intimately. Even during college, the thought of sharing a dorm room had been off-putting. But now, the idea of Jake's things mingled with mine, his presence filling every corner of my life, makes my chest flutter in a way that is both exciting and unnerving to me. I shake my head, trying to dismiss the thought. There's no use dwelling on something so far out of reach when I haven't even seen him in weeks.

After what felt like an eternity of waiting, nearly four more weeks had passed before the roads finally cleared enough to drive on. The bakery door bursts open with such force it startles me, and before I can react, Jake strides in like a man on a mission. His arms wrap around me in an instant, lifting me off the ground as his lips press against mine in a heated, desperate kiss. A surprised squeal escapes me, morphing into a laugh as he kisses every part of my face he can reach.

From behind the counter, Mrs. Anderson's sharp glare shoots daggers at us, but Mr. Walters's booming laugh fills the space. "Go on, Sarah," he says kindly, waving me off. "Take the rest of the day."

I blink at him, my gratitude momentarily leaving me speechless. "Are you sure? I can—"

"Go," he says, his tone firm but kind. "You've earned it."

Jake's hand clasps mine before I can protest further, pulling me out of the bakery amidst my breathless giggles. He guides me to his truck, opening the door like a true gentleman and helping me in before quickly circling around to his side. As the truck rumbles to life and he pulls onto the road, I can't help but steal glances at him. His lopsided grin, the way his hands grip the steering wheel—it all feels like coming home.

"Where are we going?" I ask, curiosity bubbling beneath my excitement.

He gives me a sly smile, his eyes sparkling with mischief. "Somewhere special."

The drive up the mountain feels both endless and too short. The landscape feels familiar, the snow-covered trees and winding roads sparking a memory. My heart swells as we crest a familiar hill, and the truck rolls to a stop.

"The cliffs," I breathe as I step out of the truck, the scene taking my breath away.

The last time we came here, autumn leaves painted the landscape in fiery reds and oranges, the earthy scent of pine mingling with the crispness of the air. Now, winter has transformed it into a serene wonderland. Snow blankets the ground, weighing down the branches of evergreens and leaving the world quiet and still. The air is cold and sharp, carrying with it the faint scent of pine and frost.

Jake's arms wrap around my waist from behind, pulling me against his chest. His lips find the sensitive spot where my neck meets my shoulder, his warm breath sending shivers through me. I exhale shakily, leaning into him as he kisses a trail up my neck, sending waves of anticipation coursing through me. "I've missed you," he murmurs, his lips brushing my skin. A hum of pleasure escapes me as I tilt my head, granting him better access. Each kiss he places along my neck, every flick of his tongue, leaves me aching for more. When his lips pause just behind my ear, my body responds instantly, a pulse of heat blooming low in my belly.

Then, as if on cue, the warmth disappears. My eyes fly open, and frustration swirls inside me as he steps back. The sudden absence of his heat leaves me cold and confused. I open my mouth to protest, but Jake takes my hand, threading his fingers through mine, and starts leading me toward the trail through the woods. The gesture should be comforting, but an unfamiliar pit of anxiety blooms in my stomach, twisting and turning with each step we take. My mind spirals. Why did he stop? Did I do something wrong? Where are we going? What if he's changed his mind about us? What if the time apart made him realize I'm not good enough for him?

The questions churn in an endless loop, suffocating me with their weight.

I can't take it anymore. My feet dig into the snow, halting him mid-step. Jake turns, his lips parting as if to question me, but the expression on my face must have said enough. His brows furrow, and his concerned gaze searches mine. He steps closer, one gloved hand cupping my cheek as he tips my face toward his.

"What's wrong, Little Trash Panda?" His voice, soft and full of concern, threatens to break me.

The worry in his tone forces me to shove my insecurities down, burying them beneath a forced smile. "Nothing's wrong," I say, but the breathy edge to my voice gives me away. "You just haven't given me a proper kiss since we got here."

The corners of his mouth twitch into a brief, knowing smile before his lips crash onto mine. The force of his kiss sends a shockwave through me, silencing every self-doubt that has clawed its way into my mind. My hands find his shirt, gripping it tightly as though letting go would pull me back into that spiral. His tongue slides against mine, igniting a fire that burns away the cold air around us.

He pulls me closer, one hand sliding to my waist as the other cradles my face. His touch feels electric, grounding me in the here and now. Frustrated by the layers of clothing between us, I let my gloves fall to the snow, my hands slipping under his jacket. His skin burns under my icy fingers, earning a hiss from his lips. But he doesn't stop; his mouth never leaves mine as his hands explore my back.

The heat between us quickly grows unbearable. My fingers find the waistband of his sweatpants, and I'm rewarded with the thick weight of his cock, hot and eager, against my palm. Jake groans, his head falling back as I stroke him with deliberate slowness. His reaction spurs me on, and before I could think, I sink to my knees in the snow, ignoring the wet chill that seeps through my jeans.

Pulling him free, I take him into my mouth, savoring the taste of him. His hand finds the back of my head, fingers tangling in my hair as I work him. Each groan, each hiss of pleasure that escapes him, sends a jolt of satisfaction through me. My tongue swirls around his cock, my hand cupping his balls, trying to warm them against the bite of the cold.

"Ah, fuck, Sarah," he gasps, his hips twitching against me. The sound of his voice, raw with need, is enough to send heat pooling between my legs.

Just as his breathing grows ragged, Jake pulls me to my feet, his hands firm but gentle. His mouth finds mine again; the kiss is deep and hungry, stealing what little breath I have left. When he finally pulls back, his eyes are dark with heat, and the words that follow send a shiver down my spine—not from the cold, but from the promise they carry.

"If I'm gonna cum, Little Trash Panda," he growls, voice low and rough, "it's gonna be inside that sweet little cunt."

The words punch the air from my lungs. My response is instant, voice low and breathless.

"Then fuck me, Jake."

He doesn't waste a second. Tucking himself back into his pants, he grabs my hand and leads me to the truck. The cab door flies open, and he gently guides me inside, his touch urgent but careful. I half-sit, half-lie across the bench seat, my pulse pounding as he climbs in after me—his gaze locked on mine, fierce and focused. That look sends a thrill through me, sharp and electric.

As the door slams shut behind him, Jake shrugs off his coat, tossing it behind the seat. His hands find me immediately, working fast to peel away layers until I'm left in nothing but my undershirt and panties. The air bites at my skin, but the heat in his eyes burns hotter.

He leans in close, voice low and rough against the shell of my ear.

"Fuck, you're perfect."

His grip tightens around my hips as he pushes me across the seat, pinning my back to the cold door. A flicker of worry crosses my mind—will it hold?—but it vanishes the second he drags my panties aside and dips between my thighs.

The warmth of his mouth hits me like a jolt, his tongue circling my clit with slow, practiced strokes. A strangled moan tears from my throat as my fingers tangle in his hair, hips jerking against his face. He groans in response, the vibration deep and hungry, sending pulses of pleasure through me.

Then his fingers slide inside—thick, sure, curling just right. My body arches with a gasp, head falling back against the icy window. The contrast between the cold glass and the fire building inside me is dizzying. Jake's tongue and fingers move with relentless rhythm, coaxing sounds from me I couldn't hold back if I tried.

"Oh, fuck, Jake," I gasp, barely able to breathe. "Please, please, please don't stop."

He doesn't. He drives me harder, faster, until the pressure inside me coils tight and sharp. And then—one last flick of his tongue, one perfect drag of suction over my clit—and I shatter.

My orgasm crashes through me, legs trembling, muscles clenching around his fingers as my cries echo through the cab. He doesn't stop until I'm nothing but gasps and aftershocks, sagging against the door in a haze of bliss.

As the wave fades, a new ache blooms beneath it—deeper, needier. I don't just want him now. I need him.

Jake seems to know. He withdraws his fingers slowly, dragging them from me with maddening care. Then he sucks them clean with a low groan, never breaking eye contact. The heat in his gaze steals the breath from my lungs all over again.

Without a word, he pulls me upright, wrapping me in his arms. I blink, dazed, as he shifts us until his hands settle on my thighs and lift me into his lap. My knees sink into the seat on either side of him as he shoves his pants just far enough down to free himself. The brush of rough fabric against my skin is barely a blip—I'm too focused on the heat of him against me.

One hand wraps around his cock, guiding it to my entrance. The other snakes around my back, pulling me in close as our mouths crash together again. I gasp into the kiss as he thrusts inside, stretching and filling me in one smooth motion.

The sound I make is swallowed by his mouth, my fingers digging into his shoulders as I adjust to the thick, perfect pressure of him.

His hands slide to my hips, steadying me as I start to move. I rise and fall with a slow, grinding rhythm, each stroke drawing him deeper. The friction is exquisite—enough to make me tremble, enough to drive me wild. My chest presses against his, our breath mingling in short, desperate bursts. When his teeth graze my collarbone, my whole body tightens around him.

"Fuck, Sarah," he groans, voice raw with need. His hands tighten on my hips, guiding my movements as his thrusts rise to meet mine. Each roll of his hips sends sparks shooting through me, and I can feel myself spiraling again, the pleasure building faster this time.

The truck rocks slightly with our rhythm, windows fogging as heat and breath fill the cab. The world outside disappears—just snow and silence—but inside, its heat and urgency and the ache of being reunited. All that matters is the way Jake feels inside me, the way our bodies move together, the way his voice catches when he whispers my name like a prayer.

His grip firms, lifting and lowering me with steady precision, our bodies colliding in a rhythm that leaves me breathless. The pressure builds—sharp, heady, desperate—but just as I'm about to fall, Jake stills completely.

I whimper, my body trembling with need. Confused, I meet his gaze, and the playful smirk on his lips sends a new shiver down my spine.

He leans in, voice low and commanding. "Grind on my cock, baby. Take your pleasure."

The words unravel me and hit me like a match to gasoline.

I plant my hands on his shoulders, shifting my hips into a slow, deliberate grind. The stretch, the friction—it's too much and not enough all at once. His cock hits deep with each roll, my clit brushing against him in just the right way. I gasp, hips moving in search of more.

Jake's hands slip under my shirt, cupping my breasts through my bra, his thumb teasing my nipple until it's tight and aching. Every nerve in my body feels electric, strung tight and burning. The pressure coils tighter. My rhythm falters. My thighs shake. Jake takes over. His hands clamp down on my hips, holding me steady as he thrusts upward, slow but hard. His cock drives deep, angled perfectly, and then his thumb is on my clit, rubbing firm and sure.

"Fuck, Jake," I gasp, the words nearly a sob.

He grins, wicked, then presses harder—and I shatter.

The orgasm crashes through me, hard and all-consuming. My pussy clenches around him, my hips jerking. I cry out, lifting instinctively, almost slipping off his cock.

Jake growls and pulls me back down, not letting me go.

He takes control completely, lifting me just enough to thrust up into me with punishing intensity. The sound of skin meeting skin, his deep groans, my ragged cries—it fills the cab like music, wild and breathless.

My legs are useless, trembling violently. But Jake holds me strong and steady, his focus unshakable. The next orgasm builds fast, dizzying.

"Jake," I gasp, clinging to him.

He slams into me one final time, a guttural moan tearing from his throat as he spills deep inside me—just as my climax rips through me again, raw and powerful.

Spent, I collapse against his chest, face tucked into the crook of his neck. My heartbeat thunders, echoing his. His arms close around me, and the silence that follows is thick with warmth and something deeper.

A soft laugh bubbles from my lips, hazy and breathless. "Well," I murmur, teasing, "that was... productive."

Jake chuckles, his hand tracing lazy circles on my back.

"You bring out the best in me, Little Trash Panda," he murmurs, pressing a kiss to my temple.

Chapter 29

SARAH

The air inside the cab is thick with the lingering heat of our bodies as Jake and I fumble back into our clothes. The tight space makes the task clumsy—elbows bumping, knees knocking, laughter breaking the quiet like little sparks.

Once dressed, Jake pushes open the door and steps into the cold, braving the icy air to retrieve my gloves. His breath curls in visible clouds as he bends to pluck them from the snow.

When he returns, he presses the gloves gently into my hands, then tugs me close. His lips brush mine in a kiss that's unexpectedly soft. It's not like the fiery kisses we'd shared moments ago—this one is tender, reverent. A blush creeps up my cheeks as Jake's gaze lingers on me, warm and steady. It feels like he's memorizing me. The intensity is overwhelming—but comforting. It fills the corner of my mind where he's always waiting with something bright and quiet and good.

I pull my gloves on slowly, my thoughts drifting to my parents. Their marriage had been the kind you only read about—steadfast, affectionate, the kind that made you believe in forever. Growing up watching them, I'd always wondered if a love like that was possible for me. And now, standing here with Jake, I think... maybe it is.

He crouches to retie his bootlaces, his fingers working fast, movements practiced. But there's a softness to him as he moves, a quiet thoughtfulness that tugs at something deep inside me. My heart aches in the best way. This man—this frustrating, patient, fiercely loving man—is mine. The thought is almost too much to hold.

Jake looks up and catches me staring. That boyish grin I love spreads across his face. "You ready for that walk?" he asks, teasing.

I nod, motioning toward the door. Jake opens it again, and the cold rushes in like a slap to the lungs, stealing my breath for a second. I hesitate—just for a heartbeat. But he's already holding his hand out, palm open and steady. I take it without a second thought.

His grip grounds me as I slide from the cab, boots crunching softly in the snow. The door shuts with a metallic clang, the sound loud in the quiet. Almost immediately, Jake finds my hand again, threading his fingers through mine like it's second nature.

"Come on," he murmurs, his voice low and sure. He tugs me gently toward the trail.

This time, I follow without hesitation. The doubts that clung to me earlier—questions, fears, insecurities—melt away with every step, carried off by the wind and the steadiness of Jake at my side.

The woods envelop us in a hush, everything muffled by snow. The familiar trails feel enchanted beneath winter's touch—trees cloaked in white, branches sagging with frost, the air sharp and scented with pine. Our steps fall into rhythm; the only sound is the crunch of boots over fresh snow.

I steal a glance at Jake, watching how his features soften in the quiet. For a while, he looks peaceful—his eyes calm, his mouth relaxed. But as we go deeper into the woods, something in him shifts. His shoulders draw tight. His jaw clenches. His hand grows restless in mine. There's a quiet storm building beneath his calm, and I can feel it gathering with every step.

"Jake?" My voice is tentative, barely more than a breath.

He stops walking before I can say more, clearing his throat—a sharp sound that cuts through the quiet. Then he turns to face me, eyes locking onto mine with that steady, unreadable intensity of his.

The woods are silent around us, just the crunch of snow beneath our boots and the whisper of wind through bare branches. Jake leans in slightly, his voice low and careful.

"So, what made you apply for the bakery position? I don't think we've ever really talked about it," he says. "I remember you telling me that you took a break from college after your mom died. I would've thought you'd want to pick it back up once you got settled."

It's a simple question. Casual. But it lands like a pebble tossed into still water, sending ripples out in all directions.

I glance down, fingers working nervously at the edge of my jacket. It doesn't feel like the real thing he wants to ask, but I answer anyway.

"I needed a distraction, honestly," I admit, my voice softer than I meant it to be. A faint smile touches my lips, more reflex than genuine. "Plus, the employee discount is a nice bonus."

He watches me closely, head tilted just enough to show he isn't letting it go.

"May I ask why you needed a distraction?"

The way he says it—gentle, but persistent—tightens something in my chest. I draw a shallow breath, my gaze slipping away. But when I look back at him, his expression hasn't changed. Still open. Still kind.

"My mom," I begin, and just saying it makes my throat go dry. "She was murdered... in our home."

The words hang there between us. Heavy. Final. Jake freezes. A long second passes before he exhales, sharp and shaky.

"Shit," he mutters. But something in his eyes has gone distant—like he's doing math in his head, and the numbers aren't good.

His gloved hand finds mine, our fingers intertwining with a kind of quiet urgency. The contact steadies me—grounds me—even as I start to drift.

"I... I found her body," I manage, my voice shaking. "There was so much blood."

He doesn't speak. Just steps forward and folds me into his arms. His warmth surrounds me, and his hand moves in slow, deliberate circles across my back.

"You don't have to say anything you don't want to," he murmurs, voice low, close, safe.

Part of me wants to stop there. To bury it again. But if Jake's going to be in my life, he has to know. Even the ugly parts.

"I know," I whisper. "I wanted to, though."

His arms tighten around me, the side of his face brushing gently against my hair.

"I'm so sorry, Little Trash Panda." His voice hitches on the nickname, like it catches in his throat. But he finishes it anyway, softer this time. Almost apologetic. "That must have been... God, I can't imagine."

I press my face into his chest, drawn to the steady rhythm of his heart-beat, to the way he holds me like I won't scare him off no matter what I say.

"Thank you," I murmur. "I couldn't stay in that house anymore. I was commuting to my local college at the time, and just walking in every day, seeing the place where she died—it was too much. I started failing my classes and eventually dropped out. The nightmares were constant after I found her. My dad got so worried about me that he decided we needed to move. He thought a fresh start would help... and that's how we ended up here."

Jake nods slowly, his touch still gentle on my back. He doesn't try to fix it. Doesn't rush to speak. Just listens.

"It sounds like your dad made the right call," he says, voice low but steady.

"Yeah," I breathe. "The nightmares aren't as bad anymore. And it helps that there are no predator shifters here. It feels safe."

The moment the words leave my mouth, I feel it. His hand falters. Not for long, but enough to notice.

"Predator shifters?" he asks, and something's different in his tone now. Something tight and unreadable.

"Yeah," I say. The familiar ache starts up again in my chest. "A wolf shifter killed her. My dad thought moving to a town with only humans and non-predator shifters would be the best thing for us... and he was right."

The shift in Jake is instantaneous. His body goes rigid. The comfort in his arms disappears, replaced by a tension that coils beneath his skin. His features harden—still, composed, but no longer open. He looks like someone bracing for a blow.

"Jake?" I ask, pulling back slightly to meet his eyes. Concern laces my voice as I study his suddenly unreadable face. "Are you okay?"

He blinks, shaking his head as if to clear it before forcing a smile. "Yeah... yeah, I'm okay," he says, but the unease lingers in his tone. "Predator shifters and all... Sounds like you guys picked the right place to be."

The smile he gives me doesn't quite reach his eyes, and though his arms are still around me, the warmth from his earlier embrace feels like it's slipped away.

The air between us feels heavier, despite Jake's attempt at reassurance. Something about the way his lips tug upward—strained and unsure—and the way his gaze flickers away from mine hints at an inner conflict. There's a sadness lurking in his expression, paired with a tension in his posture that wasn't there before. He's holding something back. I can feel it.

As I watch him, a thought flickers in the back of my mind—his family moved here after his brother's death. Jake never talks about it in detail. Just vague references, always brushed aside. Could a predator shifter have been involved? The way his shoulders locked up when I mentioned wolf shifters... the way his fingers twitched at his side like he was wrestling with something he couldn't say—it all feels too pointed to be coincidence.

I want to reach out. To ask. To offer him the same kind of comfort he gave me when I let my guard down. But the wall he's built around this moment is obvious. I don't want to push and make him retreat even further.

So I swallow the questions rising in my throat and let the silence settle between us—soft, but heavy. A quiet acknowledgment of the weight he's carrying.

As I study his profile, jaw tight and eyes distant, I make a silent promise: I'll be patient. When he's ready to let me in, I'll be here—steady, unwavering. Jake is worth that. Whatever he's hiding, whatever shadows he's fighting, I'll be the one who stays.

Chapter 30

The forest feels quieter now. The weight of Sarah's words lingers in the air as we make our way back to the truck. Her pain—raw and unfiltered—clings to me like a second skin, making my chest ache with a helplessness I can't shake. I tighten my arm around her, as if I can somehow shield her from the horrors of her past. I know it isn't enough. The warmth of her body pressed against mine stands in stark contrast to the cold shadows stretching across the forest floor. And yet inside me, a storm churns.

"Sarah," I murmur, the word barely making it past the knot in my throat. The truth claws at my chest, desperate to escape, but fear wraps around me like iron chains.

I don't know what terrifies me more—losing her, or watching her expression shift from warmth to fear. She looks up at me, concern softening her features. Her hand finds mine, thumb brushing gently across my knuckles in silent reassurance.

"Jake, is everything okay?"

I swallow hard. My mouth is dry, and the words I need twist in my throat, coiling tighter with every heartbeat.

"I..." My voice cracks. I want to tell her. I need to. I can't keep pretending to be someone I'm not. But the thought of her pulling away—of recoiling from me—makes my stomach turn.

"I want to be honest with you, Sarah," I blurt, the words tumbling out before I can stop them. "There's something I need to tell you."

She falters, stopping in her tracks. Her full attention turns to me, her eyes wide and searching. "What is it, Jake?"

I stare into those eyes—the ones that lit something in me the moment we met—and feel the crushing weight of my cowardice settle in again. Can I really risk dimming that light? Can I risk her seeing a monster where she sees a man now?

"Promise me," I whisper. "Promise me you'll still see me the same way."

Her brow furrows, just a flicker, before her face softens. She gives me a small, reassuring smile.

"Jake, I promise. You can trust me with anything."

I draw a shaky breath. My chest is tight, ribs locked around the truth like a cage. For one brief second, I want to tell her. I almost do. But the fear is louder. Sharper. And before I can stop myself—I backpedal.

"I found out something not too long ago," I say, forcing a smile I don't feel. "According to several people I know... soulmates are real."

Sarah gives me a look of pure disbelief—one brow raised, hip cocked. I almost laugh at how damn adorable she looks, but the humor dies before it can reach my lips. I sigh instead.

"It's true, baby," I whisper, trying my best to sound calm—even though my heart's about to beat out of my chest.

She rolls her eyes. "I know you're just being silly, Jake. Soulmates are just fairy stories told to children."

I smile at that—because I'd said the exact same thing once. Hell, I still remember how dumbfounded I felt when I first learned the truth. I reach out, gently gripping her arms and turning her to face me.

"I know it sounds ridiculous. I thought the same thing when I first found out. But it's real, Sarah." I draw in a deep breath, nerves tightening my chest. "I know you feel it. I do too. That little nagging spot in the back of your mind—that tug you can't explain? That's me. That's us."

Her eyes widen, and I know I've struck something real.

"Pay attention to it—right now," I say, my voice soft but steady. "You'll feel my nervousness. My anxiety. Everything I'm feelin' in this moment."

She closes her eyes. The quiet of the forest wraps around us, thick and heavy. I hold my breath as I wait.

Then her eyes fly open, wide and stunned. Her hands shoot up, grabbing my arms.

"I can feel it," she says, her voice trembling with awe. "Oh my God, Jake... what—what does this mean?"

"Nothin' bad, baby. I swear." I brush my thumbs over her arms. "It just means that my magic called to yours. We share a deeper connection than just love. It's... soul-deep."

Silent tears begin to roll down her cheeks, and the sight of them squeezes my chest. I know I should feel relieved, and part of me does—but the coward in me still clings to the lie I haven't told her. I've given her this piece of the truth, hoping it'll be enough. But I know it's not.

Then it hits me. That lingering warmth I feel in the back of my mind—her emotions brushing against mine—it's joy. Blinding, over-whelming joy.

She practically jumps into my arms, wrapping herself around me. Tiny sobs escape between the kisses she peppers along my jaw, and I hold her tight, letting out a shaky breath of relief. Her happiness is like sunlight breaking through storm clouds. It softens the guilt—for now.

But that guilt... it's still there. Pressing in.

I bury it, holding her tighter, resting my chin on her head as I close my eyes and try to pretend I'm not lying by omission. I know I'm being a coward. She deserves the full truth—that I'm a predator shifter. That part of me is exactly what she fears most.

I've let fear win. Again. I don't know how much longer I can keep the secret. Or what will happen when she finds out. But for now, I cling to her—and to the fragile peace between us—knowing deep down that this moment won't last forever.

The truck idles quietly as we turn onto Sarah's street; the headlights slicing through the soft glow of porch lights lining the neighborhood. The scent of pine and damp earth lingers—a subtle reminder of the time we just spent together. My grip on the steering wheel tightens as an invisible weight settles on my chest, each passing moment amplifying the internal battle I can't seem to outrun.

I kill the engine, climb out, and circle the front to help Sarah from the cab. My arm slips instinctively around her waist, pulling her close as we walk toward her door. The warmth of her body grounds me, but it does little to quiet the storm raging inside. I try to throw up some kind of mental shield—anything to keep her from sensing too much.

"Thank you for today, Jake," Sarah murmurs, her voice soft and full of quiet gratitude. Her hands grip mine, her touch a balm against the chaos in my heart. "It meant so much to me."

Her words tug at something deep inside, but the guilt simmering beneath my ribs won't let go. I squeeze her hand gently and force a smile.

"You're welcome. I'm glad we could spend part of the day together."

Her brow furrows, gaze narrowing as she studies me. "Is everything okay?"

I swallow hard, forcing the tension from my voice. "Yeah," I lie. "Just tired, that's all."

At her door, she turns to face me fully, hand still clutching mine. Her eyes search mine, looking for answers I can't give.

"You know you can talk to me, right?" she says. "Whatever's going on, I want to be here for you. I can feel the wave of emotions rolling off of you without even trying."

Her words hit me like a punch to the gut, her sincerity cutting through the defenses I've been clinging to. Her words hit like a punch to the gut—sharp, unexpected, and laced with sincerity. My throat tightens as I force a nod, mentally kicking myself for drawing attention to a bond she clearly hadn't discovered yet.

"I know, baby. I do. And I appreciate it more than you know." My voice is low, almost hoarse. "I'm just... not ready to talk about it yet. But you'll be the first person I turn to when I am."

She gives me a small, reassuring smile, but the worry in her eyes lingers. She reaches up and brushes a strand of hair from my forehead, the gesture so tender it makes my chest ache.

"I love you, Jake," she whispers. The weight in her voice nearly buckles my knees.

"I love you too," I manage, my voice barely above a breath. I lean in, kissing her softly. Her lips are warm against mine, a brief connection that leaves behind more guilt than comfort. She lingers for a moment before stepping back.

"Goodnight, Jake," she says, her voice like a soft melody.

"Goodnight," I echo, the sound of her door clicking shut ringing louder than it should.

The drive home is a blur—dark streets and suffocating silence. The hum of the engine can't drown out the war in my head. The weight of what I'm hiding crushes me, heavier now than ever. Each mile stretches the dread inside me tighter. I know what's coming. I can feel it looming—a choice I can't avoid. A decision between protecting my family... and risking everything for her.

Tears sting the corners of my eyes, blurring familiar roads. The image of Sarah looking at me with fear—pulling away in disgust—gnaws at me. The silence tonight feels like a betrayal. A lie. One that grows more dangerous with every hour I keep it.

She hates predator shifters. I saw it in her eyes when she spoke of her mother's murder. Felt it in the way her voice cracked when she said "wolf." Her hatred runs deeper than I expected, and the truth about me? About what I am? It isn't just a threat to our relationship. It's a wrecking ball aimed straight at her trust in me. My hands clench the wheel as I pull into my driveway. The tears finally spill over. In her eyes, I'll always be the wolf. The monster in the dark. And I don't know if I have the strength to tell her.

A raw scream rips from my throat, shaking the cab. "FUCK!" The word claws out of me—ragged, broken, soaked in pain. I slam my fist into the steering wheel again and again. The sting travels up my arms, but it's nothing compared to the ache inside my chest. My heart feels shredded—torn piece by piece.

I stumble out of the truck, boots crunching in the snow. My knees buckle beneath me. I collapse, the cold biting through denim and flesh, but I barely register it. My stomach heaves. I retch, choking on sobs as my hands claw at the snow like it might anchor me. But nothing helps. Nothing calms the storm inside. My magic surges. I can't stop it.

The shift tears through me—violent, primal, unrelenting. Fur explodes across my skin, my muscles stretch and snap, and a mournful howl bursts from my throat. It echoes into the sky, filled with every ounce of grief I've buried, every lie I've told, every moment of silence I've let stretch too long.

I tilt my head back and howl again—louder this time, shaking the trees. For a second, the pain lessens. But only for a second. Then—bam. A blur of fur and muscle slams into me, sending me sprawling into the snow. My wolf snarls on instinct—ready to fight—but the scent hits me fast. Familiar. Sharp. Dominant. And I hesitate.

Rolling onto my side, I catch sight of Charlie just as his wolf form shifts—his body melting back into human in one fluid, practiced motion. His breath comes in harsh, visible gasps, chest heaving as he glares down at me with a mix of fury and concern.

"What the fuck, man?!" he snaps, his voice rough and raw, cutting through the chilly night like a whip.

The words hang there—sharp, demanding. But I have no answer. My wolf crouches low in the snow, weighed down by despair, the storm inside me too loud to let anything out.

A groan escapes my lips as I roll in the bed, every movement a protest from my aching body. Before I can process anything, gravity betrays me. I'm airborne for a split second—the world tilting—before I land with a harsh thud on unforgiving hardwood. Pain shoots through my limbs, amplifying the pounding already hammering in my skull.

"Ah, fuck," I mutter, voice muffled against the floorboards. The cool wood beneath my cheek offers the faintest reprieve from the chaos in my head. I crack one eye open, squinting at the dim light filtering through heavy curtains—each ray a dagger to my brain.

Rolling onto my back, I take a moment to orient myself. Blurry surroundings. Unfamiliar. The scent of stale alcohol and a faint tang of motor oil hits me—and that's when I know.

I'm not in my room.

My gaze sweeps the floorboards. No soft rug. No familiarity. Just cold, hard reality.

"Charlie," I groan under my breath, fragments of last night snapping back in jagged pieces. His massive, furry form slamming into me. The gruff silence as he all but dragged me to his place. The blur of too many drinks going down way too fast.

My muscles scream in protest as I push myself upright. Knees shaking, I stagger to my feet and catch myself against the wall, blinking through the fog in my head.

I glance down. My shoes are gone. My belt buckle has left a bruising ache in my gut. My shirt's twisted and clinging to me like I lost a fight with a tornado. I burp, and my mouth fills with the bitter taste of old beer and worse decisions—but none of it compares to the regret simmering in my chest.

A clatter outside jerks me fully awake. Wincing, I grab my shoes from where they'd been tossed across the room and shove them on. In the kitchen, I reach for the cookie jar on the counter—and there it is. My phone, nestled like a sleeping secret. Charlie's foolproof anti-drunk-dial strategy: hide the phones where drunk brains won't look. Smart. Annoying. Effective.

I chug a glass of water, pop some pain meds, and brace myself before stepping outside.

The morning sun hits me like a hammer, and I flinch, throwing up a hand to shield my eyes. "Shit," I mutter, squinting against the glare.

A loud clang of metal on metal, followed by a colorful string of swearing, echoes from the garage.

Charlie.

Rounding the house, I find him elbow-deep under Betsy's hood, his battered Ford pickup. Tools are scattered across the bench, an oil-streaked rag dangling uselessly from his back pocket—though it hardly matters. He wipes his hands on his jeans anyway.

"Hey, man. How's the head?" he calls without looking up, voice laced with amusement and mild irritation.

"Nothing a little pain meds can't handle," I say, leaning in the doorway, trying to sound light—but last night's weight sits heavy on my shoulders. I hesitate, then clear my throat.

"Charlie, can we talk?"

He stops, straightens up, and wipes his hands on the rag before tossing it aside. His expression lands somewhere between annoyed and concerned.

"Now you want to talk," he mutters, crossing his arms. "If you'd come here first last night, I wouldn't have had to field calls all damn night. Your dad is pissed, man."

The guilt hits like a sucker punch. I reach behind my neck, rubbing it.

"Shit. Is it bad?"

His eyes narrow, but his tone softens. "No. Luckily, no one in town hit the panic button. I managed to calm everyone down when they found out you were... well, not yourself. But you need to call your dad. Sooner rather than later."

I nod, a pit settling in my stomach. "I'll handle it."

"Yeah, you'd better," he says, gruff but not unkind. "Because he's not the only one worried about you. You damn near cleared out my liquor cabinet."

"Sorry about that." I sigh. I never drink that much. This whole thing with Sarah has me twisted every which way but up.

He looks at me expectantly, like he's waiting for me to give him the answer to a puzzle on *Wheel of Fortune*. You know, fill in the blanks and all that.

The morning air bites at my skin, and Charlie's voice cuts through the stillness.

"What happened last night, Jake?" His tone is steady, but it's laced with concern.

I hesitate, the truth rising like bile in my throat.

"Sarah..." My voice falters. I trail off, not sure where the hell to start.

Charlie steps closer. His hand lifts toward my shoulder—but he stops short before making contact. His warm brown eyes meet mine, offering reassurance and silently urging me to continue. He isn't just a friend; he's family. Someone who understands the stakes of what I'm about to confess.

"Tell me," he breathes.

I draw a shaky breath, my throat dry as I force the words out. "She told me her mom was murdered by a wolf shifter. She's terrified of predator shifters, Charlie. I was going to tell her the truth yesterday, but after hearing that—" I pause, my voice cracking. "I couldn't tell her I'm a wolf shifter."

Charlie's gaze hardens, though the empathy in his eyes doesn't fade. The weight of my admission settles between us.

"Jaaake," he says with a long sigh.

"I know," I groan.

"So, let me get this straight. You didn't tell her last night because she ended up telling you how her mom died?"

"Pretty much sums it up, yeah."

"And your solution to that was to freak out, nearly out us to the whole town, and drink me out of liquor?"

A wave of heat rolls over my cheeks. I nod, embarrassed.

"Fuckin' hell." He groans. "What was the end game here? Were you gonna come out to the town just so you didn't have to come out to her directly? What was the plan here, Jake?"

"I don't fuckin' know, man. I just—" I take a deep breath, trying to gather my thoughts. "I don't know what to do."

Charlie smacks me across the back of the head.

"Ow, man—fuck!" I wince, the hit collides with my already pounding headache. "What the fuck?!"

"Don't 'what the fuck' me, Jake. You know what that was about."

"Making my headache worse?"

He grits his teeth and glares. "No, dumbass. For thinking you can keep this from her. You're trying to use her past as an excuse not to tell her—but you can't do that to her."

"Fuck you!" My voice spikes, chest burning. "I'm not using anything as an excuse! And you wanna talk about keeping shit from someone—what about you, huh?"

His head jerks back. "What about me?"

"You ever gonna tell her how you feel, or just keep drooling over her like some pathetic, lovesick puppy?"

"That's none of your—"

"It's exactly my—"

"No, it's not!" he shouts, stepping in. "What I do or don't do doesn't have a damn thing to do with this—and fuck you for even bringin' it up."

"It has everything to do with it! You wanna stand there all high and mighty when you're pulling the exact same shit!"

"It's not the same!" His voice cracks with rage. "I'm keeping my *feelings* to myself. You're keeping your *identity* from her. My secret doesn't blow her world to pieces—yours will!"

I shove him back a step. "Fuck you, Charlie."

He shoves me right back, harder. "Fuck me?"

"Yeah, fuck you. You don't know shit."

"Oh, yeah?" He crowds back in, chest to chest now. "Then tell her. Today. Right fuckin' now."

"What? Fuck no!" I snap, a sharp pain lancing through my skull. "She just told me about her mom last night!"

"And?" Charlie fires back without hesitation. "Her mom didn't die yesterday. And you're still gonna be a wolf shifter tomorrow."

"I know that, Charlie!"

"Do you?" His voice spikes, tight and raw. "Because what you're doing right now? It ain't fuckin' fair to her. She's not even in the same relationship that you are."

"I *know* it isn't fair to her. I fucking know that." My voice cracks, the exhaustion bleeding through. "But you don't know what it feels like—to know, deep in your bones, that your soulmate is gonna look you in the eye and reject you the second she finds out."

That lands. Charlie's face falters, the fire in his eyes dimming. The anger drains out of him, replaced by something softer... sadder.

"She's not going to reject you, man. And if you really believe that, then either you don't know her... or you don't trust her."

I open my mouth to argue, to say *something*—but the sharp ring of my phone cuts through the tension, jolting us both.

I fish the phone out of my pocket, squinting at the screen. 7:00 a.m. Sarah's name flashes across it, and a pang of unease shoots through me. She never calls this early.

Swiping to answer, I bring the phone to my ear. "Hey, babe. Everything okay?"

Sniffling filters down the line. The sound hits me like a jolt to the chest. My heart rate spikes.

"Sarah?" I say again, voice tight. "Babe?"

"Jake!" Her voice is frantic, panicked—shaking and sharp. It cuts straight through me.

"What's wrong?" I ask, forcing myself to stay calm even as dread claws at my insides.

She takes a few shaky breaths, sniffling again before responding.

"Can you come over? Something happened, and I need you," she says, her voice trembling with urgency.

"I'll be right there," I say, my voice steady despite the storm building inside me.

I end the call and slip the phone back into my pocket, already striding across the yard toward my house.

Charlie falls in step beside me, concern etched across his face. "Everything okay, man?"

"I don't know," I say, voice clipped. "She just asked me to come over. She sounded really panicked."

"You want me to come with you?"

I shake my head, already rolling my shoulders, stretching out the tightness in my muscles. Preparing.

"No. I don't know what's going on. I'll call you later."

Charlie nods, voice calm but firm. "Alright. Your keys are still in the truck. Be careful."

Without another word, I shift. My wolf form surges forward, powerful limbs propelling me into the trees. The cold air stings my lungs, but I barely feel it. Every instinct I have screams one thing: Get to Sarah. Her voice echoes in my head as I tear through the woods, faster and faster, the forest a blur around me.

And then it hits me—I didn't feel her panic through the bond. Not until she said my name. I was so lost in my shit, in my fear, I didn't even notice her emotions breaking through. Didn't notice she needed me. I should've felt her. The guilt sinks deeper, sharp and cold. And I run harder.

Chapter 31

SARAH

The rumble of Jake's truck has barely faded before I'm flinging the door open. Without hesitation, I sprint down the steps and throw myself into his arms, wrapping around him as tears stream down my face. His embrace tightens instinctively—a fortress against the chaos that's swallowed my morning. Normally, being held this tightly might've felt suffocating, but right now it's the only thing keeping me from falling apart.

I sob into his shoulder, my body trembling as his warmth seeps into me. His steps are soft and sure as he carries me back up the porch and into the house. Slowly, my sobs taper into hiccuping gasps, but the cold sneaks in through the open doorway, drawing a shiver from me. Jake tilts my face up, his fingers cradling my jaw with a gentleness that threatens to undo me. His eyes, steady and full of concern, seem to absorb some of the panic clinging to me.

The door resists when he tries to shut it, the wood groaning in protest. He shifts his weight, muttering under his breath as his boot thuds against the frame. The flicker of frustration that crosses his face distracts me just enough to make the fear ease, if only for a second. A tear-soaked laugh escapes before I can stop it, and Jake's lips twitch with the ghost of a smile as he finally gets the door to close.

He brushes his thumbs across my cheeks, wiping away the tears, his gaze soft but searching.

"What happened?"

His voice is low and steady, but the worry running through it is unmistakable.

I swallow hard and let myself slide down from his arms, stepping back.

"You need to see," I whisper, barely audible. There's enough fear in my voice to make him grip my hand tightly. His entire body tenses, protective instincts kicking in like a reflex. He's bracing for something—and somehow, that steadiness grounds me.

As we climb the stairs, our footsteps echo too loudly against the wooden boards. The silence stretches until Jake finally breaks it.

"Where's your dad?"

"He left a note—said he went for a run this morning," I say, my voice trembling. "He hasn't had time to shift in weeks. He was getting antsy."

Jake nods. He understands the itch of unused magic—the way it builds and coils tighter with every passing hour. I hate that part of this gift. If you don't release it, it doesn't just gnaw at you—it turns on you. When the pressure finally breaks, the magic doesn't just escape—it erupts. Violent. All-consuming. Like being yanked down a drain from the inside out. It tears your soul loose, drags it into the void, and leaves nothing but a hollow shell behind.

You feel it happen. Every second. It's not quiet. It's not peaceful.

I know, because I heard it.

Mrs. Delaney lived two doors down—sweet, fragile, always humming while she worked in her garden. She hadn't shifted for months. Said she didn't have the strength anymore. One morning, I heard her scream—this raw, ripping sound that sliced through the neighborhood like a blade. I ran over, heart pounding, but by the time I got there...

She was slumped in the soil, basket of herbs still in her lap. Eyes wide. Mouth open. Gone. Like something had hollowed her out and left the rest behind. I didn't sleep for days.

That's why Dad left. Why he risked going out alone, even with the stalker still out there. He wouldn't have left me unless he had to—and I know exactly what it means when he finally does.

At the top of the stairs, I stop cold. Panic rises, choking me, blurring my vision. My room waits just ahead, the door cracked open. The wreckage inside is still there—still real. My feet won't move. I squeeze Jake's hand, my fingers trembling, desperate for the calm he carries.

He squeezes back. Silent. Steady. Then he lets go and steps past me, his boots thudding softly as he walks toward the door. I close my eyes, trying to steel myself—but the sound of him stopping just outside my room forces them open again.

He stands in the doorway, shoulders squared, spine rigid. His eyes scan the room, and for a long moment, his face gives nothing away. But when he turns and meets my gaze, I see it—a flicker of fear, quickly hidden.

"What the hell am I looking at, Sarah?"

His voice is tight, low—controlled, but barely.

I exhale shakily and force myself to move. I reach out and grab his arm, clinging like he's the only thing keeping me upright. Without a word, he wraps an arm around me and pulls me close. His warmth seeps into me again, steadying my pulse, holding me together long enough to face the nightmare waiting on the other side of that door.

At first glance, the room seems normal. The furniture stands upright, everything clean and orderly—no signs of disarray. But when my gaze shifts to the bed, a sinking feeling grips me. The genuine horror is laid out like a grotesque masterpiece. Around the bed, a halo of flowers radiates outward, their heads meticulously arranged to point toward the center. Bright yellows, fiery oranges, and deep crimson blooms create a vivid, almost celebratory display—but something about it feels wrong.

I recognize some flowers immediately: yellow and crimson roses interspersed with orange lilies. But the others are unfamiliar. One stands out—a delicate cluster of soft petals atop slender stems, its fragile beauty betraying the menace of its placement. Another is a layered burst of yellow, each petal so precisely folded it looks sculpted, unnatural. The last is a rounded spray of tiny yellow florets, like a miniature daisy bouquet. It's as if someone plucked rays of sunlight and arranged them with surgical precision—a cruel twist on something meant to bring warmth.

It's unsettling. But it wasn't the flowers that woke me.

It was the sharp jab at my foot—the sting of tiny wood shards digging into my skin as I pulled it from beneath the blanket and set it down at the end of the bed. The sudden pain jolted me fully awake. I flinched and lifted my foot again, spotting a thin smear of blood along the arch. My breath caught. Now, my chest tightens all over again as I glance at Jake, who's stepped silently into the room behind me, his presence anchoring me in the rising tide of panic.

His gaze sweeps the bed. Then it lands on the broken pieces. His expression shifts—first confusion, then recognition. Then, a simmering anger hardens his jaw.

He moves forward, boots crunching softly against the splinters as he crouches beside the bed. With slow, careful hands, he lifts a piece of wood from the pile and turns it over. I can see the moment he recognizes it—the carving, the shape, the delicate flowers he once etched into its surface. The birdhouse. The one he made for me. Now reduced to fragments.

The grief hits him like a punch. I see it in the way his shoulders dip, in the white-knuckled grip around the wood. He stares at it for a long moment before finally looking up, his blue eyes clouded with a raw mix of sadness and fury.

"Who would do something like this?" he asks, voice low, tight—barely holding back the rage beneath it.

I hug my arms around myself, trying to trap the growing chill in my bones.

"I don't know," I whisper. My voice is shaking, just like the rest of me.

Jake's attention shifts back to the bed. His brows draw together, sharp with focus. Then he freezes. Carefully, he reaches toward something half-hidden beneath the shards. A note. He plucks it free, holding it as if it might fall apart in his hands. His eyes scan the paper. His expression darkens. Then he turns to me and holds it out. I take it with trembling hands. My breath catches as I read the words:

I can't stand the thought of you being with someone else. It makes me sick.

The sentence sears into my brain, repeating like a curse. My knees nearly give out. I can't tell if it's fear or confusion—or both—but my body trembles violently as tears blur my vision. Jake pulls me into his arms without a word. His grip is firm, grounding. I press my face to his chest, the steady rhythm of his heart thudding against my cheek. His scent—pine and earth—wraps around me, familiar and safe, even as the world spins out of control.

"You're safe," he murmurs into my hair, lips brushing the top of my head. "I've got you."

We stand there in silence, his warmth the only thing keeping me from falling apart. Gradually, the shaking fades, though fear still coils tight in my chest. Jake presses a kiss to my temple and whispers, "Talk to me, baby. This doesn't feel like a first-time thing."

Guilt twists in my gut. I pull back just enough to meet his eyes; the intensity there is both comforting and terrifying.

I sigh, breath trembling. "That's because it's not."

His grip on my shirt tightens, knuckles white. His face stays unreadable, but I feel the shift—anger, worry, something deeper moving beneath the surface.

"Tell me," he says. Firm. Calm. Unshakeable.

So I tell him.

Everything. The dead cat with the message in blood. The flowers left on my porch. The rocks beneath my window and what they mean. The feeling of being watched—the unease that's grown sharper every day. Jake doesn't interrupt. He just listens, blue eyes locked on mine, jaw clenching tighter with each detail. By the time I finish, his grip on me is so tight it hurts. I flinch, and he immediately loosens his hold, eyes flashing with apology. The silence that follows is thick, suffocating.

Jake's expression hardens. The warmth in him vanishes, replaced by something cold and focused. Not fear—fury. Quiet and lethal. I feel it crawling through me, his emotions bleeding into mine. His protective instincts have fully kicked in, and I know without a doubt—he won't let this go.

"Sarah," he says, low and sharp, his voice slicing through the tension. "I don't care who or what is behind this—I won't let anything happen to you. You have my word."

Every word lands like a strike, venomous and deadly. A promise soaked in rage.

I swallow hard. His tone terrifies me—but in the best way. His hand tightens around mine, grounding me as his anger pulses in the air. I let myself lean into him, drawing strength from the fire in his eyes.

Jake glances once more at the wreckage in my room.

"We're ending this," he says, voice like stone.

Without another word, he leads me into the living room, his presence steady and solid beside me.

"We need to call the police," he adds, brooking no argument.

I nod and pull my phone from my pocket. My fingers fumble on the screen as I dial the sheriff's office. The calm voice on the other end does little to soothe me, but the promise of a deputy coming soon offers the smallest bit of relief. Jake doesn't let go when I hang up. He pulls me onto his lap on the couch, arms wrapped tight around me.

His embrace is a comfort—and a reminder of just how serious this has become.

Restless, Jake pulls the note from my pocket and snaps a few photos. Then his focus shifts to the house itself.

"You need cameras," he says, frustration lacing his tone. "All around. Doors. Windows. Everything."

I nod. "I don't mind," I murmur. "But I'll have to talk to my dad when he gets back."

"When does he usually return from his runs?" Jake asks, his voice softening as he looks down at me.

"It depends," I admit. "It's been a while since his last shift. His magic was getting uncomfortable, so he went out to expel the excess."

Jake nods slowly, brow furrowing. "Makes sense. Overloaded magic can mess with your head. If he needed to shift, he did the right thing. But if it weren't for that..." He pauses, jaw tightening, leaving the rest unsaid. Jake doesn't know my father, but his assumptions are right. I feel the truth of that settle heavy in my chest.

Dad's been reluctant to leave me for weeks, torn between protecting me and keeping himself sane. If he hadn't been desperate—if the risk of dying hadn't outweighed everything else—he never would've gone.

A sharp knock echoes through the quiet of the house, pulling me from Jake's warm embrace. I uncurl from his lap, but before I can take more than a step toward the door, his hand gently encircles my wrist, tugging me back behind him. His broad shoulders tense as he moves to the entryway, leading the way.

Peeking through the window, Jake confirms our visitor, then pulls the door open.

Standing on the porch is a man in his mid-thirties, dressed crisply in a police uniform. His demeanor is calm but commanding—a sharp contrast to the tension thick in the room.

"Deputy Jones," Jake says curtly, stepping aside to let him in.

The officer tips his hat in acknowledgment, offering Jake a polite smile before stepping inside. As the door closes behind him, Jake moves to my side, his hand finding mine in silent reassurance.

Deputy Jones carries himself with quiet authority. His tall, slender frame gives him a somewhat lanky appearance, but the breadth of his shoulders lends him a quiet strength. His brown eyes soften slightly when they meet mine—offering a warmth that feels oddly comforting, even if his deep voice still commands attention.

"Ma'am," he greets, tipping his hat toward me.

"Officer," I reply, forcing calm into my voice I don't actually feel.

The deputy scans the room briefly before returning his attention to me.

"What seems to be the problem, miss?" he asks.

His voice resonates—low, deep, the kind that settles in your chest—but the kindness in his expression makes it feel less severe. Jake gives my hand a light squeeze, grounding me. I take a slow breath.

With his silent encouragement, I recount everything—again.

Deputy Jones pulls a small notepad from his pocket and jots down details with practiced ease. His questions are clear and methodical, each one clipped and professional, though there's a certain detachment in his tone. Efficient. Controlled. Just a job.

When I finish, he nods and gestures toward the hallway. "Would you mind showing me?"

I escort him upstairs.

The wreckage of my room feels even more stark now, more surreal, like I'm walking into a crime scene in someone else's life. Deputy Jones takes it all in with a neutral expression, snapping photos of the floral arrangement, its vivid beauty made grotesque by context.

He crouches beside the scattered shards of the birdhouse, taking close-ups before collecting them. Every move is quiet, deliberate. He carefully bags the fragments, including the note, then stands and scribbles another quick line in his notebook.

Back downstairs, Deputy Jones turns to me with a look of measured regret.

"Ms. Miller, I've done everything I can for now. I'll take the evidence to the station, see if we can lift any prints—but I'll be honest, most stalkers don't leave usable ones."

Disappointment hits hard, sinking my shoulders. Jake's arm slips around my waist, steady and solid at my back. His warmth is the only thing keeping my growing frustration from spilling over.

"Call us immediately if anything else happens," the deputy adds, tipping his hat as he heads for the door.

"That's it?"

Jake's voice is low and sharp, laced with frustration.

Deputy Jones pauses with his hand on the knob and turns back. His expression stays composed, but there's a flicker of annoyance in his eyes.

"You can't station an officer here for a few days?" Jake presses his voice rising. "She's being stalked, Ethan. You know how serious this is."

The deputy's jaw tightens. His tone turns clipped.

"I get it, Jake. I do. But without hard evidence or a direct threat, I can't justify assigning someone to sit outside her house. This isn't a big-city precinct. We're short-staffed, and I can't pull someone off patrol without cause."

Jake's grip tightens around me. I can feel his frustration vibrating beneath his skin, every muscle tense with restrained anger.

As Deputy Jones opens the door, he glances over his shoulder, voice turning serious.

"That said, I strongly suggest you both take precautions. Lock your doors and windows. Get cameras installed. And maybe consider staying somewhere else until we get a clearer picture."

I glance up at Jake. His jaw clenches. He's holding it together, but just barely. The heat of his anger rolls off him in waves.

I place a hand on his arm, trying to soothe him—as much for me as for him. The heavy silence stretches until Jake finally gives a stiff, reluctant nod. The tension in his shoulders doesn't ease.

"Thank you for your help, Deputy," I mumble, my voice steadier than I feel. It seems important to acknowledge the effort, even if it hasn't been enough.

Deputy Jones gives a brief nod, his eyes flicking to Jake before stepping out. The door shuts with a soft click that echoes through the quiet house.

Jake's composure shatters.

A low growl rumbles from his chest; the sound is raw and visceral. His jaw tightens as he stalks a few steps away, fists clenched, frustration bleeding into every movement.

The sound seeps into my bones, unsettling something deep in my chest. My muscles tense, and a chill crawls down my spine. I glance up at him just as the growl cuts off. He looks back at me, worry softening his blue eyes.

"You okay? You look a little pale."

I blink, trying to clear my head. "Yeah. I'm okay. I just thought I heard..."

"Heard what?"

I shake my head quickly. "It's nothing. Never mind. I'm just frazzled."

Jake pulls me into his arms, holding me close as he whispers, "It's alright, Sarah. Everything's going to be alright."

I wish I could believe him.

But deep down, something's screaming this is only the beginning.

Chapter 32

The door hasn't been shut long behind Deputy Jones when it flies open again. Jake and I had moved to the living room, where I sat curled into his side, his arm a steadying weight around me. At the sound of the door, my body stiffens, breath catching in my throat.

"Sarah!"

My father's voice cuts through the quiet, sharp with worry. His footsteps echo through the foyer, each one quicker than the last. Jake's arm tightens around me instinctively.

Dad appears in the doorway, his expression hardening the second his eyes land on Jake. His sharp gaze sweeps over the man beside me, his protective instincts flaring as he leans forward slightly. Jake doesn't waver. His broad shoulders are squared, blue eyes calm but alert. I can feel the tension radiating from both of them.

"Who are you?" Dad asks, his voice low—almost menacing. A stark contrast to the warmth I usually hear from him. His body is tense, coiled like a spring.

"Dad!" I exclaim, my voice cracking under the weight of the moment. I hate how small it makes me sound. "This is Jake—I called him after... after I woke up and found..."

My words falter, and I gesture weakly toward the stairs. The weight of what I saw still crushes my chest.

Dad's eyes flicker between us. His face is unreadable, but the unease is there—tight in his jaw, sharp in the way his gaze shifts from Jake to the staircase and back again. His hesitation is palpable, torn between interrogating the man in front of him and figuring out what was going on.

Sensing his conflict, I whisper, "I'll be right back," and gently untangle from Jake's arms. I feel exposed as I step away, the comfort of his warmth vanishing behind me. With a deep breath, I take Dad into the kitchen.

As soon as we cross the threshold, Dad grabs my shoulders, his voice barely a whisper. "What happened, Doodle Bug?"

I tremble, unable to fully process the morning's events. Dad wraps his arms around me, pulling me into a hug. His body is warm and solid, grounding me. I bury my face in his chest, breathing in the familiar scent of him.

"He was in the house again, Daddy," I whisper, my voice cracking with unshed tears.

Dad stiffens, his grip tightening. His large hand comes up to cradle the back of my head.

"What do you mean?" he chokes out through gritted teeth.

Tears slip free despite my best effort to blink them back. They fall onto his shirt as I recount everything—waking up alone, the writing on the wall, the sick feeling in my gut. I don't have to see his face to feel the fury simmering beneath his skin. Anger. Hate. Grief. It rolls off him in waves.

When I finish, he pulls back just enough to kiss my forehead.

"I'm so sorry, baby girl," he whispers, his voice breaking. "I should've been here. I never should've left you alone."

A sob escapes him between kisses. I cup his face in my hands, shaking my head.

"This isn't your fault, Dad. You needed to shift. I can't lose you too—not to something that could've been prevented."

"But I could've lost you," he says, voice raw. "That monster could've taken you while I was gone. I should've been here."

I lower my gaze to the floor. "We don't even know when it was done, Dad. He could've done it before you ever left."

He stiffens again, then pulls me into another crushing hug. We stay like that for a long moment, clinging to each other in silence.

Eventually, I speak again.

"Jake took pictures before the deputy got here. I think you should see them."

He nods against my shoulder, then wipes at his face with his sleeve, eyes glassy.

"Show me," he says, voice hoarse.

I take him back into the living room.

Jake stands as we enter the living room, his stance steady, though concern is etched into every line of his face. He opens his mouth to speak, but Dad cuts him off with a sharp,

"Save it."

I glance at my father, wide-eyed and open-mouthed. I've never seen him be so openly hostile. A flicker of annoyance crosses Jake's face, but he doesn't speak.

"My daughter told me you took pictures of everything. Show me," he says in a clipped tone.

I shoot Jake a pleading look, silently trying to convey that my father isn't usually like this. Jake ignores the attitude, pulls out his phone, and hands it over.

Dad swipes through each photo slowly, his expression darkening with each one. By the time he reaches the pictures of the note, his hand tightens around the phone. For a second, I worry he might crush it. But then he shoves it back into Jake's hand. Jake takes it with a nod and tucks it away.

Dad's fists clench at his sides. He paces the length of the room, back and forth, jaw tight, breath shallow. I stay silent, stunned, as I watch him unravel in front of us.

Finally, he stops. His eyes lock onto Jake, scanning him up and down. After a long breath, he says—calm, but firm—

"Thank you for being here for my daughter, Jake. But I think it's time you head out. I need to speak with her privately."

Jake nods again, then crosses the room to me. He wraps his arms around me, pulling me into a soft hug. My mouth parts in surprise when he presses a chaste kiss to my lips. I manage a small smile as he pulls away.

"Call me whenever you want, Little Trash Panda. I'll always come when you do."

"Thank you, Jake," I whisper.

Part of me wants to hold on to him and never let go, but I can see the way my father is tensing more with every passing second—and it makes me uneasy.

Jake turns toward Dad and gives him one last nod.

"I'd say it was a pleasure meeting you, Mr. Miller, but given the circumstances... well, you know."

Dad nods but says nothing.

Jake starts toward the door, Dad's eyes tracking his every step. After a beat, Dad follows.

"I'll walk you out," he says.

I trail behind them, confused and unsettled. My father's behavior doesn't add up, and the weight of that realization gnaws at me. Still, I decide not to deal with it right now.

Instead, I turn back toward the kitchen.

I need coffee if I even hope to make it through this shitastic day.

Chapter 33

I feel the prickle of eyes on the back of my neck as we make our way toward my truck. Neither of us speaks, but I can feel the tension rolling off Sarah's father in waves—like standing alone on a beach with a tsunami bearing down.

I pull the door open, and his large hand slams it shut. I whip around; disgust and anger carve deep lines into his face. My brows knit as I turn fully to the imposing man.

"Is something the matter, Mr. Miller?" I ask, keeping my voice calm. He looks ready to knock my lights out, and I want no part of that. He's like an older version of Grant—wide shoulders, bulky build, tall frame. I probably have agility on my side in a fight, but I'd rather not test that theory. Pretty sure Sarah wouldn't appreciate my hitting her father... even if he started it.

His hands curl into fists at his sides. I tense, just in case.

"Yes. Something is the matter, boy," he says through gritted teeth. My hackles rise when that word leaves his mouth. No one calls a grown man "boy" unless it's meant to insult.

I square my shoulders and stand tall, refusing to back down. I'm still in fight mode from my argument with Charlie this morning, and it won't take much to set me off.

"Oh? I don't recall doing anything to warrant this behavior. So please enlighten me—what exactly have I done to wrong you?"

Mr. Miller leans in so close his breath skims my ear. "My daughter may be shit at reading auras, but I'm not... wolf."

My eyes widen as he leans back, a self-satisfied grin on his face.

I want to deny it, but even if I could, my body language has already given me away. No point pretending.

"What of it?" I ask, quirking a brow and staring him down.

"Sarah has already been through enough. She doesn't need someone like you messing her life up even more."

"Someone like me?"

"Yes. A predator. A *wolf*. Your kind already took her mother. I'm not letting another of you take her too."

I clench my jaw until my teeth ache. My fists curl, the urge to deck the motherfucker flaring hot. I drag a few breaths through my nose, force my hands to uncurl, and keep my stance rigid.

"You know—" I give him my best glare. "A few years ago, there was a massacre down in Alabama. Real bloodbath. Papers said it was the most gruesome scene the cops had seen in fifty years."

I pause, breathe, and keep going. "You wanna know what kind of shifter did that?" I lean in the way he did to me. "A raccoon."

I pull back and watch his face. "Statistically, non-predator shifters are more likely to commit violent crimes than predator shifters. And that's ignoring the fact that raccoons are predators in nature but get labeled non-predators in shifter communities."

I smirk. "Seems like I have more to worry about than Sarah does, doesn't it?"

Mr. Miller snarls, grabs my collar, and slams me against my truck. His face is millimeters from mine. "I don't give a shit about your bullshit statistics. You stay the hell away from my daughter or I'll make sure you're never found. Is that clear, boy?"

With a calm I don't feel, I plant a hand on his chest and shove. He steps back and lets go.

"With all due respect, sir—fuck you. I'm not staying away from Sarah. She's mine to protect, and I'm not leaving that job solely up to you anymore."

"Does she even know about you? What you are?"

"Does it matter?"

He laughs. "It matters."

I say nothing. A hundred words crowd my tongue; not one makes it out.

He tilts his head, eyes like knives. "What do you think is going to happen when I tell her what you are?"

I don't blink. "You won't—she hears it from me. I'm a wolf, Mr. Miller. I'll tell her. Not you. Not Johnny whatshisface down the street. Me."

I let that settle, then add, "And since we're doing truths—there's something you should know about us." I hold his stare. "We're soulmates."

Mr. Miller's face goes granite. The muscle in his jaw jumps once. "No," he says, flat as a verdict. "You'll break it. I won't have you around my daughter."

He paces and mutters to himself. "It doesn't matter. It can wither. All I have to do is get her away from him long enough, and the bond dies. Hurts a bit, but it dies."

"You'd do that to her?" I ask. "On purpose?"

"I'd do worse to keep her breathing." His jaw ticks. "Your kind already took her mother."

"It's not that simple," I say, voice calm even though my body's wired.

"What do you mean?" he grinds out, taking a menacing step closer.

"We've solidified the bond."

"You've WHAT?!" he yells. "You little motherfucker. Do you have any idea what you've done?" The veins in his forehead bulge as he tries to process. "You've tied my daughter to you." He drags a hand through his hair, frustration in every line. "Does she know that? Does she know you're bound to each other like that? Fuck! What else doesn't she know?!"

"Sarah knows we're soulmates, and she knows it's a deeper connection," I say. "I didn't explain that we've solidified it."

His eyes flare. "Then you tell her everything. Now. And we go to a witch. We break it."

"No," I reply.

He steps in, heat rolling off him. "Yes."

"It's her body. Her magic. That spell rips people apart—fever, days of nausea, headaches, sometimes it dulls their magic for good. I won't force that on her because you hate what I am."

"I hate what your kind did to her mother," he spits. "And I will not watch you stitch yourself onto my daughter."

"You're too late for that," I say, steady. "What's done is done. Solidified means distance won't starve it. The only way out is that spell. She asks for it, I sit for it. Until then, no."

"Fine," he says at last. "You tell her. Today."

"Not with adrenaline still in her system and a deputy report drying on the table," I say. "Don't weld fear to this. Give me until Friday."

"Absolutely not." His answer hits like a hammer. "You want to stew in your story for three days while she spirals? No. You'll do it tomorrow."

"Friday," I counter. "She needs a few nights where nobody adds a new kind of terror to what has already happened."

He steps closer. "Tomorrow. In my house. I'm there."

"Friday," I repeat, steady. "You want the truth clean? Give her ground to stand on first. Let her sleep. Let you both sleep."

He paces two tight lines in the driveway, jaw pulled so tight it looks painful. "You don't go near her until then."

"I won't go inside," I say. "I won't be alone with her. But if she calls—if anything happens—I come."

His eyes cut to me, sharp. "Only if she calls or I call."

"Deal."

"And Friday," he says, voice like steel cable, "you give her both truths—wolf and bond. No softening. No half-measures. I sit in the room. You don't touch her."

"You'll get both truths." I say. "Your house, your rules."

He hesitates, like the word is stuck in his teeth. "What time?"

"Sunset," I say. "She deserves rest after."

He bites down on the decision, then nods once. "Friday. Sunset."

"Friday. Sunset," I echo.

He leans the last inch, eyes cold. "If you hedge, or she cries and can't breathe—"

"I stop," I say. "And you get your witch if she asks."

Another beat. He steps back, shoulders still wound tight. "Get off my property."

"I'm going," I tell him, turning for the truck. "I'll be back on Friday when the sun hits the trees."

He doesn't answer, but I can feel his stare between my shoulders until I close the door.

Chapter 34

My thumb hovers just above the illuminated screen of my phone, my heart pounding a frantic cadence in time with the restless drumming of my fingers against the steering wheel. The low hum of the truck's engine does little to mask the chaos in my mind. With a deep breath, I press Charlie's number, the cool edge of the phone against my ear grounding me just enough to keep my focus. My gaze flicks up to the rearview mirror, scanning the dense line of trees that frame the road, as if the shadows themselves could spring to life at any moment.

"Come on, Charlie," I mutter, the words more of a plea than a demand as the call rings through. My hand grips the wheel tighter, the leather creaking under the pressure.

Finally, his voice cuts through the static, familiar and steady. "Hey, Jake. Is everything alright? What happened with Sarah?"

Relief washes over me, momentarily loosening the knot of tension in my chest. "Hey, man." I exhale hard, my eyes darting between the mirror and the road ahead. I can almost see Charlie leaning casually against his workbench, grease-stained rag in hand, brown eyes narrowing as he reads between the lines of my tone. "Sarah's okay, but I need to talk to you about something important."

The faint rustle on his end stops, his tone shifting instantly. "Sounds serious. You okay? What's going on?"

I hesitate for a heartbeat, the weight of the words settling heavy on my tongue before I speak. "Sarah has a stalker. I'm setting up cameras around her place, but tech alone won't cut it." My voice stays low and flat, because if it shakes, I'll put my fist through the dash.

"Holy fuck, man," Charlie mutters, his voice tight with concern. I can imagine his fingers tapping nervously against the nearest surface, an unconscious rhythm that gives away his rising agitation. "You think it's that bad? That she's in real danger?"

"More than I want to admit," I confess, my grip on the wheel tightening again as I try to suppress the flash of anger that surges at the thought of Sarah being hunted by some unknown threat. "I can't get into too many details over the phone, but yeah, man. It's bad. I need your help. Your instincts."

The pause that follows is short but loaded with intent. When Charlie finally speaks, his voice is steady and resolute. "Say no more, brother. You know I'm in."

The tension in my shoulders eases, but only slightly. "I appreciate it, man. Really. Knowing you've got our backs—it means a lot."

"Always," Charlie says, his conviction unwavering. "No one messes with one of our own."

His words hit harder than I expected. One of our own. Despite the mess in my head—Sarah, the secret I'm sitting on, the threat—Charlie doesn't hesitate. He's ready to risk his neck for her because she matters to me. A lump forms in my throat, and I know no amount of gratitude could ever repay the bond we share. He'll never know how much I appreciate him. Nothing I could do would ever measure up.

"I'm going to call the twins," I say, forcing my voice to steady itself against the emotions clawing at the edges. "I'm heading to our spot now. Can you meet me there in fifteen?"

Charlie's sharp inhale echoes through the line, the telltale sign of gears turning in his head. He always does that when he's calculating something, piecing together a plan before committing to a response. The exhale comes slow and steady. "Give me about thirty, and I'll be there."

"Alright. See you soon," I reply, not waiting for more. Charlie isn't one for drawn-out goodbyes. If the details are set and no one hung up mid-sentence, he was good.

My thumb moves to dial Beau's number next. The pattern of digits is as familiar as breathing. The call connects with a faint click, followed by the muffled sounds of shuffling. Beau—always fidgeting with something, as if stillness physically pains him.

"Well, well, well," his voice comes through, laced with its usual sarcastic charm but edged with curiosity. "If it isn't Jakey boy gracing me with a call this fine morning. What's the occasion? Finally confessing your undying love for me?"

Too bad I'm not in the mood for banter. "We've got a situation," I say, my voice clipped. "Sarah's got a stalker. We need eyes on the ground."

Beau's playful tone evaporates in an instant, replaced by something sharper, more serious. "Shit. How bad we talking? You think this guy's dangerous?"

"Could be," I admit, the memory of Sarah's fear twisting in my gut. "We can't take any chances."

"Say no more. I'm in." His agreement comes without hesitation, the rhythmic shuffling on the other end of the line matching the frantic energy coursing through me.

"Good. I'm calling Buckley next. Meet us in the woods in thirty," I instruct.

"Already on it," he replies, and the line goes dead. Beau never wastes time when it matters.

Switching over to Buckley's number, I barely have time to let the line ring twice before his voice cuts through, brisk and focused. "Yo, Jake. Beau texted. What's the play?"

"Keep watch over Sarah's house," I say, the image of her trembling hands still fresh in my mind. "We're meeting at the usual spot. Can't let this guy get another opportunity."

"Understood," Buckley responds without missing a beat. I can hear a faint thud, likely the sound of him pacing. He always does that when he is locked in, a curl probably twirling around his finger like clockwork.

"Charlie's in," I add, the relief of having my pack of friends coming together steadying my nerves. "We're locking this shit down."

"Damn right we are," Buckley says, his voice low and resolute. "No one messes with us."

"Thanks, man," I say, the tension in my chest finally easing. Knowing they have my back—and by extension Sarah's—makes the weight of the situation feel a little less suffocating.

"Be there shortly," Buckley promises, his usual lightheartedness replaced with a focused determination.

The familiar stretch of northern Tennessee rolls out before me, the towering trees like sentinels guarding secrets only the woods know. The earthy scent of moss and damp leaves clings to the air, grounding me in the reality of what lies ahead. My pulse thrums in my fingertips, syncing with the rhythm of the tires crunching over loose gravel as I near our spot.

The forest breaks into a clearing dappled with sunlight, a sacred ground for countless meetings like this one. I pull the truck to a stop, the engine ticking in protest as it settles. My boots hit the ground with a muffled thud, the soft earth giving slightly underfoot. Every instinct screams for vigilance as my eyes sweep the tree line, scanning for any signs of movement. The shadows feel deeper today, like they carry the weight of Sarah's fear with them.

The low rumble of a familiar engine breaks the stillness. I turn toward the sound, catching the gleam of Charlie's beat-up Ford as it rounds the bend. That truck looks like it has survived wars—and maybe it has, given the hours Charlie has spent coaxing it back to life. Its arrival is a lifeline, the first stitch in binding the frayed threads of my control.

Charlie doesn't wait for the truck to fully stop before he throws the door open. His boots hit the ground in one fluid motion. He strides toward me, his posture taut with urgency. "Jake!" His voice carries more than just a greeting; it's a demand for answers.

"Charlie," I say, nodding in acknowledgment. "You gonna park that truck?" I ask as my eyes dart behind him to the vehicle in question.

"Tell me everything," he says, closing the distance in a few long strides while effectively ignoring my question. His warm brown eyes are sharp, scanning my face like he's trying to dismantle the situation one piece at a time. The truck comes to a slow stop behind him, making me raise my brow in question.

I sigh heavily as I drag a hand through my hair, the weight of everything pressing heavier now that I have to say it out loud. "Sarah's stalker broke in sometime last night. She woke up to find her room covered in flowers, a twisted note on her bed, and—" my voice catches for a second as anger surges "—the birdhouse I made her? Smashed to pieces. Fucker left it at the foot of her bed like some kind of sick fucking message."

"Shit," Charlie hisses, his hands disappearing into his pockets as if to keep from punching something. His jaw tightens, the tension visible in every line of his body.

"She was asleep, man," I add, the words barely above a whisper. "Asleep while someone was in her room."

Charlie shakes his head, a low curse slipping past his lips. "The fucker won't get another chance to get that close to her. Not on my watch."

"Appreciate it, man," I say, though the gratitude doesn't show on my face.

"Hey," Charlie says, his hand gripping my shoulder, firm and grounding. "We've got this."

I nod, his confidence enough to bolster my own resolve. "Beau and Buckley are on their way. Should be here any minute. Once they're here, I'll fill everyone in and we'll figure out the best way to keep her safe."

"Good," Charlie replies, his fingers tapping absently against his thigh—the same rhythmic motion he uses when troubleshooting an engine. "The more of us, the better."

"Exactly," I say, my voice hardening, conviction solidifying in my chest. My gaze flicks to the woods, the shadows stretching longer as the sun climbs higher. Somewhere out there, someone has dared to cross a line. And we are going to make damn sure they don't get the chance to do it again.

The low crunch of gravel under tires signals the arrival of Beau and Buckley. They climb out of their trucks, the familiar gleam in their green eyes dimmed as they scan the clearing.

"Hey, guys," Beau says, his body swaying side to side. His usual cocky demeanor is muted, though the faintest smirk still plays on his lips.

"What's goin' on?" Buckley asks, his hand absently twisting a curl around his finger, the repetitive motion betraying his unease.

I nod, my gaze moving between them and Charlie, who stands silently beside me. The weight of the situation sits heavy on my shoulders as I recount everything—the flowers, the shattered birdhouse, the note, and the terrifying fact that Sarah had been asleep while it all happened. My voice somehow stays steady, but I can't ignore the anger simmering beneath the surface.

"Flowers?" Buckley echoes, the single word making my shoulders tense. His confusion quickly gives way to realization. "Shit, man. That's not just creepy—it's obsessive."

"Damn right. This is serious," Beau adds, his teasing demeanor replaced by something darker. "This isn't just some prank. Whoever did this... they're escalating."

"Exactly," I say, the words sharp and deliberate. My hand moves to the back of my neck, rubbing at the tension there as I piece together the plan we need. "We're setting up cameras around her house first thing. Tech gives us an edge, but it won't be enough. We need boots on the ground too—our eyes watching her place, especially at night."

Beau's smirk creeps back for a moment, a flicker of his usual self. "Oh, I see how it is, Jakey boy. You're just wanting to spy on your girlfriend. Maybe get a little peek of her comin' out of the shower."

"For fuck's sake, Beau," Charlie groans, reaching out to smack him across the back of the head. "You're a twenty-five-year-old man! Get your head in the game; we need you to be serious right now."

"Ow, dick," he says, rubbing the spot. "I'm just trying to lighten the mood a little."

I level him with a glare that could cut through steel; to his credit, he has the decency to look ashamed. Buckley, for once, ignores his brother's antics, his gaze gone thoughtful. "Cameras are smart," he says, his voice steady. "But it's gotta be more than that. Whoever's doing this isn't gonna stop on their own."

"Exactly why we're stepping in," I say firmly. "Here's the plan: cameras for daylight coverage; after dark we run patrols—rotating shifts, staying in the shadows. No one sees us, and no one knows we're watching. If anything feels even slightly off, you call me. We don't let this bastard get near her again."

Charlie nods immediately, his jaw set with determination. "Understood. Blend in, keep quiet. I'll take first watch and head over as soon as we're done here."

"Good," I say, my gaze shifting to Beau. "We'll need high-def, motion-activated cameras. Can you handle that?"

Beau's fingers begin their familiar drumming, the rhythm signaling the wheels in his head turning. "Yeah, I've got a guy. Top-of-the-line gear. I'll call him as soon as we're done here."

"Good," I say again, letting out a slow breath. Glancing around the group, I'm thankful for each of them being ready and willing to do whatever it takes. "This is about Sarah. About keeping her safe. If we're smart and careful, this creep doesn't stand a chance."

I turn my attention back to Beau, his usual cocky grin already plastered on his face. "How soon can your guy have them installed?" My tone is sharper than I intend, but the urgency isn't something I can temper.

"Probably the next day or so. I'll know more once I call."

"Right. Right. Of course." I clench and unclench my hands, trying to calm my nerves. "There's somethin' y'all should know before we start runnin' patrols."

Every head turns my way, waiting with bated breath for what I'm sure they assume is more bad news. I take a few calming breaths. "It's about Sarah's father..." I start, then relay the conversation I had with him earlier today. I can see their faces tighten with anger the more I speak. Charlie scoffs before a long growl bursts from his chest. The twins don't make any sound, but the looks on their faces speak of agitation and anger.

"He's giving me until Friday to come clean. Otherwise, he's threatening to tell her himself."

"Motherfucker," Charlie seethes. His furious gaze finds me, and before I can blink, he has a finger pointed at my chest. "I told you..." He paces across the gravel before coming back to me and resumes his tirade. "I fucking told you! I told you to fucking tell her! You've had plenty of time, Jake! Do you have any idea how much more unnecessarily complicated you've made this entire situation!"

The twins look with matching wide-eyed confusion at Charlie's outburst.

"Jesus, Charlie!" I groan, yanking at my hair. "What crawled up your ass and died? Huh? Fuck. It's not like I could've told her anything since this morning."

He stops pacing and aims the full force of his anger at me. Part of me wants to tuck my metaphorical tail between my legs, but another part of me is pissed he keeps rubbing salt in an open wound.

Buckley—deciding to come to my rescue—takes a step forward, his hand idly twisting a curl around his finger. When he speaks, his voice carries a quiet determination that cuts through the air. "I'll take the second shift."

Charlie looks over and huffs at him. Buckley doesn't waver, though; he stands tall against Charlie's ire and the weight of my ignominy.

I reach out and clap him on the shoulder in thanks, the solid feel grounding me for a moment. "Good man. You're agile, Buckley. If that stalker shows up, you'll be able to tail them without being spotted."

Buckley nods his agreement but says nothing else.

"Alright," I say, my gaze sweeping over the group; their resolve is palpable in the way they stand—guardians in every sense of the word. "We've got work to do. Beau, I'm counting on you."

"Got it," Beau replies with a sharp nod. I can see in his eyes that he's already brimming with ideas.

I take three slow breaths and force my shoulders down. "I'll relieve Buckley," I say, steady. "Night shift is mine." I rub the back of my neck, working at the tight coil there. "If that fucker so much as sets foot near her place, I'll be there to rip him apart."

Buckley's chuckle breaks through the tension—his grin laced with approval. "Man, you don't do anything halfway, do you?"

"Halfway won't keep Sarah safe." My voice carries the certainty of that vow.

Charlie claps his hands, snapping us back to the plan. "Alright, it's settled. Y'all get some rest. I'll head over and start making the rounds." He points at each of us. "Keep your damn cells handy. I don't want to have to call you twice."

"Thanks, brother," I say, gratitude evident in my tone even though my irritation with him still burns under the surface. I'm wound tight as fence wire; every nerve is buzzing. "I need a run before I even think about resting. My magic's burnin' too hot right now."

"We'll go with you," the twins say in unison, green eyes lit with shared purpose.

Charlie gives me a tight-lipped nod as he heads for his truck. His figure disappears into the cab of his rusty pickup with a loud bang. The engine kicks over. Gravel spits. I glance at the twins.

"I've never seen Charlie with a stick up his ass like this. Wonder what's gotten into him," Beau says, staring after the cloud of dust.

"I don't know," I say, my fingers curling into a fist. "But I'm gonna do the responsible thing and run it off before I do somethin' reckless—like follow his ass into town and punch him in his stupid face."

Buckley grunts in agreement and slaps my shoulder. None of us speaks as we head to our well-used trail between the pines.

The shift rolls over me like a familiar tide, my body giving way to the pull of magic. One moment I'm a man; the next I'm on all fours, paws pressed to the soft earth. My fur ripples in the breeze, the hues blending with the natural wolves that roam these woods. No human would suspect anything unusual: just another timber wolf prowling the forest within its domain.

I glance over to find the twins already in their wolf forms, their figures taut and alert. With a flick of my tail, I take the path farther into the sanctuary of trees. The wind dances across my fur as we move, sending a shiver down my spine. You'd think the fur would keep us warm on cooler days, but since the magic is really only an illusion, our warmth is limited to what we're wearing in our human forms. The scent of pine and damp earth grounds me in the moment. The energy coursing through my veins slowly dissipates with each powerful stride, unraveling the incessant need to rip into something with my teeth.

We run together for over an hour, weaving through paths only we know. Once the restless magic in my blood finally settles, I head back to the clearing. We shift back, our clothes reappearing seamlessly as the magic washes around us. My body feels used, my muscles shaking from the strain. The twins share a glance, their teasing glint absent, replaced by a shared understanding born of the exhaustion from the run.

"Catch you later," Beau hollers, his voice rough but steady as he climbs into his truck. Buckley gives me a quick wave as he follows his brother. Their trucks rumble in tandem, then fade into the distance until the forest swallows the sound.

Alone again, I turn toward home. The plan's in motion, but there's still work to do. The drive back blurs to green and light while my thoughts map every corner of Sarah's place, marking camera mounts and sightlines around the perimeter.

By the time I pull into the shop, the blueprint is etched into my mind. The familiar clang of metal on metal guides me toward my father's work-station. I allow myself a moment to breathe before stepping inside, ready to update him on the plan and what we're up against.

He lifts his gaze as I enter, the weight of responsibility shared without a word. This is what we do: we protect those who matter most. And for me, that means protecting Sarah with everything I have, even if she hates me in the end.

Chapter 35

I glance up at the clock on the wall for the twentieth time in what feels like five minutes. I haven't been able to concentrate today, and it shows. I'd normally have three times as much work done as I do, but all I've been able to think about is how I'm going to keep Sarah safe. I'd rip out my own heart and stake it on a pole in her front yard, like some kind of morbid scarecrow, if it would keep that asshole away.

Glancing at the clock again, I sigh long and hard. It won't be too much longer before I call it a day anyway and meet up with Buckley to start my shift.

As if called on by the universe, my phone rings on the counter next to me. I glance over as I wipe my hands across my jeans. My heart drops to my stomach when I see Buckley's name flashing across the screen. I snatch the phone up so fast I almost fumble it before I recover and swipe my finger across the screen.

"Buckley. What's goin' on?"

Crackling comes from the other end of the line.

"Shit."

There's more crackling, followed by broken sounds of half words.

"I — lo — — m."

"What?"

"I f—ki—g lo—t hi—."

"Buckley? Hello. You're breaking up."

"Jake?"

Static fills my ear.

"Jake? Can — — hear — —me?"

"I can't hear you, Buck. What's happening? Did you run into trouble?"

"Shit. H—ld o — a se—."

"Buckley? Hello?"

More static floods the line, then rustling. I strain to catch anything useful. The rustling stops; harsh breathing takes over.

"Jake?! Can you hear me?"

"Fuck. Yeah, Buck. I can hear you."

"I had him, man. I fucking had him, and he slipped out of my grasp."

"What?"

"The stalker!" Buckley sighs heavily. "I caught him prowling around, watching her through the windows."

I grit my teeth as red fills my vision.

That asshole was outside her house.

My fingers grip the phone so tight that I worry for a moment it might crack under the pressure.

"Jake?" His concerned voice snaps me back to the present.

"Yeah, Buck. I'm still here."

"Good. Good. So yeah, man. I caught him peepin' like the little perv he is, and when I got closer he fuckin' bolted."

"Cowards tend to do that. You get a good look at him?"

"Nah, man. He was already in wolf form. I — I caught him for a moment. Had him by the tail."

"What happened?"

"Fucker jerked around faster than I thought was possible and bit me. Got me right on the shoulder. I'm bleedin' like a stuck pig, but I don't think it's anything serious."

"Damn it, Buckley! Why didn't you tell me before now that you got hurt?"

"'Cause it ain't that big a deal. Shit, I've had worse bites from the damn sheep. That's not the point anyway. The point is that it hasn't been long since I lost track of him, and I think we can catch up to him if we hurry."

Shit. I cursed myself.

"Where'd you lose him?"

"Just over the creek, 'bout a mile from Sarah's. I'm pretty sure he's heading toward 73."

I smirk to myself.

"He don't know what he just stepped into." I snort. "I'm on my way. Call the others and meet me just off the bridge."

He laughs like this is the best day of his life. "You got it, man. We'll see you there."

I hang up, lock the shop, and grab my keys. It's time to go hunting.

I swing my truck to the side of the road and hop out. This bridge is a popular tourist attraction during the fall months when the leaves change. It's surrounded by beech, aspen, hickory, maple, ash, and oak, which turns it into a picturesque spot perfect for those social-media photos people like to take. Not many people drive through here anymore on account of the town, but that's a problem for another day. Today the area is barren and empty, but that doesn't stop the underbrush from obscuring the trunks, though. No leaves hang from the trees—except for the evergreens—making the place feel ominous and cold.

I turn when I hear an engine behind me. Beau is pulling his truck in behind mine; I can see Buckley and Charlie in the cab with him. They all barrel out and crowd around me.

Giving them a stiff nod, I turn toward Buckley and grab his arm, turning him to inspect his injuries for myself. It's not as bad as it looks, like he said, and the sight eases the lump in my throat as I let go.

"Where'd you lose sight of him, Buck?"

He reaches up and rubs the back of his neck. "Just on the other side of the creek, headed this way."

I raise my brow at Charlie. "Think he might still be in the area?"

He shrugs. "Could be. That's why we're all here. So we might as well quit lollygaggin' and see if we can find the son of a bitch."

"Hm." I grunt. "Buckley, you come with me. We'll head toward the creek and see if we can pick up his trail." I gesture to the others. "You two go around the southwest side and see if you can spot anything there."

I take a deep breath and continue. "It's almost a new moon, so we don't have a whole lotta light tonight, but we should be okay if we shift first. With the added benefit of some night vision, we'll manage. Buckley last saw him in wolf form, so I doubt we'll have an advantage there. Keep your eyes peeled. If anyone spots anything out of the ordinary, give one sharp yip to signal the others. Agreed?"

They all nod in agreement.

"Meet back here in an hour if we don't find anything."

Beau and Charlie break away from the group and disappear into the forest. I call on the magic in my veins; it rises under my skin like a tide, and I let it take me. One breath I'm standing; the next I drop to all fours, weight settling into paws, the world sharpening at the edges. It's not pain. It's a slide into a shape my body knows as well as my own name. Buckley follows suit, then we cut toward the creek, padding side by side.

It takes us a good fifteen minutes to get to the place where Buckley lost sight of the man who's been terrorizing Sarah. We move quietly through the woods. Leaf litter rasps underpaw, the ground soft where the creek has breathed out and soaked the bank.

At the water's edge I stop. The mud is churned up, fresh. A set of prints tears from one side to the other in a straight panic line, deep at the toe, claw marks raked hard. He hit the water fast. On our side, a maple shows a new scrape where something brushed it hard enough to shave bark. A few dark hairs cling to the rough edge.

I flick my ears at Buckley and angle downstream. The current is cold and loud, chewing at stones. We parallel the bank until the prints lift out again on a gravel spit. He climbed sloppily, slipped once, then drove on. He's moving, but he wasn't careful. Cocky or rattled. I hope rattled.

I look out across the expanse of forest and know immediately where we are. If we head straight, we'll hit 73 farther down from where we parked. There are old, run-down coal mines in that direction that haven't been used in fifty years or so. They used to be the main source of income for a lot of folks around here but were closed due to structural issues. There's a possibility he has a car stashed off the road, but my gut says that's not the case.

I turn my face toward Buckley and huff. He dips his head in acknowledgment. He knows these woods as well as the rest of us. He knows where the trail is leading us as well as I do.

I raise my head and let out one sharp yip. We keep our eyes peeled as we wait for the others, in case I'm wrong and that fucker is closer than I think. Rustling comes from the underbrush a moment before Charlie and Beau emerge. I flick my head toward the mines. They bow their heads in understanding. We take off in that direction, picking up the pace from a walk to a soft trot. We make some noise as we move, but not more than a normal animal would.

We halt when the entrance of the mine comes into view. The opening is jagged from the surrounding rock and holds an air of sadness for the men who lost their lives to its brutal depths. I hesitate, not sure if we should enter such a place. The questionable structural issues make me nervous about allowing my friends to put themselves in danger for me.

Suddenly, Charlie moves, tucking his head and tail to make himself as small as possible as he creeps forward. I glance at Beau and Buckley, hoping to convey with my eyes that I'd understand if they wanted to wait this one out. They both chuff at me.

Tucking my head and tail, I follow closely behind Charlie. The smell of stale air and minerals hits me as soon as I cross the threshold. The interior is exactly what you'd expect—dark, damp, cold—with large round wooden beams at points along the walkway, holding up the walls and ceiling. At first, it doesn't look like anything disturbed the ground, then I catch sight of a paw print standing out in a patch of dirt. A few drops of fresh blood dot the path here and there, leading deeper into the mine. I crouch low as I follow the trail.

Further in, I come across a V in the path. I give a quick glance to both paths before continuing down the one the other wolf took.

A light emanates from a doorway further down the path. A man's voice echoes off the walls, his words indistinguishable as first.

I sneak up to the doorway and peek into the room. The light comes from an old lantern that he somehow managed to light. Inside is a man of average height who appears to be in his late forties. He has brown hair that is graying at the temples and appears rather thin compared to me and my friends.

This is the asshole who's been stalking Sarah?

I don't know what I expected, but it wasn't this borderline scrawny guy who looks like he'd lose a fight with a wet paper towel. He paces around the room, hissing as he holds a piece of cloth to his lower back. Spots of blood cling to the cloth.

"Ugh!" he shouts as he keeps pacing. "That little shit. I should have ripped his fucking throat out!"

I look back at Buckley, who lifts his lips in a quiet snarl.

Snarling, I step around the corner and watch with glee as his eyes fill with surprise and fear. He shoves the cloth in his pocket and shifts, his wolf form identical to mine in shape and size. He lifts his lips and growls deep, sharp teeth gleaming in the lamplight.

We duck our heads and half-circle each other, neither of us wanting to expose a vulnerable spot. He lunges at me—not attacking, testing. I nip back but don't follow. He's trying to bait me, and I won't let him.

More snarls echo through the room as my friends surround me. We have the door completely blocked, trapping him inside this small space.

He lifts his head and surveys the situation. When his eyes land on Buckley, with his bloodied shoulder, he snarls and barks in his direction, broadcasting his hatred. Buckley returns the aggression but doesn't move.

He feints a few more times before deciding there's no winning this fight. Suddenly he spins and darts toward the back of the room. We stay steady as we press farther in. The light gives way to darkness, and I see our mistake: there's a back exit, and he's headed straight for it. I let out a bellowing woof and tear after him.

The sounds of pants and claws scraping rock fill the air around us as we give chase. He's faster than I'd like as he easily out-paces me and my friends. I tuck my head and tail, dig into my determination, and gain speed, nipping at his heels. My teeth graze his leg a few times, but all I connect with is air. Beau comes up beside me. We shoot each other a look, relating our silent plan to one another. I dig my claws into the rock and drive forward; Beau does the same on his other side, boxing him in. If one of us can get ahead of him, we might slow him enough for one or both of the others to grab hold.

Just when I think we've got him, everything goes wrong. The left side of the tunnel, where Beau is, has a rock formation that juts out further than the rest of the wall. He doesn't see it until it's too late and scrambles to stay on his feet as he trips over it. He knocks into the stalker, who rams into me. The force of the hit slams me into the stone wall, knocking the breath from my lungs. My head smacks the rough rock hard enough that my vision blurs as I sag to the floor.

Charlie and Buckley halt before barreling into me. Charlie presses his nose to my side and nudges, silently asking if I'm okay. I huff and climb to my feet. My vision wobbles, the tunnel tipping side to side. I blink until it clears and shake my head. The side of my face and skull are sore, but nothing feels broken.

Beau whines as he looks from me to the stalker, who is now further down the tunnel. He huffs and growls, then takes off after him again. I yip at him to stop, but he ignores me.

Beau is several lengths ahead as I break into a run. I can't seem to gain enough speed to catch him. I don't know where he got this burst of energy, but it's like chasing a kid who just heard his mama use his full government name.

Time snaps, stuttering into slow motion without warning. The stalker glances back, a cunning glint in his eye as he sees Beau close in on his heels. He leaps and kicks off the back of one of the support posts barely holding the wall, shifting it. The rumble of movement echoes around us as the rocks start shifting. I look up as the first pebbles fall. Beau is about to be crushed under tons of rock and earth. Either he doesn't notice or he thinks he can make it before it collapses. My gut is telling me that he's not going to, and if I don't do something soon, I'm about to watch one of my best friends die. A mournful cry reverberates along the corridor as Buckley realizes the same. I'll be damned if I let this motherfucker harm one of my own.

I leap toward Beau, my paw flickering into a palm as I reach out. Wind whooshes past, and my heart fills with grief when all I am greeted with is air. Then a tickle of hair brushes across my palm. I grip it tightly, Beau's back leg caught firmly in my grasp. I pull back with all my strength and implore the heavens not to let him die. I hit the ground as a loud, pain-filled yelp resonates through-out the space and the walls cave in.

Chapter 36

The bakery is silent except for the low hum of the refrigeration units and the buzz of the fluorescent lights. The sweet scent of pastries lingers in the air—too heavy, almost cloying. I move methodically through the space, latching every lock and fastener. A prickle crawls up my spine, forcing me to check and recheck each one. My hair falls in loose waves over my shoulders, long ago released from the tight hair tie I normally wear while serving customers. Strands brush my cheek as I bend to test the last clasp. A harsh breath escapes when I find it still locked tight. I don't know why securing the display cases matters so much, but relief washes over me all the same.

"Everything's locked up tight," I whisper, a brittle mantra against the silence. But my heart won't slow, each beat hammering louder, as if trying to warn me of something waiting just beyond the glass.

My skin prickles as the feeling of being watched slams into my chest. My stalker hasn't left any flowers for the last few days, and I don't know what to make of it. Part of me is relieved, but the knot of anxiety in my stomach knows this isn't over. He hasn't given up. He's still out there. Watching. Planning. The silence of his absence feels louder than his presence ever did.

Sometimes I catch myself glancing toward dark corners, half-convinced he's already slipped inside, hiding just out of sight. I don't know what he's plotting, and the lack of knowledge has left me more on edge than ever. The mask I've been wearing for my father's sake is starting to fray. I don't want to worry him—or Jake. Especially not Jake. I haven't heard from him since yesterday, and I'm getting worried. It's not like him to not return my calls or texts.

The bakery is too quiet, every hum and creak magnified. When the sudden clatter of utensils echoes from the kitchen, my blood spikes, pounding in my ears. My mind races—even though the back door has one of those bar locks that snap shut the second it closes, I can't shake the thought that maybe I didn't hear it latch. Maybe someone found a way in. I force myself to take slow breaths as I inch closer. Peeking around the doorframe, I whisper, "Jordan?" My voice barely carries, as if the bakery itself has absorbed the burden of my fear.

Jordan looks up from where he's cleaning the prep station, hazel eyes flicking to mine. A piece of dough rests in his hands, and he rolls it between his fingers in that absent way he always does when deep in thought. The warm, earthy scent of flour and yeast clings to the room, grounding me against the chill that's seeped into my bones. I close my eyes for a moment, my body releasing some of its tension at the sight of him.

"Hey, Sarah," he says, offering me a tired but kind smile. "You done closin' up?"

"Yeah." I nod, wrapping my arms around myself, fingers twisting a strand of hair in a nervous habit. "Just wanted to make sure everything's secure. You know, with... everything."

Jordan's expression darkens briefly, a flicker of understanding passing between us. "Better safe than sorry." His voice is low, steady—almost too steady. For a moment, it carries the weight of something predatory, and unease ripples through me. I swallow hard, a sudden thought striking sharp as glass: how well do I really know him? He says he's a deer shifter, but what if he isn't?

I blink, force the thought down, and force my voice to be steady. "Do you—um, do you need help with anything else?"

He shakes his head, giving me an apologetic smile. "Nah. Thanks, but I've got it covered."

I linger a moment, glancing around as if searching for some unfinished task to justify staying longer. But there's nothing. With a reluctant nod, I murmur, "Alright, then. Take care, Jordan. See you tomorrow."

"Goodnight, Sarah," he replies, the words soft but carrying an edge of concern that follows me even as I turn away.

I move to the back door, my fingers hovering over the handle. With a small push, it swings open. The frigid night air rushes in and bites at my exposed skin, the sharp chill raising goosebumps along my arms and neck. I hesitate, my breath fogging in the icy air. Something about the darkness outside makes me uneasy, an irrational but insistent voice whispering that something isn't right.

The realization hits me—I left my coat hanging on the rack. I step back into the bakery, letting the door close behind me with a solid bam! that echoes across the small space. The sound makes me flinch —too sharp, too final, like a gunshot in the quiet.

Grabbing my coat, I wrap it tightly around myself, savoring the sudden warmth that envelopes me like a cocoon. I push the buttons through their holes, securing the jacket to my body. My phone buzzes suddenly in my pocket, startling me enough to make me jump. Pulling it out, relief washes over me when I see Jake's name light up the screen.

Jake: I need you to stay at the bakery. I'm coming to get you.

> Sarah: ?

> Sarah: What's going on, Jake?

> Jake: I'll explain when I get there, Little Trash Panda. I just need to see you.

My fingers shake as I type out a reply.

> Sarah: Ok. How far out are you?

> Jake: Not far. I'm leaving the hospital now. Should be there in about 15.

> Sarah: Hospital? What's going on? Are you hurt? Are your parents okay?

> Jake: I'm okay, baby. Something happened to Beau. I'll explain when I get there, I swear. Just stay put for me.

> Sarah: Okay.

My mind fills with worry as I grip the phone tighter in my hand. Something happened to Beau? I picture his smiling face, the mirror of his twin, that unruly mop of brunette curls always falling across his eyes when he laughs. Something serious must have happened. If it were minor, Jake would have just told me. Wouldn't he? He wouldn't let me sit here, twisting in uncertainty like this. My gut churns with the uneasy certainty that whatever happened to Beau has something to do with me. God, I hope I'm wrong.

The sharp jingle of the shop's bell above the door snaps me out of my thoughts, slicing through the quiet like a knife. My heart stutters, panic racing up my spine. I know I locked that door. No one should be able to come through it. Not unless they were let inside. Jordan is still here, but he never has company after hours. He's usually in a hurry to finish closing so he can get out. I strain my ears, every muscle taut as a bowstring.

Jordan's voice cuts through the silence, sharp and uncharacteristically aggressive. "Well. I would ask what you're doing here, but I think I already know the answer."

Lila's retort follows immediately, her tone equally biting. "Don't get too excited. I was in the neighborhood and just came to check on Sarah."

"Sure you did." His voice drips with derision. "Be honest—you just love to torture me with your presence and couldn't resist the opportunity."

A scoff rings out. "Torture you?" Her humorless laugh is bitter. "Please. You only wish I wasted my time thinking about you. You're the one always picking fights, acting like you're all high and mighty."

I debate whether to interrupt. Lila can hold her own, but she said she was here for me. My decision wavers when a shuffle and a grunt follow. I take a step toward the door, freezing at his next words.

"Only because you make it so damn easy, wabbit." His voice is low and husky, intimate in a way that doesn't belong in public.

She answers with a breathy sigh. "You're impossible."

"And yet, here you are."

What the hell is going on? It almost sounds like their bickering has shifted into something else—something dangerously close to flirting. Their banter usually teeters on hostility but never crosses the line. This feels different.

"Where's Sarah?" Lila's voice sounds wrong. Almost scared. I've never heard her falter, not once, but there's a hesitation now, a stutter in her tone that sets every nerve in me on fire.

"She left about ten minutes ago. Why? You hoping she'll save you this time?"

Her reply is lost under the *thwump* of my heartbeat pounding in my ears. Oh God. What does that mean? Is he planning to hurt her?

For a terrifying second, I see her—cornered. Caught. Prey realizing too late the predator has teeth. Teeth sinking deep, tearing flesh. Claws ripping across skin, leaving it shredded and bleeding. The image tears through me. My chest seizes. I can't breathe.

I try to suck in air, but panic claws at me, freezing me in place. *What do I do? What do I do?*

I scan the hallway in desperation, searching for something—any-thing—I can use to help Lila escape. A sudden crash from the kitchen makes me flinch, sucking in a ragged breath. I grab the closest thing at hand: the mop.

Grunts and muffled noises filter through the door. Sweat beads along my forehead as concern for Lila floods through me. I creep closer, my breath shallow, careful not to make a sound. Peering through the narrow crack, I freeze, eyes widening at the scene unfolding before me.

Jordan has his hand on Lila's back; she's bent over the prep table, her pants pushed down to her thighs. Her breath hitches as Jordan thrusts behind her. She moans as his hands grip her hips with a ferocity that matches the tension in his voice.

"God, you're such a pain in the ass," he growls, voice gruff and rumbling. "I can't stand you most of the time, but fuck..." He groans, long and throaty. "I could stay in this pussy for days."

Lila lets out sharp sounds of pleasure, her fingers curling around the edge of the table as she gasps out, "Just shut the fuck up and fuck me."

"You shut the fuck up," he snarls, movements intensifying as one hand grasps her hair and yanks her until her body bows into a perfect U. "And take every inch of me like the good little bitch you are." His words are punctuated by every slap of skin against skin. His thrusts look harsh, brutal, but the fire blazing in Lila's eyes makes it clear—she's giving as good as she gets.

"Oh God! Yes! Yes! Yes!" Lila cries, her voice desperate and raw.

My stomach flips, a cocktail of shock and discomfort churning within me. Heat prickles up the back of my neck as I realize what I'm witnessing. They're tangled in a moment so intimate, so raw, that it feels like a violation just to be present.

I step back slowly, careful not to make a sound. My breath catches in my throat as I replace the mop and tiptoe toward the back exit, the revelation of what I've just seen stealing every thought from my mind. My fingers fumble as I slip through the door and out into the night, easing it closed with the softest click.

Snow squeaks beneath my shoes as I rush across the empty lot behind the bakery. The freezing air sweeps through me, sharp enough to make my teeth chatter as if the cold itself is warning me off. I wrap my arms around myself, shivering. For a moment, I consider going back inside for warmth—but the thought of hearing them again makes my stomach knot. I'd rather freeze my toes off than walk back into that. My brain is still struggling to process what I saw. Lila and Jordan together. Like *together together*.

Soft, visible puffs leave my mouth as I glance around the shadowy lot. I debate for a moment—should I wait here or head out front? The shadows in the back parking lot unnerve me. The woods beyond loom dense and dark, tugging at the memory of the night I found my mother. A chill runs down my spine that has nothing to do with the cold. The idea of the streetlamps out front, casting their reassuring light across the main road, feels like a much safer bet. Decision made, I head toward the narrow drive between the building leading out to the street.

The sudden snap of a branch breaks the silence. My breath stutters, heart fluttering like a trapped bird. I freeze, ears straining for any other sound. Slowly, I turn toward the source, eyes darting to the edge of the light's reach. It gets dark too quickly this time of year; the shadows stretching longer, thicker, as if hiding something—or someone—just beyond sight.

Nothing moves.

Exhaling shakily, I force myself to take a few deep breaths. *It's nothing,* I tell myself, trying to brush off the unease settling like a stone in my gut. Probably just a stray dog or something. I turn back toward the alleyway, quickening my pace, boots crunching loud against the packed snow.

Snap.

The sound is closer this time.

I whirl around, wide eyes scanning the darkness. The shadows feel alive now, prickling against my skin. My breaths puff in rapid swirls, hot and frantic in the freezing air. The sensation of eyes crawling down my back makes the hair at my nape stand on end. Every nerve in my body screams, run.

I spin toward the alleyway and break into a sprint. Each step purposeful, my stride born of the gnawing fear clawing at my insides.

Snap.

The sound comes from right behind me, at the edge of the small parking lot.

I jerk my head toward it, twisting—my heel hits a patch of ice hidden beneath the snow. The darkness erupts with movement as a massive, hairy creature lunges from the shadows. Before I can react, it collides with me. Heavy paws slam into my side with crushing force. What little balance I had vanishes, and I tumble backward into the snow, the cold wetness biting through my clothes.

A scream tears from my throat, raw and desperate. My head cracks against the unforgiving asphalt beneath the snow. Stars burst in my vision; my skull rings like a struck bell. Disoriented and stunned, I barely register the crushing weight pressing on my chest. *Am I dying?* The thought flashes through my mind, wild and unbidden, as my scrambled brain fights to process what's happening.

My blurred vision clears just enough to make out the hulking figure above me — a wolf, massive and menacing. His dark fur bristles as it snarls down at me, razor-sharp teeth bared mere inches from my face. Hot, foul breath washes over me, and I flinch as a string of saliva drips from his jaws, landing on my cheek like a scalding brand.

A whimper escapes me as I lift trembling hands, instinctively trying to shove the beast away. His snarl deepens, the feral sound vibrating in my bones, and he snaps his teeth dangerously close to my face. I squeal, fear smothering any rational thought, and fling my arms over my head in a desperate attempt to shield myself.

The crushing weight on my chest vanishes. I gasp for air, each breath a cold, sharp gulp of relief. My trembling arms move cautiously away from my face — but the reprieve is short-lived. A sudden, searing pain rips through my leg like shards of glass tearing flesh. The sensation is sickeningly familiar. A pained cry rips from me as I snap my gaze downward and lock onto the horrifying sight.

The wolf has clamped his powerful jaws around my calf, teeth piercing deep into muscle. Blood seeps from around his teeth, staining the pristine snow. My breaths are shaky gasps. Panic seizes me, and I thrash against his hold; every movement only drives the teeth deeper, sending fresh waves of agony up my leg.

"Let go!" I grind out through clenched teeth, desperation shredding my voice. My hands scrabble to grip my leg just above the wolf's snout. I try to yank my leg again, but I remember the first pull—how it only drove the teeth in farther—and I choke back the motion. Tears blur my vision and spill unchecked down my cheeks.

The wolf jerks, dragging me across the frozen ground. The snow, once a soft cushion, becomes an icy burn against my exposed skin as my clothes ride up with every savage tug. I twist, fingers clawing at the slick surface, digging into snow and asphalt in a futile attempt to anchor myself.

"Help!" I scream, my voice raw with terror as it echoes into the night. The sound rings hollow, swallowed by the stillness of the empty parking lot. "Help me!"

The cold seeps into my bones, fear grinding against every nerve. My mind races, flickering between frantic thoughts—Jordan and Lila, surely they hear me... or Jake... Jake, please get here... please.

Another wrench of the wolf's jaws sends me sliding farther, my body twisting unnaturally as I fight against him. My leg feels like it's on fire, the relentless pressure of his teeth a cruel reminder of how powerless I am.

"Let me go!" I sob, voice cracking as exhaustion drains my strength. "Please, I didn't do anything—please!"

The edge of the asphalt looms, the dense shadows of the tree line creeping closer. The wolf drags me without pause, each tug a nightmare of being hauled to a den, kept alive only to be devoured later.

Panic surges as dirt replaces pavement. Darkness folds in, swallowing everything. My free leg kicks wildly, but each strike only provokes a vicious shake of his head. Pain detonates through me in unbearable waves, but I push through, kicking again and again.

Sobs rack my chest as I thrash, claw, scream—anything to make him release me. "Jake!" I cry, the name leaving my lips like a prayer, a fragile hope clinging to the edges of despair.

My eyes dart wildly as I reach again—anything, anything—my fingers finally collide with something solid. A bush. Its thick limbs barren and outstretched like skeletal arms against the night sky.

With everything I have left, I latch onto it. The bark bites into my frozen palms, rough and unyielding, but I barely register the sting. I can't feel my fingers anymore, but I hold on; my arms tremble as I strain against the wolf's hold.

The creature growls, low and furious, tugging harder, jerking my body like a rag doll. I clench my teeth and refuse to let go. This bush is my savior, my last chance, and I cling to it like my life depends on it—because it does.

The wolf snarls, his jaw releasing my leg with a sickening squelch. My calf throbs violently, each heartbeat sending fresh waves of agony through shredded muscle. Blood seeps out in sluggish rivulets as cold air bites the open wounds, freezing the sticky trails to my skin.

The beast stares, its menacing gaze pinning me in place as it stalks forward. His frame blocks the faint light filtering through the trees, and his breath puffs in hot, cloudy bursts that hover inches from my face. A deep, guttural rumble rolls from his chest, vibrating through the air and straight into my stomach.

His eyes flick to my hands, still gripping the rough bark. He trails his snout along my arm, hot breath raising goosebumps as he pauses. Then, with slow, deliberate precision, he parts his jaws and eases them over my forearm.

Razor-sharp teeth slice through my jacket, pricking the tender flesh beneath. A low hiss of pain escapes me; my grip tightens until my hands go white. The wolf's teeth press harder—a warning, a challenge—but I don't let go. If this beast wants me, he's going to have to kill me here and now—I won't be dragged another inch without a fight.

Just as his teeth dig in, the screech of tires splits the night. A metallic squeal follows, a vehicle skidding to a halt, the noise tearing through the tension like a blade.

"Sarah!" Jake's voice rips across the lot—raw, frantic, steeped in fear and fury. Relief jolts through me like lightning. The wolf's ears twitch at the sound, and for the first time, he hesitates.

He releases my arm with a final snarl, frustration rumbling low in his chest. Heavy boots pound the asphalt—Jake. The rhythm shifts to a crunch as his steps hit snow. The wolf throws one last huff, then pivots and slips into the underbrush, his tail vanishing into the shadows just as Jake bursts through the trees.

The color drains from his face the moment he sees me. His frantic gaze sweeps the scene—my blood staining the snow, paw prints vanishing into the woods. My eyes widen when I realize he's holding a gun, a pistol gripped tight and aimed where the wolf had disappeared. His jaw clenches, and without hesitation he fires. Two sharp cracks split the night, followed by a high-pitched yelp. My heart lurches, hoping he'd hit the bastard dead center.

A hiccuping sob escapes as relief floods me. Jake's head snaps back toward me, a curse slipping through his teeth. He shoves the gun into the waistband of his jeans and drops to his knees in the snow. His hands hover, trembling, as his blue eyes dart over the damage. Gentle pressure traces down my leg until his fingers brush torn flesh, drawing a hiss from me. He curses again—low, vicious words meant for himself—before shifting to brush damp strands of hair from my face. Tears pour freely down my cheeks, my chest convulsing with ragged, uncontrollable sobs.

"Sarah," Jake murmurs, soft but steady. His powerful arms wrap around me, his warmth bleeding through my frozen, shaking form as he pulls me close. I bury my face in his neck, clinging to him.

The bakery door slams open, reverberating off the brick and sending a fresh jolt of adrenaline through me. Lila and Jordan's panicked voices cut through the night, calling my name.

"Over here!" Jake barks, his voice stronger now, carrying in the cold air.

Brush thrashes as Jordan bursts into view, a rifle clutched in his hands, pants half-open and eyes wild. "We heard gunshots," he pants, gaze locking on me. "Jesus fuck!"

Lila almost barrels into him as she clears the undergrowth, shirt buttoned crooked, hair askew. She gasps sharply, hand flying to her mouth. Her face pales at the sight of my blood coating the ground. Jeans torn.

Jake's eyes flick over them both. If he has an opinion about their state of undress, he keeps it to himself.

"Pass me your belt, Jordan," he snaps, tightening his hold around my waist.

"What?" Jordan says, giving him a perplexed look.

"Your belt, Jordan! Give me your belt."

Jordan fumbles, passing the rifle to Lila before yanking at his belt. "Jesus, dude. You don't have to yell."

He hands his belt to Jake, who practically rips it from his grasp. Jake wraps the belt around my calf and pulls it tight, causing me to cry out from the sharp burst of pain.

"I know, baby. I know," he coos. "I've got to slow the bleeding."

Lila drops to her knees and seizes my hands, squeezing tight. I crush her fingers in a death grip as Jake cinches the belt. She winces but holds firm, offering me a shaky smile.

"We need to call the cops," Jordan croaks. His face has gone a sickly shade of green, his expression wavering between panic and disgust. He looks like he's one deep breath away from either passing out or throwing up.

Jake shifts, sliding his arms beneath me. His movements are deliberate, protective. "Good idea," he says firmly. "You and Lila call and wait for them here. I'm taking Sarah to the hospital."

Without another word, he strides into the underbrush, carrying me with long, steady steps.

As we clear the treeline, Jake's truck comes into view. The driver's door hangs open, the insistent ding-ding-ding chime filling the night. Smoke curls from the exhaust, the engine rumbling. The scene tells its own story—the urgency that brought him running.

Chapter 37

It's been three days since the incident. Thankfully, despite how terrible my leg looked—swollen, bruised, mangled—I only needed a few stitches. Most of the wolf's teeth hit scar tissue from his previous attack, so I only picked up a few fresh additions to my already scarred leg. The entire ordeal was tense; Jake and Dad pacing like caged animals. By the time we left, their smothering presence had left me drained.

The police came by while I was getting stitched up. They'd found a trail of blood where Jake shot my stalker, but it disappeared once it reached the road. He was nowhere to be found.

Ever since then, they've been suffocating me. Jake comes over every morning and stays with me until Dad gets home from work. Dad doesn't seem to like Jake being around at all; he gives him hard looks every time he sees him. Jake just gestures to me and shakes his head. I have no idea what that's about, but I can tell Dad gets more frustrated with it every day. Suddenly, I'm a prisoner in my own life and I just want to punch someone in the face. I don't even care who at this point.

Buckley came by yesterday with a friend to install cameras. He looked ragged and worn, his eyes bloodshot with dark circles framing them. That's when I found out from him that Beau was in a coma, and they have no idea if he will ever wake up. His hand has been crushed too, and they've already done surgery to repair some of the damage. I hugged Buckley tight, and he broke down, sobbing against my shoulder. Jake wore a grief- and guilt-filled face the entire time he was there, and I finally got him to tell me exactly what happened.

This morning I force myself back into routine. Back to work. The smell of coffee and sugar greets me the moment I push through the bakery's back door, but it doesn't comfort me the way it used to. The air feels heavier, like even the sweetness has been weighed down.

Jordan glances up from the counter where he's scribbling notes; his usual easygoing grin flickers before settling into something more careful. Like he's not sure if he should joke with me or keep his mouth shut. I wave him off before he can say anything and slip into the apron hanging by the door. Normal. I need normal.

The bell over the front door jingles, and a couple of regulars shuffle in, stomping snow off their boots. My hands move automatically—pour coffee, bag muffins, take cash—but my mind keeps drifting back to Buckley's hollow eyes, the way he crumpled when I hugged him. Beau's in a coma. His hand crushed. The words circle me like vultures.

I catch myself staring too long at the pastry case, lost in thought, until Jordan nudges me with his elbow. "You good?" he mutters, low enough so the customers don't hear.

I force a smile, brittle around the edges. "Yeah. Just... tired."

He studies me for a beat longer, like he doesn't buy it, but he doesn't push. I'm grateful. Still, when the rush dies down and I find myself wiping the same counter three times over, the truth presses in: normal doesn't feel like normal anymore. It feels like pretending.

The back door of the bakery thuds shut behind me. I take a deep, shuddering breath of pre-spring air. A shiver runs down my spine—not just from the lingering cold, but from the knot of unease twisting in my stomach. My leg throbs, a deep, pulsing ache that beats in time with every step.

I pushed myself too hard today, and now I feel the consequences with every minute that passes. Mr. Walters had tried to coax me into taking breaks, urging me to sit and rest, but I waved him off like a fool. Now I'm paying for it, my leg screaming for mercy with every weight-bearing step.

"Rough day?" Mr. Walters' voice cuts through my thoughts. I look up, startled, to see him leaning casually in the doorway, his white apron dusted with flour. His hazel eyes crease with concern, soft and steady as always.

"Something like that," I reply, forcing a smile that doesn't reach my eyes. "Just... a lot on my mind, I guess."

"Want to talk about it?" he asks warmly, his voice carrying the familiar, fatherly comfort he always seems to exude. "A problem shared is a problem halved, as they say."

I let out a breathy, humorless laugh. "Thanks, Mr. Walters, but I think this one might need to be quartered before it's manageable."

His lips twitch at the corners, though his gaze stays heavy with concern. "Sarah," he says softly, taking a step closer, "If you need some more time off, all you've gotta do is say so. Anytime, kiddo."

I don't know how to feel or what to say to that, so I just go with the polite thing. "Thank you."

"Would you like a hug?" he offers, holding his arms out in invitation.

The gesture unravels me. I don't hesitate. Stepping into his embrace, I let his arms fold around me, solid and warm. The scent of cinnamon and sugar clings to him like a second skin, soothing and familiar. For a fleeting moment, it's a balm against the rawness I carry inside. It isn't quite the same as Dad's bear hugs, but it's close. Mr. Walters' hugs are more like Christmas morning, while Dads are more like soaking in sunshine on the first warm day of spring.

When he pulls back, he holds me at arm's length, studying my face. "Take care getting home, alright?" he says with a gentle smile.

"Always do," I breathe.

"Ready to go, Doodle Bug?" Dad's voice interrupts the moment, his familiar figure stepping into view beside me.

I nod, forcing a smile for Mr. Walters as I wave goodbye. "See you tomorrow."

Dad's arm slips around my shoulders, pulling me close as he guides me toward the alleyway that leads to Main Street.

We clear the alleyway to find Jake's truck parked in a parallel spot out front. Jake leans casually against the side, his sharp blue eyes locking onto me the moment we step onto the sidewalk.

The casual stance doesn't last long. As soon as he sees me limping, he springs into motion, yanking the passenger door open before I can take another step. Dad scowls, silent disapproval radiating off him like a storm cloud, but he doesn't say a word. Instead, he steps in beside me and helps me climb into the seat, effectively blocking Jake from doing so.

"Careful, Doodle Bug," Dad murmurs. I wince as my leg throbs but manage to settle in with only a quiet hiss of discomfort.

The back door slams as Dad climbs into the seat behind me. I lean back against the headrest with a sigh, the tension in my shoulders easing slightly. I don't have to walk the few blocks home today—thank God.

"Thanks for the ride, Jake," I say, glancing toward him.

He offers me a small, lopsided smile—one that doesn't need words to carry its meaning. "Anytime, baby."

Dad scoffs, but Jake ignores him. Without another word, the engine rumbles to life. As he pulls into traffic, I feel the faintest flicker of peace.

Chapter 38

SARAH

Dinner is tense. I can practically feel the air growing thicker the longer we sit at the table. Neither man has said a word since we came into the house. I invited Jake to stay, wanting his presence close after the day I'd had, but now I'm wondering if I made the right call. Whatever is brewing between these two, it's only a matter of time before it blows.

Dad scrapes his chair back; the sound is sharp enough to make me flinch. "I'll handle the dishes tonight."

He's gathering plates when Jake reaches out, placing a hand on his arm.

"I'll take care of it, Mr. Miller. It's the least I can do after being provided such a fine meal this evenin'."

Dad sneers as he wrenches his arm free. "Fine. Dish towels are in the drawer by the fridge."

Their eyes lock for a fraction too long, sharp and unyielding. The current between them crackles, hot and dangerous, until Dad finally tears his gaze away.

Then his face softens the instant he looks at me, shifting from storm to sunshine. He holds his hand out. "Come on, Doodle Bug. Let's get you settled on the couch for a bit."

I glance at Jake, who gives me an encouraging smile, then take Dad's hand and let him lead me into the living room. He settles me onto the couch, flopping into the seat beside me.

I open my mouth to ask what the hell is going on between them when a sharp knock sounds at the door.

Dad goes to open the door, his shoulder stiff as he leaves the room. A moment later, I hear the deep tenor of male voices, then the click of the door shutting and two sets of footsteps approaching. Dad reappears, followed closely by Deputy Jones.

I scrunch my brows in confusion and call out a greeting. "Good evening, Deputy Jones."

"Sarah..." His voice falters, heavy with something I'm not ready to hear. "I'm sorry to tell you this, but there's been an incident. Mr. Walters... he's been found dead."

The air thins around me as the world tilts sideways. My lungs refuse to work. For a moment I fight my body before dragging in a desperate breath.

"Dead?" I croak, the word splintering in my throat. "But... I just saw him. This afternoon."

A warm hand lands on my shoulder—Jake's. His fingers squeeze softly, grounding me against the numb shock spreading like ice through my chest.

"What's this got to do with Sarah?" Dad asks.

I want to scold him for being so callous in a moment like this, but part of me is just as desperate to know why Deputy Jones is telling me.

The deputy takes a deep breath, like he's forcing the words out. "There was a note left at the scene... addressed to your daughter."

"What?!" Dad explodes.

I drop my gaze to the floor, trying to wrestle my emotions under control. Images of Mr. Walters flood me: his warm hazel eyes, his kind smile, the cinnamon-and-sugar scent that always clung to him. I had just hugged him, felt the steady comfort of his arms around me, and now... he's gone.

"Can we see it?" Jake asks, his voice calm against the backdrop of my dad's outburst.

Deputy Jones nods, pulls out his phone, and hands it to me. I close my eyes for a moment, then take in the image. The picture shows a small slip of paper sitting on top of two flowers. An orange lily and a yellow hyacinth. Blood paints the ground beneath them. I concentrate on the scrawled writing; my throat tightens as I read the words aloud.

"He paid the price for touching what is mine." My voice shakes with every syllable, and I swallow hard, forcing myself to keep reading. "He dared to lay hands on you, Sarah. Remember, you belong to me."

The last sentence hits like a punch to the gut. My grip on the phone wavers; my breaths come shallow and uneven. Jake shifts closer, his presence a solid anchor against the horror pulsing through my veins.

"Jesus Christ," he mutters, fury lacing his voice.

I hand the phone back, my movements jerky and unsteady. "He...he killed Mr. Walters because of *me*?" I stammer, my words barely audible.

"No," Jake barks, his blue eyes blazing as he faces me, anger aimed at the monster lurking in the shadows, not at me. "This isn't on *you*. This is on *him*. Whoever he is—he's the one doing this, Sarah. You're not to blame for his sick games."

Deputy Jones nods. "Jake's right. Don't let him twist this to make you feel responsible. The blame lies squarely with the person who's leaving these notes and orchestrating these attacks."

I pull my arms tight around myself, shivering despite the warmth of the room. Every inch of my body aches with exhaustion. There is no safety, no distance between me and the predator who lurks just out of reach.

"Whoever he is..." I whisper, voice trembling, "he's not going to stop, is he?"

I can practically hear my father's teeth grinding together. All three men stand silent above me, a quiet conversation taking place just over my head.

"Mr. Miller, it's come to my attention that you recently had security cameras installed on the property. Is that correct?" Deputy Jones says, breaking the tense silence.

"We have."

"Mind if I take a look at it?"

He gestures toward the hallway that leads to the back of the house, where the security system is set up in the office. I follow, Jake close at my side, our footsteps too loud in the tension-filled silence.

Once in the office, Dad sits in front of the computer, his movements methodical as he navigates the system. The glow of the screen illuminates his furrowed brow and tight jaw—the only outward signs of his turmoil. With a few clicks, he pulls up the footage in several small boxes across the screen.

Deputy Jones leans forward, his eyes glued to every motion.

"Can you start from this mornin', when y'all left for work, and fast-forward it through now."

The only reply Dad gives is the click of the mouse as he does what the deputy asks.

"Is that..." My voice falters, the words strangling in my throat as I stare at the screen, disbelieving.

"It could be," Deputy Jones replies, his tone grim.

My skin prickles with unease, my pulse a frantic rhythm pounding in my ears. Jake's fists curl at his sides, his body practically vibrating with barely contained anger. Then he does something I never thought he would do in a million years.

He growls.

Chapter 39

The weather is surprisingly warm today, and that doesn't feel right. It shouldn't be warm today, not when we're burying the kindest man I've ever met. It should be storming. Gushing rain and lightning, not this. I glance around the cemetery at all the people gathering for the funeral; practically the whole town showed up. Several groups of people are sharing memories from his life and talking about how wonderful his bakery was. I want to smile at those comments, but I can't bring myself to do it. It feels wrong to smile when a man like Mr. Walters' light was stolen. Too soon, much too soon.

I stand there and listen for a while longer. It's easy to imagine Mr. Walters laughing amongst these people, offering comfort and joy in the simplest of ways. Yet, beneath the shared nostalgia, my heart aches with the thought of never walking through those bakery doors to his bright smile again. My heart also aches for another reason. It's been about a week since someone murdered Mr. Walters, and I haven't spoken to Jake since then. All I can think about is the way he growled when he saw the camera footage. My body immediately went into lockdown. I started having a panic attack and pushing him away. Deputy Jones didn't look pleased, but my father had a smug grin on his face in the beginning. Soon after, his worry for me took over. He kicked Jake out of our house before he could get a word in. He's called and texted, but I haven't replied. I know what he is now, and all I can think about is how he's lied to me this entire time. I trusted him, loved him, and he shredded that trust with his lies.

My skin prickles with awareness, turning I find Jake standing behind me. Close but not close enough to crowd me. I look him up and down; he looks handsome in his black suit. Tie snug against his throat, his hair styled with product. It is shocking to see him outside of his usual flannel and jeans combo. My heart swells in my chest, and tears cling to my eyes for an entirely different reason now. It feels like my body is trying to pull itself toward him, but I don't move. He's looking at me with so much longing in his eyes that it's hard to resist the urge to forget everything. To throw my arms around him and sink into his warmth. Somehow, I do.

"Sarah, I..." he starts. I throw my hand up, stopping his words before they can leave his mouth.

"Not now, Jake. Please."

A few tears trickle down my cheeks, and he hangs his head. I can see the hurt on his face, but I just can't do this today. I already feel so guilty for my part in Mr. Walters' death. I can't handle anything else.

A murmur breaks through the hum of somber recollections, snagging my attention. I turn toward the two women standing closest to me; their heads are bowed together in conspiracy as they gossip amongst themselves.

"Did you hear? Jordan's planning to close the bakery...," one whispers, her voice leaking disbelief.

My breath hitches, a cold dagger of shock piercing through the fog of grief. The bakery. The thought of its doors shuttering is inconceivable. And what about Sam? Surely Jordan wouldn't do that to Sam. Sam had dreams of taking over when his father retired. Except he isn't retiring now. Panic flutters in my chest, like a caged sparrow battering against its confines. This can't be happening.

"Are you sure?" The second woman asks, her question mirroring the tremor in my heart.

"I overheard him talking to Noah outside his office this morning. It's happening." The first woman says.

I look to Jake, seeking confirmation that I didn't just hear what I think I heard.

"Did you—" He starts, but is cut off by a sudden commotion.

"Jordan, you can't do this!" Sam's voice rises above the whispers, raw and edged with betrayal.

I whip my head toward the commotion. Sam stands toe-to-toe with his brother, hands clenched at his sides, breathing ragged. His bright blue eyes, usually so full of light, now shimmer with tears held back by sheer force of will. "That bakery is everything Dad built—it's our legacy!"

"It's not that simple, Sam," Jordan replies, his tone aggressive. The lines etched on his brow speak of sleepless nights and heavy burdens. "I've got no choice."

"You always have a choice!" Sam shoots back, his youthful face contorting in distress. "What about your promises? What about my dreams?"

"Promises aren't gonna pay the bills, Sam!" Jordan shouts, his voice strained.

Sam shrinks back from his brother. Jordan pinches the bridge of his nose; the tension in his shoulders speaks to the stress he must be feeling.

"Sam, please understand," Jordan pleads in a softer tone.

"Understand?" Sam's voice wavers, a crescendo of hurt breaking free. "How can I understand when it feels like you're giving up on everything we are?"

The words hang heavy between them, laden with years of unspoken fears and unmet expectations. The bakery isn't just a building; it's the heart of their family. Or, at least it is for Sam.

Lila stands from comforting their mother, Amelia, and walks over to the boys.

"Now is not the time for this," she hisses. "Pull your shit together; your mother needs you right now."

Sam has the decency to look ashamed while Jordan shoots daggers at Lila before storming off toward his mother. She cast me a glance, a silent question in her eyes. I know she sees the tension between Jake and I but we haven't even had time to talk about what's happening with her and Jordan, much less what is going on in my life.

Jake stays close to me throughout the service. He doesn't try to say anything else or to touch me. He's just there, quiet, steady. My emotions are conflicted when it comes to him, but I can't think of that now. Not now. Not when the sound of Amelia's sobs are filling the air and the guilt is eating at my stomach with every tear she cries.

Once the service ends, the crowd departs. I hang back, my gaze drifting to the closed doors of the bakery across the street. That sign unknowingly marks the end of more than just a business—it is the coup de grâce for the life I have found, the sanctuary I've come to know in the warm kitchen where flour dusted every surface like a fresh coat of snow.

I jerk my eyes away and scan the remaining crowd.

Sam stands a short distance away, his youthful features etched with a pain too heavy for his shoulders to bear. I watch him discreetly, my heart aching for the boy who seems lost in a sea of adult sorrows. I witness the exact moment he brushes away a tear, his attempt at composure slipping.

Resolving to act, I step away from Jake and cross the short distance to where Sam stands alone. I don't want it to be, but Jake's presence is a comforting warmth behind me as he follows. Sam must sense my approach as he turns to face me.

"Sam," I begin tentatively, reaching out to place a hand on his shoulder but think better of it. The last time I touched someone, they ended up dead. "I... I'm so sorry about your dad. If there's anything I can do to help..."

He looks at me, grief flickering across his features before something else takes its place—gratitude. "Thanks, Sarah. Dad always said you were one of the good ones."

"Your father was very special to all of us. He left big shoes to fill, but... but you're not alone in this." My voice is solemn but careful not to intrude too much into his grief.

"Feels like it sometimes," Sam admits with a crack in his voice. "Feels like the whole world's just... crumbling."

"Maybe," I concede. My thoughts turn to the early days after losing my mother. "But it won't feel that way forever. There will always be a hole in your life, but it will get less burdensome, little by little."

Sam manages a weak smile, nodding. It's an insignificant gesture, but at the moment, it feels like the most significant thing I can offer—a promise of solidarity in the face of loss.

Sam's freckled cheeks glisten with tears that he stubbornly tries to blink away.

"I don't know how to keep the bakery going without him," he confesses, his voice barely above a whisper. His hands, dressed in the somber fabric of his suit rather than the usual flour-dusted apron, now fumble with the hem of his jacket, twisting and pulling as if trying to seek solace from the familiar feel.

My heart aches at Sam's anguish. "I know how much the bakery means to you, Sam. It's your dream, too."

Sam nods, his gaze distant. "Yeah... Dad and I, we talked about expanding, about making it more than just a small town place."

"It still can be," I reassure him, my voice gentle yet determined. "You have all of his knowledge and passion. You can carry on what he started. You just need a little guidance."

"Jordan..." Sam's voice quivers with anger, his brow furrowing deeply. "He's selling. He's claiming it's because of money, but I know he wants out. I can't believe he's just gonna give up on Dad's dream like that."

"Talk to him, Sam," I urge softly. "Maybe he just needs time to come around. Your dad's legacy means everything to you both."

Sam's fists clench at his sides, his eyes flashing with frustration. "I can't let him walk away from this. Not after everything Dad built."

His bright blue eyes, usually so full of life and mischief, meet mine. They're like clear windows into his soul, revealing the tumultuous storm of doubt and fear within. "But what if that's not enough?"

"I'm sure—"

"Stay the fuck away from my brother." Jordan's voice suddenly cuts through our exchange, sharp and commanding. He looms over us, his chestnut hair showing no hint of the usual flour dust.

I step back reflexively, my gaze shifting to meet Jordan's stern hazel eyes. There's no warmth there, only a protective ferocity that seems incongruous with the somber setting of the funeral. "Jordan, I was just—"

"Whatever you were 'just,' it doesn't involve Sam." Jordan's firm hands, usually precise and gentle enough to craft the most delicate pastries, clench into fists at his side. "This is a family matter. Last I checked, you're not family."

"She was just trying to help," Sam interjects, his tone turning into a quiet plea.

"Help?" Jordan scoffs, stepping between me and his younger brother. "We don't need help. Especially not from her."

I've known about Jordan's dream—to leave Willow's Haven and the bakery behind—for awhile now. I just never thought that he would do so this quickly. He's not even letting the grass grow over his father's grave before he's uprooting everything in his life. And Sam's.

Jordan glares at me, his eyes holding a hatred that freezes my blood. "If you hadn't come into our lives, my father would still be alive."

I gasp as my hands tremble. The accusation stings like a physical blow. I twist a lock of hair around my finger, struggling to compose myself.

"Enough, Jordan!" Sam's outburst slices through the tension. His eyes flicker between us. "This isn't her fault."

I look at Sam; the pain in his gaze mirrors my own. "I'm so sorry," I whisper, though I know my guilt does nothing to undo the harm.

"Sorry won't bring him back," Jordan spits bitterly; his hands relax only to knead imaginary dough as he struggles to rein in his emotions. "He was fine before you came along, before you brought your... your complications into our lives."

"Complications?" Jake says. In all the conflict, I forgot he was standing next to me.

"Jordan," Sam pleads, stepping closer to his brother. "She cared about Dad. She's hurting too."

"Is she?" Jordan raises a brow.

Jake's jaw clenches, his hand absently rubs the back of his neck. The muscles in his arms tense, a protective instinct flaring within him as Jordan's harsh words slice through the air.

"Or is she just worried about herself? About her job?"

"That's enough!" Jake says, his voice strains with barely contained anger. He steps forward, positioning himself as a barrier between me and Jordan. "You're out of line."

"Stay out of this, Walker," Jordan spits. He pushes past Jake, inching dangerously close to me.

"Jordan, stop!" I plead.

"Your pity won't bring my father back!" He points his finger accusingly at me as his grief manifests into palpable rage.

Before another word can be exchanged, Jake's fist slams into Jordan's jaw; the crack echoes through the space. Jordan stumbles back, shock etched on his face as much from the blow as from the realization of who hit him. Sam gasps and reaches for his brother.

"Jake!" I cry, my voice trembling with fear and confusion.

Jake turns to me, his anger dissipating as quickly as it surged. "I'm sorry, I couldn't let him—"

"Everything okay here?" Lila's piercing blue eyes flick between all of us before settling on Jordan. His hand rubs his jaw as he glares back at her.

"Fuck off, Lila! Nothing is fucking okay! Why don't you stay out of shit that doesn't concern you?!" Jordan's voice rises as he shakes off Sam's grip.

Lila bristles; hurt flashes across her face before she schools her features. She huffs a breath. "You want me to leave it alone, Jordan? Fine, have it your way. But just know you're the one making an ass of yourself at your own father's funeral. Hope you're happy." She seethes, throwing Jake a hard glare as she walks away.

"Let's get out of here," I plead to Jake, my eyes brimming with tears that threaten to spill over. I glance once more at the brothers. Jordan is watching Lila. He shakes his head then stalks back across the grass to his mother. Sam sighs, he shoots me a pleading look and quietly followed.

We walk away in silence. His hand finds mine, and I let him grasp it. I may not know what I'm going to do about Jake and all his lies, but I do know that I need his strong touch at the moment. Mrs. Walters' sobs follow us like an oppressive fog, making my insides twist. Jordan's accusation reverberates in my mind, intensifying my guilt. My stalker echoed the same haunting sentiment in his note. If I hadn't hugged Henry, hadn't accepted that brief moment of solace, he would still be alive. I wonder how many others silently blame me for the loss of such a gentle soul. Lord knows I deserve all their ire.

"Sarah," Jake says softly as we reach the edge of the cemetery. "None of this is your fault. You know that, right?"

I attempt to swallow the lump in my throat, shaking my head slightly. "But it is, Jake. Jordan is right. If I hadn't come here, hadn't gotten close to his family, then none of this would have happened."

"Hey." Jake stops, turning to face me and ensuring I meet his gaze. "Don't do that to yourself. You have no control over the whims of a madman. It could have just as easily been anyone else."

I don't say anything, just nod. Jake will never understand the weight of the guilt I feel. And I'm not sure I want him to. This is my burden to bear, and I will bear it in silence. I release his hand and leave him standing in front of the entrance gate. He doesn't follow me, but I feel his eyes track me until I turn a corner out of sight.

Chapter 40

SARAH

Three days have crawled by since I left Jake standing on that sidewalk. Most of it I've spent in bed, drowning in guilt and grief, ignoring every message he's sent. I know we need to talk, but I can't bring myself to do it. A small part of me wants to pretend I don't know what I know, but there's no putting that genie back into its bottle.

Jake is a wolf shifter. He's been lying to me from the start.

I want to smack myself for being so stupid. Of course, I would be the one to come to a town famous for being predator-free and fall in love with one. I felt the danger in his aura on our first date, but I ignored it, chalking it up to nerves. I should've listened to my instincts. I should've run as far and fast as I could.

I sigh. No, that isn't fair. I know it isn't. I can't help feeling betrayed, but part of me still wants to believe Jake had no ill intentions in not telling me. My head and my heart are at war: one reminding me how wonderful he's been, how much I love him; the other whispering that everything I know is a lie. Can I even love him if I've never known the real him? That question gnaws at me. How well do I truly know Jake if I've never known this huge part of him?

I need coffee.

Flinging the covers off, I pad down to the kitchen. The machine has just started when a knock rattles the front door. The hairs on my neck lift. Everyone I know is at work or school; no one should be knocking at this hour. I grab the biggest knife from the block and head toward the door.

I feel ridiculous clutching it while someone pounds on the wood, but the irrational—or maybe rational—part of my brain says it could be my stalker. Surely a stalker wouldn't knock all politely... Would they?

Relief floods me when I peek through the curtain and see Jake on my porch. I unlock and swing the door open, meeting his somber eyes.

"Sarah." He breathes my name like seeing me is some kind of divine gift.

"Jake." I reply, somehow keeping my voice cooler than I feel inside.

"Can I come in?"

I open the door wider and step aside, with no hesitation or apprehension in my movements. My brain screams not to let him in, but my body fully trusts this man. I know in my soul that despite what Jake is, he would never hurt me — not with violence, anyway.

Jake scans the entryway as I close the door behind him.

"I was just making coffee. You want some?" I call over my shoulder as I head back to the kitchen.

"That would be nice, thanks."

I gesture toward the table for him to sit. He gives me a soft smile.

"You gonna stab me with that thing?"

I look down and realize I'm still holding the knife, and not only holding it but gesturing with it like some crazed psycho ordering around their victim.

"Oh." I shove the knife back into its spot. "Sorry. I guess I've gotten a bit jumpy with everything that's happened."

Jake nods and lowers himself into the closest chair. I busy myself making our drinks, then hand him a mug before sitting down across from him.

I blow on the rim a few times while looking anywhere but at him.

"Sarah, baby. Can you look at me?"

I do. God help me, but I do. What I see staring back at me guts me. He looks tired; his eyes are rimmed in black, and his face is sporting stubble he clearly hasn't shaved in several days. My heart clenches when I look at him, but I don't move, stay silent — just meet his eyes and continue to nurse my coffee.

He looks away first with a sigh before meeting my eyes again.

"I'm sorry I didn't tell you. I wanted to, but..."

"But what?"

"At first, I just didn't think anything of it. I was in the middle of telling you that first day when the twins interrupted. After that, I just couldn't bring it up. I was being a coward, I know."

He sighs, long and somber.

"When you told me about your mom, I got scared. Scared you'd see me as a monster, like the one who..."

"Who killed her?" I finish for him, setting my mug down on the table with a soft thwack. "And you thought lying would be better?"

He jerks back as if I'd slapped him. "No! No, nothing like that. I just..."

He takes a deep breath. "Every day I wanted to tell you. I fought myself on it so many times, but every time I saw the fear in your eyes, the scars that bastard left on your heart, I couldn't add to your pain."

I scoff, feeling both betrayed and foolish. "Were you really trying to protect me from more pain, or were you just protecting yourself?"

"Both," he admits, his shoulders sagging. "I was selfish, but I also wanted to shield you from more hurt. I thought if I could just show you the good in me, in us, maybe you could look past the wolf shifter part. You've seen how this town reacts to my kind. You yourself are terrified of us. I never intended to keep it a secret, but after you told me about your mom... I couldn't."

"That wasn't your decision to make!" Tears sting my eyes, blurring his pained face. "You don't get to choose what I can or can't handle. You took that choice away from me."

"I know," he breathes. "I'm sorry, Sarah, truly. If I could take it all back, I would."

I want to scream at the cliché of his words. If he could take it all back, humph. He's only feeling this way now because he got caught in it. If he had never revealed himself, how long would he have kept it from me? Endless questions nag at my mind, but one forces its way past my lips before I can stop it.

"How can I trust anything you say now?"

My voice breaks. "Being a wolf shifter isn't just a minor detail, Jake! It changes everything." I look away, unable to bear the intensity of his gaze. "You might not be a predator by choice, but you chose to deceive me. Did you think I wouldn't find out?" The questions flow from my lips, loosened by the immensity of his betrayal. "Or were you ever really planning on telling me someday? When? After we had a life together?"

"I always planned on telling you," he says, his voice cracking under the strain of his emotions. "I just... couldn't find the words. I've lived in fear of others in this town finding out for so long..."

My eyes fill with tears. I blink them away, unwilling to let them fall. "So instead, you lied to me. For months, Jake. Months!"

He winces under the intensity of my words.

"Speaking of this town, how does everyone think you're a non-predator?"

He looks taken aback by the question, his mouth parting before he finally exhales.

"For the most part, they don't ask," he says quietly. "They see what they want to see. Most shifters can't read auras well enough to tell the difference, and the ones who can, are easy to fool if you know how to mask it. It's not hard to hide when people already believe what they want to believe."

I cross my arms. "And what would happen if they didn't?"

His expression hardens, something dark flickering behind his eyes. "You really don't know, do you?"

I shake my head, the silence between us stretching thin.

"They don't just run predators out of town," he says, voice low and heavy. "They hunt them out. Threats. Slurs carved into doors. Rocks through windows. Refusing business until families starve. Stuffed animals strung up from trees and set on fire like trophies. Sometimes people disappear in the middle of the night, and everyone just pretends they never existed. No one stops it. No one even talks about it."

"They call this place safe," he continues, almost to himself. "But safety built on hate isn't safety at all."

I can't find the words. My throat burns, shame mixing with the sting of betrayal.

"So you hid," I manage finally.

"I had to," he says. "It was the only way to stay alive."

He looks at me then, and there's nothing defensive in his gaze. Just exhaustion. "I wasn't trying to deceive you, Sarah. I was trying to survive in a town that would rather see me hanging from a tree than sitting in your kitchen."

He pauses, his gaze distant. "Sheriff Anderson's the only one who ever tries to keep things fair. He's strict about the law, by-the-book to the core, but he's one man trying to hold back a mob. Most of the deputies don't share his morals."

My pulse quickens. "You mean Deputy Jones?"

Jake nods. "Yeah. Ethan's been here longer than I have. Keeps things polite on the surface, but I've never heard him say a kind word about predators. He doesn't need to. Everyone knows where he stands. And now..." He swallows hard. "After what happened with Mr. Walters, I'm sure he has suspicions."

A chill runs through me. I can still hear that growl in my head, low and raw, the sound that made my blood run cold. Ethan had been right there beside us when it happened. Watching. Listening.

"You think he realized what it was?" I ask quietly.

Jake nods, the movement tense. "He's not stupid, Sarah. He might not say anything outright, but he knows something's off. And that's bad enough."

I study him for a long moment. The fear in his eyes is real, but so is the pain in my chest. Everything I thought I knew about him feels like it's shifting beneath my feet.

"How am I supposed to live with that?" I whisper. "How can I ever feel safe with you again?"

"Because I love you," he says, his voice breaking as the words leave him. They hang between us, heavy with truth and sorrow.

"Love isn't built on lies, Jake." My voice shakes, but it still carries the weight of my shattered trust. "And right now, I don't know if it can be rebuilt at all."

"I should have told you sooner," he says. "I can't change that. All I can do is promise you that from now on, I'll be honest. Completely."

"From now on?" My eyes narrow, the hurt bleeding into anger.

"Yes," he says, meeting my gaze without flinching. "I don't want to lose you. I'd rather face whatever this town throws at me than keep lying to you."

My lips tremble as I look at him, torn between anger and the ache of what we used to be. I want to believe him. I want to trust in our love. But could I? Could I really look past the lie that had been woven into the very fabric of us? Predator shifters are dangerous and cruel. One murdered my mother in cold blood. But this is Jake. My Jake.

"Jake," I whisper, my voice barely audible. "I need time. To think. To process all of this."

He nods slowly, eyes glassy with emotion. "Of course. Take all the time you need, Little Trash Panda. You're my soulmate. I'll be here when you're ready to talk. And if you decide I'm not what you want, then I'll call a witch and we'll get rid of the bond."

He stands, the chair legs scraping softly against the floor. For a second, it looks like he wants to reach for me, but he doesn't. His hand falls back to his side.

"Goodbye, Sarah."

I don't answer. I just watch as he turns and walks out the door, his footsteps fading down the porch steps. The silence he leaves behind is deafening, a hollow ache settling where his presence used to be.

Chapter 41

I feel like Atlas in this moment, the pressure of everything suddenly bearing down on me. The sensory details of the town—the rustle of leaves, the distant call of a bird—fade into the background as I struggle to process the emotional maelstrom swirling inside.

"Dammit," I curse, pounding my fist against the steering wheel. I want nothing more than to turn this truck around and wrap Sarah in my arms until she melts into me. But that won't help the situation. She asked for space, and I promised her that. I can't go back on my word now, especially not after the way things ended. I promised her honesty from here on out, and I am going to keep that promise come hell or high water.

Instead, I steer toward the mountains. I need guidance. Someone to help me through this maze of guilt and longing. But not my parents, not yet. My thoughts drift to Charlie.

Charlie always knows what to say. Somehow he cuts through the noise and gets straight to the heart of things. Dude's going to make an excellent dad one day. Lord knows he gets plenty of practice between me and the twins.

Reaching out to him means facing the truth of my own failings, admitting how badly I've messed up. I can't undo the past, but maybe, just maybe, I can find a way to mend the future. With a heavy heart, I press harder on the gas, hoping Charlie's steady presence at the end of the road will offer some kind of clarity.

The gravel crunches beneath my boots as I approach the dimly lit garage. The glow of a single bulb casts long shadows across the concrete floor where Betsy, his old Ford truck, sits. I can hear the clink of tools and Charlie's low humming before I spot his grease-stained boots poking out from beneath the vehicle.

"Charlie?" I call out, hesitating at the door.

"Yeah!" comes the slightly muffled reply. "What brings you out this way, Jake?"

I crouch down, peering under the truck to see Charlie's face illuminated by a drop light. There's not much light, but enough to notice the lines of concentration around his eyes.

"Need to talk," I say, my voice coming out more strained than I intend.

Charlie slides out, pushing himself up to sit on the cold floor while wiping his hands on a grease-stained rag. "Trouble with Sarah?"

"Yeah. Sorta." I rub the back of my neck, my gaze dropping to the oil-streaked ground. "She knows about me now."

"Ah." Charlie's eyes soften with understanding. "How'd she take it?"

"About as well as a cornered cat. I've hurt her, man." My voice breaks slightly. "I never meant for any of this to happen."

Charlie shakes his head, giving me a shit-eating grin. "You know, I could say I told you so, but I'm a better friend than that."

I groan and flip him the bird.

Charlie chuckles and leans against the truck's tire, tapping his fingers rhythmically on the rubber. "You feel any better?"

"Fuck no," I mutter, frustration bleeding into my tone.

"Yeah, didn't think so. Can't say you don't deserve it for putting it off for so long."

Rather than punch him in his smug face, I kick the truck tire and start pacing around the garage with my fingers linked behind my head.

"Dammit, Jake!" Charlie yells, crouching down to inspect the tire for damage. "I know you're pissed, but don't take it out on Betsy. She didn't do shit to you."

I stop pacing and meet his eyes. "I don't know what bug crawled up your ass lately, but I didn't come here to get berated for shit I can't change. I came here for my friend. Now if you can't be that for me right now, then I can just leave."

"Fair enough," he says as he stands and wipes some invisible dirt off the side of the truck.

He sighs. "Just give her time, Jake. From what you've told me, this was a big deal for her, and you deliberately kept it from her. She's feeling betrayed right now, and the wounds are fresh."

"I already agreed to give her space," I say, the words tasting bitter in my mouth. "But what if space just makes her realize she's better off without me?"

"Then you'll respect that decision," Charlie says, his tone firm but gentle. "Patience, Jake. Understanding. Those are your strengths. Use them."

The silence hangs between us until I finally break it. "You heard anything new on Beau?"

Charlie's expression shifts, the humor draining out of him. He drops the rag onto the workbench and leans back against Betsy's fender, letting out a slow sigh. "Not much. Buckley called this morning. They took Beau in for another surgery on his hand. Docs think he might get to keep it, but they don't expect much movement. Still no change otherwise."

My throat tightens. "Still in a coma?"

Charlie nods, eyes fixed on the floor. "Yeah. Buckley hasn't left the hospital since it happened. Mama Annie takes him food every night, says he just sits there talking to Beau like he's gonna wake up any second."

Guilt twists in my gut. I drag a hand down my face, my fingers digging into the stubble along my jaw. "If they hadn't been out helping me track that bastard, Beau wouldn't be lying in that hospital bed right now. It should've been me, not him."

Charlie's head lifts, his eyes steady and unflinching. "You don't get to shoulder that, Jake. We all made that call. Beau knew the risks, same as the rest of us."

"Doesn't make it easier to live with," I mutter.

"Never does," Charlie says quietly. "Every damn day I pray he wakes up. He's too damn stubborn not to. But you're not the one who put him there. Don't start thinking like you are."

We fall silent again. The garage smells of oil and cold steel, the faint buzz of the drop light filling the silent space between us. For a moment, neither of us knows what to say, because what else is there? Some things you can't fix. You just wait and hope like hell the world shows a little mercy.

Chapter 42

SARAH

The lamplight casts a golden hue over the room, throwing shadows behind the overstuffed armchairs where we sit. I can feel the warmth of the room on my skin, a comforting presence in the cozy space Lila has created. But even amidst the softness of the cushions and the familiarity of our shared silence, my fingers betray me—twining and untwining a lock of dark hair that's escaped my ponytail.

It's been four days since my confrontation with Jake, and he has yet to reach out. I know I told him I needed space, but a small part of me hoped he would anyway. Just a text to say he was thinking of me. Instead, I've heard nothing. I don't know why that upsets me so much. He's doing exactly what I asked him to do. But I'm not here for me. Tonight I am here for Lila.

I watch as she fumbles with a lock of golden hair, twirling it around her finger in a way that says her thoughts are miles away. The lamplight cast a warm glow on her face, etching soft shadows into the lines of worry creeping over her usually cheerful features.

I quietly tap my fingers against my jeans, waiting for her to start the conversation she called me over for. Her shoulders sag, and when she finally lifts her eyes to meet mine, they're heavy with sorrow.

"He's gone." Her voice is so soft, I'm not sure I heard her right.

"Who is?"

"Jordan..." she replies, looking down at her hands.

My eyes widen. I lean forward, resting my elbows on my knees. I can't say I'm surprised that Jordan left; the way everyone talked at the funeral, it sounded like he couldn't wait to get out of this town, but I didn't think he'd drop everything so fast. Or that he'd abandon Lila. Or Sam.

"Did he say anything to you? Before he disappeared?" I ask, my heart aching for both of my friends.

She swallows hard, lifting her gaze again. Her eyes shimmer with a mix of defiance and pain. "Nothing. He just left, Sarah. No explanation, no goodbye. Just vanished."

"Nothing?"

She shakes her head. "I only found out because Sam told me. He came in to see Noah yesterday about the will."

She lets out a bitter snort. "I'm not an idiot. I know our relationship was... complicated. We've always had this push-and-pull thing. One minute we're trading barbs, the next we're sharing flour-dusted kisses and hate-fucking whenever we get the chance. Lord knows we don't love each other, but I thought I meant enough to him to at least get a goodbye call."

"Have you tried calling him?" I ask gently, knowing all too well the torment of unanswered questions.

She huffs, frustration etching lines across her face. "Yes. Asshole either blocked me or turned off his phone. Every call goes straight to voicemail."

I clasp my fingers together to keep from letting them curl into fists. "What an asshat!" I snap, my voice sharper than I intend.

Lila hiccups and nods as tears stream down her face.

"There's more," she says between quiet sobs.

I move to her chair and nudge her over to make room, wrapping my arms around her in a tight embrace. My fingers trace slow, soothing circles on her back. She clings to me, her sobs growing louder in the quiet space. I say nothing — I know she'll tell me the rest when she's ready. Right now, she just needs this.

I hold her for several long minutes until she finally leans back, wiping her face with trembling hands. She grabs a tissue from the box on the end table and blows her nose. After a few deep breaths, she looks up at me — shame flickering in her eyes.

"I think I'm pregnant."

Her words hit me like a brick to the heart. I pull her close again as another wave of sobs shakes her. When I draw back, I wipe the tears from her cheeks.

"Hey. Hey, it's okay. You don't know for sure yet, right? You might not be. And if you are, we'll figure it out. It's not the end of the world."

She stands, pacing the room, sniffling and brushing away stray tears.

"No. I don't know for sure, but I have this gut feeling. I even stopped and bought a few tests on the way home today."

"Well," I say, trying to sound reassuring, "then it sounds like we won't know for certain until you take one. For all we know, you're worrying about nothing."

Fifteen minutes later, I'm holding Lila as she cries hysterically into my shoulder. I try to focus on anything else—the dripping faucet, the sound of her hiccuping breaths—but my eyes keep drifting back to the three pregnancy tests lined up on the counter.

Two vivid lines stare back at me from each one. There's no mistaking it.

Lila is pregnant.

Chapter 43

The shrill sound of my phone ringing pulls me out of a dead sleep. I smack my hand along the nightstand until I find the smooth surface of glass. My heart rate spikes when I read the name flashing across the screen—Sam. A quick glance at the clock tells me it's 10:50 p.m. I answer as I throw the covers off my body.

"Sam? What's going on? Is everything ok?"

Sniffling comes from the other end of the line, followed by a pained moan.

"I'm so sorry," Sam blubbers. "I didn't know who else to call. It's my mom. Something's wrong with her."

I search around my room for my robe and throw it on. "It's alright, Sam. Have you called an ambulance?"

The sound of him murmuring reassurances to his mom fills my ear before he comes back on the line.

"No." His voice is shaky and terrified. "It's a shifter problem, not a medical one. There's nothing they'll be able to do for her."

"Ok." I run my hands through my hair, trying to think of what I need to grab. "Send me your address and I'll be there as soon as I can."

"Okay," he breathes. "I'll text it to you now."

Neither of us says goodbye before hanging up. I fling open my closet and grab the first pair of shoes I see. They're ratty flip-flops I usually only wear in the summer, but they'll do. Slipping my phone into my pocket, I frantically search for my car keys. A ping comes from my phone, and I don't have to look to know it's Sam. I pause for a moment, letting my brain catch up to the situation. Then I remember—my keys are on the ring by the garage door.

Flinging my bedroom door open, I come face to chest with a warm body. I know instantly who it is when he speaks.

"Whoa. Where's the fire, Doodle Bug? What's going on?"

"Dad!" I practically shout in relief. "It's Sam. He called and said there's something wrong with his mom. I could hear her in the background; she sounded like she was in a lot of pain."

He places steadying hands on my shoulders. "Breath, baby." He demonstrates with slow, even breaths. "That's it. Nice and deep."

I nod, following his lead. My heart rate slows closer to normal, though it does nothing for my nerves.

"Give me a minute to throw on some shoes, and we'll head out."

"Wha... Dad, no. You don't have to go. I can handle it."

He gives me a stern look, one brow raised. "If you think I'm letting my daughter leave this house in the middle of the night alone, much less to the same house where her stalker killed a man, you're sorely mistaken. I. Am. Coming."

I shrink back a little from his intensity. "Fair point."

Without another word, he stalks back to his bedroom and returns a moment later with shoes on his feet. He gestures for me to lead the way, following me down the stairs and into the night.

I barely throw the car in park before I'm out of the vehicle, Dad hot on my heels. My knuckles scantily brush the door when it swings open, revealing a disheveled and terrified Sam. He grabs my hand and pulls me into the house, leaving Dad to close the door behind us.

A pain-filled cry echoes from down the hall as Sam drags me toward the open bedroom. My lungs seize up the moment I pass the threshold.

Curled on the floor is Mrs. Walters. Her nightdress sticking to her sweaty skin, her hair knotted and unwashed. She clutches her stomach as another wail passes her lips. Ripples of fur flicker across her skin as her magic surges.

"Christ." Dad mutters, stepping fully into the room. "How long has she been like this?"

Sam shakes his head. "I'm not sure. She started screaming about an hour ago."

Dad kneels beside her, checking her pulse and pressing the back of his hand to her forehead.

"Is it...?" I can't bring myself to finish the question. My heart hammers and my palms sweat as memories of Mrs. Delaney flood my mind. My eyes snap to Sam. "How long has it been since she's shifted?"

He clinches his fist a few times, then wipes his eyes with the sleeve of his shirt. "She's been fighting it. Her magic forced a shift a few days ago, right before Jordan left, but ever since Dad..." his voice cracks "...she's been...off;"

I shake my head, confusion and dread churning in my gut. It's obvious Mrs. Walters is grieving the loss of her husband and refusing to shift. What makes no sense is why Jordan would leave during a time like this.

"Does Jordan know this is happening?"

Sam nods but won't meet my eyes. There's something more he's not saying. Amelia screams again as Dad tries to soothe her, his voice low and calm against the chaos.

I rack my brain for a solution to this problem. Her husband, the man she loved, just died, and then her eldest son up and left. She's in a lot of emotional pain right now, and Jordan leaving sure as hell didn't help. If I had to guess, she's probably depressed, like the world drained every reason she had to keep going. Not even for Sam. Poor Sam. If that's the case, he's probably going to feel like shit about it for a long time.

"I'll be right back," I say, already halfway out the door. In the living room, I pull out my phone with shaking hands and call the one person I know might actually be able to help.

I stand back, clutching Sam's hand in mine while Lila kneels next to Amelia. Dad has stepped back to give her space but stays close in case he's needed. He has a strange look on his face that I can't quite decipher.

Lila reaches out and brushes a strand of hair from Amelia's face.

"Amelia, honey," she says in a calm, soothing tone. "I know you're hurting right now, but I need you to shift for me."

Amelia sobs and shakes her head. "Just. Let. Me. Die," she chokes out between sobs.

"I can't do that, sweetie." Lila takes a deep breath, steadying herself for her next words. She takes Amelia's hand and places it over her still-flat stomach.

"I can't raise this baby alone, and they're going to need their grandma to help me look after them."

Sam squeezes my hand tighter as shock flashes across his face.

Amelia looks at Lila with wide eyes. She sits up and wraps an arm around Lila's shoulders, pulling her close, her other hand still resting on her stomach.

"I'm going to be a grandma?" she sniffles.

Lila nods, her hand rubbing gentle circles down Amelia's back. Amelia sobs into her shoulder—this time the sound is different, still broken but no longer hopeless.

"Henry is going to miss seeing his first grand-baby."

"I know," Lila says, tears streaming down her cheeks in silent rivers. "But they'll have me, you, and Sam. We'll give them all the love they'll ever need and tell them all about their grandpa."

Amelia pulls back and wipes her eyes. "And Jordan?"

Lila lowers her head for a moment, composing herself before she looks up with a sad smile. "If he ever comes back, I don't plan on keeping him away from his kid, Amelia."

Amelia pulls Lila into another hug and kisses her cheek. "Thank you," she whispers, then gently pushes her away.

Amelia grits her teeth, grunting through the pain as she shifts. One minute she's curled on the floor, and the next, a sleek golden colored cougar lies in her place.

Holy fucking shit.

Sam pulls me into the hall and grabs my shoulders, his face a mix of worry and panic.

"Breathe, Sarah."

I suck in a deep breath and exhale sharply.

"Your mom is a—"

"I know."

"Are you a...?"

"No. Jordan and I are deer shifters, like our dad."

From where we're standing, I can still see into the bedroom. Lila's talking softly to Amelia while my dad runs his hands over her head, scratching gently behind her ears. She lets out a low grunt—more like a chuff—every now and then.

What the hell is going on? How is he *not* freaking out right now?

Sam grabs my face and turns me toward him. "You good?"

I nod, surprised to realize it's true. I guess finding out your boyfriend's the kind of shifter you hate most takes the panic right out of you. I'm more shocked by Amelia's other form than anything. My stomach twists a little—because, yeah, technically she *could* eat me—but that's ridiculous. This is Amelia. She's an amazing mom to Sam and Jordan. She was married to Henry, the sweetest man I've ever known. She's an elementary school teacher, for Christ's sake. Surely, if she were dangerous, everyone would know by now. Right?

I take a few more steadying breaths. Sam gives me a small, relieved smile when he sees I've calmed down.

I peek back into the bedroom; nothing's changed. Amelia's still making those soft chuffing noises, which is... a bit concerning.

"It's part of the reason Jordan left," Sam whispers. His voice is heavy with sadness, and when I face him again, I can see it in his eyes too.

"What is?" I ask, confused.

"'Cause of Mom." He shrugs like it's nothing, but the tight set of his shoulders says otherwise. The poor kid's barely holding it together.

"What do you mean, Sam?"

"We didn't know." His eyes drop to the floor as he speaks. "A few days ago, when she was forced to shift—that was the first time we'd ever seen her like that. Dad always took Jordan and me out for our shifts since we were deer like him. We thought she was a badger. That's what Dad always told us."

"What?" My brows furrow.

Sam lets out an exasperated sigh and pinches the bridge of his nose. "It's a lot, I know. You've seen what this town is like, Sarah. Imagine if people found out about Mom. She's never harmed a fly—okay, well maybe a fly, but you get the drift."

I nod slowly, unsure of where he's going with this.

"Anyway," he continues, "Mom told me they always planned to tell us when we were older. They were worried we might accidentally say something as kids."

Sam grabs the back of his neck and squeezes. "They were planning to tell us when we hit puberty, but when we both ended up being deer shifters, they decided to wait."

He shrugs, looking exhausted. "I think Jordan turning out more anti-predator didn't help the situation."

"What do you mean?"

Sam gives me a sad look and shakes his head. "I mean that despite our parents trying to steer us away from all that anti-predator crap, Jordan drank the Kool-Aid, so to speak."

I lower my head, a sudden rush of shame washing over me. My cheeks burn. I think about Jake—and how I've treated him. I want to say I'm more upset about the lies than the fact he's a predator shifter, but honestly? I'm not sure that's true.

"Shit. No. Hey, hey." Sam lifts my chin with his fingers until our eyes meet. "You are *not* like the ones in this town. You went through something awful. It's understandable that you'd be... wary."

I glance away, nodding, eyes flicking toward the bedroom. The scene inside hasn't changed.

Sam follows my gaze. "We need help. She's not expelling the magic fast enough. She needs to run."

Chapter 44

I grunt and groan as a catchy pop song blares across my bedroom.

"Who the fuck—?" I grumble, throwing the covers off and sitting up. The glow from my phone makes me squint as I grab it off the nightstand.

My heart slams against my ribs when I see her name on the screen. I don't even think—I just swipe.

"Sarah?" My voice cracks, a hint of panic slipping through.

"Hey. Sorry to call so late."

Her voice filling my ear feels like the first breath after nearly drowning—sharp, exhilarating, life-giving.

"No, no, it's okay. Never apologize for calling me."

Fuck, I sound like a simp.

She goes quiet for a moment, and I worry I've said too much.

"We need your help."

The sound of my knocks reverberates down the quiet street. Sam throws the door open and ushers me inside, leaning out to check the street before closing it again. I follow him down the hall to the primary bedroom—and the scene inside takes me off guard.

Amelia is lying on the floor in her cougar form, alternating between chuffs and pants. Lila kneels beside her, speaking in a soothing tone, but it's Thomas running his fingers through her fur and scratching her ears that surprises me most. Sarah stands near the wall, arms folded tight, her worry written plain across her face.

I kneel next to Lila, placing a hand on Amelia's shoulder as I lean in to speak.

"Hey, Amelia. I heard you need a little assistance tonight."

She blinks, eyes glassy and distant, but doesn't make another sound.

"I'm going to get you somewhere safe where you can expel this excess, alright? Just lay there for a few more minutes while I get everything worked out."

Thomas cuts me a sideways glare, his jaw tight, but he doesn't stop petting her. Something is definitely going on there, but right now it's none of my business. My priority is getting Amelia out of this house without half the neighborhood catching a glimpse. Even at this hour, there are *Nosy Nancys* who live for porchlight drama.

I make my way over to Sarah. She offers me a small smile that makes my breath catch for a moment. I'd started to forget how beautiful her smile is in person—but even a glimpse of it feels like looking directly at the sun.

"I need to borrow your SUV," I whisper. "It's the biggest vehicle here with any covering. My truck will work in a pinch, but I don't want to risk someone seeing her in the bed while I'm driving out of town."

She immediately nods. "Whatever you need."

I motion for Sam, relaying the plan. He leaves to move the car out of the carport, Sarah following close behind.

I pull a clean sheet from the closet and spread it on the floor behind Amelia, tucking part of it under her back.

"Alright, Amelia. Thomas and I are going to grab you by your front and hind legs—"

Thomas hisses at me, and I have to do everything in my power not to roll my eyes.

"Lila's going to slide her hands underneath you and grab the sheet. When I count to three, Thomas and I will pull our way, and Lila will pull hers. Once the cars are in place, we'll lift you and get you into the SUV."

I crouch into position, hands poised just above her fur, feeling the faint tremor of magic under her skin.

"One, two, three."

I grunt with the effort. If you ever want to really test your strength, try moving someone's deadweight. Even with help, it isn't easy. Hopefully lifting her won't be too straining.

Sam and Sarah clear the doorway.

"We're ready," she says.

I nod, repositioning myself to lift a corner of the sheet. Sam grabs his corner, then glares at Lila. "Uh-uh. You let Sarah take that spot. You're carrying my nephew, and there's no way you're lifting anything if I have any say in the matter."

My eyes widen. "You're pregnant?"

She glares at Sam, then at me, reluctantly releasing the sheet and stepping back. "That is *private information*, Jake Walker. It does not leave this room, you understand?"

I would never tell someone else's business like that. I'm not some geriatric church lady who can't hold water in her mouth. I say the only thing I know that will appease her. "Yes, ma'am."

Sarah adjusts her hold, trying not to giggle. I want to give her a playful smile, but with Lila still glaring daggers at me, I don't dare.

"On three." I take a few deep breaths, steadying myself. "One, two... three."

My arms strain under the exertion, but we manage to lift her. Carefully, we move down the hall and through the living room. Lila jogs ahead, opening the side door. She glances around, then gives us a thumbs-up. We maneuver through the doorway, making our way to the back of the SUV.

Thomas and I trade corners so we can get in one at a time. We gently pull Amelia across the carpet until she's far enough inside to shut the door. I climb over the middle seats, wiggling and contorting my body in ways I never thought possible. By the time I make it out, Thomas has climbed out the back and closed the door.

I glance around the street and carport. Sam and Lila stand shoulder to shoulder by the door, while Thomas lingers near the rear of the SUV. Sarah stands next to me, holding up her keys.

"You want me to drive?"

She nods. "I figured you know where you're going, so you might as well." She drops them into my hand.

"You ready to go, then?"

She opens her mouth to answer just as Thomas comes barreling around the side of the car. "She's not going anywhere with you."

I practically shake with the effort not to sigh dramatically. Sarah reaches out, placing her delicate hand on my bicep, and I can't help but smile down at her.

"I... um." Her eyes flick around before finally landing on mine. I see her gather her resolve as she takes a shuddering breath. "I think it's time we had a talk."

I can't help teasing her. "You think?"

She shakes her head, her slender fingers coming up to rest across those delightfully plump lips of hers. Smirking, I wait patiently. "Not think—*need*. We need to talk."

My heart stutters in my chest. Part of me is afraid that whatever she has to say will be the end of us—that she wants to find a witch to sever our bond. But another part is hopeful. Maybe her wanting to talk is a good thing. Maybe she's had time to come to terms with everything... and maybe I'm enough for her. Beyond the doubts, beyond the fears, *I am enough*.

"I'd like that, Little Trash Panda."

I don't get to say anything else before Thomas cuts in. "Alright, enough dillydallying. We need to get this show on the road. The sooner we get Amelia somewhere safe, the sooner she can feel better."

Guilt swarms me for a moment, but I can't find it in me to truly regret it. Amelia's going to be just fine. A few extra minutes to talk to my girl isn't going to hurt.

I dig around in my pocket, pulling out my truck keys. Dropping them into Sarah's hand, I curl her fingers around them. "Be extra careful with her, alright? She's my baby."

Lila snorts. "I think Charlie's got you beat on the human–automotive lovers scale."

Sarah smiles brightly as I shake my head.

Climbing into the SUV, I twist around to check on Amelia. She's not making that chuffing noise anymore, which is a good sign. Her eyes are closed, though she's not asleep—*yet*. I imagine after this, she'll probably sleep for days.

I reach to put the vehicle in gear when the passenger door slams shut against its frame. A quick glance reveals Thomas in the seat beside me. I arch a brow but keep my mouth shut.

He doesn't either as he snaps his belt into place. Pulling the gearshift, I ease out into the night, checking the rearview as we drive off. Sarah stands at the end of the driveway, those delicate fingers once again resting across her lips.

I don't know why, but a sudden urge hits me—strong and relentless—to keep her close. It's like an itch under my skin, buzzing louder the farther I get from her. The feeling makes no sense; everything's fine. She's safe. We all are. Still, the night feels wrong somehow—too quiet, too still. I shake it off, telling myself it's just the adrenaline wearing thin, but the thought lingers like a shadow at the edge of my mind, whispering that peace never lasts long in this town.

Chapter 45

SARAH

The engine dies with a low rumble as I turn the key. I sit there for a moment, breathing deep, letting the night sounds slip through the cracked window. It took some convincing to get Sam and Lila to let me drive home alone, but I needed this—quiet, distance, room to breathe. Everything feels so suffocating lately, and I can't handle anymore right now.

We haven't seen or heard anything from my stalker since he killed Mr. Walters. There isn't a blizzard keeping him away this time, and I'm hoping that the bullet he got from Jake was enough to deter him any further.

Doubtful since it didn't stop him from killing an innocent man, but one can dream. Still, I am cautious. I give the yard and surrounding neighborhood a thorough once over before I leave the truck. Once again as I walk across my yard and once more when I make it to my door.

As I slide the key into the lock, the hairs on the back of my neck suddenly stand on end. Before I can turn, strong arms wrap around me, a gloved hand clamping over my mouth. A husky male voice whispers in my ear.

"I finally got you, My Flower. You played one hell of a game, but now that I've caught you, I'm never letting you go."

I scream into his palm, thrashing. His shushing only fuels my panic. Sucking in as much air as I can through his fingers, I scream louder.

"Fuck," he mutters behind me before one arm leaves my waist and begins fumbling around.

I jerk forward, trying to break his hold on my jaw. His fingers dig deep into my skin as he holds me against him. My heel makes contact with his foot, and he hisses, muttering curses as his fumbling intensifies. A sharp prick against my neck has me kicking my feet backward harder.

"Shh, My Flower. Everything will be alright. You'll see."

My heart is pounding against my chest as my body weakens. I kick, flail, claw for purchase, but my limbs turn heavy like they've been filled with wet cement. Gradually, my vision darkens, and the sound fades into a dull rush before my body goes slack in his hold. The scent of his gloves, the rasp of his breath, the world narrowing to the pulse in my throat—then his voice, low and satisfied, just before everything stops.

Chapter 46

Amelia darts in front of me once more, her long, lithe body blurring against the backdrop of the darkened trees as she runs. This is her tenth cycle through the pre-laid paths. It took a few years for all our friends and family to make these natural trails through the forest, but it was well worth it. They're easy to follow and provide a safe space to let your mind wander without worry. I'm a bit surprised that Henry never asked for access, but that's neither here nor there. What matters right now is that Amelia is safe.

Thomas is leaning against the side of the SUV, arms crossed, watching Amelia make her rounds. His tall body is taut with tension as she zooms past. He hasn't spoken since he got into the vehicle. I can't say if that is a good thing or a bad one. Most of my interactions with this man have been less than ideal, but he is Sarah's father—a father that she loves dearly. The last thing I want to do is come between the two of them.

I let my mind wander to the conversation earlier. She said she wanted to talk to me. I'm trying so hard not to let my heart hope, but damn it's difficult. It's like trying to plug a drain with a colander. She's got me wrapped around her fingers, and I can't say that I'm mad about it. It's the best place in this world to be. I knew from the moment that I saw her that she was it. There ain't a damn thing in this world that I wouldn't give her if she asked. Even walking away. It would break me—God knows it would—but I don't have it in me to deny her anything. She could walk across my naked body in stilettos and I would only beg her for more, and I'd thank her for the pain. Because it'd still be her touch.

Fuck, I really am a simp.

A smile curves my lips. But I'm *her* simp.

Thomas glances over at me, his body tightening further. It's like the man forgot I was here. I open my mouth to say something—what; I don't know—when the air shifts, heavy and sharp, crawling over my skin like static. The bond between Sarah and me pulls tight, sudden and wrong, like a wire yanked too hard—dragging in a direction she isn't supposed to be in. My brows furrow as I turn toward Willow's Haven. I can't see the town from here, but I know which direction it's situated in. Turning toward it fully, my confusion only grows. She's headed southwest. The pull gets more and more taut the further away she moves. The sensation is weird; I can't tell exactly where she is, just the general area. It's like Dad said—it's not like a GPS.

Something's wrong. The thought hits before I can even name why. I fumble in my pocket for my phone, pulling it free. Thomas turns fully toward me, curiosity written on his features. The line rings and rings, finally connecting to a voicemail that rattles off the number I just called. I pull the phone away and dial again. The same happens. Muttering a curse, I turn to Thomas.

"Something is wrong."

He stands up straighter, unfolding his arms as worry fills his features.

"What does that mean exactly?" he grumbles, his voice low and rough. With danger or fear—or both—I don't know.

"I mean, she isn't where she is supposed to be, and Charlie isn't answering his phone."

Thomas wastes no time rounding the car, hopping into the driver's seat. I scramble after him, barely closing the door before he takes off. I look back and see Amelia's cougar standing at the edge of the woods watching us. She doesn't appear distressed as she turns and heads back into the underbrush. Still, my gut twists. The pull in my chest doesn't fade—it tightens, like a warning I can't ignore. I make a mental note to call Sam.

The streetlamps cast an eerie glow across the street as we pull up in front of the house. At first glance, nothing looks amiss, but that pull is still there— but that pull is still there, stretching tighter with every passing second, like a rubber band drawn to its breaking point. I jump from the vehicle the second it stops, Thomas hot on my heels, as I race across the yard. Everything looks so peaceful that you wouldn't assume anything was wrong. That illusion shatters when the faint clink of metal reaches my ears as my boot strikes something solid. Moving back, I crouch, picking up a small ring of keys. Thomas takes them from my hands, almost reverently, and inspects them.

A choked noise leaves his throat. "These are hers."

I just nod as my gut bottoms out. I knew before he said it, but hearing the words aloud is a separate punch to the gut. I pull my phone out, calling Charlie once more. This time I don't just hear the ringing over the speaker—I hear it close by.

I scramble off the porch, trying to locate the source.

"Charlie!" I yell.

When he doesn't reply, I start to panic. *Fuck. Fuck fuck fuck.* I've already got one of my friends hurt. I don't know if I could live with myself if another one did too.

I keep redialing the number while frantically searching. Once I round the side of the house, the shrill sound gets louder. I take off in that direction, shouting his name every few moments.

The phone goes to voicemail once more, and I fumble to call again. A large hand rests on my shoulder, making me jump. Thomas gives me a light squeeze and points to an area just inside the tree line.

"There," he says. "That looks like a cream-colored sweater."

I snap my gaze toward where he's pointing. Recognition slams into me and I bolt.

"Charlie!" I cry, not stopping until I breach the tree line. I drop to my knees, skidding to a stop beside him in a slide that would make any MLB player jealous. My hands land on his arm, and I shake him, calling his name.

"Charlie. Charlie. Charlie. Come on, man, wake up."

There's blood in his hair and running down the skin on his neck. It looks bad, but I know even minor head wounds can bleed like a river during the rainy season. Still, the sight of it sends my stomach twisting, fear rising like bile.

The sound of ringing swallows the quiet of the night, followed by Thomas's rumbling voice.

"Yes, I need an ambulance at..."

His voice fades as I refocus on Charlie. I reach for the pulse point on his neck but pull back before my fingers touch it. I need to know if he's alive, but the dread that he isn't sits heavy on my chest as grief and fear batter at my senses like waves slamming against a dam. There's a crack forming—small, splintered—and I can feel it widening. Any moment those feelings are going to break free, and when they do, I'll be useless, swallowed whole.

I grit my teeth and reach out once more, this time placing my fingers against his skin. His heartbeat flutters strong under my touch. The sigh of relief that leaves my lips is like coming out of a hurricane. Everything is still raw and wrecked, but the battering has stopped—at least for now.

Sirens split the night, coming closer. Tears drip down my face, and I wipe them away with my shoulder. The despair of the night presses down, heavy and unrelenting. Beau is still in a coma because of me. Charlie is lying in the dirt, hurt because of me. And Sarah... Sarah is gone.

A low sound breaks through the noise—a groan, rough but alive. My breath catches, the smallest flicker of hope cutting through the dark.

Charlie groans.

Chapter 47

JAKE

WEEK 1

I run my hands through my hair again. The tresses lie haphazardly across my head, but I don't have it in me to give a damn. Sarah's been gone for a week. One whole fucking week, and we have zero leads and not a snowball's chance in hell of finding her.

I'm pacing the living room of her home, feeling more and more agitated the longer we don't have answers. The pull from the mate bond is still to the southwest, but that doesn't tell me shit other than she's southwest of me. Thomas has a map of the United States laid across the coffee table, staring at it like it'll give him the answers. I stop and stare at it again. Thin black lines form a V from Willow's Haven down to the Florida and Mississippi coasts. It's a lot of land to cover. 72,085 mi^2 give or that. I can't tell how far away she is, so we have to narrow it down the best we can.

Fuck.

I want to kick myself for allowing her to be alone. I know Lila and Sam feel guilty, but I'd rather they felt guilty than be dead. Charlie escaped with only a minor concussion, but that whole thing could have been worse. Beau's still in a coma from our last encounter, and the longer he doesn't wake up, the more we lose hope that he ever will. Buckley's a fucking mess because of it, and I can't do anything except sit back and watch.

To make matters worse, Deputy Jones refuses to even acknowledge my presence. When he stopped by to get statements after Sarah was kidnapped, he just gave me a disgusted look and only asked Thomas questions. It was infuriating. I want to punch him in his stupid face, but he has leverage over me now. He doesn't have to say anything—I know that if I do anything but play by his rules, he'll let the whole town know what I am. I'm walking a tightrope and I can feel it wobbling. Only time will tell if I manage to save myself or if I fall to my impending doom.

"Take some breaths, Jake," Charlie says calmly behind me. He's been with me since he was released from the hospital, trying to help me find her.

I glare at him, then resume pacing. He sighs—long, loud, and over-exaggerated. I ignore him.

"Mr. Miller, would you mind replaying the footage?" he asks.

I huff. We've reviewed that footage forward and backward and every direction in between. Both from the day Mr. Walters was murdered and the night Sarah was taken. It tells us fuck all. The guy's wearing a hoodie pulled so low over his face you can only make out his chin in the first footage, and in the second, he's got on one of those ski masks burglars wear in movies. We have no footage of his car, no identifying marks. We have nothing. Jack shit.

Thomas grabs the remote and plays the footage. We moved the DVR into the living room days ago—trying to watch on the tiny screen in the office wasn't cutting it.

The sound of Sarah's muffled screams explodes across the room, and my head jerks up. I don't know why I can't look away from the screen. I watch as she struggles, stomps on his foot, and fights with everything she has. Then I watch as he plunges that needle into her neck, and she goes limp in his arms. He drags her off screen, then nothing. The sheriff questioned all the neighbors, but no one saw anything.

I grit my teeth and turn away from the screen to pace once more.

Chapter 48

WEEK 2

We made progress. Thank fuck, we made progress.

I wipe the tears from my eyes before they can fall. They're happy tears, but I don't have time for them. I've been fighting them for hours, and they'll just have to wait.

My fist pounds on the door. It's early evening, so I know he shouldn't be in bed yet. When there's no sound from the other side, I hit it again, harder this time.

"I'm coming!"

The door swings open, and I'm faced with a disheveled Thomas. His hair is a greasy mess on top of his head, while his eyes sport dark circles, telling me the man hasn't been sleeping much. The smell of strong bourbon wafts off of him, but I clamp down on the urge to speak. It's taken every piece of my desperation and hope not to fall down the same rabbit hole. I can't fault the man; much more of this and I'd be joining him.

"Can I come in?"

He swings the door open further and gestures. I step in, heading straight to the living room where the map of the U.S. is still spread out across the coffee table. My foot comes into contact with an empty bottle that rolls along the floor before getting caught on the edge of the couch. Again, I keep my mouth shut.

I motion him over and grab the yellow highlighter. Leaning down, I make a small mark on the map.

"We've got something. I don't know if I'd call it a lead, but it's something."

He grunts as he stands behind me, leaning over my shoulder.

"Charlie thought it'd be a good idea to take me for a drive. Clear my head, you know."

He stays quiet, so I continue.

"We didn't have a destination in mind—ended up on 81, then took 40 toward Knoxville."

I look over my shoulder at him. "That's when the pull started changing direction. It shifted more in a southerly direction."

Thomas's eyes widened, his big hand resting on my shoulder. "What else?"

"We followed 40 into a little town called Kingston. It pulled directly south. We kept going, and by the time we hit Monterey, it was pulling back the other way."

Thomas glances at the map, then at me, and back at the map. He puts his finger where I marked Kingston and grabs the ruler. He lines it up and draws a straight line from there all the way to the coast. Then he circles two cities.

Athens and Atlanta.

The room goes still. Thomas doesn't speak right away, just stares at the names like they've reached out and grabbed him. His throat works as he swallows, eyes flicking toward the window as if half-expecting to see someone standing there.

"You said it pulled back after Monterey?" he asks quietly.

"Yeah. Why?"

He sets the ruler down, his hand trembling just slightly. "Because if she's anywhere near there…" His voice trails off, rough and thin. "Then she's closer to something we left behind."

He looks up at me, eyes glassy with something I can't name, but whatever it is, it scares the hell out of me.

The answer hits me like a brick to the face. I whisper it before I can stop myself. "Her mother."

Chapter 49

WEEK 3

I'm exhausted. I rub my face, fighting to keep my eyes open after a week of re-checking every scrap for a clue. Narrowing it down to two cities is amazing progress, but there are roughly 520,000 people in Atlanta alone. Honestly, I haven't put effort into Athens. Thomas and Charlie both say that we need to cover all our bases, but I just feel it in my bones that she's in Atlanta. It's too coincidental for it not to be.

"I'm going to make some more coffee," Thomas states as he heads toward the kitchen.

My phone vibrates on the coffee table. Reaching over, I see Buckley's name on the screen and my stomach dips. I show the screen to Charlie, who drops what he's doing and comes to sit next to me.

I send up a quick prayer. *Please let Beau be okay.*

"Hey, Buck." I answer, trying not to let the exhaustion and panic fill my voice.

"Jake? Fuck, man. You've got to come to the hospital right now."

I swallow hard.

"Is it Beau?"

"Hell yeah, it's Beau!" Buckley shouts, making me wince. "He woke up! Jake. He fuckin'..."

Buckley's voice cracks; he takes a deep breath. "He woke up," he croaks out.

"That's..." Words jam in my throat, useless. Relief, disbelief, gratitude—they all crash into me at once. Tears start streaming down my face. Charlie gives me a panicked look; I shake my head.

"Beau woke up," I state to him.

He lets out a deep sigh, his eyes turning upward as he sends up a quiet thank you to the heavens.

"Charlie there with you?"

"Yeah. Charlie's here with me."

"Great! Saves me a phone call. Get your asses down here. He's askin' about ya. Ouch—shit, Momma. What was that for?"

"Buckley Troy Wilson! We are in a hospital. You know better than to be doin' all that cussin'. There're children in here!"

I snicker at the use of his full government name. Buckley's done stepped in it now.

"Yeah, Buckley. Think of the children."

"Not helping, asshole. Oww, ok, ok. I get it. I'm sorry. Momma, stop. Jesus."

"Don't you take that tone with me, young man. You're never too old for me to whip that backside."

I glance at Charlie, who has the same gleam in his eyes as me. This is good. This is so good — we're going to tease him until the end of time over this one.

"I'm grabbing my keys. We'll see y'all in a few."

"Thanks, man."

I look up to find Thomas standing in the doorway, coffee mug in hand. "It was time to call it a night anyway, boys. That's wonderful news you got. Go spend time with your friend."

Hospitals always feel the same—cold, sterile, humming with quiet dread. I round the corner and am engulfed by a warm, tight hug. I embrace the person back. I'd know this little body anywhere—it's the twins' mom, Annie.She steps back and hugs Charlie. He returns the hug, giving her a kiss on the cheek when they part. Buckley comes out of a door farther down the hallway. His smile brightens when he sees us. This is the most life I've seen in him since Beau got hurt. A small feeling of relief washes over me at the sight. He jogs down the hall, pulling both Charlie and me into an embrace.

"I'm so glad you two could come. Come on, he's waiting on you."

We follow Buckley back down the hall. I stop outside his door, guilt twisting in my gut. If it weren't for me, Beau wouldn't be in this mess. A small hand slips into mine and squeezes. Annie gives me a small smile. She knows how I'm feeling, and she has never once blamed me for what happened. Taking a steadying breath, I squeeze back gently, taking some of her strength before walking into the room.

Everything in the room is the same as it has been for months—except this time, when I cross the threshold, Beau is sitting up in bed, talking low to Charlie. His hand is no longer bandaged, but the scars along it are still very noticeable. Two of his fingers are permanently bent; seeing them brings those guilty feelings right back to the forefront. He looks smaller than he used to. It doesn't take long for your muscles to atrophy. He's in for a long recovery. There will be months of physical therapy to gain his strength back.

Annie's hand comes to rest on my back as Beau turns to me. He smiles. I rush over, enveloping him in a hug. His arms come around me, but they're weak—so weak.

"Welcome back, brother."

"It's good to be back."

I release him and stand, wiping my eyes. I open my mouth to speak when it feels like my chest has been hit by a bolt of lightning.

I grit my teeth and clutch at it. My knees hit the floor before I even register them buckling. Sounds are coming from all around me, but I can't make out the words. All I can hear is a loud ringing. My chest burns as my whole body aches. Coolness touches my cheek—my brain barely recognizes that I'm on the floor before hands are touching me everywhere. I can't speak, only scream. It feels like every muscle in my body has locked up at once, and I can't breathe. The only thing I know now is pain; everything else is distant and murky. My muscles release, and I take a much-needed breath. My vision wobbles around the edges, darkness seeping in. I comprehend a sense of relief as my world turns black.

Chapter 50

JAKE

WEEK 4

Three days. Three days I've spent in that damn hospital getting an unending number of tests run, scaring the hell out of my mother—all for nothing. A witch just happened to pass me in the hall on the way to see her grandmother, and problem solved.

I knock on the door. Thomas opens it and motions me inside. He's looking better—hair clean, face shaved, dark circles fading. I guess hope's enough to pull a man out of his wallowing.

I follow him into the living room and stop short. Pictures and yearbooks cover every surface. My brows pull together. He shrugs.

"It's our wedding anniversary today."

He offers no other explanation.

Alrighty then.

"I've got news."

Thomas sits in the recliner he seems to favor and laces his fingers together, waiting. Smart man.

"I've been in the hospital the last few days. Felt like my chest was on fire for a while there."

I pause for a moment, waiting. When he doesn't say anything, I continue.

"Doctors ran all kinds of tests, couldn't find anything wrong. Then I ran into a witch."

He raises his brow, his face showing impatience.

"Right. She asked me why I wasn't with my soulmate while the bond was being severed."

"What." His voice is venom—all the anger and frustration I've been feeling bleed out in that one word.

"According to her, the two parties have to be in attendance to sever it completely. I almost shifted in the middle of the hallway I was so pissed."

I cross my arms, locking eyes with him.

"I know in my soul that Sarah isn't the one trying to force the break, that motherfucker who has her is."

Forceful breaths leave his nose; he sounds like a bull getting ready to charge. His jaw flexes, teeth grinding, then he shuts his eyes and breathes deep, steadying himself. When he looks at me again, his voice is low.

"What you were feeling, she was feeling too. Having a bond broken is painful on its own—forcing one is ten times worse."

I nod. I could have guessed that was the case, but I had hoped I was wrong. The thought of her going through that kind of pain sets my blood to boiling. I clench my fists, digging my jagged nails into my palms until they sting.

Thomas stands, crossing the room.

"I'm gonna grab a cold one. Want one?"

"Sure," I reply. I'm not sure I want one, but I'm not saying no if he's offering.

Unclenching my fists, I let my gaze travel around the room. There are photo albums scattered across the couch, yearbooks, and loose photos covering the coffee table. I walk around the room, glancing at each one in turn. A lot of them are family photos from over the years—pictures of Sarah growing up, birthday parties, vacations, holidays. All feature her mother. She's smiling brightly in every single one. That same smile lives in Sarah. God, it's beautiful. The kind of smile I yearn to wake up to every morning.

My eyes roam over the wedding photos. Thomas was a broad man even then, beaming, and the way he looked at his bride is indescribable. It's the kind of look that women dream of seeing on their husbands' faces on their wedding day—pure, unadulterated joy and love. I pull my gaze away, my heart aching for his loss.

My eyes find the open yearbooks as Thomas comes back into the room. He hands me a cold beer. Popping the top, I take a long swig. With my next drink, I nearly spit it right back out. I choke as I swallow, then cough deeply. Thomas smacks his hand across my back.

"You alright?"

I cough a few more times, taking in much-needed air. Wiping my mouth on my sleeve, I point to the picture that caught my eye. In it is Sarah's mother, Katherine, but next to her is the much younger face of a man I will never forget. Next to her is Sarah's stalker.

Setting the beer down forcefully on the end table, I pull the album closer. My finger presses against the man's face.

"Who is that?"

Thomas grunts as he looks over while taking a sip of his beer. "That is an old friend of Kitty's she went to high school with. They ended up at the same college too. Only met him a time or two. Bit shy, kinda nerdy, but otherwise he was a nice guy."

He frowns. "His name is Nick... or Vick... something like that."

"That's Sarah's stalker."

Semi-warm beer splatters across my face. I blink a few droplets out of my eyes before wiping it away with my shirt.

"What?!"

"That's the man who's been stalking your daughter."

Thomas shoves his beer at my chest. I barely grab it before he's snatching up the album, flipping pages until he finds the senior portraits. He scans the pictures, his finger landing on one.

"Victor Langley."

He stares at it, brow furrowed. He drops the book, bolting across the room.

"Be right back!" he hollers.

His footsteps thunder across the house and up the stairs. There are sounds of things dropping or being thrown, followed by his returning steps. His chest is heaving as he crosses the threshold, handing me a thick stack of papers opened to a specific page.

"The name sounded too familiar, like I'd heard it recently, and I was right."

He jabs a finger at the signature line on the bottom.

"It's the same motherfucker who bought my house."

The air leaves my lungs in a rush. For a second, all I can do is stare at the name scrawled across the page. *Victor Langley*. The stalker. The man who took Sarah.

My pulse hammers as the pieces slam into place—her mother's death, the house, every damn note left on her door. He's been circling her family for decades. Hunting them.

Rage floods every vein, hot and unrelenting. He didn't just steal Sarah; he desecrated everything she ever loved. Her mother. Her childhood home.

I meet Thomas's eyes, and for the first time, I see the same fury I feel reflected back at me.

"We're bringing her home," I say, voice rough. "And when we do, he'll never touch her again."

Chapter 51

SARAH

It's getting dark out. He'll be back any minute, and I'll have to pretend again. He's had me for a month now. I've been trying to hold out hope that Dad or Jake will come for me, but it's getting harder with each day that passes. I absentmindedly press my hand to my chest. The bond is still there, pulling toward Jake. It's weaker than before, though. I don't remember much from that day—just pain and someone with long blonde hair soothing me.

A door closes on the other side of the house. My palms grow clammy as my heart rate picks up. I have a few more seconds alone before he comes into the room. I've searched every square inch from top to bottom and have found nothing that will help me escape. He has an iron collar around my neck attached to a heavy-duty chain bolted into the wall. He's given me just enough slack to move around the room and into the en-suite. It's strange being in this room—it used to be my parents'. Everything's the same except the life that once filled it. When we started fresh, we truly started fresh. We sold the house fully furnished, taking only mementos and clothes.

I stand as the doorknob rattles. It creaks on its hinges, revealing Victor standing in the doorway. He's wearing a white long-sleeve button-up shirt with gray slacks. His tie, a dark green color, hangs loosely around his neck. In his long, elegant fingers, he twirls a single red salvia.

His dress shoes click against the hardwood floor, coming to a stop in front of me.

"Good evening, my Flower. How was your day today?"

I grit my teeth, holding perfectly still as he places the flower behind my ear.

"The same as yesterday and the day before," I reply, doing my best to keep the tartness out of my voice.

He smirks, like he knows how hard I'm trying.

He pulls a leash out of his pocket, clipping it to my collar.

"Come. Let's have dinner together," he says as he unlocks the heavy chain. I roll my stiff shoulders. It's not easy carrying around the extra weight all day. If not for the company, I might even welcome the relief.

He tugs gently on the leash. I follow absentmindedly down the hall, scanning my surroundings once again as we walk. Nothing. No pictures on the walls, no candleholders or lamps within reach. The place has the absolute bare minimum. Every single decorative item my mother once had hanging on the walls has been removed, along with the nails that held them there. Each day I search. Each day, nothing. Hope is a habit I can't kill.

He guides me to a kitchen chair, attaching my collar to another leash that's been tied to the chair in such a way that I can't reach it and am only allowed miniscule movements. He unhooks his walking leash, hanging it up on the key holder by the door. It's the same door I came through the night I found my mother dead on the floor. My gaze finds the spot before I can stop it. I look away fast.

Victor smirks but stays silent. He turns to the counter and starts unpacking food from plastic bags, plating them, then setting a steaming plate in front of me. It's some sort of Thai dish with noodles, eggs, chicken, and veggies. Thai isn't my favorite, but I don't tell him that. I'm his prisoner, after all, what good would it do me?

I eat with the plastic fork he allows me to have. Hunger has been chewing at my belly for hours. He only feeds me twice a day. Each morning, he drags me in here as he cooks breakfast before chaining me to the wall in my parents' room. Then he leaves for the day to go God knows where, leaving me with a single plastic cup for water. Every day I pace the room, trying to come up with some way to escape. He's removed the lamps from the bedside tables, the walls are as blank as everywhere else in the house, and he's made sure that my chain is just long enough to open the drawers on the armoire, but not long enough to reach the glass on top. The bathroom is empty of everything except the essentials. No cleaner, no bleach, not even a toilet brush.

On days he has a maid come clean, he locks me into the room that used to be my dad's office. That room has been padded—every wall, including the floor and ceiling, covered in a spongy type of material. There used to be a window, but even that's been sealed. When he shuts the door, it looks like a literal padded cell. The chain in that room ensures I can't reach the door. I don't think it would do me any good even if I could; I'm sure he locks it. The padding in there has got to be some type of soundproofing. I've tried screaming and yelling at the top of my lungs with no results. When he opens the door, I can always tell someone's been here. The house smells clean. The floors shine. No one ever hears me.

I don't know how he gets away with having chains bolted to the walls, though. Maybe they don't see. Maybe they don't want to.

As I finish my dinner, he reaches his hand out and cups my cheek, rubbing his thumb across my skin. I grit my teeth to keep from flinching. He smiles at me, and I give him a soft smile back.

Just pretend. Keep pretending. It's only for a little longer.

"Yes, dear?" I ask with a sweet tone. He likes it when I call him that, so I keep doing it even though it turns my stomach.

He leans in, kissing my other cheek. "How would you like to watch a movie tonight, My Flower?"

It's a battle not to spit in his face. *Comply. Be good. Pretend.* I repeat the words in my head over and over.

"That sounds amazing. Thank you, dear."

He boops my nose. "I thought you'd like that idea. Stay here, Flower. I'll get everything ready."

I nod, and he takes the plate away, the only thing I might hurt him with if I could smash it on the floor. I watch as he cleans up the kitchen. I can't do anything but watch anyway. Once he finishes there, he moves over to the living room, turning on the TV and finding a movie on one of the streaming channels. I'm not really paying attention to the unimportant details anyway. He cleans. I watch. That's all there ever is to do.

He comes back with my walking leash, unhooks me from the chair, and leads me to the couch. He sits, slinging one long leg over the length of it and patting the space near his lap for me to sit.

I grit my teeth as I do so. He pulls me down over his chest before wrapping his other leg over mine. If he were someone I cared about, someone like Jake. No, not *like* Jake. *Jake.* This would be relaxing and sweet. Instead, it makes my skin crawl.

He starts the movie and begins running his fingers through my hair. His nails brush along my scalp, and God, it feels good even though I don't want it to. When he starts running his fingers along the skin behind my ear and down my neck, I can't help the goosebumps that rise along my flesh. I shiver involuntarily, then shove the feeling away with thoughts of who this man is and what he's done.

I swallow hard as his fingers trail across my arm and under my ribs, his hand coming to rest just below the crease of my breast. I know all it would take is a twitch of his fingers and he'd be groping me. He doesn't move, though; his hand stays resting across my ribs as he rubs lazy circles just under my breast.

My body stiffens.

He reaches out and grasps me under my arms with both hands, pulling and turning me until we're chest to chest, our faces only inches apart. He tucks my hair behind my ears, looking at me with so much adoration that it breaks my heart. I know that it's really his madness shining in his eyes, but I feel for him all the same. He looks at me like I'm the only thing keeping him sane. Maybe that's the cruelest part, because he's still a monster.

"You haven't given me a welcome-home kiss yet, Kat," he murmurs.

I will my body not to stiffen as he wraps one hand around the base of my neck and pulls me closer. His lips brush mine in a gentle caress before he devours me.

Comply. Be good. Pretend.

I repeat.

Comply. Be good. Pretend.

I force myself to open for him, his tongue raking across mine the moment I do. I go lax, pretending to melt into his kiss. It's only when I feel his hard cock press firmly against me that I pull back.

I pant loudly, like he just gave me the best kiss of my life. Inside my mouth, I'm scraping my tongue with my teeth, trying to remove the taste of him. No matter how hard I scrape, the taste stays.

I lower my lids, putting on my best sultry look.

"Why me, Victor?"

He leans in, trailing kisses along my jaw.

"Why you what, Kat?" he whispers in my ear. His hot breath fans across my skin, sending waves of tingles in its wake.

"Why did you choose me?"

He pulls back, both hands coming to rest on my cheeks.

"You know why, My Flower."

He smiles, his entire face warm and inviting.

"But if you want to hear it again, I'll tell you."

He leans in once more to rub his nose against mine.

"I've been in love with you since the eighth grade. You were the only one who even looked at me, who noticed me. How could I not love you?"

I don't answer. It sounded like a rhetorical question anyway. I'm proved right when he continues after a breath, not waiting for a reply.

"You became my best friend. And when I asked you to homecoming, and you agreed, I knew you loved me too."

His eyes darken, his face twisting into a scowl.

"Then you started hanging out with that Johnny Carson kid. Hugging him, kissing him, fucking him. It broke my heart. You were mine." He growls out the last word. The growl isn't human; it's a sound scraped up from somewhere feral inside him.

"You told me we'd always be together. You promised. So when that fool inevitably broke your heart, I was there to pick up the pieces. I was the one who held you while you cried. I was the one who brought you back. Me. Not him. *Me.*"

He kisses me, soft and gentle, a complete contrast to the look on his face.

"I even changed my major so we could go to the same college. I wanted you to see me the way I saw you. To love me like I knew you could. Like you did before he came around."

He grips my hair in a tight fist.

"Then you just had to betray me once again, didn't you, you whore? You started seeing that... that fuckboy, Thomas. Suddenly he was all you talked about. *Thomas this and Thomas that.* It took everything in me not to murder him then."

He yanks harder, and a cry escapes before I can swallow it.

"I tried to talk to you, Kat. Tried to explain how we were meant to be together, that he would only break your heart the same way Johnny did. But you didn't listen, did you? Instead, you ran off with him. Disappeared and left me behind. It took years for me to find you. *Years.*"

He crashes his lips against mine in a bruising kiss, forcing his tongue between my lips.

Comply. Be good. Pretend.

I soften my body, leaning into his and running my tongue along his. When he finally pulls back, I pant.

"I'm sorry, Victor. I'm so, so sorry."

He hums his approval, his face a mirror of satisfaction.

"I know you are, My Flower."

He loosens his grip on my hair slightly, caressing my face once more.

"I'll get us some wine," he murmurs, brushing his lips against my forehead before standing.

My body is frozen on the couch, but my heartbeat is anything but. The leash still hangs from my collar, the end resting against the cushion. He left me here alone. He didn't drag me with him. I stare at it, pulse pounding in my ears.

He hums to himself as he moves around the kitchen. I hear the soft clink of glass, the twist of a cork, liquid pouring.

Now.

I rise slowly, my legs trembling. Every movement feels too loud. The leash at my throat drags along the floor, scraping, faint but sharp. He doesn't react. I take one step, then another.

The front door isn't far, just on the other side of the room.

I glance over my shoulder. His back is turned to me. I move faster, breath shallow, every sound amplified. My fingers brush the door handle. It doesn't budge. Locked.

My fingers fumble along the door, finding the deadbolt. I flick it. The lock slides open.

I pull it wide, stepping into the night air. Cool wind rushes against my face, wet and real. My body shudders with relief as a tear slides down my cheek.

I take three hurried steps out the door. Then, my body jerks backward. I groan and gasp, pain blooming through every muscle.

Victor's face comes into view above me.

"I'm disappointed, My Flower," he says softly. "You almost made me spill the wine."

He crouches beside me, stroking my hair as I writhe.

He's back up in an instant, the leash in hand as he pulls. The collar tightens around my throat, cutting off air. I claw at it, gasping, pleading with him with my eyes. He loosens his hold.

"Get up," he grits out, all signs of patience gone.

I stumble to my feet, rubbing my throat around the collar. His fingers dig into my arm as he drags me away from the door, slamming it behind him.

"I think it's about time I taught you a lesson in trying to leave me again, Kat."

I tug against his grip, frustration and fear and anger flooding through me.

"I'm not Kat, you crazy asshole. You *MURDERED* her!"

He jerks my body close, grabbing my throat and slamming me against the wall. His fingers squeeze just above the collar, bruising my skin but firm enough to cut off my air again.

"Oh, I know." He spits in my face. "I watched her expression shift from terror to confusion as her warm blood leaked from my claws. Turns out she wasn't worthy of my love."

His other hand comes into view, fingers tipped with sharp claws. He drags them along my jaw, scratching but not breaking the skin. I avert my gaze from them.

He chuckles, low and menacing.

"But her blood runs through your veins, My Flower. Through you, I have a second chance. You will be my Katherine and live the life we were meant to live."

I try to shake my head. His grip tightens as he growls. He plucks the flower that is somehow still in my hair, twirling it between his fingers.

"You are mine. Forever."

He smirks, then releases his hold on my throat. Pulling on my collar, he beckons me to follow. I fall into step behind him. My mind races with each step down the hall. I was almost free. I felt the fresh air on my face for the first time in months.

Crossing the threshold into my parents' old room, he grabs me by the back of the neck, pushing me toward the bed. Panic fills me as my mind conjures every possible scenario, none of them good. I reach back and grab his hand with both of mine, struggling against his grip.

He throws me onto the bed face down, grabbing my wrist and jerking it toward the corner. The feel of the cuff against my skin makes me thrash harder against his hold. I can't go through that again. Not again.

"Please!" I cry out. "Please, Victor. Don't. I'll be good, I swear!"

He had bound me to this bed for a week straight when he first brought me here. Only being able to barely move had driven me to the brink of madness.

He's never assaulted me, but I can't guarantee he won't this time. He's a monster, but a monster with limits. Or at least, that's what I've been telling myself to survive.

He falters at my words, his grip loosening slightly. I take advantage of his mistake, jerking my wrist free. Rolling onto my back, I scramble across the bed. I pull my leg back and kick as he tries to grab me, nailing him right in the balls. He lets out a sharp *oomph*, hitting his knees hard. His face turns red as he struggles to regain control.

Twisting, I fling myself off the other side of the bed. My feet slap against the floor as I run. The sound of his pursuit follows me down the hall.

I make it to the kitchen, grabbing a chair and hurling it in his direction. It doesn't go far, but the hit is enough to stun him momentarily. I dart toward the side door, grasping the knob and twisting. It opens. I didn't even think about the deadbolt in my panic, but it doesn't matter. He left it unlocked.

It doesn't escape my notice that my thoughts mirror the ones from the night my mom was murdered. *Run. Get to the trees. Climb.*

I fling the door wide, sprinting through it, straight into a hard chest.

Chapter 52

JAKE

The drive was brutal. Five hours of fear, hope, and helplessness, all packed into a metal box hurtling down the highway. We didn't waste time, just got in my truck and took off. As the minutes ticked into hours, it felt like I would be trapped in this cab forever, stuck in some perpetual loop of racing toward the woman I love and not knowing what I'd find on the other end. It's a special kind of torture.

I glance around as we pull into the driveway of Thomas's old house. Sarah said there were woods surrounding the property, but I don't know if these thin patches of trees qualify. There's barely enough to block out the neighboring houses.

I kill the engine and hop out, Thomas meeting me in front of the hood. We survey the area, taking in the fancy BMW parked out front. It's flashy and not something that would go unnoticed in Willow's Haven. Worry churns in my gut that we were wrong. Then I catch a flash of brown hair dart by an open window.

Almost by instinct, I rush toward the side door. I'm just about to reach for the knob when it flings open, and a soft body I'd know anywhere collides with mine. I wrap my arms around her, pulling her further out the door as the bond flares back up in full force.

She gasps in my arms, pulling back to look at my face. Tears start streaming down her cheeks. I want to wipe them away, but she's still in danger. Thomas's hand lands on my shoulder as he races past.

"Get her in the truck, Jake. I'm not letting this son of a bitch get away this time," he shouts.

I hurry her to the truck without hesitation. Urging her into the cab, I take a moment, just one moment, to kiss her forehead.

"The keys are still in the ignition. Lock the doors behind me, baby."

She gives me a shaky nod.

A loud crash comes from the house, followed by the sound of glass breaking. I make sure she's locked the door, then rush back across the yard.

The sounds grow clearer once I push through the open door. Glass is shattered across the kitchen floor, red wine bleeding across the tile. Across the way, the table lies in pieces, the two men grappling with each other as they roll across it. Victor's hands are shifted into claws, but Thomas somehow avoids getting scratched.

Victor lands a heavy punch to Thomas's face. Thomas reels back, giving Victor just enough time to grab the large chef's knife lying on the floor. I call out a warning as Victor swings it through the air. Thomas jerks his body back, barely avoiding the strike. Victor corrects his motion, stabbing Thomas in the thigh. The blade sinks deep, crimson flooding out around it.

I move across the room, refusing to let Thomas be murdered by this man too. Everything slows. Thomas grits his teeth, rage burning in his eyes as he grips the knife handle and yanks it free. He grabs Victor by the shirt, meaty fingers digging into the fabric as he jerks him closer. The knife plunges into Victor's chest, deep enough to pierce his heart.

Victor's limbs go slack. He looks down at the knife, then back up at Thomas. A gurgling sound rattles in his throat before he slumps forward, landing on top of him.

I grab Victor's body, heaving him off Thomas. Dropping to my knees, I inspect the thigh wound.

"Sarah?" Thomas asks between sharp, panting breaths.

"She's alright. She's locked in the truck."

Then Thomas does something I never thought he'd do in a million years. He reaches out, wraps his arms around me, and pulls me into a tight hug. I stiffen at the unexpected touch but don't pull away.

"Thank you, Jake," he murmurs in my ear, voice rough with unshed tears.

I hug him back. When he finally releases me, he sets both hands on my face. Looking me in the eye, he says, "You're exactly the kind of man I always hoped my daughter would find. If she still wants you, I won't stand in your way."

I nod, speechless for a moment.

"That's all well and good, Thomas, but let's get you patched up before you bleed out all over the floor."

Chapter 53

SARAH

My eyes are glued to the door Jake went through. I swallow a sob as I blink tears away. I need to be able to see. Both of the men I love are inside with that madman. I spot Jake's phone lying in the seat and snatch it up, my fingers shaking as I type in his code. A shaky breath escapes me when it unlocks.

I dial 911. The line rings so long I start to worry no one's going to answer.

"911, what's your emergency?"

A sob breaks loose before I can stop it, and I start frantically recounting the events. The operator stays calm and patient as she takes my information. Hearing that help is on the way gives me a small sense of relief.

"Ma'am, can you stay on the line while we wait?"

I open my mouth to answer when two figures stumble out the side door, one with an arm slung over the other.

"Dad?" I say absentmindedly when I realize it's him who's limping.

"Ma'am?" comes from the phone as it slips from my fingers. I scramble for the door handle, missing twice before I finally get it open.

I rush across the yard, hitting my knees beside my father, where Jake has just eased him down.

"Dad!" I exclaim, my eyes scanning over him. There are minor cuts and bruises, but it's the blood covering a large section of his pants that draws my eye. A belt's pulled tight above the injury.

I fling myself into his arms, sobbing against his chest. He pulls me close, pressing a kiss to the top of my head.

"It's alright, baby. We've got you."

The words break me all over again. He doesn't say anything else, just rocks me until my sobs slow.

Sirens wail in the distance, growing louder until blue and red lights flash across the yard. The sound rips through the night, dragging me back to another one just like it. That night, it was me injured and covered in blood. Tonight it's my father. The same man was responsible for both. Anger simmers below the surface at the thought of what he took from me, and what more he could have done.

Jake helps me stand as they stop a few feet away.

Everything after that blurs together.

The police ask questions, Jake an ever-present shadow by my side. I only catch part of the conversation with my father.

"Mr. Miller, how do you know the deceased?"

"He's just some little piss ant my wife was friends with in college. After we started dating, he got aggressive. He was forward, possessive, made her uncomfortable. We moved as soon as she graduated, and she went no contact with him. I haven't seen or heard of him in about twenty-five years."

His eyes find mine, the depth of his anguish shining through as he adds, "I should've known a little cockroach like him would eventually come crawling out of the woodwork."

That one sentence is enough to show the enormity of the guilt he's carrying.

I lean on Jake, his presence a comfort in ways I didn't know I needed. He holds me as they take Dad away in the ambulance, followed closely by

Victor's body. Jake gave me a quick rundown of what happened, and I can't bring myself to feel an ounce of sympathy for the man.

They had to use bolt cutters to remove the fucking collar from my neck. Hours later, I can still feel the weight of it pressing against my skin like a noose waiting to tighten.

I only have a few precious minutes left with Jake before they haul us to the police station. I grab both of Jake's hands, desperate to express everything I'm feeling but don't have time for.

I take a breath; the words catching in my throat.

"You're not him," I whisper. "You'll never be like him. I'm safe with you."

For a heartbeat, Jake just stares at me, his eyes searching mine like he's afraid he misheard. Then his lips curve into a smile—soft, unsteady, full of relief and something that feels like hope.

Six Months Later

I groan as the truck bounces along the back roads of Tennessee. About a mile or so off the highway, there's a little white church where a sweet, perfect, beautiful woman is waiting for me. I curse myself and my friends as I wipe sweat off my brow. It's a balmy August evening, and the sun's casting its golden glow across the landscape. Sweat's runnin' down every crack and crevice on my body. By the time we actually make it to the church, I'm gonna smell about as wonderful as a dumpster.

Charlie's behind the wheel of his beat-up old Ford pickup he lovingly named Betsy. I call her Ol' Unfaithful, 'cause he's constantly workin' on the damn thing. If I weren't thanking my lucky stars right now, I'd be surprised it's running at all. We couldn't find the keys to any of the other cars. They weren't in the cookie jar where they were supposed to be. I've got a feeling that has something to do with the twins, but I don't have time to worry about it.

Inside the cab, the air's thick with anticipation, nervous energy and a hint of reckless excitement. My other friends, Buckley, Beau, and Grant, are sprawled across the worn-out seats in the back. How they all fit back there, I'll never know. There's too many limbs and not enough space. Maybe it's wedding-day magic or somethin'. Who knows?

Buckley's passed out, his snoring harmonizing with the engine's rattling. Drool leaks from his mouth onto Grant's shirt. Grant's holding his head, groaning something I can't make out, while Beau's clinging to the door, his face a shade paler than the ass of a Californian surfer. I want to laugh at the ridiculousness of it all, but I don't want to jinx my luck. This truck's held together with a wing and a prayer. Any sudden movement might make it fall apart around me—and I need, more than anything, to get to that church in one piece.

The truck starts to shake, the speedometer flirting with ninety-five.

"What's the matter with you, man?" I call out to Charlie, who's wrestling to keep the old truck *on* the dusty road. "I thought you said you could drive!"

Charlie flips me the bird between the bounce of the worn-out shocks, his grin wide with amusement.

"Fuck you, Jake!" he hollers, his words barely audible over the rumbling engine. "I oughta make your ass get out and walk!"

He risks a quick, sharp glare my way.

I chuckle; there's a nervous edge to my laugh. "Well, that's not gonna stop me, Charlie. Not today."

I chew on the skin around my thumbnail.

"Do you think it'd be faster if I shifted and ran the rest of the way?" I yell over the sound of the wind blowing through the windows.

Charlie sends me another glare.

"First of all, don't you fucking dare, Jake. Even if I let you jump out of a moving vehicle, there ain't no way in hell you can outrun Betsy. Secondly, it's not my fault you let these idiots keep us up all damn night."

Beau lets out a bellowing laugh, then immediately retches.

"Hey! Hey! Stop laughing; bad idea; knock it off!" I holler back at him. "It's bad enough I look like shit; I don't need to smell like it too."

Charlie snorts. "Too late for that, buddy!"

I flip him the bird and try my best to rein myself in.

As the miles roll by, my mind drifts to the woman waiting for me at the end of this road. Sarah. The woman of my dreams. I proposed not long after her father was acquitted on the grounds of self-defense. It was a pretty cut and dry case in my opinion. In addition, Victor's DNA matched samples from his wife's murder, and from Mr. Walters.

His living in their old house was an extra layer of crazy, too. He had a whole hydroponic flower garden set up in what used to be Sarah's bedroom. It explained how he was giving her flowers in the dead of winter. We're damn lucky he wasn't crazier than he already was.

"Uh-oh," I mutter, gripping the *oh-shit* handle as we hit a pothole big enough to swallow a tire.

"Fuck," Charlie hisses, a loud squeal tearing from the engine.

That sounds expensive.

"Careful now. We don't want this worn-out piece of shit thinking you don't love her," I say, voice dripping with mirth as I try to lighten the mood.

Charlie clenches his teeth, fighting not to snap back. This truck's his baby, and he'd be damned if anyone talked shit about it. It's like one of those *only-I-can-insult-my-sibling* kind of relationships.

Beau, now a shade greener than before, manages a weak nod. "Yeah, man, you've got to love her right."

I reach back and smack him. "You shut up. I don't need a tie-dyed shirt."

Beau laughs and retches again. I barely manage to move out of the way as he leans farther out the window and empties his guts along the road. Charlie laughs loudly, the sound bouncing off the truck walls. Buckley snorts in alarm, then promptly begins snoring again. I shake my head, leaning as far forward as I can to stay away from the mess. It's good to see

Beau acting so lively again. It's just a shame that his joy is more often found at the bottom of a bottle.

The minutes drag by before the dirt road gives way to pavement. The church looms on the horizon, its steeple reaching toward the sky. My pulse quickens as adrenaline courses through my veins. I envision the moment I sweep Sarah off her feet and make her mine forever. Then I see her beautiful face turn into a scowl. We are so late.

With a final burst of determination, the truck lurches into the church's parking lot, skidding to a halt in a cloud of dust and gravel, then promptly dies. I spring from the cab, my eyes scanning the crowd standing behind a barrier at the edge of the lot. A handful of people hold up various versions of "No Predator Shifters" signs while booing at us.

Sheriff Anderson, a tall, muscular man with gray hair and a no-nonsense demeanor, stands in front of the barrier with a shotgun in hand. He has a well-groomed mustache and deep-set, expressive eyes that shine bright blue in the light. Although his face has weathered with age, he's still considered handsome among the ladies of the town. That weathered look only adds to his rugged charm.

He grabs the edge of his hat, tipping it at me. I offer him a smile along with a two-finger salute. Those assholes aren't going to dampen this glorious day, and I know without a doubt the sheriff will keep them in line. He's more than done with the bigotry in this town.

The church doors bang open, drawing my gaze. Sarah comes flying out, her veil swirling behind her on the breeze. More people pour out of the church as she runs toward me. I catch her in my arms, pulling her in for a fervent kiss.

She breaks the kiss, eyes scanning me from head to toe. I'm a mess of haphazardly thrown-on clothes and uncombed hair. She doesn't care. She just smiles at me, her face radiant enough to rival the sun.

"Jake," she whispers, her voice barely audible over the thumping of my heart. "You made it."

"I wouldn't miss this for the world, Little Trash Panda," I reply, giving her one more soft, gentle kiss.

I make the mistake of looking behind her and glimpse her father's irritated scowl. My mother wears a matching one, while my father sports a shit-eating grin. Lila, heavily pregnant, stands close by with her hands on her hips, a disappointed frown marring her face. I know I'll hear about this later, but for now, I need to make the stunning creature in my arms my wife.

I smile at our parents and nod toward the church.

"Let's go do this thing," I practically shout.

Sarah's laughter fills the air. We move toward the church as my grooms-men stagger after us.

The familiar sound of tires on gravel reaches my ears. I turn to see a very expensive car pulling into a parking spot. I glance at the rest of the crowd, but they all have the same confused expression as me. The door opens, and a tall, trim blonde woman steps out. Her hair is pulled into a sleek high ponytail, and she's wearing a form-fitting dress with what has to be four-inch stilettos. She doesn't need them for the added height—she'd be tall even without them. She's got sunglasses that cover most of her face. I have no idea who this woman is, but when she smiles, it looks so familiar.

She stops about ten steps away.

"I heard someone decided to get married without me. I'm a little hurt I didn't get an invite," she says, removing her sunglasses.

I hear Buckley let out a low, "Holy shit."

Charlie pushes through the crowd.

"Ro!"

"Hey, Char-Char," she says, holding her arms out. Charlie engulfs her in a hug, and she laughs.

Sarah leans into me, whispering, "Who is that?"

I lean toward her.

"That, Little Trash Panda, is Charlie's twin sister, Aurora."

The Tale of Gaia's Mercy

Before the written word, before the rise of kings and crowns, there was war.

Not for land, nor gold, but for cruelty's sake.

Men burned what they could not own and slaughtered what they did not understand.

And the innocent?

They cried out, their blood seeping into the soil like prayers unspoken.

The Earth heard them.

Gaia, Mother of All, stirred in her rootbound slumber and wept.

She could not change men's hearts;

But she could grant her children the means to survive.

From stone and storm, from beast and bloom, she wove a gift—

Not of flesh, but of illusion born from truth.

She split the gift into two:

To the weak, the sick, the young—

She gave the forms of prey;

Soft-footed and quick,
Rabbits, squirrels, deer, and mice—
So they could vanish into brush and burrow,
Too swift to slaughter.

To the strong, the protectors,
She granted the guise of predator—
Wolf and lion, fox and bear,
Claws sharp as mercy's edge,
Fangs that gleamed with resolve.
Not to dominate, but to defend.

The magic was not in their muscle;
But in the illusion itself—
So real it fooled the eye, the hand, the world.
So strong it lent the speed of the fox and the teeth of the bear.
They wore their shapes like prayers;
Each shift a hymn to survival.

And from this gift, passed down like stories by firelight,
There bloomed something deeper:
The Bond.

When two threads of Gaia's magic sang the same song—
They tangled.
Knotted.
Their magic reached like roots beneath the soil,
Seeking one another, yearning.
They were called **soulmates**;
Not bound by fate,
But by choice.

By the slow-growing ache to know one another whole.

If nurtured, the bond deepened—
A tether that shimmered like dew on a spider's web.
They could sense danger, feel joy like an echo through bone.
But magic is not a jailer.
They could walk away.
And if they stayed apart long enough,
The thread frayed.
The ache dulled.
The bond withered,
As all untended things do.

A gift born of mercy.
A bond born of magic.
And a choice born of love.

Some called it myth.
Others felt it bloom in their chest and knew:
Gaia's mercy still lingers.

Acknowledgements

Special thanks go out to my friend, Sara, who encouraged me and became my unintentional editor/beta reader. Her notes in

the margins brought me smiles and laughter, as well as some frustration. She's very skilled at finding consistency issues, even in

the smallest things. Even though she has a full-time job, a family, and she suffers from health issues that keep her unwell for days

on end, she still found time in her busy schedule to be there. May I always have you and your illustrious hip to lean on.

Special thanks also go out to my husband/partner, James, who has supported me every step of the way in achieving my dreams.

He let me bounce plot points off of him at the strangest of times and told me to stop rewriting the prologue for this novel (I rewrote

it five times). He always finds a way to bring joy in the frustrating times and create new inside jokes we can share. May we always

have (in my best Vin Diesel voice) family.

About the author

Clara James writes steamy, high-emotion romance that lingers long after the last page. Her stories blend grit and heart across sub-genres—rock-band romance, gritty biker vibes, and small-town mountain shifters. Expect deep chemistry, found family, fierce loyalty, and endings that feel earned. She is obsessed with characters who fight for the love they choose and with the consequences that make their victories matter.

Clara lives in a rural community with her spouse, their child, and a small menagerie: three dogs, a snake, and a chinchilla. Writing has been her first love since childhood. As a kid, she wore out a gifted typewriter, clacking away into the early hours while everyone else tried to sleep. After years of waiting, she is finally pursuing the passion she always knew was hers. She swears the words flow better with a caramel coffee at her elbow.

When she isn't drafting, she is storyboarding songs and mapping worlds so every road, bar stool, and back alley feels lived-in. Readers come for the heat and stay for the heartbreak that heals.

Also by

More titles coming soon!